# Erotic Tales of the Knights Templar in the Holy Land

## Jay Starre

STARbooks Press
Herndon, VA

Published in the United States
STARbooks Press
PO Box 711612
Herndon VA 20171
Printed in the United States

Many thanks to graphic artist John Nail for the cover design. Mr. Nail may be reached at: tojonail@bellsouth.net.

Book and text design by Milton Stern. Mr. Stern can be reached at miltonstern@miltonstern.com.

# Contents

# Tale One: Sir Guy Becomes Master

*In which Sir Guy de Brussiers, a Frankish Knight from the heartland of France, returns home to Castle Rock on the Palestine coast. He has recently been made a Master of the Order of the Knights Templar. He dallies in the bath with his Arabic slave, Mamluk.*

Guy de Brussiers, a sturdy and upright member of the Knights Templar, gazed out from his stone balcony over the pale blue Mediterranean Sea, which washed against the coast of the Latin Kingdom in the Holy Land. He had just removed his heavy helmet and shook out his shoulder-length blond hair in the freshness of the ocean breeze. He sighed with contentment as he breathed in the moisture-laden air that promised a rare rainstorm in this dry land. Massive thunderclouds piled up in the north, now threatening to block out the desert sun.

"Master, do you require assistance? May I help you disrobe?" a voice called from behind him. Guy recognized the husky tones, and the soft Arabic accent that enriched the perfect French. He turned away from the brilliant scene to confront his slave. Mamluk bowed deferentially and smiled humbly as his master's eyes turned upon him.

"Yes. I am tired and hot, and desire a bath, Mamluk. Would you please ready the water after you assist me?" Guy replied graciously, gazing down at the shorter Arabic servant.

The Knight had just returned from a long journey, the dust and grit of the road still clinging to him. The sight of this ever-immaculate and smiling Arab made him feel welcome, more than any other single thing. He was glad to be home in his castle by the sea.

Mamluk worked efficiently and with practiced consideration as he aided the Knight with his traveling clothes of heavy mail and thick wool. As usual, the slave marveled at the madness of wearing such clothing in the searing heat of the Arab lands. But he said nothing, merely smiling and agreeing with whatever utterances his Master offered.

Mamluk removed the clothing piece by piece, laying them out for later cleaning on a stone bench in the open air of the balcony. As his fingers grazed the blond Frenchman's bare arms and then his unclothed shoulders, he shuddered inwardly at the sensual feel of Sir Guy's firm muscles beneath flesh of silken suppleness. He had been undressing Sir Guy for a year now, since the Knight had journeyed from his home in far off France to this Arabic Castle. Mamluk had not ceased to enjoy every precious moment of it.

Sir Guy allowed the servant to remove his clothes passively. His thoughts were on the business he had just been conducting and the work he must do to further his Order's schemes. The Frenchman was unusually pensive, due to the seriousness of what had occurred on that recent journey. Guy had met with the Grand Master himself, called personally from Castle Rock to the great man's presence to discuss an important matter. At this meeting, the Grand Master informed Sir Guy he was now elevated to the rank of Master. Guy was to oversee a Cell of Knights here at Castle Rock. It was a tremendous honor, but also a serious responsibility. A Master! He was not quite certain of what that entailed, not yet at any rate.

When he had been stripped completely, he happened to glance at Mamluk and was surprised to notice the man's gaze focused on Guy's prick and balls. The French Knight smiled, as always proud of his large member and his huge ball sack. Unfortunately, the potent cock and balls had seen little action

2

since he had come to this land and taken his vows as a member of the Knights Templar.

Mamluk realized his Master was watching him and managed to withdraw with grace, bowing and offering Sir Guy a soft linen gown to pull over him until the bath was readied. Guy thanked Mamluk and then turned away to watch the building storm. His thoughts returned to money and power and politics, the matters with which the Knights Templar concerned themselves.

The thunderclouds battled with the sun in the distance like two mighty armies, one of darkness and shadow and one of light and golden vistas. Neither triumphed before Mamluk interrupted Guy once again.

"Master Guy. Your bath is ready," he murmured, his sultry voice close to the French Knight's ear.

Guy followed his servant to the next room where the sunken tub was steaming with beckoning warmth. Two large apertures in the stone wall allowed in the stimulating breeze while offering a stupendous view of the storm clouds on the horizon and the sparkling ocean beneath. After removing his Arab gown, Guy sank into the pool to sit waist deep in hot water. He sighed with satisfaction as the soothing water surrounded him while he was offered that pleasant breeze and the agreeable view. Guy leaned back against the tiles, stretching out his long arms on the cool marbled floor at the edge of the pool.

Mamluk had been watching when Sir Guy first dropped his gown. The Arab slave's large eyes fixed with keen relish on the glorious sight revealed. The cheeks of the Knight's thick buttocks were incredibly pale, while the Frenchman's huge, dangling nut sack was exposed from behind when Guy bent to step into the tiled tub. Mamluk longed to run his hands over that solid-yet-smooth bottom. He grinned secretly, knowing he would soon be doing so in the course of his duties.

Bending over the seated Knight from behind, Mamluk began to massage soap into his shoulders. As Guy closed his

Jay Starre

eyes and groaned with pleasure, Mamluk kneaded the taut muscles expertly. The Arab slave worked lather into every inch of his master's shoulders and arms, even to the fingertips and nails of each thick digit. Guy lay passively savoring the bath, occasionally opening his eyes to observe the gathering storm outside their windows.

Mamluk worked deft fingers along Sir Guy's bull neck and then down to his chest, massaging each thick pectoral muscle, grazing his fingers across the nipples hiding in the light curls of his master's chest hair. Leaning close beside the Knight's ears as he worked, Mamluk breathed in the air that Guy breathed out, reveling in its scent and the intimacy of its warmth. He worked his way down to Sir Guy's flat stomach and then ceased at the water line, just above the genitals he could see floating beneath the translucent surface.

Mamluk proceeded to gently move his master's trunk forward without disturbing his thoughts. He added more scented soap and massaged the lather into the thick knots of Guy's upper back and spine. The Knight sighed as Mamluk pressed firmly into his exhausted back muscles. Guy leaned further forward, slumping languidly with his head dropping almost to his chest. There was nothing as pleasant as this long-awaited bath and Mamluk's perfect attentions. The French Knight had been dreaming of this for the last four days while riding across the burning deserts of Palestine.

Mamluk lowered his hands to knead at Guy's waist and lower back just above his pale buttocks, staring down at the cleft that was just out of his reach. He lingered there, knowing it to be a tender and aching area of his master's anatomy. Ministering to those muscles was just what the travel-weary Knight required.

When he finished, Mamluk rose and deftly slipped off his own soft gown. Nude, he stepped into the pool to stand before his seated master. Guy opened his eyes to see Mamluk hovering in the pool before him and sighed. With a lazy smile and light chuckle he said, "I suppose I must stand now."

4

Sir Guy rose from the pool, scented water sliding off his powerful frame. He stood in front of his slave to allow Mamluk to soap his lower body. The Arab attentively lathered the Knight's cock and balls. Mamluk savored the moment as he handled the thick girth of male prick and then held in his palm the heavy sack of knightly seed and soaped the pair of balls tenderly. Mamluk's fingers reluctantly abandoned the cock and balls, moving between Guy's legs and down his thighs. The Knight closed his eyes again and luxuriated in the tender caresses of his slave's hands before turning his back and allowing Mamluk to offer the same attention to his muscular buttocks.

Mamluk took his time soaping up the firm buttocks. He slid his hands between the cleft, working on the blond curls snaking in the center of the crack and down to the balls hanging below. He knelt in the water to work his hands up and down the burly legs of his master, probing and pinching, peering up in fascinated wonder at Sir Guy's large white ass hovering above him. The Knight leaned over to rest his hands on the tiles at the side of the pool and had presented to the Arab servant a sight Mamluk could never get enough of.

Yet Mamluk knew his place and continued with his duties heedfully. With gentle persuasion, he turned the big Frenchman around and sat him on the edge of the pool. Mamluk lifted one beefy leg to work on Sir Guy's foot and toes, pressing the tender instep and working lather into every spot and crevice.

Guy opened his eyes at that point. Leaning back on his strong arms and big hands, Guy thoughtfully observed his loyal servant as Mamluk expertly manipulated Guy's feet and toes. Guy admitted to himself he found the dusky skin of the slave, as well as his hairless muscularity, both beautiful and sensual. Almost like that of a fine horse or hound. The light black curls perched on the top of Mamluk's head were always clean and scented, and his smile forever kind and obedient. Mamluk was a good soul, but an infidel and a slave. Yes, he was Sir Guy's slave, but what that meant exactly, the Knight was not certain. Guy had never owned slaves until he came to this desert land.

"Mamluk. Have you always been a slave?" Sir Guy found himself asking, his eyes half closed as he watched the Arab soap his legs and feet.

Mamluk glanced up at the Knight's exotic blond-bearded face and smiled easily, answering at once, as was required. "Yes. My parents were slaves as well but not my grandparents."

"Yes. And what were they?" Guy pursued, content to let Mamluk wash his feet until doomsday, it was such a luxurious sensation.

"My grandparents were members of a wealthy Caliphate family in Mesopotamia, far from here near Baghdad. We suffered misfortune at the hands of a rival tribe and lost everything. I was sold as a child to the Sultan of Acre, and then won in battle by the Knight Sir Harold Seanaulut de Burgundy who owned this Castle before your Knights Templar," Mamluk explained patiently, moving to work on Sir Guy's other foot.

Guy languidly observed the graceful servant as he spoke, admiring the smooth hands and strong fingers as they laved soap in and around his toes. He was an infidel, but his family had once been free men in far off Mesopotamia and fabled Baghdad. Guy was intrigued and wanted to hear more.

But Mamluk managed to scatter the Knight's thoughts by moving his soapy hands sensually up Guy's aching legs and settling around his crotch to knead and pinch the tender muscles between his now widespread thighs. Guy groaned with delight and closed his eyes once more.

This time as Mamluk's hands moved across his fat ball sack and massaged the pair of semen lemons firmly, Guy's thoughts abruptly became sensual and disturbing. His shaft, nestling beside Mamluk's busy hands, suddenly began to lengthen with unbidden lust.

Guy felt no shame. As a matter of course, he did not find bodily functions or sexual desires unnatural or abhorrent. On

6

the contrary, he was intrigued further, allowing his mind to dwell on the delicious feel of his slave's fingers manipulating his hardening cock and tender inner thighs. After all, Mamluk was Guy's to do with as the Knight pleased. At least that was the basic premise of slavery, he assumed.

Guy opened his eyes. He peered down at the top of Mamluk's finely shaped head. He gazed contemplatively down at the gleaming black hair, the delicate and perfectly formed ears, and the face that was undeniably beautiful in an exotic and foreign way.

Mamluk looked up to see his master staring down at him, and he smiled agreeably as he gently pulled the Knight back down to sink into the warm water again. Mamluk stood and rose from the pool, Sir Guy now gazing at the hairless brown cock and balls that dangled between his slave's legs. He had never really looked at them before, and now found the sight of them arousing. But those tantalizing body parts rose along with Mamluk and out of sight as the slave stepped out of the tiled pool. Mamluk knelt behind his master and began to massage scented soap into his thick blond locks.

Mamluk now took his turn at gazing thoughtfully. He stared down at Sir Guy's face as he worked the lather into Guy's hair. The slave found himself transfixed by the look of pleasure and the strange aspect of surrender playing across the Knight's features as his eyes closed and his mouth hung half open. The full lips parted, glistening wet between the luxurious curls of his soft beard.

"Are you unhappy being a slave?" Sir Guy murmured, without opening his eyes.

Mamluk replied in a low voice. His head now bent close to his master's, their breaths mingled. "No, master. For now I am not."

A sudden crack of thunder boomed, and a flash of lightning illuminated the room.

Sir Guy's eyes flew open to witness the sudden gloom that heralded the fury of the rainstorm's arrival. Clouds opened and sheets of blessedly cool rain poured in torrents from the heavy sky. The redolent scent of new moisture blew across them in a wild gust.

Mamluk, although momentarily startled by the thunder and lightning, had not ceased in his labor of love. He continued to manipulate the scented lather into Sir Guy's temples as the Knight gazed in awe at the magnificent scene unfolding beyond their window.

Guy grinned with a mixture of sensual pleasure from Mamluk's competent hands, and excitement from the rainstorm. He relaxed, giving himself up to his Arab servant's ministrations. As his head tumbled back to be held by Mamluk's delicate hands, Guy found himself gazing up at the face that bent over him. At that very moment, another strike of lightning and peal of thunder shook the stone walls of their fortress to their very foundations.

Heavy rain poured down outside their window, and thunder crashed as Guy continued to gaze up into Mamluk's deep amber eyes. The roaring chaos of nature outside drowned any words he might have uttered. Guy had no conscious realization of his hands rising to grasp his slave's head and pull it down to cover his own. He gave no thought to why he placed his lips over Mamluk's soft, dusky ones. The wet heat of the slave's mouth drowned him as the rain drowned the world outside. Guy opened to the snaking tongue that entered him and probed deep inside.

More thunder boomed around them. A torrent of need flooded Sir Guy's entire body. He seized his Arab slave with both hands and dragged Mamluk down to join him in the hot bath. Guy ran his hands feverishly up and down the smooth dark limbs, clasping the slave to his own larger body without compromise.

Mamluk was equally incensed. He sucked at the French Knight's mouth with his own, jabbing his tongue in the wet opening as far as he could. He gripped Sir Guy's head with his gentle-yet-strong hands, and began to shamelessly rub his

8

suddenly stiff cock up against the powerful body holding him captive.

Sir Guy moaned inaudibly, the sound of pouring rain and crashing thunder overwhelming any of his groans as his mouth was ravaged by the slave he held. He roamed his hands up and down Mamluk's smooth back, amazed at its firmness beneath the flesh. Guy grasped Mamluk's plump buttocks, thrusting his own hard meat against Mamluk's belly as he did. The feel of those ample ass cheeks maddened Guy much like an enraged bull. He rolled and pinched the satiny mounds between his calloused hands, finally digging between them and sliding possessively through the slick crack. He discovered the puckered opening and without hesitation drove a thick finger inside, feeling the hot inner muscle give way to his insistent pressure.

This is my slave, Guy thought madly. I can do anything I want with him!

Mamluk groaned out loud as Sir Guy's finger invaded his butt hole, but his utterances also were drowned by the violence of the rainstorm outside. As mad as his master, Mamluk pushed back against Guy's hand and fucked himself lustfully on that huge finger while sucking his master's tongue deep into his own hot mouth.

Sir Guy stuck two, and then three fingers up his slave's asshole, reveling in the way it opened willingly as Mamluk pressed back against the probing hand. For some reason, the anal orifice must have been previously oiled or greased. Guy's fingers slipped and slid without dragging friction. He gave no thought to why Mamluk would have greased his ass channel, but instead enjoyed the lubricated slide as he managed to drive three fingers deep inside the slave's quivering anus.

Mamluk reached beneath Sir Guy's body and searched for the big white ass submerged below the water. He found it and immediately grasped one massive butt cheek. Mamluk pinched and squeezed the chunky mound as his own ass was violated. Without relinquishing the Knight's hot mouth,

9

Mamluk pulled Sir Guy up to a standing position. The slave clutched both Guy's butt cheeks while driving his own ass back at the same time into the thick trio of fingers impaling him.

Guy pulled his mouth from his slave's and laughed out loud, the gleeful sound entirely overshadowed by the pelting rainstorm and continual peals of thunder. With a sense of overwhelming power, he pivoted Mamluk in his arms and bent him over the edge of the pool.

His hand slid from inside the slave's quivering asshole as they moved, but Guy immediately forced one calloused finger back inside, plunging it to the hilt. With the storm crashing around them, Sir Guy drove that cruel finger in and out of Mamluk's chocolate-brown ass, forcing another along side it, and then another. In his heated madness, Guy noticed the tub of scented soap on the edge of the pool and he reached out to scoop up a generous handful of the slippery substance. Guy poked a well-soaped hand back up into Mamluk's parted butt cheeks and crammed three massive fingers up the hot orifice nestled between them.

Guy gazed down with fascination at the prostrate slave as his ass was steadily violated. The Knight added a forth finger. He added a fifth! Mamluk groaned, his head craned around to regard Sir Guy with pleading eyes while lustily pressing his beautiful, dusky ass backward into the probing hand of his master.

Guy was completely amazed when the frothing hole opened further, and he was able to slide his thumb inside. He was further aroused when he felt that gaping slash back against the pressure, and then against all odds, swallow his entire fist. The Knight was beyond himself as he felt his hand move inside his slave's compliant asshole, completely enveloped in the drooling, pulsing opening.

Guy shouted for his infidel slave to take his hand up his ass, but neither could hear the words as thunder drowned them out. Neither could they hear Mamluk's response, wild pleas for his master to fuck him with his big French fist.

Sir Guy drove his big hand in and out of his slave's squirming ass, rubbing his dripping cock up against the satin-smooth butt cheeks, reveling in the sight of his hand disappearing and reappearing from that willing butt. The pliant anal walls were a squishy, soapy quagmire that Guy found to be the sexiest, most sensual flesh he had ever stroked. He twisted, poked and massaged his slave's insides while staring in awe at the lush brown butt cheeks. Coated with foamy suds, Mamluk's plump ass writhed and bucked with frenzied and unmistakable pleasure.

For his part, Mamluk spread his legs wider and pushed up, swallowing the Knight's hand and sucking it inside his gaping hole with all the expertise he could summon. Lust, and love, drove him to fuck himself senseless. Never had he felt such a powerful force filling him and controlling him. He sobbed with unparalleled joy, unable to believe his beloved Knight and Master was finally fucking him. And with such unbelievable forcefulness!

Thunder shook the solid stones around them and lightning flashed explosively. Sir Guy's enraged lust erupted in a spray of cum. The seed splatted all over his slave's smooth butt cheeks, Guy's fist planted deep inside the Arab's twitching ass.

Mamluk screamed as the Knight yanked a monstrous hand from his dripping hole. The Arab spurted his own load down his legs as another bright flash of lightning blinding them both.

Later, they lay together in Sir Guy's soft bed.

The rainstorm still drowned the world outside. Mamluk was allowed to explore, and eventually invade his master's virgin butt hole during the course of the ecstatic night. Mamluk felt the power of Sir Guy's thick French cock as it slithered between his full, sensual lips.

Altogether they left no territory unexplored as they passed the night in their Palestine Castle redefining the

11

relationship between master and slave, infidel and Christian, lover and friend.

Even later, Sir Guy stood by the balcony and watched the red sunrise wash over a rain-drenched desert land.

He was so far from his home on another continent. He was a Master now, and soon Knights would come to Castle Rock for him to command. Men would offer themselves to the Templar as initiates. Guy would train them. Guy would rule them. That last night with his Arabic slave he had tasted what that would mean.

He laughed in the dawn light.

He could not wait.

# Tale Two: The Initiation of Philippe

*In which Sir Guy de Brussiers, Master at Castle Rock, initiates the first new member under his jurisdiction, Sir Philippe de Chanson of Burgundy.*

From the vantage point of his Castle balcony, Sir Guy de Brussiers observed the first of the stars sparkle into existence in the Palestine sky across the expanse of the blue-green Mediterranean Sea. Other stars quickly followed as darkness descended rapidly, the sea turning blue-black, and only the distant sight of goatherds' campfires remaining to cast any light on the darkened landscape. He smiled to himself, anticipating the night's events that were about to begin.

The tall Knight stretched his thick arms above his head and turned from the fascinating sky scape to meet the eyes of his waiting manservant, the darkly immaculate Mamluk.

"All is prepared. The Knights are gathered below in the confines of the lower feast hall. Sir Philippe de Chanson waits in the chamber adjacent," Mamluk pronounced, his inky-dark eyes smiling, his fluid Arabic-accented French soft to his master's ears.

"Very well, Mamluk. Let's proceed, then, as I'm also ready."

Guy spoke with an affectionate grin, running a hand through the black curls of his servant's scalp. The only hair on Mamluk's otherwise shaved body. Guy loved those tight, short curls. Truthfully, though, he was just as fond of the silken hairlessness of Mamluk's other body parts.

Mamluk obediently led the Master Knight to the appointed chamber, there to bow to the Burgundian Knight awaiting them. The slave then discreetly ensconced himself in a quiet spot in a dimly lit corner of the room.

Sir Guy gazed with silent contemplation at the man who paced the room's small confines. The Knight he observed turned with nervous anticipation to greet him.

"Sir Guy! Is all ready? I admit, I am nervous to begin and cannot stand to wait much longer!" In his exuberance, Philippe's deep voice echoed against the thick stone walls.

Guy smiled enigmatically, but did not answer at once, preferring to continue his perusal of the prospective initiate to their Order. The Knights Templar were a secretive and dedicated group, and Philippe must be wholeheartedly theirs before he could be accepted.

The young Knight had been dispatched to Guy by a relative in France. Guy's cousin had sworn to the upright character and bravery of this particular knight. He had also hinted at Philippe's sexual proclivities. Philippe was unmarried at twenty-two, five years shy of Guy's age. The Knight Templar looked the prospective initiate up and down, pleased at the handsome aspect the Burgundian exhibited. Auburn curls and a neat goatee accented his sensual, full lips, and a hook nose and piercing green eyes fit pleasingly into a strong face. He was tall, taller even than Guy, with long limbs that appeared muscular and fit. The manner in which he paced the room was reminiscent of some fine beast eager to be at its activity, whatever that may be.

"So. You are prepared for your initiation, Philippe de Chanson?" Guy asked quietly, his voice as soft as the dim light cast by the flickering wall torches.

Philippe halted his aimless pacing. He faced Guy squarely, not shy to gaze directly into the older Knight's eyes,

14

before falling to his knees and reaching out to take one of Guy's hands in both of his.

"I'm prepared to take my vows. I desire this with all my heart," Philippe swore in an eager steady voice, although his hands quaked with apparent trepidation.

Guy smiled, not unhappy on noting Philippe's fear. If the Knight was afraid, but managed to overcome his fear, he was a brave man and worthy of their company.

"You must strip then. You go into the initiation as a child from the womb. Nothing of your former life must accompany you." Guy's command was firm, although he had yet to raise his voice.

It was obvious Philippe was not prepared for this order. He momentarily faltered in his obedience as he remained kneeling, gawking up at the blond Knight in confusion. But when Guy said nothing more, Philippe shook his head as if to clear it, then abruptly rose and began to peel off his clothing hastily, ashamed at his fleeting lapse in obedience.

Guy observed intently, while Mamluk did the same from the corner of the chamber. Philippe removed his boots and pantaloons, then blouse and jerkin. Soon he stood erect before them completely nude and unashamed, his large cock flopping in the close heat, his balls pulled up in some measure of fear close against his crotch. A broad back which had seen much sun, and equally tanned arms contrasted with a pale lower body. A slight sheen of sweat glistened where it had gathered just at the junction of his high, tight buttocks. Lean and long, like a fine horse, he was undoubtedly athletic. And virile, which was immediately evident. His flopping prick thickened and threatened to become hard as he sweated under the scrutiny of both his Teacher and his Teacher's slave.

Guy grinned easily, reaching out to touch that hardening cock with his fingertips, which caused it to jerk and stiffen fully. Philippe's body broke out into a more profuse sweat as he allowed the touch and uttered not a word.

15

"Come, Philippe, you will now enter the Chamber of Initiation!" Guy commanded. He pulled the young Knight ahead by the shoulder, and then when he was in front of him, pushed him by a palm placed on one cheek of Philippe's naked buttocks.

The door that led to the Chamber of Initiation was only a scant few feet away. Philippe reached it at once, unhesitating as he opened it. He was greeted by the sounds of male voices chanting, their Latin words blurring together in a deep and thrilling unison.

Two braziers provided sputtering light to the chamber, one in the center of the room and another on a raised dais before an empty hearth. Six Knights, clad in their Templar jerkins with the red crosses emblazoned on white, stood in a line facing Philippe as he entered. It was their voices that boomed out the chant, which resonated around the emptiness of the room.

Guy pushed the naked initiate forward by the buttocks, one of his hands grasping a tight, sweaty cheek and squeezing firmly. Philippe was acutely aware of that hand, and how his cock had not softened, but was painfully erect and bouncing in plain sight before the assembly awaiting him.

The Knights' voices rose higher, the timbre of their chant deeper and more insistent. One of them sprinkled some kind of incense over the brazier they stood behind. Pungent smoke rose to envelope Philippe's nostrils, causing him to sway for a moment as the herb's effects stimulated his faculties.

Guy's hand remained on his buttock, but another found his shoulder and firmly guided him down to his knees, then forced him to place his hands on the rough stones of the floor as well. He was now on his hands and knees like some forest beast. Utterly naked, his head swam from a heady combination of the vibrations of the deep male chant and the smoky incense assailing his nostrils. One of Sir Guy's hands continued to grasp Philippe's naked butt cheek, while the other moved to clasp him in an unyielding grip by the neck. By these two implacable holds, Guy forced Philippe to crawl forward toward the brazier and the six Knights awaiting them.

When they reached the first man in line, Guy thrust Philippe's face down to the tall Knight's feet. His cheeks and mouth were forced to rub across the leather boots the Knight wore. Philippe instinctively understood what was required of him. His tongue darted out to lick and slobber over the smooth black leather of the boot Guy mashed his face into. While he did so, he felt Guy's hand move from the cheek of his ass to the slippery cleft of his buttocks and remain there, pressing against his crack and tender butt hole.

After a moment of this boot attention, Guy abruptly hauled Philippe up by the neck and shoved his face directly into the crotch of the chanting Knight whose leather boot he had just been licking. A cock throbbed beneath the man's pantaloons and Guy pressed Philippe's face into it, rubbing his cheeks and nose along its turgid length. Without a break in the rhythm of his chant, the Knight swiftly dropped his pants, revealing a fat, pulsing prick. The released member leapt out like a striking snake and smacked against Philippe's flushed face.

No directions were uttered, but Sir Guy's guiding hand on his neck was message enough. Guy placed Philippe's mouth directly on the prick that jerked in his face. Philippe opened wide to take the hot phallus inside and swallowed to the full root of it at once. He gobbled and snorted without any sign of reservation.

Slightly dizzy from incense, trepidation, and rising lust, Philippe inhaled deeply through flared nostrils. The ripe scent of the Knight's sexual odor assailed his senses. He tasted the warm cum that leaked from that potent prick, as the fierce chanting continued to echo in his ears. The hazy smoke from the burning incense blurred his eyes and brought tears to them. His mouth was completely stuffed with drooling prick. While he sucked greedily, he felt the hand in his ass crack press against his butt hole. Obligingly, Philippe spread his knees wider to allow that powerful palm to rub against his slick anal opening. Philippe trembled as he felt a thick finger tease his asshole while the rest of that big hand pressed against his parted butt crack.

A bombardment of erotic thoughts confused him as he sucked and licked the first Knight's prick. He was only vaguely aware of being moved to the next Knight in line and being forced to swallow his member in turn. The finger in his ass crack invaded his hole just as the second prick was forced against his face and found his throat. He gagged with submission as he was entered from both ends.

Philippe's ass slot was slippery and heated as Sir Guy slid a finger into its depths. Guy frigged upwards into the naked body of the obedient Knight as Philippe laved attention on the steely rod Sir Duncan was feeding him. Guy observed avidly as Philippe's goateed mouth sucked and grunted. Guy continued to slowly finger the initiate's warm butt hole while his own prick grew rock hard beneath his pantaloons.

The circle of Knights' chanting voices rose higher in a new pitch of sexual excitement as they witnessed Sir Philippe service their fellow Knights. Anticipation of their own forthcoming enjoyment instilled rising vigor in their song.

One of them sprinkled more of the pungent herb over the brazier's flames. Philippe nearly swooned when he inhaled this fresh intoxicant. He slobbered with increased fervor as he worked on the third Knight's long, slim meat. Sir Guy pinned Philippe with his thick finger, working it in and out of the young man's moist butt hole as he moved him to the next Knight in line.

Through the fog of sensations bombarding his pulsing, finger-fucked butt hole, and slobbering prick-fed lips, Philippe realized he had sucked all six of the Knights. Yet he also realized they had not cum in his mouth, nor had he yet. His own prick pulsed stiffly, so far untouched.

Philippe sprawled on his knees naked and half senseless before the Knights. Their pricks pointed at him in erect hardness like steely swords. Their nude, hairy thighs moved slightly up and down in an erotic rhythm as they chanted. Sir Guy held him by the neck and fucked his aching butt hole with that insistent finger. Philippe's now empty mouth drooled and salivated until Sir Guy stuck two fingers in it for him to suck on while one of the Knights stepped toward him.

The chanting did not falter as Philippe felt a white jerkin being dropped over his head, the Templar red cross emblazoned across its front and back. The new cloth only half-covered his nakedness, while his ass continued to experience that intense finger-fuck and his mouth was forcefully violated by two of Sir Guy's other large digits.

The chanting grew louder. He was pushed back onto his hands and knees and compelled to crawl forward toward the dais and the remaining brazier. Sir Guy withdrew his finger from Philippe's sweaty asshole and stood over him as Philippe continued to crawl forward. Somehow, Philippe understood what he should be doing, and he remained on his hands and knees. He clambered up onto the dais before halting at the foot of the burning brazier. Philippe dropped his head to the stone floor, displaying his naked buttocks for the Knights who were moving forward to surround him.

Dressed now only in his new Templar jerkin, he knelt compliantly while the Knights hovered behind him. More of the herb was thrown on the fire, and a burning brand was stuck before his face so that he inhaled great gulps of the intoxicating smoke. He felt a strong hand rubbing some hot, stinging grease along his ass crack, then between his spread legs along his dangling balls and up to his throbbing prick.

His legs were spread wider to allow easier access to his balls and prick for those behind him. The unusual grease was rubbed all along his inner thighs. A big finger pressed some of it inside his tender butt hole, which immediately began tensing and then throbbing as the grease melted. The hand and finger pulled away, and Philippe felt the grease begin to heat up and tingle, then to burn and itch, making him wish with all his might he could rub and fondle himself to relieve the sensation.

19

But he believed he shouldn't – that it was not allowed. In his drugged fog, he began to writhe and moan – the heat and itching on his prick, balls and asshole nearly unbearable. The Knights chanted louder, stroking each other's pricks through joined hands, each pumping his neighbor's on the left. They observed Philippe's writhing contortions with breathless fascination.

Eventually Philippe could no longer resist and drove his hands up under his belly to grasp and rub his own prick. He reached further between his spread thighs from beneath and obscenely dug a finger deep into his own tortured asshole in search of some measure of relief. The Knights watched Philippe's animalistic manipulations with greedy interest, stroking one another's cocks with increased fervor.

But Philippe was not allowed that relief. Sir Guy reached down to remove his hands and place them back at his head. Philippe continued to writhe and twitch, humping his ass in the air, the now distended and reddened butt hole visible as it drooled hot grease, opening and closing with the beat of Philippe's uncontrollable sexual hunger.

Guy removed his own clothing while he gazed down at the prostrate initiate. Philippe appeared as some crazed animal, moaning and grunting, his ass waving in the air, his entire body writhing as if it was crying out to be violated. Guy was naked in moments, his huge, blond-furred body glistening in the smoke and firelight as he planted his feet directly behind Philippe. His crotch was level with Philippe's squirming ass poised above the floor on the raised dais.

Philippe stared with wild eyes back at his naked Master. He moaned loudly at the sight of the fat prick that dripped precum directly onto the entrance to his anus. Philippe could not control himself and mindlessly humped up and down. Guy merely had to stick his hard member against that heaving ass to have it rubbed in the slick grease that leaked from the younger Knight's reddened butt hole and dripped from his swollen ball sack.

Guy did not wait long, though, before seizing the writhing ass and holding it still. His powerful hips thrust forward, and he drove the purple crown of his fuck sword into the warm folds of Philippe's butt-ring. Philippe mewled with intense pleasure, the maddening itch all at once absolved by the insertion of hot prick. He let out an obscene grunt as the lips of his hole were pleasurably distended by the slow but steady introduction of Guy's big pole.

That exquisite sensation was prolonged as Sir Guy fed him his manhood inch by fat inch. Finally, the Master Knight's balls slapped against the greasy crack of Philippe's plump ass. Philippe let out another feverish grunt as Guy's prick hit bottom. As he snorted in air, another Knight yanked up his head and stuffed prick into Philippe's gaping mouth.

Philippe grunted and mewled around the hard flesh that had invaded his mouth. His heated asshole accommodated Sir Guy's enormous, pulsing prick, which was now driving in and out in measured strokes. His guts were aflame, yet now the insane itching became a sweet, moist pleasure. Groaning, Philippe worked avidly with his mouth and tongue over the stiff meat of the Knight he knelt before.

When a stream of sticky cum spurted inside his mouth, he sucked it up and swallowed it greedily, only to have that prick withdrawn from his mouth and another crammed inside. This one soon filled him with warm cum as well, while Sir Guy relentlessly and steadily fucked Philippe's upturned, willing butt.

All six Knights took their turn face-fucking Philippe. Their Master, Sir Guy, observed with profound gratification as he himself continued to thrust his powerful hips forward, driving stiff cock up the slobbering initiate's ass without respite. The burning grease affected him, too, but he was able to hold off his own ejaculation long enough to witness all the other Knights fill Philippe's gaping, beard-rimmed mouth with man-seed.

21

Jay Starre

When the last of the ejaculating Knights withdrew, Philippe moaned feverishly and lay his face down between his folded arms. Cum drooled out from between his lush lips onto the stone floor. One of the Knights knelt beside him and began to jack the kneeling man's greased prick, eliciting incoherent moans from the prostate Philippe. He slobbered on the floor like a beast, then began licking back up the cum that had dribbled from his slack lips. Another Knight took mercy on him and stuck two fingers in his open mouth. In that manner Philippe was provided something to work on while his ass was deep-drilled and his prick was rubbed and twisted torturously.

Philippe screamed out around the fingers in his mouth as he felt his orgasm ripped from him. Hot cum sprayed the floor and even up onto his belly beneath the new jerkin. Sir Guy could hold back no longer when the asshole he pumped began twitching wildly in paroxysms of orgasm. Guy shot spurt after spurt of man juice deep into Philippe's hot, plump butt, while the young Knight flailed and groaned beneath him.

All six Knights gathered around the incoherent and still-twitching initiate. Chanting with increased tempo, they lifted him and carried him to a corner of the chamber where a table had been covered with a soft mat of rushes. They lay the moaning man there tenderly, then finished disrobing and surrounded him. Sir Guy climbed upon the table and sat directly down on Philippe's flushed face, burying the man's mouth and nose with his own widespread butt cheeks.

For the next hour, all six Knights took their turns fucking Philippe's well-juiced ass. Two held his legs up and apart while Guy remained seated on his face. Philippe contented himself with licking and sucking his new Master's warm asshole while cock after cock pumped into his own swollen, tender asshole.

Finally the chanting subsided, the embers of the braziers died out, and the last man erupted up Philippe's tenderized, dripping hole. Sir Guy stretched out beside the young

22

Burgundian Knight in the silence, the other Knights withdrawing and leaving them alone.

Sir Guy's deep voice whispered in the younger man's ear. "You are now a member of the Order of the Knights Templar. Ours fully, obedient and forever marked as our man. You will never divulge the events of this initiation to any man and will participate in future initiations as one of the Teachers. Do you comply, Sir Philippe?"

Philippe sighed, half asleep and totally satiated. He was content to be in the strong arms of his heroic master and mentor, and would willingly follow him anywhere.

"Yes, Master. Yes, Sir Guy. I will obey you forever," he mumbled, then to his surprise and disbelief, he felt pulsing flesh once again pressing against his wet and distended asshole. He sighed and surrendered to Sir Guy's deep kiss as he felt himself sinking again.

The torrid desire of his master's monstrous prick fucked him into sated unconsciousness.

# Tale Three: The Knight's Witchcraft

*In which the youthful German Baron, Siegfried von Bartlet experiences the mystic embraces of the Knight Templar, Sir Gerhardt Slalciz, on the shores of the Palestine Sea.*

The young German Baron, Siegfried von Bartlet of Saxony, was just eighteen years old the day he set sail for the Holy Land from Sicily with his equally young wife. His father had sent him, after arranging his marriage with a Lombard princess, Livonia Emeche. From his castle in the northern forests of Germany, the older Baron directed his son's life without a qualm or thought to the boy's own desires. Siegfried obeyed, as ever he did his father's wishes, without vocally questioning the man's indomitable will.

Secretly, he was despondent.

That night as they sailed across the tranquil seas of the Mediterranean, Siegfried stood alone gazing out toward the half moon that nearly touched the darkly placid waters. A gentle breeze touched his soft blond beard and rustled the shoulder-length golden curls that graced his handsome head. A strapping young man, of renowned abilities in the field with horse and sword, he had only just learned of the duties of husband, and under the spell of the liquid moon was contemplating his ungratifying accomplishments. He was not happy. The third night now with his new wife had proved as unsatisfactory as the first two. Livonia had lain passive while he thrust himself within her, finally achieving orgasm after much sweating and intense concentration. She had not even fully unclothed herself, nor uttered a single word of encouragement or love.

It was to be expected. They had only just met, and the Lombard princess was uncomfortable. But in his heart, he knew it was more. He was not terribly excited about all of it anyway, although he had hoped he would have been. He desired an heir and children. After all, that was the purpose of marriage, at least with Royal families. But he was a lusty young man and felt somehow cheated.

At that moment he spied his companion and fellow Knight across the bow, staring at the same moon he himself was infatuated with on that hushed evening.

Siegfried silently contemplated the figure of the Swabian Knight. Gerhardt Slalciz was his accountant and servant, and a member of the infamous Order of the Knights Templar. He had met up with him on the journey south from Saxony, as also arranged by his father.

They had spoken together amiably from the start, but Gerhardt was a quiet and solitary man, not given to drink or cards or other frivolity, bearing his duties with measured gravity. Darkly handsome with short raven hair and a neat goatee, his smile when displayed was white with innocent generosity. Older than the young German Baron by at least five years, Gerhardt was a qualified and observant advisor for the Baron. He was in charge of their finances on this trip to the Holy Land, where they would do business after engaging in an obligatory battle with the heathen Moslems. They were to seek out a certain Castle Rock, and a Master of the Order of Knights Templar, Sir Guy de Brussiers of France. Gerhardt was to join Sir Guy's cell. The Knights Templar were renowned bankers, and Siegfried was to conduct his Father's business with Sir Guy then return to Saxony.

Siegfried thought of these things briefly as he watched the enigmatic Gerhardt. The Swabian appeared to be completely fascinated by the floating moon and did not realize the young Baron was watching him. He made no attempt to hide his worshipful demeanor as he knelt against the wooden ship's gently rocking railing and raised his hands in prayer, eyes fixed on the moon's luminescent glow.

Siegfried gasped as he witnessed the display, realizing it for the rumored trances of which many of the ship's men had been whispering. His own wife had made fearful utterances on the subject that very morning.

"The Knight Templar serves the devil! He communes with the moon at night and falls into a strange trance. He must not be trusted! Send him away to battle when we reach the Holy Land. Let the infidels kill him. We all know of the strange and unholy doings of those Knights Templar," Livonia had argued in her Latin-accented German.

Siegfried found himself unable to tear his eyes away from the scene. An eerie glow seemed to emanate from the kneeling Knight. He shook his head and laughed at himself. The moon was merely casting its peculiar light on Gerhardt, and he was praying to God most likely, not Satan. Siegfried genuinely enjoyed the man and instinctively trusted him. Trust was not an easy commodity to acquire in the life of a German Prince.

After a few moments, Gerhardt rose from his spot and turned away from Siegfried who continued to watch with interest as the lithe man strode off in the opposite direction. Siegfried's eyes unerringly searched out the rounded, muscular globes of the Swabian Knight's buttocks in their tight breeches. His cock hardened instantly, unslaked by the evening's sexual encounter with his new wife. Siegfried sighed and turned back to contemplate the moon further, ashamed of his lusty thoughts.

The voyage continued with other late evenings when Siegfried would pace the decks of their ship. Sometimes he spoke with Gerhardt openly, and other times Siegfried observed him from a hidden spot in the shadows. Gerhardt invariably prayed to the moon, if he believed no one was watching. Whenever Siegfried observed this prayerful trance, the young Baron found himself unduly stimulated. Hovering in the shadows, Siegfried began one of these nights to pleasure himself. He let a hand slide down into his breeches where he fondled and manipulated his aching flesh. With eyes peering through the night toward the object of his fascination, Siegfried gazed at the Knight Templar who in turn gazed at the moon with unwavering, ecstatic eyes.

Once, near the end of their voyage, Siegfried became so involved with his own manipulations, he spilled his seed over his own pumping hand as he regarded Gerhardt kneeling alone communing with God. It seemed a sacrilege, but the young Baron couldn't deny it had been very gratifying.

When they made landfall in Palestine, they were all similarly possessed by the holiness of their journey and descended to the sandy shore with reverent emotions ruling their hearts. The sun-beaten land was blistering hot, yet strangely beautiful in its historic and wondrous aspect. Siegfried escorted his diminutive Italian wife, who with the rest of the crew knelt and prayed when they touched the sand of the Holy Land. Gerhardt was the exception. He bowed to the Baron and asked to be excused for a brief time to pray alone on this momentous occasion.

"He goes to perform the work of the devil!" Livonia hissed in her husband's ear.

Others of the crew cast glances at the mysterious Knight themselves, but when Siegfried paid no attention, they returned to their duties at once.

Their camp was set up on a rise of ground while messengers were dispatched to alert the local Christian Maronite authorities of their arrival. Siegfried decided to take a walk himself and ascertain the whereabouts of his liege Knight and accountant. He said nothing to his wife who was ensconced within the protection of an amply supplied and commodious tent.

Siegfried had removed some of his cumbersome clothing, stripping down to a bare undershirt, sleeveless in the warmth, and light breeches. His muscular arms were tanned from the summer's sun in Saxony. As he was a young man who enjoyed the outdoors, he had no trouble traversing the rocky seashore to the north in the direction Gerhardt had taken.

It was many minutes and nearly a mile before Siegfried clambered over a rocky trail and spotted the Knight Templar at a distance below him on a secluded strand of beach. For some reason Siegfried remained where he was and hid himself. He reasoned with himself that he was merely allowing the Knight his privacy. He was ashamed to admit he enjoyed observing Gerhardt without the Knight's permission, even though he had been doing just that for many nights aboard ship.

On the shore below, the tall, dark-haired Knight Gerhardt knelt just out of reach of the waves. Obviously praying, his hands pressed together while his gaze turned upwards toward the empty heavens. His strong back was bent, and he bowed periodically, so his forehead would nearly touch the sandy beach. In obeisance to God, Siegfried imagined. Or the Devil, as Siegfried's wife would have it.

The young Baron felt certain, though, it was to God whom Gerhardt prayed. He was a kind and unassuming man with a special aspect of wisdom that Siegfried envied. There could be no evil lurking in that generous soul.

Gerhardt abruptly rose from his supine position. While Siegfried watched, the Knight removed first his tunic with its holy emblem of the red cross, and then his undershirt to stand naked to the waist. His back was clean and hairless, and both broad and muscular. A narrow waist divided the wide back from the swell of rounded, powerful buttocks. Siegfried had no time to grow accustomed to the sight before the Knight inexplicably removed his breeches as well, and stood completely nude in the Palestine sunlight.

Siegfried was both stunned and enthralled. Having never seen the man completely disrobed, his hungry eyes darted around, taking in everything at once. The white buttocks gleamed in the sunlight. Strong, lightly-haired hamstrings led to thick calves and naked feet now burrowed in the sandy beach. Totally naked in the open daylight under the sun, Gerhardt emanated a sensual aura that captivated the spying Siegfried. The German swiftly pulled his raging prick from beneath his breeches and began to rub and stroke its length. His breath came in gasps as he gawked hungrily at the naked Knight below him.

Gerhardt strode forward, his ass muscles rippling in beautiful display of muscularity. When reaching the ocean, he knelt in the water and again raised his hands in prayer. His legs were widespread, and Siegfried strained to see what appeared to be Gerhardt's man sack dangling between the magnificent globes of his ass.

While Siegfried peered from his high spot, Gerhardt unashamedly took his own member in his hand and began to stroke it. At least, that was what Siegfried believed he was doing. The Baron could not see Gerhardt's front, but Gerhardt's hands were moving at his waist, and his ass was clenching and unclenching in rhythmic spasms. Gerhardt's body bent forward and his back tensed as his elbows moved rapidly up and down.

Siegfried moved closer, stealthily clambering down the rocky slope until he was within ten feet of the man. He moved as silently as he would have when hunting a boar in the forest of Saxony. Siegfried was out of the wind now and could hear the kneeling Knight's gasping breath, and even what he perceived to be the slapping of Gerhardt's hands as they massaged his prick. Siegfried stood absolutely still, resisting the powerful urge to manipulate his own cock, instead devoting his entire attention on the sensual sight in front of him.

Gerhardt spread his legs wider in the shallow water and bent forward, straining to achieve an orgasm as he mumbled prayers between grunts and gasps. The young Baron was amazed when Gerhardt employed one strong hand to reach around between his own buttocks, seeking with eager fingers deep into the crack of his own ample ass. Those fingers found the puckered hole there while Siegfried watched, his eyes nearly popping out of his head. When Gerhardt inserted two large digits up between the crinkled lips of his own asshole, quite plainly for the German prince to witness, Siegfried was overcome, and at once ejaculated mightily without even touching his own cock.

Siegfried attempted to breathe without sound, even as his balls and cock exploded in orgasm. The Baron continued to watch until the kneeling Knight had jerked and spasmed himself into his own ecstasy, unaware that he was being observed from only a few feet away.

Gerhardt leaned forward and groaned loudly, his fingers still deep between his own white, clenching ass, his body convulsing in the shallow waters of Palestine, naked under the harsh light of the afternoon sun. While he did so, Siegfried made his silent escape, clambering up and over the rough escarpment to hide once again above the kneeling Knight.

For some time Gerhardt remained naked and kneeling at the edge of the water before he plunged into its blue-green depths and swam out to nearly disappear in the distance. Siegfried looked on, breathing hard and again taking his own youthful member in his hands to play with it. He could not get enough of the sight of the naked Knight, but eventually he had to return to his camp or be missed.

That night while they sat at dinner and afterward when they sat in council, Gerhardt appeared as serene as ever. Siegfried spoke with him as often as possible, jesting with him in an extremely amiable manner, pouring him wine and entertaining him with stories. All the while Siegfried undressed the dark Swabian Knight with his imagination, recalling the man's fingers jabbing up his own pulsing butt hole on the edge of the Palestine Sea. Finally, when it was necessary to seek his own bed, the German Baron attempted to copulate with his young wife. Livonia lay still as a stone, as usual. Siegfried yearned to plunge into her and violently relieve his desires but was afraid of her fragility. And, he was unwilling to coerce her into something she seemed not to desire.

He achieved another orgasm, which he found satisfactory only in the feeling that he may have got his wife with child as was his duty. But as he drifted off to sleep his thoughts were not of heirs or his wife. They danced with memories of the handsome and serene Knight of the Order Templar, and his exquisite naked back and buttocks.

Over the next few days, they reconnoitered the area and met with envoys of the Christians living nearby. The two men worked together daily, planning their strategies and performing their diplomatic work amiably. But Siegfried's mind would inexplicably picture the sturdy Knight naked before him and his cock would strain and harden beneath his trousers. Or when the Swabian Knight was walking ahead of him or bending to some task, Siegfried would see the form of his buttocks and suddenly imagine the man's own hands digging between those lush globes and inserting themselves in his own private hole.

Siegfried was filled with lusty thoughts whenever the two men were together, which was almost all the time. When he took some object from Gerhardt's hand, he would picture the fingers of that hand digging into the Knight's own white ass and then into the red and puckered hole Siegfried had glimpsed briefly on the Palestine beach.

When several days of this agony/ecstasy had gone by, Gerhardt asked the Baron to be excused, as he wished to be alone and pray. Siegfried readily acquiesced, allowing the Knight to leave but then hastening to follow him at once. A stealthy and accomplished stalker, Siegfried was easily able to track the Knight to a secluded spot on the Palestine shore.

From his hidden vantage point Siegfried regarded the praying Knight with keen attention, pulling out his own thick and drooling prick. Again, he was rewarded as the Swabian Knight of the Templar stripped, his nudity an obscene yet wondrous sight in the stark clarity of the afternoon light. As Gerhardt knelt once more in the shallows, Siegfried moved forward to stand as close behind the man as he could, this time only four or five feet away.

Almost immediately, Gerhardt's elbows and arms began their movements, and the Knight's back and buttocks clenched and strained in sexual contortions. But this time when the

Knight once more sought out his butt hole with one of his hands, Siegfried could not hold back a barely audible groan of lust. When the Swabian had pulled apart a white cheek to display his tender red asshole, bare and hairless, Siegfried's groan was loud in the silence, and hearing himself, the young Baron froze in fear.

To Siegfried's utter humiliation, the kneeling Knight turned and caught sight of him.

Siegfried's fat cock was in one hand while his frightened eyes stared directly into the innocent blue ones of the man of the Templar. For a brief moment their gazes locked. Then inexplicably, Gerhardt slowly turned away, and bending gracefully at the waist, displayed his spread butt cheeks without so much as a word.

The hand that had been pulling apart those substantial mounds continued to do just that. Seeking out and finding the red asshole, Gerhardt fingered it lasciviously right before Siegfried's stunned eyes. He could not move, rooted to the spot as he witnessed his friend's fingers circle and rub across the lips of his puckered and twitching butt hole.

Finally, as if in a dream, Siegfried did move forward. Kneeling without conscious volition behind the Knight's widespread legs, he found himself dropping his face ever so slowly. Eventually his cheeks grazed against the naked flesh of Gerhardt's ass.

Gerhardt glanced backwards briefly, then leaned forward. His face nearly kissed the shallow water of the Mediterranean Sea, his butt now higher in the air. The young Baron knelt behind him, Siegfried's face barely an inch from the hand that played so provocatively with his liege Knight's puckered asshole. Breathing in gasps, Siegfried was riveted by that sight as Gerhardt's fingers teased the twitching opening, one finally dipping inside where the fingernail and then part of the knuckle disappeared. He gasped again as that finger moved slowly deeper. When it popped out and the red hole was momentarily open to the air, Siegfried threw all his reservations

33

to the wind and lunged forward to drive his tongue within the hot, sweating confines of Gerhardt's sweet butt hole.

Slobbering, the Baron licked and sucked greedily, amazed at the heat and the slickness of what he found between Gerhardt's widespread cheeks. He reached out to clutch the Knight's naked back, and then gripping him with all his considerable strength, pulled back on the man as he pressed his face deep into Gerhardt's pale butt.

At that moment, as Siegfried slid his tongue up into Gerhardt's pulsing anus, the mystical Swabian spoke for the first time.

"Yes! That's it my young friend. Taste the gate of heaven before you enter. Drive your tongue into the holy sacrament before your angry member violates its ramparts!"

Gerhardt's husky voice was a loud whisper, his silken tones and outrageous commands further inflaming the Baron's lust.

Of course Gerhardt himself was in heaven already, staring behind himself at the blond German's face buried in his butt, the handsome youth's hot tongue digging into his asshole. It was undoubtedly the single most wondrous feeling he had ever experienced. The bearded, muscular nobleman eating out his ass was a sight to see, and Gerhardt shoved backwards with rapturous glee as the Baron gripped his back fiercely and held Gerhardt's ass against his face. Gerhardt had dreamed of such a moment and prayed for it on many a moonlit night since becoming acquainted with the beautiful young nobleman. But the reality was beyond any fantasy. He nearly sobbed with the power of his joy.

Meanwhile Siegfried could not get enough of the taste of Gerhardt's firm butt, licking up and down the crack, biting at the solid but pliable cheeks, and then seeking out and rimming deep into the warmth of the dark hole. All the while he grasped the Knight's back and ribs firmly in his hands so that he could neither move nor resist. No need for that fierce grip, though, as

Gerhardt wanted that face in his ass as much as Siegfried wanted to be eating ass.

"Yes, Siegfried! Bite my buttocks, lick my private entrance, tongue my insides while I obey your commands and allow you whatever you desire. Plunder me with your hot mouth!" Gerhardt moaned the lewd words, pressing backwards, grunting with bestial lust as the Baron's tongue penetrated his butt hole again and again.

The heat of the sun was mellowed by the cool waters of the sea that washed their knees, and the soft wet sand against their feet. But their sexual craving created more heat and sweat until it became unbearable for the Baron, who was still clothed. He pulled his mouth reluctantly from the butt feast he savored. Feverishly, he tore his clothing from his body. In front of him, Gerhardt remained kneeling with legs wide and ass open, his butt hole wet and dripping from the Baron's mouth juices.

"Enter me! Drive your member deep into my soul, Siegfried!" Gerhardt gasped, waving his ass and staring back at the now naked young German. The thickly muscled youth was a vision, blond hair covering his pectorals and thighs, his cock twitching and straining, poking obscenely from his hips, while his huge furry balls swelled in eager anticipation. That sight transformed Gerhardt into a pleading worshipper.

"Please! I need you deep in me. I've wanted you since I first laid eyes on you! Fuck me, Siegfried," he groaned.

The Baron wasted no time in idle chatter. He lunged forward to encompass the Knight Templar in his powerful embrace, his cock heading straight for its intended target between Gerhardt's spread-eagled thighs. When the heat and tightness of Gerhardt's butt hole encompassed the tip of the Baron's dripping dick, he thought he would die. But before that unlikely event could transpire, Siegfried drove deeper, and then deeper, spreading the hole with his girth until he had violated Gerhardt completely, his balls firm against the Knight's sweat-soaked butt cheeks.

Gerhardt grunted with the force of the penetration, then emitted a mewling sound of utter surrender as he felt the thick hardness pulsing inside him. In his spiritual frenzy, he felt himself to be a beast spread out on the beach and fucked by a stronger and more powerful animal. Siegfried pumped into him, lunging and driving eagerly, his violence and joy intermixed, holding back nothing. Gerhardt was impaled, speared, gored, and reveled in it.

Siegfried couldn't get enough of the kneeling Knight's wondrous body. His hands searched around Gerhardt's taut ribs and took hold of the Knight's tender pointed nipples. Pinching those sensitive tit nibs harshly while grunting with savage pleasure, Siegfried fucked relentlessly, his cock pounding Gerhardt's willing hole without cessation.

"Yes! Yes! Aagggghh! Fuck my ass! Stick it in me. I want it!" Gerhardt gasped out, his breath knocked violently from his lungs with every powerful thrust of the Baron's thick rod.

Siegfried responded to the gasped pleas with guttural joy, whispering into his friend's ears as he covered Gerhard's naked body with his own. "Take it! Take it like a Knight Templar! Take my big prick up your hole. You want it, you slattern. You want me to pound your sweet ass with all my might!"

Siegfried held nothing back. Unafraid of hurting the tall Knight beneath him, he pounded his hole with abandon. He pinched Gerhardt's tender tits, and then seized Gerhardt's long slimy cock and squeezed it fiercely, eliciting a cry of mixed pain and pleasure from the man's drooling lips.

He sought out and discovered Gerhardt's dangling ball sack next, pulling and torturing those hefty nuts violently while yanking on the Knight's twitching prick. Gerhardt shouted out, ramming his ass back for deeper thrusts in an attempt to alleviate some of the agonizing pressure now engulfing his entire crotch, from his throbbing prick and tortured balls to his battered asshole.

Gerhardt muttered and screamed at each new sensation. "Oh yes, please, oh no, don't, yes, no, oh, ahhh…" As his ass was rammed, his balls were stretched back and his cock was pinched and slapped, arousing opposing and gut-churning sensations. His butt hole was on fire. The snug slot had transformed into an open, sloppy doorway that Siegfried had no trouble driving into to the hilt with his fat prick. The feelings of cock stuffing Gerhardt's guts was searing and delicious, but the constant pain of the Baron's manipulations of his sensitive cock and balls drove him to both distraction, and a fierce joy.

As Gerhardt felt his prostate being battered with a raging violence, his balls roiled with cum about to erupt. He let out a whimpering gurgle as jism spurted upwards to shoot out of the tip of his tortured prick being yanked by Siegfried's strong fist. Gerhardt bucked beneath the Baron and cried out, drooling into the waves lapping over his knees and legs.

Siegfried's own grunts of bestial joy joined Gerhardt's as the ejaculating Knight's asshole convulsed around his pounding member. Siegfried, with his cock already on fire from the pounding he applied to Gerhardt's sweet butt hole, spewed an abrupt river of semen. Deep into the violated Knight's tender insides, the seed gushed and spurted. At the same time, Siegfried felt slimy cum erupting from the prick he gripped in one flailing hand. He was incensed by this obvious signal of Gerhardt's lusty surrender. Siegfried drove his shaft deeper and harder up the Knight's ass while his own man scum pumped into Gerhardt's reamed-out hole.

Withdrawing while still shooting, Siegfried yanked the Knight around roughly and embraced him face to face. He thrust his tongue inside Gerhardt's hot, slack mouth, his cum spraying over the man's belly and chest in spurt after copious spurt.

Rubbing together like animals they tongue-fucked each other's mouths while their sperm ran out between their mashed stomachs. Both men twitched and jerked, their bare butts clenching and unclenching as their forceful orgasms slowly subsided.

After some moments, while they still kissed, Gerhardt's hands found their way between the pliable young buttocks of the Baron, and boldly played with the virgin hole, now sweaty and soft. Siegfried groaned while Gerhardt's mouth still sucked on his own, allowing and anticipating the fingers that rubbed against his tender fuck hole.

Gerhardt pulled his mouth away and laughed out loud, his fingers playing with his Master's young asshole. Siegfried joined his exuberant laughter, willingly shoving his virgin butt back against the teasing fingers.

"You'll make an excellent Knight of the Order Templar. Let me prove it to you!" Gerhardt grinned, his voice low and husky, his fingers speaking volumes as they did their tantalizing work exploring the Baron's sweet young asshole.

Siegfried sighed with delight. Lying in the arms of his new masculine lover, under the exotic Palestine sun and washed by the gentle waves of the Palestine shore, he experienced a profound sense of relief.

His life would not be as barren as he had feared.

The future definitely appeared more promising now. Who knew what this Castle Rock would prove to be? Or how magnificent this mysterious Sir Guy whom Gerhardt spoke of in such reverent tones?

Siegfried could not wait to find out.

# Tale Four: In Ethiopia

*In which four Knights Templar explore the hidden lands of Ethiopia and discover Black priests and an unexpected orgy.*

The four Knights abandoned their slaves and servants on the coastal plain before ascending the mountains of fabled Ethiopia. They also left behind the sweltering heat and encountered instead a welcome moisture-laden breeze. The forest was thick around them, but the escarpment they traveled was giving way to a pleasant track. They had been promised this narrow trail would eventually lead them to their destination.

They sought a mysterious holy monastery of Christian black men, spoken of in whispers throughout the Holy Land. The Knights' Master, Sir Guy de Brussiers, had commanded them to seek it out and ascertain if there was some merit to the rumors.

As usual, the Knights Templar who trekked through the African jungle also had a hidden agenda. Their order was secretive and ambitious, beyond what they would claim they performed for their Christian God. This afternoon the Knight who led them, Sir Daignold Assnault of Toulouse, was contemplating the feasibility of economic gain in the hidden jungles of black Africa. His thoughts were abruptly disrupted when he rounded a turn in the path and encountered a wondrous opening in the forest canopy.

There, in magnificent splendor lay a hidden lake of serene, aquamarine waters. In its center floated an island surrounded and nearly obscured by all manner of flying fowl.

Every hue of the rainbow flitted through the air as the amazing array of bird life sailed and soared over the lake.

"Miene Gott!" Sir Daignold heard at his shoulder. It was his fellow Knight, Heinz Brauhauf of Bavaria uttering the expletive, the German's big hand snaking out with supple alacrity to land and rest on the shorter Captain's shoulder.

"Magnifique, oui, Heinz! The fabled Lake of the Monastery. Look there in the center of the island, the rooftops of some type of structure!" Daignold replied. He was completely comfortable with the nearness of his companion who leaned up against his back with such familiarity.

Two other men crowded close and gazed in awe at the splendid scene. They also spotted the golden domes of some structure half-hidden by green jungle out on the island. They, too, watched in wonder as the thousands upon thousands of lake birds rose and fell in waves across the placid lake. These two brother Knights from Aragon were named Sir Alfonse Della and Sir Jaime Della. Twins, they had dusty Spanish complexions with nearly identical features. Both boasted amber eyes of dreamlike beauty, which now gazed in wide-eyed marvel at the serene lake and its island. Those pairs of beautiful eyes widened considerably when a delicate barque sailed out from a cove to their left only a scant few hundred yards away, startling the sturdy Knights with its inexplicable appearance.

Astounding the gathered men, a clear voice cried out in melodious and unmistakable French. "Hail, mighty Knights of the Order Templar!" The owner of that voice was a tall half-nude African, his skin of such a shining obsidian it seemed to glow in the afternoon sunlight. A half dozen other men, equally as black and half-naked manned the boat, working the sail and the set of oars.

"And hail to you, whoever you may be, kind sir. How do you know us?" Sir Daignold replied on the instant, his quick wits the reason for his leadership of the quest.

The smiling African answered as quickly, just as the boat struck the shoreline before the gathered Knights. "I am

40

Dado. At your service. We're here to welcome you for our Holy Master, Miseria, whom has sent us to fetch you to the Holy House of the Island."

Ferried to the mysterious island, the Knights spent the initial hour in illuminating conversation with the intelligent black man, Dado. He revealed tantalizing glimpses of secrets which only whetted the Knights' appetites for more. Refusing to elaborate, instead he eventually ushered the four travelers into the presence of his Holy Master.

Somewhat of a disappointment, he was seated humbly on the floor amidst an open chamber that looked out over the lake and the distant jungle.

The ancient Master scattered bread crumbs and fruit pits before him, all manner of birds alighting from the balcony window to taste of his generosity. He merely glanced at the strange Knights and cackled, speaking in his African tongue to Dado, who bowed and chuckled in return.

"The Holy Master bids me welcome you to his island. He has never seen Franks in the flesh before," Dado translated.

The inhabitants of the Holy Land labeled all Europeans who traveled to their lands "Franks," even though the Knights were of many different nations. What surprised the four Knights, though, was the fact these isolated monks had even heard of Franks, and Knights Templar. Daignold was about to ask just this, when Dado held up a hand to silence him.

"I'm to be your guide while you remain on the Holy Island. I'll answer all your queries and offer to you our hospitalities." Dado smiled and bowed politely, but it was clear their interview, such as it was, with the Holy Master was at an end. The handsome Dado escorted the Knights from the Master's room and further beyond, into the monastery.

Immaculate and beautiful, the building was the essence of simplicity with little adornments or comforts throughout its whitewashed rooms. Shortly, the intrigued Knights were gathered together in another large chamber as simple and clean as the others.

41

Dado clapped his hands, and several strapping young black men appeared instantly. Naked as Adam in the Garden of Eden, they bore baskets of fruits, sweet and full of scent, jugs of aromatic liquids, steaming bowls of exotic meats and soups, and finally breads and puddings. All was laid on the floor atop a marvelously woven rug that would no doubt serve as banquet table.

"Relax. Eat and drink. We'll attend to your clothing and washing needs at your leisure," Dado said pleasantly. Again bowing politely, he caught Daignold's eye and offered an enigmatic wink.

The Knights grinned at one another and set to with relish, unafraid of strange foods. They were avid explorers, which is why Sir Guy had dispatched them on this particular mission. Whatever came their way they would surely make the most of it. What actually came their way, proved to be far beyond their wildest expectations.

While they dined casually on the floor, the naked black men saw to all their needs. Hovering over the Knights with bright smiles and ready hands, Daignold was awed by their glistening beauty. Muscular and hairless, their bodies were close to perfection, although none was as tall and mighty as the breathtaking Dado who stood by and watched over them with massive arms crossed over his black chest. Daignold was amused by the way their cocks and balls swung freely while they moved back and forth or bent to offer more food or drink. All boasted lengthy, thick members, covered over by dangling foreskins the likes of which he had never seen.

Another astonishing sight that titillated Daignold was the way their naked bodies were adorned with one simple embellishment. Their hairless black chests were each pierced through the nipples, thick silver or gold rings inserted in the holes. The adornments made their taut nipples stand out almost an inch with erect lushness.

Heinz Brauhauf was equally entranced by the black servants' nipple rings. He commented on it to his Captain, leaning close to murmur in his thick Bavarian-accented French, "Sir Daignold, but how strange these forest men are! Their tits are ringed in this bizarre manner. I'd like to feel one of them. They have an enticing look about them."

"Go ahead. You may do so," Dado called out from across the banquet rug, miraculously having overheard the German Knight's whisper.

Heinz' blond head shot up in consternation, surprised the black man could have heard him. But his handsome countenance lit up in a delighted smile when one of the black servants leaned over to press his be-ringed chest directly into the Bavarian's face.

Heinz obliged the man by reaching up to fondle and tug on the gold rings he presented to the leering Knight. The Bavarian's face flushed with sensual glee at the pliable feel of those erect nipples as he stretched them out from the ebony man's muscular breast.

The Della brothers stared wide-eyed at their companion as he manipulated the African's chest, their bodies leaning close as they often did when they were thinking alike. Their liquid brown eyes dropped as one to gaze at the servant's crotch as his lengthy cock began to rise and thicken under Heinz' nipple manipulation. In a matter of seconds, each of the four Knights had a black servant standing in front of him. Each one obligingly bent over to present their chests for the Franks' explorations.

Daignold reached out for the chest of the man hovering over him, tugging at the silver rings that dangled before his eyes. He pulled and twisted them, glancing up to see the black servant's eyes open wide and his mouth turn slack from the fierce manipulation. Daignold decided to tug the rings and then to pinch the extended nipple with the nails of his fingers. He was fascinated by the paleness of his fingers against the African's deep black flesh. Daignold was also aware of the cock that had begun to swell between the man's legs. As the man's nipples were lightly tortured and stimulated, that black dick

43

swiftly engorged with blood and became a throbbing column of fuck meat. Utterly amazed, Daignold twisted harder.

The Della brothers had gone farther. Leaning upwards with like minds they sucked and bit on the men's tits, playing with their tit rings with their white Spanish teeth and mouthing the black nipples eagerly. Hard, jutting black cocks waved between the black men's thighs while the Della brothers slurped and sucked the natives' sensitive tits.

Totally entranced by the nipple rings and bobbing cock, Daignold was startled when he heard a loud clapping from Dado. The servants instantly responded by rising up to disengage themselves from the Frankish Knights' eager ministrations. Swiftly, they cleared away the food, their big hard cocks swaying between their legs while they worked. Not knowing what to expect next, the Knights stood up and congregated in the center of the room.

They turned toward Dado. The towering man offered his usual smile and bow, "Please come with me. You must be eager to remove your soiled clothing and bathe. The Holy Master's servants will assist you."

After glancing at their Captain who nodded his assent, the Franks followed without objection. In an adjoining room they met back up with the identical black men who had just been serving them, each beautiful and glowing with ebony manliness.

The Knights were assisted to disrobe, their cumbersome leather jerkins and leggings pulled swiftly from their bodies by the deft servants. In moments, the Knights were stripped entirely naked and being urged into a large steaming pool overlooking the lake and the jungle. While birds flew by and called out in their raucous voices, the Knights splashed and cavorted in the luke-warm water of the pool. All the while the compliant servants massaged and lathered their bodies with perfumed soaps.

Although Daignold was powerfully built, he was the shortest of the four Franks. He was dwarfed by the tall black men, the one assisting him towering at least a foot and a half above him. Dark haired himself, with a neat goatee of auburn curls, Daignold was a handsome man, bordering on pretty with his delicate features and mouth. In comparison, the black man hovering over him as he sprawled languidly on the side of the pool was huge. Next to the smaller Knight, the black man appeared almost as a potent, masculine giant.

From his spot across the pool, Heinz stared at the Captain, taking in the curious sight of the two so very different men. He grew lusty as he observed the black servant lean over to massage the Captain's small head. Big, black beastly balls dangled close to the French Knight's delicate mouth.

Heinz gasped at what he saw next. The servant's mammoth cock swelled and bobbed, grazing one of the Captain's cheeks. At that moment, Daignold turned and caught Heinz's eyes. With a mischievous grin and with his eyes still on Heinz, Daignold opened up his mouth and took the tip of that black cock between his small, but full lips. Still eyeing Heinz, Daignold sucked the big cock deep into his mouth.

Heinz's jaw dropped open and his own cock hardened with pounding lust. The sight of that enormous ebony meat beginning to slide inside Daignold's delicate mouth excited him so much he couldn't contain himself. He rose up and splashed his way through the warm pool toward the Captain. Once there, he stood over the two men and watched his Captain suck the big black cock. Heinz rubbed his own substantial, although ivory pale, cock with both his beefy hands while he watched the stimulating suck-job.

Daignold's eyes were on his blond friend while he attempted to engulf the mighty African cock being stuffed between his lips. He snorted and almost gagged as it drove deeper and deeper down his willing throat. As he swallowed the meat, the scent of jungle flowers and masculine musk combined in his flared nostrils. The proximity of his tall Bavarian companion, especially with Heinz manipulating his own fat cock close to Daignold's face, sent a gratified thrill through the French Knight's naked body.

Heinz gawked, enthralled at the picture of his Captain's face rape, but was at that moment experiencing another incredible sensation. Behind him, his own servant was running soft but expert hands over him while a massive intruder thrust up between Heinz's pale butt cheeks.

In the blink of an eye, the servant had his cock stuck directly between Heinz's muscular ass cheeks, banging up against his sensitive anal hole. Heinz yelped and attempted to move forward, but the African pinned the Knight Templar's powerful frame with his long black arms. Heinz surrendered without much of a struggle, his cock unexpectedly seized by the Captain's outstretched hand, which sent a shiver of delight coursing through him. The giant slab of flesh rubbing in his ass crack was hot and wet, some kind of lubricant making it slippery as it prodded his tender hole. Heinz's mouth opened and a groan escaped his lips as he capitulated to his lust and sat back to allow the tip of the black cock to penetrate his butt hole.

Heinz's eyes were locked on the sight of Daignold being force-fed a long ebony rod, the small mouth opening impossibly wide. The Captain's muffled gags and moans only served to further energize the watching German Knight.

As black cock began to push into Heinz, and the pain seemed too great to be accepted, he lurched forward and grasped the big black butt hovering over Daignold's face. His white hands slid between those smooth, perfect cheeks and discovered the puckered opening hidden between. He dug deep with two fingers of each hand just as he felt himself being impaled fully by the dark invader from behind. As the huge servant fucked Heinz, he in turn forced his fingers into the pliant hole of the servant who fucked Daignold's mouth. Somehow, the mere fact he was violating a black asshole while his own white one was being stuffed with black cock made it easier to take.

The hot confines of the servant's hole Heinz fingered were like liquid fire, no doubt because of the exotic lubricant they employed. His own hole writhed and contracted over a massive girth of invading cock, but also pulsed with a bizarre blend of heat and pleasure. The strange lubricant allowed slick access for the servant's thick black shaft.

Heinz began to yelp with each thrust of cock up his pale ass. He shoved into the Captain's servant at the same time, which also forced more and more of the lengthy cock into Daignold's expanding mouth. Daignold snorted and mewled, his own shaft raging hard beneath the surface of the warm waters where he was sprawled naked. Daignold whipped one hand up and down Heinz's cock, while his other frantically manipulated his own more slender rod.

Stimulated beyond belief, both Knights shot cum simultaneously. Heinz shouted out in grunting ecstasy, while Daignold moaned around the black boner that was also shooting jets of steaming cream, that load spewing down his throat and deep into his stomach. Heinz felt himself being force-fed African cum as well. The Bavarian's sore ass bobbed up and down over a shooting shaft, his personal servant continuing to offer him a violent and lusty pounding even while cuming himself. Such service, Heinz marveled through the fog of his orgasm.

After a gasping few moments, the Franks disengaged themselves and fell into each other's arms. Their bodies shook with the power of their orgasms. The stench of male seed was rich in their nostrils. They gazed into each other's eyes and shared a moment of satiated joy, which proved to be only short-lived.

Crazed yelps emanating from another corner of the room startled them from their blissful interlude. They looked over toward the blood-curdling sounds, and were astonished at what they saw.

The Spanish Della twins were spread out on the tiled floor. Their naked, dusky butts were receiving a lusty pummeling by two impossibly long black pricks, driving in and out of the men's asses like glistening snakes. That in itself was a riveting sight, but what the enigmatic Dado was doing as he leaned over the men was something altogether different.

The two servants who fucked the hapless Spanish Knights had the brothers pinned to the floor. With their arms spread wide, the Della brothers' chests were exposed to the ministrations of Dado and another naked black man assisting him.

The screams the Spanish brothers uttered were not due to the depth those black cocks stuffed their willing and pliant butt holes. The shrieks were because at that instant, Dado was piercing each of their pinched-out nipples with bright silver needles. Deftly, Dado and his assistant inserted thick gold and silver rings into the brother's sensitive protuberances.

Heinz and Daignold both shouted out, leaping from the pool and striding forward naked to rescue their compatriots, if they were not too late already. But they were absolutely astounded at what they next witnessed. The writhing Spanish brothers abruptly jerked and bucked in uncanny unison. The muscles of their taut bodies convulsed in a bizarrely matching rhythm as simultaneously they squirted gobs of cum high in the air. Their own semen splattered their pierced nipples and chests.

They were strangely aroused by the sight of their fellow Knights ejaculating and bleeding. Both men were already racing forward, but rather than coming to the rescue of their fellows, Daignold and Heinz dropped to their knees behind the bobbing asses of the black men raping the shrieking Della brothers.

With perverse grins, the two Franks drove their reawakened cocks deep into the black butts in front of them. The Africans howled with obscene pleasure at the unexpected intrusion and lunged forward, drilling the impaled Spanish brothers with renewed vigor. The snake-like black cocks continued pounding into the wailing Spanish Knights, whose own cum-slimed cocks remained stiff throughout the next half

48

hour while Dado soothed their pierced nipples by bathing them with cool compresses.

Heinz and Daignold discovered their own stamina, drilling the two servant's well-lubed and steaming black asses. Those two servants continued thrusting up the Spaniards' asses all the while. Finally, as Dado rose from his handiwork, the Franks simultaneously grunted out and spurted a load of spunk up the men's butt holes.

Scummed deep with Frankish seed, the Ethiopians immediately withdrew from the Spanish Knights' reddened and stretched asses and spewed gobs of their own creamy cum all over the prostrate brothers from crotch to face.

The following week was a feast for all their senses. The simplicity of life at the monastery did not preclude lavish meals, lavish baths, and more lusty fucking. Eventually, it was time for the Franks to depart. The four Knights left the island and its beautiful lake and extraordinary bird sanctuary behind.

Daignold was pleased, as they had accomplished their goals of exploration and discovery, and more. They succeeded in forging a bond with the smiling and enigmatic Dado, who was in truth the power behind the aging Holy Master. There would be a strong alliance between the Knights Templar at Castle Rock and these Ethiopians, henceforth.

But beyond furthering Sir Guy's aims, two of the Knights had something more intimate than politics on their minds.

They shared a secret smile as they marched away, touching their breasts lightly and shivering as they experienced strange and provocative sensations elicited from that touch. Beneath their leather jerkins, Jaime and Alfonse each boasted two shiny new rings to show off when they returned to the Holy Land and their Master, Sir Guy.

One gold and one silver in each nipple, they were now even more alike.

# Tale Five: The Caliph Captures Sir Philippe

*Sir Philippe de Chanson, with five other Knights Templar under his command, has been wined and dined by the Caliph of Cairo late into the Egyptian night. The last thing he recalls is the strange taste of the wine he has imbibed, an offering of the sly Caliph to him and his men.*

Sir Philippe awoke with his head still foggy. An aching and tingling coursed through his entire body. His mind cleared slightly, enough for him to ascertain that he was bound in a strange manner, his arms stretched high above his head, his feet clamped to the floor and spread wide apart. He was not uncomfortable, but testing his ropes, discovered he could move only a little. He also discovered he was unclothed. Glancing around as his awareness increased, he was aghast to determine that his fellow Knights were likewise bound, only they were not trussed upright but were kneeling with arms tied behind their backs. They knelt several yards away from him, each of them staring at him with wide, fearful eyes.

"Fellow Knights, what is happening?" Philippe managed to call out, his voice sticky and his throat dry.

Before any of the Knights could reply, a honey-smooth voice interrupted him from the doorway just beyond the bound men.

"Ah, Sir Philippe! You're awake! Excellent. We'll begin our discussions!" That voice belonged to the tall but plump

Caliph of Cairo, standing now at the doorway. An equally tall and plump black man hovered subserviently at his side.

"What is the meaning of this?" Philippe cried out. Obvious indignation vibrated in the timbre of his strengthening voice.

The Caliph laughed uproariously. His sycophantic attendant grinned at the Caliph's humor. Once the Caliph's bout of laughter subsided, he bowed with a flourish and replied to Philippe's indignant query. "We only desire to forge an agreement with the Knights Templar as regards to trading and banking. In that regard we've merely taken the opportunity to place you and your men in a position of bargaining."

"What is it you want?" Philippe asked, his eyes narrowing but his voice calm. He realized if they were to come out of this whole, he must be an example to his men.

"Concessions, and your slavish obedience to me in front of your men. Or else, they will all suffer worse than you will now," the Caliph threatened with a cruel smile.

Before Philippe could gather his wits for a reply, the towering black man approached him, his white eyes and bald obsidian head gleaming in the diffused light. Philippe's mind wandered strangely; he realized it was day, and probably midmorning. The room was flooded by light from high windows, the floor tiled in exotic and wondrous patterns, graceful fronds of green plants lining the walls. Lemon scents wafted in from the outside, emanating from the Caliph's extensive gardens, no doubt.

All these sensations flooded his awakening consciousness at once, before he was abruptly brought back to reality. Lightning-like pain lanced through his chest and he looked down to see the black slave who stood before him attaching silver clamps to each of his nipples. The man screwed the clamps tightly over the sensitive areas, eliciting gasps of sudden pain from the bound Knight. Before Philippe could gather his senses to protest, the efficient slave hooked a silver chain to rings in the clamps and strung it downwards. He deftly grasped Sir Philippe's dangling ball sack in one hand and wrapped a leather strap of some kind between it and his limp prick. He attached the hanging chain to a ring in the leather ball restrainer and yanked it tight. Philippe groaned in a sudden conflict of pain as his nipples were drawn downwards while his ball sack was stretched upwards.

The black giant moved away for a moment to survey his handiwork, while the Caliph looked on with avid interest. Philippe shuddered with tingling agony, which only intensified the pulling and pinching of his responsive tits and balls. Through his pain, he first glanced at the leering Caliph before turning his head and looking toward his kneeling men. With the part of his mind that was not drugged or in pain, he realized the five Knights were all still wearing their white jerkins with their distinctive red crosses, but were otherwise naked from the waist down, their own crotches and asses bare to the morning air.

But before Philippe could think of some reassuring words to offer his men, his mind and body were again assaulted. The black giant came forward and pried open his lips to place a wineskin in his mouth and squeeze a sweet tasting liquid down his throat. Philippe was actually glad for the drink. He was extremely thirsty and guzzled it down. The slave then went to the kneeling Knights and performed the same to each, squeezing the bladder and forcing the unknown liquid into their open mouths.

Philippe instantly experienced a flooding warmth coursing through him. His vision cleared somewhat, and his body felt revitalized. Strangely, the pain in his nipples and balls was transformed to a throbbing heat that made his prick swell, while a throaty sigh escaped his lush lips.

But the bizarre sensation was quickly dispelled as the Caliph laughed aloud and handed a long-handled whip to his black slave, the ends of silk and leather strips. At once, he began to assault Philippe's naked body with it.

Philippe did not scream as the initial blows fell, but his unprotected body did jerk and spasm, the movements causing

53

his clamped nipples to burn and his ball sack to ache. The blows were sharply stinging and landed indiscriminately about his chest, stomach and legs. The anticipation of where they would next strike proved nearly as terrible as the pain.

The Caliph observed with relish. The sight of the naked Burgundian Knight being whipped as he dangled from the ceiling caused his own member to swell and tighten beneath his silken pantaloons. His slave knew how to flagellate the man without cutting or marking him, as they were reluctant to disfigure their slaves, yet still the naked Knight's skin was a mass of red streaks and flushed skin. The Caliph drank in the sight of the Knight's muscular arms and legs spread wide and bound tightly by the leather straps that held him. He shivered with delight at the way Philippe's nipples were stretched and pulled by the silver chain that attached to his now swollen ball sack. Philippe's long prick jerked and twitched at each blow, half hard as conflicting feelings wove through the captured man's consciousness. The Caliph stared lustfully at Sir Philippe's handsome face, with his head of lustrous auburn hair and neat goatee, which surrounded his full lips. The depraved Caliph was totally entranced by the look of pain that passed over the man's features at every strike of the silken whip.

At an imperative gesture from the Caliph, the whipping abruptly ceased. Philippe slumped in his ropes, his breath coming in ragged gasps. Yet he had not screamed or uttered a single word. His watching men were astounded, their own minds fuddled by the drink they had just imbibed.

At a signal from the fat Caliph, the giant black man knelt at Philippe's feet, releasing the clamps which held them in place. A rotating ring in the ceiling allowed him to swivel the Knight's body. Philippe now faced away from his men and the Caliph, although he was such at an angle where he could see them out the corners of his eyes.

Philippe's broad back, high taut butt, and muscular legs were displayed for the Caliph and the bound Franks. Philippe expected further blows from the stinging whip and attempted to prepare himself. But instead to his shock, he felt something slick and hard being rubbed up in the crack between his widespread ass cheeks.

The bound Knights were horrified when the black slave produced a long leather instrument, a series of ripples on one end, and a thick handle on the other. Under the influence of the liquid drug, their horror was tinged with fascination as they witnessed the slave rub some sort of sickly-sweet lilac-scented oil over the rippled end. The slave's mammoth black hands massaged the strange dildo sensually before he placed the tip between Sir Philippe's powerful, ivory-white ass cheeks. The handle in one hand, the slave rubbed the tip into the white butt crack, searching out the hole that was hidden there. In an instant, he found Philippe's tender slot. Pressing the smooth tip against the anal entrance, he wasted no time, plunging it within the puckered opening.

Philippe was dismayed at the brutal pain that ripped into his guts as the unknown invader pushed past his sensitive ass lips. Instinctively, he relaxed and allowed his tight ring to open and ease the pain, but the pressure intensified incredibly as he was stretched even wider with each succeedingly larger ripple of the black dildo.

The Caliph grinned lustfully as he watched his slave violate his captive's firm white ass. He sighed with pleasure when the black man stepped away to leave the long dildo hanging obscenely from between the Knight's widespread buttocks. The ripples in the shaft had allowed the first third of the dildo to be captured by Philippe's straining butt hole and prevented it from falling back out as it hung from his bound body. The kneeling Knights were appalled as they regarded the monstrous dildo and contemplated how the remaining two thirds could possibly fit, each ripple larger than the last.

At once the slave recommenced the whipping, allowing Philippe no respite from painful stimulation. Philippe still did not cry out. Although, when the silken bite found his swollen and stretched ball sack now dangling between his legs, he had to swallow a scream that sought to escape from deep within his aching lungs.

His senses were heightened by the drugs. The scent of the lemon trees and the aromatic lilac odor rising from the oiled dildo blended with the stench of his own sweat and the black slave's reek as he lustily employed the whip. Those powerful stenches entwined with the pain wracking his entire body, elevating it to another plane. Philippe almost found himself welcoming each blow of the whip and each burning sensation in his nipples when his body jerked under the assault.

Yet his tortured senses were to be further goaded. The slave abruptly halted the whipping and leaned against Philippe in his chains. The black man reached around him to grasp each tit-clamp and screw it agonizingly tighter, then shorten the chain that connected them to his balls. And as if that were not enough, he drove the leather butt plug deeper by another two ripples. Philippe's aching asshole convulsed and clamped around the now even larger invader.

The whipping began again. Philippe dripped copious sweat, his mouth hanging open, his thoughts a blur. The Caliph observed it all with intense fascination, ordering his slave to proceed to the next step. The whipping halted. Philippe looked down with horror to see the slave attaching a heavy round weight to a ring in the leather that surrounded his balls. He released it to dangle heavily between Philippe's thighs, causing his balls and nipples to stretch atrociously. The brave Knight was forced to bite back a shriek, his muffled gasp of pain audible to all in the room.

The bound Knight was given no time to assimilate this new torture as the slave drove the dildo even deeper, now two thirds within Philippe's straining butt hole. The whipping continued.

The Caliph watched his muscular black slave expertly attacking the infidel Knight, lusting after Philippe's pink skin that glistened exotically in the morning light with sweat and oil. The black dildo danced as it dangled from the Knight's quivering, flushed ass. The round weight attached to Philippe's balls bounced as it pulled and stretched the swollen sack. The plump Caliph laughed aloud then ordered the action to escalate.

The giant slave again tightened the screws of Philippe's tit-clamps and shortened the chain that pulled up his balls. He added even more weight to the leather ball stretcher. Philippe moaned and shook with the waves of pain and freakish agony that wracked his body from these torture implements. He hung suspended, enduring these agonizing sensations while his whipping was momentarily delayed.

At another order from the drooling Caliph, each of the bound Knights was dragged before Philippe. He had no choice but to watch. Each of the Knight's forearms and thighs had been wrapped in lengths of leather thong, which forced them into their kneeling positions. Their faces were pressed to the floor so that their bare ass cheeks rode high in the air.

One by one the fat slave drove a thick butt plug up between their widespread asses. The rank stench of the exotic lilac-scented oil filled the air as the Knights were fucked full by leather butt plugs one after the other. Their faces to the floor, their upended white muscular asses now sported the black plugs. Unlike Philippe, the men did scream. Each and every one cried out for mercy. The Caliph enjoyed tremendously the sounds of their pleas, deigning to reach down and rub his hands across their slick and violated butts with depraved pleasure.

Even after this, Philippe's torture was not at an end. More weight was added to his ball sack, nearly causing him to faint, while he was forced to watch his men moan and mutter at his feet. Then he was whipped mercilessly before the final last inches of the monstrous dildo were driven up his battered asshole. Philippe finally screamed himself and begged for the Caliph to allow him to surrender. He promised to do whatever was asked of him.

"Let me down! I will be your lowly slave and suck your lordly prick willingly. Let me wrap my sweet lips around your enormous shaft! Please, I beg you of you mighty Caliph,"

Philippe whimpered, albeit eloquently, for all the strange and erotic mixture of pleasure and pain his body was undergoing.

"Ah yes, my fine white Frankish plaything. Yes! Come to me on your knees!" The Caliph chortled with ecstatic triumph, signaling to the slave. At once he released Sir Philippe's restraints, the Knight instantly tumbling to the floor at the Caliph's feet.

"Master! Let me lick and suck your infidel prick. Please," Sir Philippe begged, crawling forward to grasp the Caliph's silk-encased legs.

The Caliph gazed hungrily down at the sweat-soaked Knight groveling at his feet. The handle of the black dildo protruded from Philippe's violated asshole, and he was forced to drag the weights attached to his swollen ball sack as he crawled forward. The Caliph gloated happily as he dropped his soft pantaloons and exposed his substantial brown thighs, hairless and plump, yet sturdy and exotic. His huge member stood erect, dripping precum and lurching obscenely before the vanquished Knight's face. Sir Philippe pulled himself up to stare at the thick rod. The crown shone with drooling liquid before he wrapped his full lips around it and swallowed it to the root.

Philippe's Knights groaned with dismay as they watched their leader sucking the Caliph's monstrous prick, but then themselves crawled forward to beg and plead at his feet for a turn to suck their new master's hard flesh.

The Caliph laughed with unbounded joy. His power was now proven! His cock twitched and throbbed between the beautiful lips of the Burgundian Knight's drooling mouth. The black slave moved closer to watch eagerly as the formerly arrogant Knights begged at his master's feet. Obscene black butt plugs filled every white asshole, while the six inch handle of Philippe's protruding dildo bobbed and jerked as he moved his mouth up and down over the Caliph's spit-slick shaft.

The Caliph and his slave were so engrossed in the erotic scene, they were caught totally unprepared when Philippe pulled his mouth from the Caliph's prick and launched himself in a blur of athletic speed.

He seized the Arab ruler by the thighs, turning him and tossing him onto his fat belly on the floor. As Philippe leaped onto the sprawled Caliph's large ass, he also managed to twist his body and strike out with a fist at the surprised black slave. The giant was knocked senseless with that one swift blow. Ignoring the pain of his nipples, ass, and weighted ball sack, Sir Philippe speedily tied the Caliph's hands behind his back and gagged him with his own silken pantaloons. Philippe remained seated on the prostrate Caliph, who squirmed beneath him, while still managing to untie his bound Knights. Once freed, they assisted him in completing the job of tying up the Caliph and his huge slave.

Sir Philippe and his Knights wasted no time in removing their firmly planted butt plugs. Instead, they barred the door and then lustily attacked the bound figures of the Caliph and his slave. The Caliph boasted a huge and exotically beautiful ass, which jiggled as the Knights each took turns driving their oil-slicked pricks in and out of the brown hole between those enormous cheeks. The slave's ass was just as large and pliable. It was spread out and tied apart, fucked repeatedly, and then had the largest of the butt plugs inserted and tied in place with an ingenious use of leather straps around balls and prick.

When woken, the slave was forced to watch as Sir Philippe rode his master's ass. The other Knights stood in a circle and watched as well, avidly drinking in the sight of Philippe's powerful pumping white buttocks, which still had the black handle of the dildo protruding from between them. His thighs were spread wide as he straddled the fat Caliph, so his leather bound balls with the heavy weights stretching them dangled visibly onto the tiled floor. Philippe's tits remained clamped and the chain pulled against his captured balls with every thrust of his erect prick up the Caliph's slippery fuck hole. To Philippe, pain and pleasure were no longer distinguishable. He shouted with agonized pleasure as he spurted cum deep inside the slick hole he pounded.

All around him, the other Knights jerked off to spray their own cum on the figures at their feet. Gobs landed indiscriminately on Sir Philippe's white butt and stretched balls and on his red-streaked back and legs. The Caliph himself grunted and shuddered beneath his violator, obviously cuming himself against the slick tiles of his own torture chamber.

Hours later, the naked Knights and the equally naked Caliph and his black slave, ate and drank merrily from a banquet in the Caliph's private bed chambers. Happily, they celebrated the culmination of their new trade agreements, all sides content at the outcome.

Sir Philippe would return to Castle Rock and his beloved Master, Sir Guy, with a hard-won victory under his belt. Plus, Philippe could boast a delightful new experience to recall to his other Knights Templar, and the well abused body to prove his bizarre claims!

"Do nothing to antagonize them for now, Alfonse," Jaime whispered.

He was instantly punished for his words. A huge Arab sneered in his face after yanking him roughly forward. The man then strung a silver chain through a ring in the leather collar around Jaime's neck.

The same was done to Alfonse while Jaime watched stoically. The sight of his brother completely unclad, other than a leather collar around his neck, was dismaying to say the least. A silver chain dangling from that collar and gripped in the cruel hand of a large Arab infidel only added to the horror of the image.

But there was more. Jaime looked on helplessly while Alfonse was held immobile by two of the Arabs. A third stood in front of him. This third Arab reached out to clutch at the delicate nipples rings on Alfonse's chest. With an evil grin and glaring into the tall Knight's amber orbs, the foul Arab used his dark fingers to yank on the rings brutally. Although Alfonse gave no sign of the pain he felt, the Arab continued sneering evilly as he pulled another more delicate silver chain from the pouch at his side. In seconds he had connected it to each of the rings in Alfonse's chest. Taking the long end, he moved to Jaime. Offering the older brother his nasty grin, the Arab connected the end of the chain to Jaime's identical nipple rings. Now, the two brothers were bound together by a long silver chain, their nipples attached to one another in an obscene yet bizarrely erotic manner.

When previously exploring in Ethiopia, the brothers from Aragon had suffered their breasts to be adorned by these nipple rings. Thereafter, they became enamored with the curious body decorations. The pair spent many a night exploring the sensations the rings could elicit. Now, they only thought of the dangerous circumstance they found themselves in, at the mercy of these brutal Arabs.

The thicker chains attached to the Knights' neck collars were clamped together. They were ordered to march forward,

Alfonse before Jaime, the ten foot length of their nipple chains adequate to allow them room enough to move without undue difficulty.

Jaime stared at his brother's nude back and haunches as they walked through an open doorway, admiring the smooth muscles of his butt globes as they pumped up and down. His brother's naked flesh, similar to his own, was the dusty color of coffee and without hair or blemish. Alfonse was the younger, although only by a minute, but Jaime always felt protective of him because of this. He ached at the sight of his humiliated brother and prayed for his safety in the trial that was sure to lie ahead. He also experienced a strange moment of unexpected sexual stirring as he gazed at his brother's naked back, with the thick collar encasing his neck and his elegant hands tightly bound behind him. It was profoundly unsettling that he found the degrading sight erotic.

The Arabs led them through various rooms in a large building. It must be the Emir's palace, Jaime surmised. They passed other Arab men who jeered at them when they passed, but saw no evidence of any women. Light streaming in from windows told them it was late morning. They eventually reached a wide portico that although open to the west away from the rising sun proved very bright. It was pleasantly cool from the shade of scattered lemon trees and swaying date palms. A large pool fronted it with a small fountain splashing in its center.

The men who led them forced them to descend into the cool waters of the pool. The Knights from Aragon were not unhappy to enter this sparkling pool, although they were a trifle leery with their hands bound helplessly behind them.

Two of the Arabs casually disrobed and strode into the water beside the Knights. Seizing their naked bodies, they set to rubbing them vigorously with scented soaps. All their Arab captors were large and muscular. In fact they were so bulky they could have been described as fat, but were undoubtedly powerful men. They proved this strength as they manipulated the slenderer Frankish soldiers easily, rudely laving soap between their legs and up into their butt-cracks. Jaime nodded to Alfonse, who understood and offered no resistance to the demeaning treatment.

Rinsed without fanfare the brothers were dragged from the pool, their dusky flesh glowing and clean from their forced bath. Jaime and Alfonse shared a brief, secretive smirk as they both noticed the rising pricks of the Arab soldiers who held them when their plumper bodies brushed against their captives' leaner forms.

While they were bathed a crowd gathered. A score of Arab men lined the far walls of the outdoor patio. Leering at the naked Knights and talking among themselves they obviously awaited some event.

Jaime and Alfonse were forced to stand side by side and wait as well. The brother's chains and the rings attaching them together gleamed silver in the morning light. Naked and chained thus, the pair nevertheless stood tall and proud even under these dire circumstances. Their handsome faces, usually clean-shaven but now with a day's growth of beard, were solemn yet elegant. Their black hair was a mass of wet curls falling down to just above the thick collar surrounding each of their necks. Lustrous, those heads of hair gleamed darkly from the bath. They appeared as a pair of fine exotic animals might, naked and sublime.

Yet on either side stood the equally naked Arab soldiers, near to twice the bulk of their captives. Chains, collars and leather bound the Spaniards. They may have appeared proud, but there was no denying they were at the mercy of the Arabs surrounding them.

One of the onlookers was apparently in charge. He nodded with a haughty smile toward the four other Arab guards surrounding the Della brothers. The appointed men disappeared briefly, returning with a low table of gleaming, aromatic juniper wood that they placed in front of the Knights.

The younger Alfonse was seized by the hulking naked Arabs and spread out on the table. His bound arms were beneath his straining chest, which was forced upwards in an arc. His be-ringed and chained nipples pointed high in the air. His legs were left to drape over one end of the table while his head was pulled backward to dangle over the opposite end.

While Jaime was compelled to stand over his brother, their chests and necks still attached by the silver chains, the four remaining Arab guards stripped off their own garments. Naked as their companions, they also were of monstrous girth. Several sported enormous pricks, which already thrust out before their rotund bellies in aroused agitation.

"It will be all right, Brother. We can withstand whatever torture they strive to inflict on us," Jaime murmured as he smiled down at Alfonse. Their smoky-pale amber eyes met, sharing a silent communication. It had always been so, ever since they were mere babes in their Father's castle in far Aragon.

Jaime was cruelly forced to abandon the momentary intimacy with his brother. One of the nude Arabs violently gripped his dangling ball sack and began to bind the hefty man nuts with strips of black leather. The Knight gasped at the sharp pain, but his mind was distracted as he realized his spread-eagled brother suffered a similar fate.

Two naked Arabs seized Alfonse's balls, stretching them out and binding them with similar black leather strips. Alfonse's face screwed up in a pained grimace until he met his brother's stoic gaze. Jamie's example helped his twin to breath deep and attempt an equal composure. It was not easy to imitate his fearless brother while his balls were wrenched and twisted by the Arabs as they mercilessly wrapped them in the tight straps.

Both men's nut sacks were wrapped, so they distended several inches away from the base of their pricks. The tender balls themselves were swollen and tight. There were silver rings embedded in the leather bindings, and Jaime could only imagine what purpose they would serve. The Knight was impelled to spread his legs farther apart to ease some of the pressure permeating his swollen balls. As he did, the naked Arabs behind him laughed, propelling him forward at the same time so that his distended sack hovered directly over his brother's dangling head.

Savage hands grasped his shoulders and buttocks. He was forced downward so that his flopping prick pressed against his brother's lips. Jaime groaned when one of the Arabs pried open Alfonse's mouth and fed that long flesh between the finely formed Spanish lips. His legs shook as the wet heat of his brother's mouth enveloped his stalk. Jaime stared down at Alfonse's drooping head. His strong, collared neck was exposed and his nipples chained and straining. An unbidden, but irresistible rush of burning passion engorged Jamie's prick. Alfonse's mouth and throat were wide open at the angle his head was forced into, and Jaime's lengthening prick thrust past the younger brother's tongue and into that warm channel.

Jaime was propelled forward almost at once. His face was mashed into his brother's crotch. Ferocious Arab hands pried open his mouth and Alfonse's prick was stuffed inside it. Already semi-hard, it too swelled and pulsed as it filled Jaime's mouth. With his hands bound behind him, he could only flop himself across his brother's hot body. Jaime was unable to prevent his weight from crushing down and pinning the younger Knight to the table beneath. Both men's ringed nipples were cruelly pinched between their sandwiched bodies as they were compelled to swallow each other's Spanish fuck stalks.

Gagging over his brother's stiff meat, Jaime felt another sensation bombarding his body. His balls were being yanked, and he realized that one of the rings attached to the leather straps there was being connected to something. Immediately, he felt a strap sliding upwards between his widespread butt cheeks and then across his broad back. The collar around his neck was pulled on, and he understood that they had attached his nuts to his neck by that same long strap.

Jay Starre

When they began to tighten the leather, he almost bit down on his brother's hard shaft in agony. Slowly and inexorably, his balls were pulled backwards as the strip of leather was shortened between his balls and his neck. That same strap also pressed intimately against his exposed butt hole, placed ingeniously so that it parted his tender ass lips and dug deep into his hole. When they finished, he was bound tightly from crotch to neck. Intense pressure in his balls, asshole and neck vied for his attention even as his brother's pulsing throat enveloped his prick.

And this was not the end of the Arabs' cruel manipulations.

Alfonse's muscular legs were raised up and bent backwards. They were then strapped to Jaime's back by more lengths of black leather, which also wrapped around both their bodies and was secured beneath the juniper table. The Spaniards were crushed together, their nipple rings mashed against each other's bellies.

With his legs forced back and held in place against his brother's back, Alfonse's ass was exposed to the view of all. Dangling before his tortured eyes, Jaime could see his brother's tightly distended balls in their black leather constraints. He watched helplessly as a ring there was attached to another leather strip and Alfonse's balls were stretched upwards. The binding was pulled over Jaime's forehead and attached to the ring in his collar behind his head. Tightened cruelly, this new restraint forced his face deep into his brother's crotch and Alfonse's hard prick deep into his throat. Alfonse's straining balls were pulled high up nearly between Jaime's eyes, pressing against his nose so that he inhaled his brother's masculine scent with every breath.

Alfonse's hairless butt hole was also directly in Jaime's sight. The stretched lips convulsed and pulsed with obvious tension due to the painful bondage he experienced.

They were now pressed together so tightly, their bodies bound from crotch to crotch, any tiny movement either made could be felt in numerous tender spots on their bodies. Even their labored breathing caused jolting twinges of sensation and pain. Both men were barely able to breath around the hard pricks filling their mouths, but because of their mysterious mental connection, they managed to maneuver their bound heads and crotches just enough to allow for easier breathing. Otherwise, they might have suffocated under the constricting bondage.

The six naked Arabs hovered around them, sporting huge erections. The on looking Moslems laughed among themselves as they moved closer. Jaime was aware of the men surrounding them and imagined what they thought. He and his brother must have formed an exotic picture, the two Spanish Knights naked and defenseless, bound together with their pricks planted firmly in each other's mouths. The fact that they were twins excited them even more so.

Their cruel treatment was only in its first stages. A beefy naked Arab placed himself at either end of the bound Knights. As Jaime watched powerlessly, they wielded wide leather paddles, striking out to land a swift blow against each of the brother's exposed buttocks.

Jaime could barely restrain a muffled scream as he felt his own ass suffer the harsh blow. He could hear Alfonse gagging out a stifled shriek of his own. With the blows, they both had jerked spontaneously and thus sent sharp stabs of agony throughout their mutually bound bodies. More blows followed. The two Knights writhed in profound shock as their entire bodies experienced the inevitable results of their unwilling movements. Jaime's nuts were yanked as his body convulsed and the leather strap between his butt cheeks bit deep into his asshole. Alfonse's nuts were pulled forward agonizingly with every twitch of his brother's head.

Yet all these tortured movements caused other sensations as well. Both their stiff pricks were forced in and out of their trapped throats, eliciting a passionate pleasure to mingle with the tormenting sensations emanating from other areas of their tightly constricted bodies.

The beating ceased abruptly. The Knights' frantic movements subsided into exhausted twitches and deep heaving breaths around the pricks stuffed in their mouths. Through the fog of his agony Jaime watched the hovering Arabs. Both those naked and those clothed masturbated their own rampant flesh. Oiled palms rubbed up and down distended erections as they gazed lustfully at the Spaniards' powerless bondage.

The Arab standing between Alfonse's legs gripped his fat meat in a big paw. He lewdly rubbed the glistening, knobby tip directly in front of Jaime's eyes. He had dropped his paddle and was now oiling up the hand that was not busy at his swollen prick.

Jaime had no choice but to watch as the Arab reached forward and ran his oiled fingers across his brother's paddle-flushed, exposed butt cheeks. At that same moment he felt slick fingers grazing his own widespread ass cheeks. While he gazed down in horror, the Arab's fat fingers zeroed in on Alfonse's defenseless asshole. The fingers worked around the pulsing hole, which alternately snapped closed or gaped open nervously. Jaime felt fingers rubbing against his own hole, pressing the leather strap that separated his ass lips deeper into his crack with maddening intensity.

Jaime's eyes bulged when the Arab dipped one of his big blunt fingers into the yawning opening of his brother's butt hole. Jaime was stabbed with instant pain as Alfonse jerked in response to the brutal invasion and their shared bindings yanked on his own balls and butt hole. Jaime stared downwards as that huge finger was inserted deeper and deeper. At the same time he felt his own butt hole being pried apart. Either side of the leather strip guarding it was being teased with cruel Arab fingers.

The fucking began in earnest. The Moslems' invading fingers worked in and out of the Knights' defenseless assholes. Searing pain in their bum holes was only part of their agony.

The men responded to the fingering by instinctively bucking their hips and thus driving their fuck sticks deeper into each other's throats. Their bindings dug into their writhing bodies and their pricks impaled each other involuntarily.

The vile Arabs surrounding them raised their voices in a cacophony of jeering laughter.

Jaime was forced to watch as the monstrous Arab finger-fucked his brother's slippery hole, which gaped wider with every violent thrust. The Arab's big shaft was thrust close in Jaime's face, the glistening knob slipping and slapping under the Arab's fevered masturbation. Out of the corner of his eyes he could see other Arabs working their rampant pricks, moving closer and closer to the bound Knights.

Jaime's ass was on fire as two fingers inserted into it on either side of the tight leather binding that still restricted his movements He bucked forward without volition, driving his prick deep into his brother's dangling face. Alfonse was unable to stop himself from bucking away from the invading fingers raping his butt hole as well, driving his own long shaft up into his brother's tightly bound face.

Heat suffused both Knights' entire bodies under the cruel punishment. Yet, due to its very intensity, the wracking pain was inexorably transforming into a bizarre pleasure. Their pricks swelled in each other's throats. Their butt holes expanded to accept the Arabs probing fingers. Jaime realized he was no longer pulling away from the Arab violating his ass, but meeting the penetrating fingers with willing, backwards thrusts. Rather than fighting his brother's meat in his mouth, he was sucking on it with wanton lust. His own shaft slid eagerly between Alfonse's suckling lips.

And all the while he stared at the huge Arab prick being manipulated inches from his bound face.

The brother's torrid excitement built to a crescendo of agonizing pleasure. Both their bodies writhed eagerly against their various restraints. Their bound butts worked against the Arabs' violating fingers. Their pricks pounded deep into each other's gurgling mouths. Jaime felt his own sperm building from a spot inside his penetrated butt hole. Up through his stretched and tightly bound balls and surging through his hard prick, the spew flowed directly into his brother's hot throat. It was at that instant of bizarre ecstasy he felt Alfonse's cock spasm and spurt creamy cum into his own mouth.

While they squirmed under simultaneous orgasms, feeding hot spunk into each other, their assholes tightened and pulsed around their Arab captors' driving fingers. Jaime was suddenly splattered with a geyser of hot white cum as the Arab finger-fucking his brother's spasming hole ejaculated gobs of ropy sperm over his flushed face.

The other Arabs surrounding the bound Knights achieved orgasms of their own. Pounded members began to shoot over Jaime's broad back as it convulsed in wild abandon. Jamie felt all that sticky cream running down his shoulders and ass.

The onlookers were treated to the sight of the muscular, leather bound Knights writhing under their punishment, being finger-fucked and yet through it all, reaching orgasm and each cuming in his own brother's mouth. The tight black bindings that constrained them gleamed in the morning light, while their dusky skins were coated in spurt after spurt of Arab sperm.

\* \* \*

A month later, the Della twins were roused from a night's sleep, and hustled naked to an empty room in the dawn light. Believing they were to be sold due to the remarks of their captors, they gazed at each other in silent support, standing upright and prepared for the worst.

Their joy was unimaginable as they were greeted not by some beastly Moslem slave traders, but rather by their fellow Knights of the Templar entering the doorway.

Sir Guy de Brussiers, tall and blond, was accompanied by the shorter Frenchman Daignold Assnault. Daignold grinned from ear to ear as he strode to embrace the Spanish Knights with unrestrained love and relief. Having finally tracked them down, Daignold had alerted the Knights Templar Master, Sir Guy, and together they had negotiated the brave Aragon twins' release.

For his part, Sir Guy was astounded by the rescued Knights' appearance. Although obviously in good health, clean and muscular from good food and forced exercise, they were all the same naked and bound with humiliating chains of silver. He had not yet seen their nipple rings acquired in Ethiopia. That in itself would have been shocking enough.

But the hapless Spanish Knights had been further decorated during their captivity in the Arab palace. Both men stood naked and proud before their leader, chained together by neck, nipples and now incredibly by cocks as well. A large golden ring dangled from the tip of each of the twins large pricks!

The intrigued Templar leader felt his own cock stiffening beneath his breeches at the sight of the naked twins, who were now pierced so exotically. New and exciting possibilities flooded his mind, and his happiness at the rescue of the brave Spanish twins merged with the lustful thoughts centering on the heat between his legs.

Guy smiled with pleasure as he contemplated their return to his Castle. The joyous Della Knights obviously would have many experiences to share, and a few things to teach their fellow Knights as well!

# Tale Seven: The Virgin Knight

*A tender story involving Sir Guy de Brussiers and a virginal young recruit. Sir Guy opens up Eric von Bartell beside a fire at night in the wilderness when they are alone, after tying him up and lashing him for disobedience.*

Sir Guy rode upwards through the narrow canyon, urging his steed over the rocky trail, intent upon reaching their goal before nightfall. Behind him trailed Eric von Bartell on a diminutive donkey well able to negotiate the rough ground. Eric stared ahead at his new liege Lord, the handsome Sir Guy de Brussiers, whose shoulder-length blond curls gleamed in the last rays of the spring sunshine like a halo. Eric was in awe of the renowned Knight who was a Master of the Knights Templar in the Holy Land. Sir Guy was Lord of the formidable Castle Rock, which was behind them now a score of miles away on the coastal plain.

As they ascended through the constricting walls of the canyon, Eric continued to gaze up at his Master. Eric observed every move of Guy's powerful body. Sir Guy's back was wide, but tapered to a narrow waist, and then spread again around broad hips and a pair of hefty buttocks that moved in perfect rhythm with the gate of his mount. Each cheek of that stupendous ass rose and fell in an entrancing cadence that utterly fascinated the German acolyte.

Eric was both excited and frightened, although less frightened than excited. He should have been petrified; Sir Guy had been livid with anger when he had dictated Eric's punishment. But surveying Sir Guy's masculine form from behind, Eric was keenly aware of how much he worshipped the Templar Master. The German youth was far too inflamed by the prospect of being alone with Sir Guy and spending the night in the hills with him, to allow fear to ruin the opportunity. As well, the Master of Castle Rock was known for his fairness and merciful nature. He had been jovial and kind to Eric ever since the young German had arrived in the Holy Land. Eric could not conceive of the man being cruel.

At that time, Eric knew little of Guy's implacable nature when it came to discipline among his Knights.

It had begun the previous day when Sir Guy had dispatched Eric on a mission. The German was to deliver a contract and sum of money to a local Christian Maronite Priest. But Eric had been careless enough to stop at an inn on the way to the Maronite village. He was pick-pocketed, forfeiting both the money and the message. When Eric had returned to report the mishap, Sir Guy had stood quietly over Eric's kneeling form. With deceptive composure, Guy had commanded this punishment – a night alone with Sir Guy to offer up Eric's submission and penance. To Eric, it had sounded portentous, but vague.

As they approached their destination, Eric's thoughts ran wild over the question of what punishment the Knight Templar would mete out during the course of the night. His own fantasies leaned toward sexual tortures, but as a virgin his thoughts were admittedly unclear on the matter. Riding through the mountain evening and contemplating the possibility of simply being unclothed in the presence of the mighty Sir Guy had Eric's love-member hard as desert stone.

"We've arrived, Eric. Make camp and prepare a fire and supper. I'll pray for your salvation, and that you will benefit from this night's discipline," Sir Guy ordered.

Guy turned his eyes on the young knight. His smoky-grey gaze penetrated deep into Eric's heart, and Eric instantly leaped from his donkey to obey. They had reached a secluded opening in the mountain ravine, a flat area surrounded by high sandstone walls and containing an exquisite pool of crystal clear water fed by a bubbling spring at its far perimeter. There was a campsite with rough wooden benches and table, and a brick fireplace. As well, Eric spotted a lean-to with space to sleep several occupants. A pile of firewood stocked the camp. It was plain this was a place often used.

Eric set to work directly, while Guy removed his Templar jerkin, and after that all the garments covering his upper body. The afternoon sun had been hot and Sir Guy's body was beaded with sweat. The blond curls on his massive chest glistened with drops of moisture. Sir Guy knelt and prayed on a rock overlooking the placid pond. Eric made an effort to concentrate on his work but was hard-pressed to keep his eyes off the muscular form of his Master.

Eric recalled that this must be the place referred to as the "High Pond," which he had overheard mentioned on numerous occasions by knights at Castle Rock. The knights journeyed here to meditate, several of them spending the desert nights in prayer. Or whatever else they might think to do in the secluded spot. Again, Eric's mind wandered into fantasies of sexual fulfillment. He realized he should have been meditating on his errors and his determination to never repeat any such transgressions. Instead, he was still wrapped up in lustful thoughts when he completed preparing their camp and supper.

When he tapped the praying Sir Guy on the shoulder to inform him he had completed his tasks, his hand trembled violently as it grazed the bare flesh. The shoulder was soft and smooth, and yet hard as marble. Eric's cock swelled painfully within the confines of his leather breeches.

Sir Guy rose and nodded sternly to his acolyte. While they ate in silence, the profound stillness of their retreat permeated the air and seeped into their thoughts. Eric contemplated the evening ahead with lustful speculation intermingled with the added stimulus of fear. After some time though, Sir Guy's absolute silence and stern gazes began to erode the German's trust. He thought Sir Guy too benevolent to mete out harsh punishment. But now under that forbidding silence, fear began to dominate Eric's thoughts.

In turn, Guy reflected on the nature of his companion while they ate, recalling when he had first come to Castle Rock two months earlier. Eric's father, the Baron Harold von Bartell, from the northern German land of Saxony, had sent the 19-year old to Guy. His letter had listed Eric's shortcomings. He had been spoiled by his wealthy parents and had done little but carouse and practice swordplay. According to the father, Eric had gambled and drank to excess for the previous two years. The Baron hoped Sir Guy could take him in hand and train him for a useful career in the Knights Templar.

Guy had noted the young Eric's behavior over the past two months heedfully, and as yesterday's events had proved, judged that he required discipline in his life. Discipline was what this night would be all about. Sir Guy also sensed that Eric had a joyous heart, and he did not want to stifle that. A proper combination of obedience and that personal joy would be required if the young nobleman was allowed to permanently join the ranks of the Knights Templar.

"Enough now. Clean up and we'll begin. Stoke up the fire, Eric," Guy ordered, standing and stretching his large arms over his head.

Eric trembled as he prepared the camp for the night, which had settled over them in subtle stealth. He built up the fire so that it crackled lustily, along with his stiff cock. As the light of their bonfire increased, so the last vestiges of the day slipped away and darkness surrounded their refuge.

Eric straightened and approached Guy. The Knight was again kneeling beside the pool.

"All is complete, Sir," Eric reported. He bowed his head with what he deemed the proper submission.

"All right then. We must bathe first, to cleanse our bodies for the ritual ahead. Disrobe, boy," Sir Guy ordered, his stern command breaking the serenity of the desert night like shattering glass.

Eric obeyed with shaking hands. He peered from the corners of his eyes at Guy as the Master Knight pulled his heavy leather boots off then removed his leather breeches and woolen underwear. Bulging thighs glowed in the flickering firelight as the French knight strode into the stillness of the pool. Eric caught a tantalizing glimpse of his fat cock and hefty ball sack before they were submerged in the still water.

His own cock jutted out in an irreverent display as he peeled off his remaining clothing and he swiftly descended into the pool to hide it below the waterline. The water was icy, and Eric shivered but said nothing, attempting to imitate Guy's stoic example. As the Knight Templar scrubbed his beefy body with a boar's bristle brush, Eric gazed hungrily at his astonishing beauty.

Sir Guy stood in shallow water and worked the abrasive brush over his muscular limbs. Eric drank up the sight and nearly gasped when Guy ran the brush up into the crevice between his ass globes. The boar brush rose up under his arms into the heavy pits then higher and into the curls of his short beard that framed his handsome features. The firelight played across Guy's brawny form as he rinsed the soap away and his body glowed with health in the aftermath of the scrubbing.

The knight stepped close to the unmoving Eric and handed him the scrub brush and the soap, locking eyes and silently commanding the youth. Eric obeyed without a word. He scrubbed his body with exuberance in an attempt to wash away the immobilizing miasma of lust and dread threatening to overwhelm him.

When he was finished his cock had subsided from the rough treatment he had awarded it. As he strode from the pool, he was able to stand before the naked Guy without demeaning himself by flaunting a depraved erection.

"Kneel and pray for enlightenment. Pray for your mind and heart to accept this punishment and to learn from it," Guy commanded severely.

Eric did so, his bare knees on the stone beside the pool, his head bowed only inches from the crotch of the towering knight that was to be his Master if he was accepted into the Knights Templar.

Guy inspected the naked Saxon. His body was undeniably strong yet also soft with extra fat from easy living. Eric was also wanly pale from little exposure to sun during the past winter in the northern state of Saxony. His hair was a full mass of straight flaxen gold, cut short above his ears. A clean-shaven face revealed a boyish but handsome countenance. His arms were strong and graced with light blond hair, but the rest of him was devoid of it and appeared even softer without any cover of manly fur. Guy's own cock twitched appreciatively as he scrutinized the kneeling Saxon.

"Rise!"

Eric obeyed the peremptory command without hesitation, gasping as his eyes fell upon his Master's hardening flesh that bobbed only inches from his rising body.

"Prostrate yourself on the table, face up!"

Eric's legs shook as he stepped over to the wooden table and clambered up to lie back upon it. He was prone upon the table with his arms across his chest and his legs raised so that his feet would have a place to rest. The crackling bonfire was close enough that he could feel its welcome warmth, yet he still shivered, naked as he was and bursting with trepidation.

Guy observed the nude nobleman for a moment, a smile fleeting across his otherwise stern features. Then he set to work. Reaching into his goatskin pack of supplies, he firstly pulled out a black leather collar.

Stepping up to the recumbent Saxon, Guy peered down at him while displaying the collar before his face. His voice was silken but firm. "You will be secured tonight with earthly bindings so that your heart may learn to be bound by the rules of our Order."

With that, he strapped the collar around Eric's shivering neck and attached it to a metal ring embedded in the planking of the wooden table. Eric's head was now fastened to that slab of wood, and he could neither rise nor escape.

When he realized that harsh fact, Eric's limbs began to shake with real violence. Guy could not mistake the young man's fear. He did nothing to allay that fear, rather he gazed into Eric's eyes with increased severity.

"Do you understand?" he demanded, grasping Eric's face with one large hand.

"Yes, Sir," Eric just managed to reply.

Guy smiled then, but it was a menacing grimace that did nothing to calm the bound youth. Eric could lift his head only a foot before the chain attaching him to the table halted his movements. He felt it pull on his neck as he tried to follow Sir Guy with his eyes. The naked knight shimmered in the fire's flickering glow. The blond hair on Guy's limbs caught the light, his muscles bulging while he dug through his leather bag.

Guy turned to the collared acolyte with two pair of leather restraints in his hands, which he displayed to the Saxon.

"To bind your hands and feet so that you recognize the restrictions placed on your movements throughout your life as a servant of the Knights Templar," Guy intoned.

Guy seized Eric's shaking arm and snapped one of the leather bracelets over his wrist, then followed by binding Eric's other wrist, and then his ankles with the second pair of leather cuffs. With his eyes boring into the prostrate youth's, Guy then raised up each of his legs and attached them by leather straps to each of his wrists beside his shoulders. Eric's ass was exposed as his thighs were stretched backwards over his chest. Eric shivered with fear. An utter sense of helplessness flooded his mind as he accepted the fact his legs and arms were irrevocably locked together by short chains and leather straps.

Guy stood back for a moment and considered his companion who was bound and unable to evade his looming punishment. Eric's long limbs, muscular and hairless, shone in the firelight. Their tremulous movements accentuated the captive's plight. Eric's crotch was exposed as well as the plump cheeks of his pale buttocks. His cock had swollen so that it dangled down half-hard between his thighs.

Guy reached into his bag and removed a long wooden bar, which he deftly attached to either of Eric's bound ankles, stretching them nearly three feet apart. A groan escaped Eric's lips as he experienced this further restriction. It was not painful, but his ass now felt wide open and vulnerable. His cock and balls, which lay down between his thighs, felt totally unprotected as well.

Sir Guy had one more form of bondage to inflict upon his disobedient servant, and this was the most intimate thus far. Guy seized the Saxon's ball sack and twisted a length of leather strap around the base of it, then wound it up to encircle the root of his half-swollen cock. Guy attached a small silver chain to the leather through a ring embedded within it. While Eric gasped with bated breath, Guy stretched the attached chain upwards to loop it over the center of the wooden bar and clip it to a metal ring there. He tightened it until Eric's balls and cock were stretched tightly away from his body, held firmly by the wooden bar between his ankles. A groan escaped the bound youth's lips. Although this too was not painful, it was restrictive to the extreme.

And bizarrely humiliating.

But Eric's humiliation was only just beginning. He was terrified of that prospect as his bound limbs trembled with weakness and forbidden desire. He could move little, and could not escape the punishment to come, whatever it was that his new Master, Sir Guy, was determined to mete out to him. No one was nearby to rescue him or even hear him cry out.

Nothing like this had ever occurred in the entirety of his spoiled, wealthy existence, and his mind struggled to cope with the enormity of it. But Sir Guy was looming over him again, holding a wooden paddle in his hands, which he placed directly before Eric's wide eyes.

"Now, Eric von Bartell, you will prove your mettle. I'll begin your punishment and expect you to take it like a man. You must submit to my will and in this way prove your worth. If you are to become a knight worthy of the Templar, tonight's outcome will determine that fact."

Guy explained carefully, his voice no longer stern, but strangely gentle. That silken voice was totally at odds with the violence of the image he presented; naked, massive and wielding a large and threatening wooden paddle.

Eric was close to swooning for a heartbeat, his eyes actually going out of focus. He was brought back to reality by a sudden impact of mind-numbing force smashing against his bare buttocks. He gasped, his eyes snapping open and a shriek on the tip of his tongue. But when another blow of the paddle landed on his uncovered buttocks, he clamped down on his teeth and held back the wail that strove to escape from deep within his confused soul.

He could see the mighty Sir Guy, in all his nakedness, his arms raised high as they prepared to deliver another blow to Eric's ass. Eric focused on the man's savage strength and thus was able to stifle any outcry. As each blow landed, his body vibrated with the pain, and his mind rebelled at the humiliation, but the only sounds he emitted were loud gasps. He did not cry out nor did he beg for mercy.

Guy observed his bound captive attentively as he employed the flat of the paddle to strike Eric's unclad and vulnerable buttocks. He was gratified by Eric's display of will. It was clear the pain was great; the Saxon's body rocked with each stroke. Yet he took it well. Guy halted his punishment after ten strokes and allowed Eric a moment to recover. The knight stared down at the flushed butt cheeks, smooth and hairless. By the light of the fire he could see the hole in the center of those pink cheeks. The small orifice quivered with pain just as the rest of the man's body did. There was a sheen of sweat breaking out on Eric's bound form, and a tiny rivulet ran down between his legs to run across the pink lips of his asshole. Guy ran his fingers over the wet skin of Eric's ass crevice, crossing over the pursed lips and lingering there to rub that bead of sweat gently into the convulsing hole.

Eric's gasps were transmuted to a low moan when Guy's finger caressed his fluttering slot. Eric jerked involuntarily, which sent a jolt of pain through his balls and cock as they yanked against their restraints. The double sensations elicited another stifled moan, and when Guy's finger pressed into his anal cleft, his violent shivering threatened to topple him from the table.

Guy was absorbed in his exploration of the virgin butt hole, but when Eric jerked and would have fallen, he relented and grasped the wooden bar that spread his ankles to steady the youth. Guy stepped back and summarily began a renewal of the Saxon's punishment, inflicting ten more blows one after the other. Guy keenly regarded the young noble as he struggled to maintain his equilibrium, the wooden bar preventing him from closing his legs and protecting himself, his cuffed hands permitting him no possible response other than to simply submit.

Sir Guy ceased his beating once more and hovered silently over his captive while Eric inhaled vehemently in an attempt to catch his breath. Guy surmised that another humiliation was required in order to instruct the youth in the art of obedience. He plucked a wooden butt plug from his pack. Encased in fine black leather, it was several inches in length and tapered from a narrow tip to a wide end and a flange. After dripping a vial of scented olive oil over the object, Guy placed it between Eric's pink ass cheeks. The Knight inserted the smaller tip between Eric's sweat-drenched anal lips.

Eric had raised his head as far as he could and had seen the strange object in Sir Guy's hands. He felt it being pressed against his asshole, and he fervently willed his body to relax.

All his resolve centered on that tender area as the steadily penetrating plug pried it apart.

Guy was pleased to see the black plug invading Eric's hole so effortlessly, the slickness of Eric's copious sweating and the scented oil aiding the entrance. He was proud of Eric, who emitted only muffled gasps as the plug stretched his nether lips wider and wider. Guy approved as Eric bit back any outcry. Even when the fattest part of the plug disappeared and the narrower end popped inside Eric's muscled ass ring, finally captured by those tight lips. A small, square black flange remained visible, obscenely planted in the center of the Saxon's widespread butt crack. Guy imagined what sensations Eric was experiencing within those puckered lips. The big knight watched the visible end of the plug move slightly in and out as Eric's asshole fluttered around the foreign object in an attempt to cope with its harsh invasion.

But Guy hardened his heart to mercy, and once more began to beat Eric's ass. This time he landed several blows directly on the plug, sending tremors of both agony and ecstasy through the youth's body. Guy even landed several blows upon the balls that hung stretched above Eric's crotch, observing the fevered twitching of the young noble's limbs in reaction. Yet no pleas for mercy sprang from the poor Saxon's gaping mouth. Rather, his loud gasps became less those of pain and more those of rapture. Guy intuitively recognized when this was so, and laid another score of heavy strikes upon the shuddering youth without pausing.

When Guy did cease, Eric was a quaking mass of moaning muscle. His ass continued to move and thrust as if he were still being beaten. Wondrously, his cock had actually hardened as it was stretched upwards, now jutting into the air like a disembodied spear. The butt plug up Eric's ass moved in and out as if he was fucking himself. His head tossed back and forth, moans continuing to spew from his drooling lips.

Guy realized it was time for the final humiliation, and he set the paddle aside. Standing directly between his captive's bound legs, he gazed down at Eric's tossing, sweat-covered face.

Guy murmured into Eric's face, his breath hot against Eric's open mouth and lolling tongue. "Now is the time for complete subjugation to my will. Are you prepared to submit?"

Eric peered through dazed eyes upwards. At that precise moment, a full moon appeared over the rim of the high canyon walls. Its light glowed directly behind the face hovering so close above him. A luminescent halo surrounded Sir Guy's head as Eric gazed up at him.

"Yes, Master. Do what you will with me. I'm yours. I'll always obey you. I'm yours willingly. I'm yours," Eric blubbered, tears streaming from his eyes.

Guy leaned closer and planted his lips on his captive's wet mouth, kissing him gently. Guy licked the tips of Eric's teeth and ran his tongue lightly across Eric's parted lips. After a moment of tantalizing tongue-play, Guy rose and stood back, his massive body planted firmly between Eric's bound thighs. Eric stared up at his master. The light of the moon cast a soft and almost spiritual glow around his muscled figure. His arms appeared too huge to be human as he raised them to clasp Eric's bound ankles and hold them immobile.

Eric felt the butt plug embedded within his tight asshole being pried out. The widest section of the slippery plug stretched his tender butt lips with a mixture of odd pleasure and aching pain. Eric submitted, unable to prevent it anyway. After the plug slipped free and Eric's asshole became a sudden palpitating void, the young Saxon realized the emptiness was only temporary. His master's cock would fill that hollow next.

Eric resisted the impulse to close his eyes and instead focused on the silence of the desert night, the moonlit form of his Master hovering over him, and the impending violation of his virginity. He had dreamed of this exact moment and for it to be at the hands of Sir Guy, whom he admired and worshipped more than any other man alive. An overwhelming emotion of gratitude and love poured out from deep within Eric's beaten soul. His body shook and his heart ached. He was ready.

When Eric felt Guy's blunt fingers working oil into his butt hole, he gave himself up to the sensation. All memory of pain dissipated in the sensuous probing. He relaxed against his bondage, allowing his master to hold him up, and pressed back against the invading fingers that teased his ass entrance.

They were removed after only a brief exploration of the rim of Eric's hole, followed by Sir Guy's cock head. Eric felt the power of that potent member as it pressed against his stretched and puckered ass lips. He responded with a lust that overwhelmed every other emotion.

Guy gazed down at his bound student, sensitive to the profound emotions that had vanquished Eric's resistance. The Saxon's body had gone slack with capitulation, and then taut with eagerness as Guy's plum-head rubbed against his tender butt lips. Guy was not immune to the provocative wonder of the scene; his captive's bound body was exceedingly erotic under the soft moonlight. The sweat that covered his muscular, yet plump, body lent Eric a sheen of sexual heat that blazed ethereally in the desert night. His ample butt cheeks, glowing red from Guy's beating, were luscious and sensual, and his inability to defend himself or resist Guy's impending violation was supremely arousing.

Guy's shank swelled with lust, grossly huge as it crowded between Eric's widespread butt cheeks. Guy willed himself not to plunge the heated head inside in one swift stroke. Instead, he rubbed it across the puckered lips slowly, teasing and testing the young man's resolve.

Eric moaned aloud and for the first time begged his master. "Please, Sir Guy. Violate me now. Violate me now."

Guy grinned with delight. He pressed his knobbed cock head between Eric's oiled ass lips and shoved beyond into the hot anal channel. Eric responded with unequivocal capitulation. His ass ring unfolded and widened as a willing accomplice to his own violation. Eric was astonished by the intense pleasure he experienced within that palpitating slot. The width of Guy's cock penetrated him and filled him to a point he hadn't known possible. He welcomed the invading shaft as it plowed deeper and deeper, inexorably plumbing the depths of his guts and his soul.

Guy in his turn was amazed at the ease of his penetration. He worked his cock fully into Eric's captive ass. Eric's expression of rapture allowed Guy to throw off his own inner tension. With complete abandon, he set about fucking the Saxon's oiled quim.

Eric moaned and begged, his body wracked with sensations of unbounded wonderment, overwhelmed with the power of utter surrender. His entire being submitted to the Knight Templar's reaming. Eric yielded to every thrust and stab that ploughed his pliant anus.

Under that vigorous pummeling, bound and chained, Eric reached a threshold of rapture. In the midst of that unimaginable joy, he abruptly succumbed to a volcanic orgasm and ejaculation. Eric's cock was erupting, his balls were churning and his ass was spasming all at the same moment. He vaguely discerned a roar in his ears and realized Sir Guy was shouting. The knight's thrusting shaft was spewing deep within Eric's clamping fuck hole.

Guy witnessed Eric's violent ejaculation. Eric's tightly stretched cock sprayed jism high in the air to land in gobs upon his pale, sweating chest. That incredible sight had elicited the Knight Templar's own eruption. He poured cum deep into Eric's willing asshole. Cum erupted and splattered, flowed and filled, saturating the night air with its rank scent.

The cry of a wild dog disturbed the desert stillness that followed. A desert owl hooted in response. The two men, absolved by their mutual orgasm, finally found rest.

The moonlight shone down on their naked forms as they lay together upon the rough wooden table, freed from their restraints and slumbering beside the low fire. A new Knight for the Templar had been born during that evening's activities, created out of young innocence and melded by punishment and correction at the hand of a Master.

The aftermath was this simple joy of two bodies entwined. One obedient to the other forever.

# Tale Eight: Philippe Punishes the German Knights

*Return of the Baron Siegfried von Bartlet of Saxony and Sir Gerhardt Slalciz of Swabia from tale three. A three way ensues where they are lustfully pounded by a double dildo by the second-in-command, Sir Philippe de Chanson who has had his sadomasochistic tendencies stimulated by his experience with the Caliph of Cairo in tale five.*

Sir Philippe de Chanson sat across the table from the two young men. Gazing sternly at them, a frown graced his handsome face. It was supposed to be an imitation of his beloved Master Sir Guy's most severe look, but it was mostly feigned. He was not unhappy at the company he found himself with, but it suited his purposes to appear so. The minute the two young Knights had entered Castle Rock, Philippe had decided on this ploy. Now that he was close to the strapping young Knights, he gave himself over to it wholeheartedly.

Continuing with his stern ploy, Philippe chastised the young Knights. "Sir Guy will be very displeased that you haven't come to him earlier with this information. It's vital that he is aware of all doings in the Holy Land!"

"We're very sorry, Lord, but the Baron was forced to find a safe haven for his wife while the two of us searched out Sir Guy and Castle Rock as speedily as possible on horse. Forgive us. It's entirely my fault, and not the Baron's," Gerhardt Slalciz replied contritely in his soft, diffident voice.

Philippe was not about to accept any apologies from the Knight Templar. He lashed out with his tongue, his voice harsh in the candlelight. "You are both to blame and must be punished!"

The men blanched at the anger in Sir Philippe's voice. Bowing their heads, they contritely accepted the chastisement. Philippe could barely suppress a grin of satisfaction as he continued. "Young Baron, tell me what's more important. Is it the soft luxuries of your wife or the service to God and the Knights Templar who protect Christian travelers from the infidels?"

With those words, he rose and reached across the table to grasp the Baron's sweet face in his hands firmly. His supple fingers tangled in the light blond beard gracing those youthful cheeks.

"Forgive me. It's all my fault! Sir Gerhardt was obeying my orders!" Siegfried von Bartlet appealed, his eyes imploring as he gazed up at the fierce Burgundian Knight that hovered over him.

This Knight was the second-in-command of the Knights Templar in this coastal area of the Holy Land. Only Sir Guy de Brussiers was more senior. The young Baron wished heartily to join these famous Knights, especially so he could remain at the side of his companion, Gerhardt, whom he had fallen deeply in love with.

Philippe released the Baron's cheeks but did not relent. "Well, well. The two of you are obviously willing to shoulder the blame for this mishap, and that is commendable. But you will have to be disciplined, or I'll be remiss in my own duties. Let's retire to the next room. Both of you must remove your garments at the door and enter naked, so that your humility and submission before the Order is pure."

Philippe commanded this with a flourish, his tall form towering over the seated men. He knew his imitation of Sir Guy was far off the mark, but he enjoyed it anyway.

They rose and obeyed with alacrity, hastening to the indicated wooden door and disrobing without so much as a whimper of protest. Philippe watched as the young men stripped. His piercing green eyes filled with lust as their asses and dicks were exposed to his appreciative perusal.

"Go inside and await me. Kneel on the floor before the brazier! I'll arrive with the instruments of your correction momentarily. Pray for forgiveness."

Baron Siegfried von Bartlet led the way. His companion and liege servant, Sir Gerhardt Slalciz was right behind, their naked limbs rosy by the light of the dim candles. Entering the next room, they were confronted by another dimly lit chamber. Torches burned on bare stone walls. Two braziers flamed at one end of the room beside a rough wooden table and several wooden benches.

They made their way to the braziers and knelt on the cold stone floor where they remained naked and silent beside one another. They were almost touching as it were, when Gerhardt reached out and placed one comforting palm on his youthful friend's trembling shoulder. Siegfried turned and smiled with gratitude at the Swabian Knight, his courage bolstered by that heartening touch. He had indeed grown to love this quiet Knight and would endure anything for him. If they were to be punished, so be it. At least they would suffer it together.

Philippe arrived after only a short time. He entered the room quietly, but then shut the door with a loud bang to startle the fearful young miscreants. He smiled with wicked glee as both their backs jerked due to their nervous states of mind. He inhaled appreciatively at the sight of their kneeling nudity.

Philippe was dressed in only a leather harness, which he had constructed himself. Black straps crisscrossed his strong chest and encircled his narrow waist. Similar black leather straps wrapped tightly around the outside of his high, hard buttocks, and then ran between his legs and encircled the base of his stiffened dick and dangling balls. He wore knee-high

Jay Starre

black boots, but other than the outlandish leather garb was as nude as the two Germans. In his hands, he held several of his "instruments." He strode forward and placed the things on the wooden table before the eyes of his startled victims.

Both young Knights' eyes widened at Philippe's appearance. The bizarre leather accoutrement was extremely exciting and provocative. The leather straps did little to conceal Philippe's own nudity, and in fact accentuated the sensuality of his thick chest, potent crotch and powerful buttocks. The tools in his hands were also bizarre, inflaming their already fevered imaginations. Philippe smiled at the dismay in their eyes and moved to stand behind them.

"Put your heads to the floor and stretch your arms out to the side," he instructed sharply, his voice lashing out in the quiet of the room. Both men obeyed at once, and Philippe ogled them with more wicked satisfaction.

The two men were comely specimens of youthful vigor.

Gerhardt was the taller of the two, very lean and dark with a small goatee and raven hair. He reminded Philippe of himself in looks, and his lean body was indeed similar to Philippe's tall litheness, although Gerhardt was not so substantially muscular as the Burgundian. Philippe admired the Swabian's wide yet firm buttocks that were now pointing up into the air, hairless, plump and inviting.

The young Baron was fair in contrast with an unruly thatch of blond hair on his head. His thighs were also graced with blond fur. The golden hair snaked up into his ass crack and covered his furry ball sack, which hung down between his parted legs. His upended butt was even paler than the Swabian's and delectably plumper. His back was thick with youthful muscle, much more so than the leaner, older Gerhardt.

Lustfully absorbed in the spectacle of the healthy young knights with their heads to the floor and their arms akimbo in a position of submission, Philippe was not surprised to feel his dick harden further, twitch and even drool. It stood out from his leather-garbed body in all its curved, sword-like glory. He

94

smirked lewdly at the sight of the Germans' firm asses in the air, their legs apart and their balls and dicks dangling defenselessly between their legs. He contemplated the pleasant sight several minutes before returning to the table and fetching the first of the tools he intended to employ for their correction.

Philippe returned to his position behind the crouching pair and shouted at them. "You must put your duty to the Order of the Knights Templar first. Do you understand?"

"Yes, sir," the two men chimed together. Their replies ended in startled screams as they felt the harsh sting of a whip strike each man's bare shoulders in swift succession.

Philippe clutched a leather-tipped whip in his hands. He wielded it with precision, lashing out to strike either of the young knights at random across their unclad shoulders and backs. He grinned as he observed their twitching muscles and reddening flesh in the flickering firelight. The whip did not break the skin as he had no intention of scarring these beautiful young men, but it did inflict some pain. That pain was a delectation he reveled in.

Philippe's passion was further inflamed as the whip he wielded struck out to lash at the quivering buttocks of both men alternately, leaving rosy stripes across their perfect ass globes. Once commenced, he gave himself up entirely to the whipping. His dick twitched and drooled precum with every luscious assault he inflicted on the bodies of the prone knights. Every scream uttered by the hapless young men evoked memories of Philippe's previous experience at the hands of the Caliph of Cairo.

Philippe had since that time contrived to expand and experiment within the limits of this sadomasochistic experience and now was living a fantasy he had lusted for over these past months. He was fully aware it was his superior's duty to punish any of the Knights at Castle Rock. But Philippe had hungered for this opportunity many a night while observing Sir Guy inflict discipline or while receiving such punishment himself freely, and joyfully, from his Master's strong hands.

Jay Starre

Now Philippe sweated profusely in the confines of the dimly lit room, savoring the lashing and the howling. He relished the sight of those beautiful young men writhing on the floor before him under his severe instruction. He undertook to increase his expertise with the whip, managing to strike their pulsing butt holes exactly, shrieks of dismay rewarding him. He teased their dangling balls with the tip of his whip, inducing the young men to jerk spasmodically, and when he grazed their hanging, swollen dicks with the whip's harsh caress, they both begged and shouted for mercy.

Philippe did notice one surprising fact about the young men's shrieked pleas for mercy. Neither cried out for their own clemency, but for the other's. It was admirable, but Philippe really didn't care either way. The screams themselves were what heated his ardor.

"It's time for the next stage in your correction, lads!" Philippe finally huffed, his arms exhausted from the exuberant whipping. Sweat coated his semi-naked form. He stared lustfully down at the two asses flushed with rosy stripes, quaking with agony and trepidation. He was so aroused by this, his dick jerked and spasmed in an unintended orgasm.

Philippe stood stiffly with his legs wide and groaned as his seed shot out to spill over the quivering pink buttocks at his feet.

This uncalled for orgasm did almost nothing to alleviate Philippe's unbounded appetites. When its power had subsided and he had caught his breath, he moved forward and fetched another of his instruments of torment from the wooden table.

"Get up on the bench! Face away from each other and spread your legs. Press your guilty faces to the wood and raise your asses in the air," Philippe barked harshly. He was enjoying the sound of his own voice!

The two Knights rose, momentarily leaning upon one another for strength. Their backs, buttocks, and balls were on fire from the recent lashing. Yet their previously flaccid dicks began to stiffen as they peered at the depraved tool Philippe

96

displayed before them. With their dicks rising, they obeyed their superior. With their naked butts toward each other and their cheeks pressed to the smooth wood, they prostrated themselves obediently on the bench

Philippe grinned. He licked his lips lasciviously before he leaned over to place the sexual instrument on the bench between the two men's parted ass cheeks. Philippe had placed an enormous dildo at the entrance to Sir Gerhardt's pulsing asshole, as well as at the furred nether lips of Baron Siegfried's butt hole. This dildo had been carved for him from fragrant sandalwood, a double headed monster of ivory-yellow, veined beauty. Now it lay between the two Knights, their exposed asses quaking with dreadful expectation.

"You will punish yourselves upon this dick of God, each of you straining to drive the wooden shaft into the ass of his partner. In turn you will be punishing each other for your transgressions," Philippe commanded in a lordly boom. A gleam of lustful joy lit his emerald eyes.

With that order, he placed one end of the dildo directly at the entrance to each of their tender butt holes. He held it with his leather-gloved hands. Its prodigious length, a full three feet, was obscenely displayed in preparation for its no-doubt brutal introduction into the confines of the young men's guts.

Philippe had rubbed scented oil into the torture tool beforehand. The slippery round knobs at each end of the dildo were very realistic, appearing exactly like two mammoth dickheads poised to part the tender lips of the Knights' assholes.

Already their backs and asses blazed crimson from the whipping they had just received. Their bodies flushed further, from the nearby heat of the brazier, and from the fresh strain of attempting to obey Philippe's command and impale themselves on the immense dildo.

Gerhardt was the first to succeed in accepting the wooden cock head. A loud groan of anguish escaped his lips as he pressed back to encompass its hard girth. Philippe groaned himself at the wondrously crude sight of that flared head slipping inside the hairless asshole. The opening stretched impossibly in an effort to encircle the monster dildo head.

The young Baron grunted and pushed with his hips. Yet no matter how hard his plump blond-furred ass shoved, the tight anal lips were unable to accept the dildo head's girth. Instead his gyrations pushed the opposite end further into the heat of his friend's ass. This induced Gerhardt to emit ragged pants of agony in response to the invasion. In an effort to obey Philippe's orders, they both shoved harder, and finally Siegfried's asshole could not withstand the pressure. With a slick plop, the dildo head disappeared inside the young man's churning anal orifice.

Once both men had been impaled, their guttural groans rose up an octave. They mashed their cheeks into the bench they were spread across and gnashed their teeth. Their bodies were wracked with a violent shuddering as they held themselves immobile and attempted to catch their breaths. Philippe stared appreciatively down at the huge wooden shaft that connected the two nude Knights' assholes. Their tender butt lips stretched widely around its enormous girth and their spread-eagled bodies quivered on the bare wooden bench. Philippe began to pray over them sanctimoniously. Latin tomes of punishment and forgiveness rang out. He barely concealed another wicked grin as he slapped them both on their asses with his gloved hand, thus encouraging them to continue their self-abuse.

The two Knights complied. They strained to press back and further swallow the dildo while their teacher chanted over them. They grunted in unison with every inch of hard wood they managed to imbibe with their nether holes, but it was slow progress. Those holes toiled to stretch enough to accommodate the elephantine instrument.

Philippe was merciless. He took hold of the shining dildo in his gloved hand and lifted it up while he prayed. This forced the poor men's impaled asses to rise with it, their grunts swelling into howls. Philippe's chants only increased in fake sanctimoniousness. He released the dildo, allowing their plugged asses to drop back down to the bench. But he immediately used his gloved hands to grasp each man by the hair, yanking backwards and compelling the men to thrust backwards harder as he forced them closer to one another.

Gerhardt and Siegfried obeyed to the best of their abilities. Pressing backwards, they fucked themselves on the invading double dick. Inexorably, they moved closer and closer to one another. Their explosive grunts became exhausted moans as their butts touched, the dildo planted firmly between them, having finally disappeared between their solid young ass cheeks.

Philippe was amazed. He had not dreamed they could take the entire length, but they had. Although he appreciated their compliance, he was by no means ready to put an end to their sexual torment. With a shout of glee, he slapped them both soundly on their sweat-soaked asses and commanded them to fuck themselves. Even though exhausted and stuffed to the gills, the two Knights struggled to comply with Philippe's harsh orders.

Both Knights had labored to accept the gross dildo only because they were ordered to do it. But they now found themselves experiencing a bizarre and unexpected pleasure. They felt the warmth of each other's buttocks pressing together, sensual and exciting. And they each keenly felt the totality of having their holes filled with such a large shaft. Their moans were now of pleasure as they wholeheartedly thrust back against each other, their sweat-drenched bottoms slapping obscenely in the dimly lit chamber.

Philippe was so engrossed in the arousing vision, he was caught completely unprepared when a pair of strong hands grasped each of his outstretched arms.

He looked up to see Sir Guy de Brussiers standing before him, his eyes blazing with fury.

Philippe's heart skipped a beat, and his own eyes widened with terror. He had been caught red-handed by his Lord and Master! What would Sir Guy do to him now?

Philippe had no time to contemplate this turn of events. Sir Guy instantly yanked him off his feet and tossed him atop the writhing young Knights who were still impaled on the dildo Philippe had ordered them to spear themselves on. Philippe trembled with alarm as he allowed himself to be quickly tied in that position, each of his outstretched arms roped to an opposite leg of the wooden bench by an expert Master, Sir Guy.

He said nothing, afraid of further indicting himself. Instead, he lay submissively atop the hot squirming bodies of the young Knights he had just been whipping. They had no idea Philippe was not supposed to be punishing them. They continued their vigorously mutual dildo fucking unabated. Even though Philippe was of course terrified of Guy's wrath, those sweating, heated bodies writhing beneath him couldn't help but feel wickedly pleasurable.

Philippe's thoughts returned to his own plight. He stared down at the stone floor as he felt his legs stretched behind him. His quaking ass was roughly pinched and prodded. An agonizing sensation assaulted him as his asshole was penetrated by a large object. He was certain Sir Guy had taken the leather butt plug Philippe had been intending to use on the young Knights, and instead stuck it up Philippe's hole. His asshole was on fire as it stretched in an effort to accommodate the giant invader, but then immediately blazed with multiplied heat as he felt the sting of a paddle slapping him with resounding force.

The first whack of that paddle, another instrument of torture Philippe had been intending for use upon the hapless German Knights, drove the butt plug deep into his quivering asshole. Subsequent blows slammed it completely home, decisively imbedded inside his warm guts.

Philippe shrieked, realizing Sir Guy would require him to do just that, and begged for mercy, again as he knew Sir Guy would wish. Mixed with the loud moans of the dildo-stuffed men squirming beneath him, a cacophony of pain and rapture echoed in the small chamber.

100

Sir Guy smirked broadly, delighted to have caught Philippe in the act of such flagrant misbehavior. He was glad for the excuse to punish the tall Burgundian Knight, who obviously reveled in the entire scene. He had arrived at Castle Rock in the night, unexpectedly, and his loyal servant Mamluk had informed him of Sir Philippe's midnight carousing. He employed the paddle with red-blooded joy. His own dick drooled precum as he noted the delicious writhing of the three Knights sweaty, masculine bodies evoked by his not-so-gentle ministrations.

After satisfying himself that Philippe had been adequately paddled, Guy released him from his bonds and ordered him to turn the dildo-speared Germans on their backs, keeping them attached to that monster dick throughout. Philippe obeyed with alacrity, the substantial butt plug up his ass filling his guts as he moved over the moaning young Knights.

They were laid on their backs, their legs raised and placed so the soles of their feet were against one another. Sir Guy and Philippe stood over them side by side. Guy's big paw formed a steely grip around the Burgundian's neck but otherwise he offered no word of chastisement to his erring friend in front of the sweating Germans. Unlike the imitation of himself Philippe had been attempting, Guy was not one to belabor a point.

The two Knights silently watched the wooden dildo as it disappeared and reappeared between the young men's quivering butt holes. Unaware of Philippe's little deception, they sought to obey the Burgundian's last order and continued fucking themselves with vigor. Guy nodded to Philippe, and the Knight intuitively understood as they each stood at one of the Germans' heads and pulled them further apart on the bench. Two feet of slippery dildo was exposed. Guy then ordered the poor Germans to work the length back inside their straining holes. They obeyed amidst grunts and squeals of mixed delight and agony.

"Bring yourselves to orgasm. Spill your seed as atonement for the error you have committed," Sir Guy ordered,

101

although he was completely unaware of what Philippe was punishing them for.

Guy didn't really care. Later he would easily elicit a confession, but for now he was content to enjoy the spectacle of these handsome young men in such a sexually exciting situation.

Guy towered over the shaking men. They gazed up with awe at his blond comeliness, his brawny girth, and his unequivocally commanding presence. There was no question of disobedience.

As for Philippe, Guy grasped him by the leather harness he wore and forced his head down between the men's legs as they obeyed their undisputed Master. Slowly they re-impaled themselves on the huge wooden dildo, their muscles tensing, their hands working their own hard dicks, and their mouths spewing out a constant and incoherent chorus of agonized howls.

Philippe's face was pressed between the young men's sweating ass cheeks as they fucked themselves together. He nearly suffocated in the slippery heat of their plump flesh. Guy was behind him using the palm of his hand to slap directly on the huge plug planted between his hard butt mounds, causing the thing to ram ever deeper up his brutalized anus.

Abruptly, the two young Germans ejaculated simultaneously. Ropes of slimy cum shot into the air and landed on the back of Philippe's head. The thought of that gooey cream running down his neck was the added stimulus that drove the Burgundian Knight to his own sublime orgasm. He felt his asshole contract around the mammoth plug with quivering pleasure, his balls tighten, and his dick erupt between his widespread thighs. Hot cum splattered over his leather boots.

Philippe felt his head being yanked up by the hair, and his face forced over first Gerhardt's spewing cock, and then the young Baron's fat dick. He slurped and licked their jism as loudly as possible, begging Sir Guy for forgiveness as he did. He knew the Knights Templar Master would expect as much.

Philippe intended on doing his utter best to placate the powerful man.

The hapless Knights had the thick dildo withdrawn from their anuses, amidst groaning sighs. Sir Guy had them kneel beside Sir Philippe on the floor and fucked each in turn while they promised absolute obedience in the future between their grunts of pleasure. After shoving his meaty dick up each of their assholes and pumping them a satisfying amount, Guy rose and stood over them. He was so inflamed by the sight of their dripping and just-fucked assholes, he was overcome by his own orgasm.

Guy sprayed his liberal seed over their up-thrust pink buttocks.

Sir Philippe was thoroughly chastened and promised with loud oaths he would inflict no more secret punishments. The young German Knights agreed to obey their Masters in the future.

Sir Guy was satisfied all was well with the Knights Templar once more.

# Tale Nine: The Arab Slave Spies

*In which Mamluk spies upon an unusual feast. It involves the recently initiated Eric von Bartell and various other manly Knights who are intent upon instructing the delectable youth on the proper manners at supper.*

Mamluk spied on the intriguing proceedings from his secret hiding place. Ensconced in a small anteroom slightly above the dining hall, a facade of intricate stonework hid him well. He had exploited that very same hideout for identical purposes before his current Master, Sir Guy, had taken over Castle Rock for the Knights Templar. At that moment, his sultry orbs fixed greedily on the scene unfolding below. His hand was busy at his smoothly-shaved crotch, manipulating his stiffening cock while he observed four of the Castle Knights at their meal.

More than casual dining and good-natured bantering transpired in the feast hall that late Palestine evening. Much more, three of the Knights had come in after dark and wearily ordered a late supper. Upon recognizing the newest of the Knights Templar in attendance, the young Eric von Bartell, they had peremptorily ordered him to serve them their supper as their junior and inferior.

Of course, he obeyed speedily. Eric hoped to please the older and more experienced Knights with prompt and consummate obedience. But he had not realized to what extent their demands would test that proffered obedience.

The sly Mamluk had more than an inkling of what was about to occur. He had rushed up to this private spot to witness it all, eagerly anticipating some interesting action. He was not to be disappointed.

"Stoke up the braziers. We're cold this evening, young Eric," Sir Jan Hansen had commanded Eric on entering the dining hall. A short and muscular Dane, with shoulder-length copper locks, Jan was handsome and cheerful. He was already slightly inebriated. He eyed his companions with a wicked grin and added a bizarre twist to their servant's duties. "We require that you perform your service unclothed, as a mark of your humility. So make sure those braziers burn hot, or your plump young ass may get cold tonight."

The other two Knights guffawed with delight at Jan's unusual instructions. Seating themselves at the heavy wooden dining table, they exchanged smirking nods, in silent and mutual accord. They would continue in the vein Jan had begun for the remainder of the evening.

Eric's mouth dropped open briefly before he clamped it shut and hastened to obey Sir Jan. Eric stripped off his woolen tunic and drawers with tremulous hands while the three Templar scrutinized his every move with leering grins. He lastly removed his boots, and completely nude, ran to the waiting braziers and stirred up the quiet coals into blazing sparks. His youthful buttocks quivered as he trotted around the room, eliciting further rude guffaws from the seated Knights. Eric was a handsome young Saxon, yet maintained a pampered plumpness due to his wealthy upbringing. This luxurious plumpness was now readily apparent through his total nudity.

"Good work, lad. Now fetch us our supper," Sir Brian Howard barked out along with a guttural chuckle. Although hailing from England, he spoke in German. It was the common tongue among the four men present.

The third Knight seated at the supper table was the handsome blond Sir Heinz Brauhauf of Bavaria, another whose mother tongue was German. Sir Heinz had recently returned from Ethiopia where he had participated in a barbarous week-long orgy with several giant black men. Surveying the pampered, plump young Eric, with his lush white flesh, his manly libido was pleasantly stimulated by the contrast between the Ethiopians of his memory and the Saxon of the here and now.

While the three Knights chuckled over their wine, Eric obeyed their commands swiftly. He eagerly served them up heaping plates of fowl, fat dripping lamb with fruit, and breads and steaming vegetables. As he made the rounds of the table, each of the men thanked him with laughter and good natured heckling. Heinz Brauhauf was the first to slap his ample butt cheeks. The stinging sound was loud in the chamber.

"Good job, lad! You've got to work off some fat from these chubby butt cheeks," Heinz teased. Grasping one plump globe with his thick hand he squeezed. The rear muscle jiggled obscenely.

The others burst into gales of laughter. On the instant they joined in the frivolity as they each in turn slapped Eric's ass or groped his reddening butt cheeks while he continued serving them. He was wise enough to offer no resistance. Instead he grinned obligingly although his face flamed with embarrassment as rosily as his well-spanked bottom.

Above them all, the Arab slave Mamluk was delighted at the sight of the young Saxon princeling serving his betters naked as the day he came squalling into the world. His luscious ass suffering those rough slaps and rude grabs was a sublimely titillating sight. Mamluk stroked his long satiny shaft eagerly while he spied unnoticed.

Meanwhile, Jan Hansen, the copper-haired Dane, had decided to escalate the activities. "Are you hungry, too, young Eric? You may be allowed to have some of our food. But, you'll have to get up on the table like the slave you are. And eat out of a bowl like a dog," he commanded with a merry whoop. He emphasized his nasty command by slapping Eric's available ass and urging him up with that hand onto the wide wooden supper table.

"Excellent idea. Let's have the rich young princeling learn his place and eat his supper like an obedient cur," Sir Brian Howard agreed.

The Englishman leaped up from his seat drunkenly to place a bowl with chunks of meat and bits of bread in the center of the table. The Knight had quaffed several cups of wine one after the other and had lost any sense of the usual propriety his naturally dour English nature bestowed on him. The big, bear-like man was almost growling with lusty exuberance as he banged down the proffered bowl in front of Eric.

Eric knew enough not to dither. He hastily clambered up to the top of the table, not escaping without another slap across his quivering buttocks from Jan Hansen's ready hand. He knelt on hands and knees over the bowl placed in front of him and without the slightest hesitation lowered his flaxen head to eat out of it.

Brian's voice boomed drunkenly as he reached out to slap the widespread butt only a few feet from his face. "Good boy! Eat your supper like a proper pet!"

Eric complied, gulping down the meat and bread without a word of protest. His balls and cock dangled between his spread-eagled legs as he buried his face in the bowl, presenting an enticing target for Sir Brian's large, hairy-knuckled hands. Brian reached out and yanked on Eric's hairless balls, engendering a muffled groan from the crouching young Saxon as he gobbled the meat in the bowl before him.

"Give him a bowl of wine so he can lap it up like the hungry mutt he is," Jan suggested as he also reached out to fondle the pitiful Saxon's seed sack and dangling member.

Heinz, the blond Bavarian, slipped a bowl of spiced wine under the lowered nose of the piteously crouching Knight and forced his flushed face into it. Eric began lapping up the liquid, his tongue snaking out so all could see, his loud slurping eliciting another round of strident laughter.

"That's right! Slurp up your dinner like a good little bitch," Heinz grinned. His hand on the back of Eric's plump neck compelled him to concur.

Jan had been eyeing the perfect winking butt hole presented by Eric's kneeling posture. He couldn't resist probing it with a thick finger. At the sudden intrusion, Eric gasped, inadvertently sucking up and swallowing more of the intoxicating liquor.

"Give him some more wine. Make the slut bitch lap it up," Sir Jan ordered, fingering Eric's tight anus while Brian zealously continued to yank on the youth's silky balls and pinch his stiffening cock.

Eric had no choice but to lap up the wine and accept the degrading abuse the three Knights meted out to him. At first Eric merely wished to be properly obedient, but as he inhaled the liquor and the heat of the braziers intensified, the swimming of his head blended with the pinching of his balls, squeezing of his cock and probing of his asshole by the Dane's insistent finger. Eric found himself growing suddenly wanton from the intensity of the combined physical sensations and his position of subservience. He began to lap up the wine with loud obscene snorts and to lewdly wiggle his delectable ass, which was already raised in the air and accessible for the eager probes and slaps of the surrounding Knights.

"Oh yes! Look at the slut dog, like a bitch in heat. He needs something more to suck on besides that bowl of wine," Heinz suggested.

Already standing, he released Eric's neck to undo his own woolen clothing. All but his thick leather boots were abandoned in a matter of seconds. Naked, he got up on the table and knelt in front of Eric, his fat cock soft, yet beginning to wax erect as he waved it over the young Saxon's bowed head. Heinz yanked up Eric's head by his mop of short blond hair and pried open his wine-wet lips to insert his own large meat. Heinz had an unusually long and fat cock. The German meat grew swiftly as he fed it to the kneeling young Saxon, spreading his cheeks and literally stuffing his face. Eric suckled piggishly. The taste of wine was still in his throat while the scent of manly cock invaded his nostrils.

The others were inspired by the sight of the big Bavarian kneeling on the table with his huge cock being sucked by the servile Eric. Both men were blond and Germanic, although Heinz had a rippled body of cut muscularity and Eric was a chunkier, smaller version of that nationality. The vision of one on his hands and knees like a dog slurping up the other's monster cock excited the two onlookers to such an extent they also rose and ripped off their clothing in a frenzy of lust.

The room had become hot and with their lusts inflamed as well, the three Knights let loose their erotic fantasies and made gratifying use of their obliging slave.

"Wiggle your fat ass like the eager young pup we know you are," Jan instructed, reinserting his finger up Eric's hairless asshole. Jan's nude body glistened in the firelight, sweat running down his slender sides as he leaned over to finger fuck the sweet and tempting butt before him. Eric complied, wagging his quivering butt while he gulped down the huge tool planted between his lush lips.

Brian was likewise undressed. His considerable bulk, covered in dark hair like a bear, along with his thick beard and long black hair presented an aspect of brute animal strength. He crawled drunkenly up on the table, knocking plates and bowls aside and placed himself between Eric's widespread legs, pointing his cock at the hole Jan was forcing his finger in and out of.

"Fuck the bitch boy," Sir Jan enthused, grasping Brian's throbbing cock with his free hand and jacking it while he fingered Eric's pulsing butt hole.

The brawny Englishman lustily scooped up a generous dollop of meat drippings from a bowl at Eric's feet and slathered the greasy substance over his cock, allowing Jan to work it in. Then he pasted more of the grease onto Eric's wiggling butt, rubbing it across his ivory-pale cheeks with a large paw. Jan packed the dripping semi-liquid into Eric's asshole with his finger, working the slackening slot into a greasy pit for Brian's rock-hard fuck tube.

While Sir Heinz continued to feed his cock between the moaning Saxon's lips, Jan removed his probing finger from Eric's butt and pressed the cock he held in his hands up against the lad's pulsing hole.

"Stick my rammer up the bitch's greasy butt hole," Brian gasped, thrusting forward with his cock.

Jan grinned, obligingly spreading Eric's red ass lips with his fingers. He pried the greased lips apart to insert Brian's throbbing knob between them.

"Take that stiff bone, bitch puppy! Swallow it with your anal lips like you're swallowing that Bavarian sausage with your mouth. Take some hot meat up both ends at once," Brian Howard grunted in his guttural English-accented German.

Eric nearly screamed around the flesh filling his mouth as Brian's big cock head was crammed up his asshole. Fortunately the pain was immediately replaced by incredible pleasure as he felt his hole stretch and accommodate the cock that stuffed it. He slurped up Heinz' huge member as he was ordered and willingly crowded back to take Brian's equally large flesh up his butt.

Jan fed the English Knight's cock to the willing young Saxon, forcing it deeper inside the greasy red fuck hole with his fist, mesmerized by the image of the fat knob disappearing inside the tiny, hairless aperture.

A loud grunt welled up from deep in Eric's chest to escape around the Bavarian cock that filled his mouth, and with an abdicating shove of his luscious ass, he swallowed up Sir Howard's shaft with one great thrust.

Above it all, Mamluk still observed, afire with lust. He was lambasting his slick cock with abandon as he spied down on the four Knights. He had feverishly stripped off his own garb, the heat from the room rising to envelop him there in his hiding spot. His dusky, hairless body sweated in the confining space of the antechamber as he worked his cock and emitted muffled pants of passion. The delectably pale and plump young Saxon was on the table on all fours, getting his face stuffed with cock by the muscular Bavarian, while the hairy English giant was feeding him cock from behind. The thin Dane had his face buried in the hairy ass of the Englishman at that point and was licking his hefty butt while Brian enthusiastically ploughed into Eric's upturned bum.

Mamluk was unexpectedly startled out of his exciting perusal by a firm hand grasping his smooth buttocks from behind. Another strong palm covered his mouth and his head was drawn back. His eyes were wide as he faced his Master, Sir Guy, glaring down at him. He had been caught! What would Sir Guy do?

Mamluk was not left to ponder the situation for more than a brief second. Sir Guy's hand on his ass probed between the smooth cheeks and pressed into his hot crack, searching out the hairless hole hidden there. Guy inserted two blunt fingers deep inside in one swift plunge. Mamluk groaned, the sound luckily muffled by the hand over his mouth so that those below could not hear him. Sir Guy uttered no words himself, but rather turned Mamluck's head so that he could observe the proceedings below once again. While Mamluk watched the Saxon princeling being fucked like a dog, he mewled with agony around the hand over his mouth as he was forced to accept Sir Guy's throbbing cock up the butt in one gut-wrenching shove.

Back on the dining table, the four men were spiritedly enjoying their sexual antics. Eric whimpered like a beaten cur as he was stuffed from both ends by huge, insistent cock. Jan slobbered over Brian's solid butt cheeks, biting and licking while he dove deeper between the hairy mounds to seek out the man's warm asshole. When Jan found the Englishman's slot with that lapping appendage, Brian shouted out loud and drove his cock deeper into Eric the Saxon's tender young butt.

Heinz pillaged Eric's throat with equal fervor. The lad was pounded betwixt them, his body shoved about the table, knocking plates of food every which way as he accepted his superior's humiliating treatment.

"Fuck the dog! Pound his greasy hole," Heinz shouted, leaning forward to grasp the big Englishman by the shoulders, then planting a sloppy kiss on his beard-ringed lips.

The two men sucked each other's hot mouths as they drove their cocks into opposite ends of their fuck-slave's body. The naked Dane continued to drool and slobber over Brian's pulsing asshole. Food was scattered everywhere, Eric's body splatted by the various dishes, meat grease running down between his spread legs to coat his balls and thighs, wine splashed over his soft, smooth belly and his dangling cock. By that point, Eric had opened his mouth and his ass completely, allowing cocks to slide in and out without resistance, his body slack between the brawny Knights that fucked him.

Eric's cock inexplicably erupted in streams of sticky cum, although it had never gotten completely hard, splashing over the table and the scattered plates of food. The Knights fucking him sensed as much as Eric's body became entirely limp, and he twitched with spasmodic convulsions beneath them. With one mind they pulled apart and withdrew their slick members. Jan rose up as well to hover over the ejaculating young slave.

"Look at him cum, the horny slut, dripping juice all over the table. He loves it! Nothing better for him than a good reaming out," Jan guffawed.

Eric was moaning, his mouth drooling where it had dropped to the table, his legs sprawled apart as grease ran out of the just-fucked opening between his ass cheeks. His cock still leaked copiously onto the wooden table.

"Make him lick it up. The dog can clean up his own mess," Brian insisted with a wicked leer.

The others joined in with a cheer, seizing the young Knight's naked body, pulling him back so that his face was right in the middle of the cum-covered pile of food that he had just sprayed.

In a daze, Eric obeyed. He gobbled up the sticky mess, a mix of his own cum and chunks of meat and bread hot with the slimy cream. He grunted and mewled like a dog, eager to please his masters and intuitively understanding what they required.

Fits of hysterical laughter convulsed the three Knights. Brian and Heinz gripped each other's slick cocks and pounded them frantically over the pale body of the sprawling Saxon. Jan sat back on his haunches behind Eric and poked into his throbbing butt hole with four of his slim fingers, digging deep while stroking his own hard shaft. Jan searched for Eric's prostate with his invading fingers, spreading impossibly wide the young man's straining ass lips. Eric let out one prolonged groan, pressing back on that penetrating hand. Such a profound sensation forced Eric to ejaculate one more time across his quaking thighs and the table beneath him, his cock abruptly hard for that brief instant as it again shot out gobs of slime.

"Oh yes! Good doggie," the men shouted out in unison, shooting their own cum over Eric's shuddering body.

Above them, Mamluk was experiencing an orgasm of his own. Sir Guy's fat member was planted deep inside his butt, his large hands jerking the Arab's smooth cock to explosion as they spied upon the bizarre scene below. Eric's degradation, his snuffling over his own cum-splattered food and fierce fingering by the lean Dane were too much for Mamluk. The sight of those quivering ass cheeks accepting four fingers and doting on it enough to cum for a second time sent the Arab slave over the brink. Sir Guy's cock also played its part, reaming Mamluk's willing butt hole with steady, powerful jabs.

Before even half his pent-up jism had time to exit his throbbing cock, Mamluk was forced aside as Sir Guy released him. Guy leaned out to hover over the decadent scene below. He bellowed out in his battle voice, startling the laughing Knights out of their mutual orgasms with one mighty cry.

"Hold!"

The three Knights surrounding the hapless Eric froze at the unmistakable sound of their Master's voice. Looking up as one they spied his handsome head and shoulders protruding from a niche in the gloomy facade of the upper walls. It was as if an apparition had inexplicably appeared, and terror gripped their hearts alike.

Only Eric did not look up, his degradation and humiliation complete, no longer caring what would happen next to him. But he was not prepared for the words that followed.

"You three will clean up this mess you've made, and apologize to Sir Eric at once. You can remain as you are, without a stitch of your clothing until the job is done! Do you understand?" Sir Guy's steely voice was thunder from the heavens as it rained down on them.

The men blanched and hastened to obey, lifting Eric up and profusely offering their apologies, cleaning him off with their towels and bowing before him when they had finished. Sir Guy observed for a few moments, then shouted down to the men once more.

"Eric, you will come to my chambers, as you are. You have been admirable in the performance of duties this eve. None of this is your fault. I will reward you privately."

Eric had gathered his wits by this time. Although having just been butt fucked and humiliated in front of his Master, and still entirely naked, he managed a shaky grin. He looked up at Sir Guy and accepted his commands with a polite bow.

When he saw that Sir Guy had withdrawn, he turned to the three Knights surrounding him. He reached over to the table and lifted up a plate of food, his cum coating the greasy meat.

"I think you haven't finished your supper yet, Sirs. One last bite?" His grin was wicked as he raised up the plate and offered it to the chagrined Knights.

True to their orders, each of them bowed in turn. Only slightly disconcerted they strode forward one at a time to kneel before Eric and lower their heads to the befouled plate of food.

They all ate their fill under the smirking regard of their former dog slave.

Eric was laughing as he left them there to clean up the evening's meal. And Mamluk was chuckling as well, Sir Guy at his side as they secretly watched the three miscreant Knights' accept that final humiliation.

# Tale Ten: The Rapist Is Chastised

*Sir Jonas Dambrusk of Lithuania undergoes chastisement from Sir Guy for his rape of a Muslim woman.*

Sir Jonas Dambrusk of Lithuania languished in an agony of remorse in a dark dungeon cell below Castle Rock. With those tormented thoughts of repentance his punishment had already commenced. He prayed to his Christian God for forgiveness and contemplated the well-deserved penalties he would no doubt be soon experiencing. Sir Guy had been harsh when he was informed about Jonas' crime, rising at supper and bellowing for the other Knights to drag Jonas away and deposit him in this fetid cell.

Jonas was young. Just eighteen, he was unfamiliar with the complicated nuances of the Holy Land and new to battle as well. He had fought admirably beside his compatriots against the infidels at a Muslim village the past week. In the aftermath of the bloody conflict, he came on a lithe young Arab woman hiding in her brother's villa. Jonas was inflamed with bloodlust, his breath heaving from the act of hacking to death two Arab warriors. He barely escaped their cruel swords with his own life intact. When he discovered the quaking young woman, he ripped away her gossamer gown and plunged his potent prick inside her. It was as if he was once more stabbing to death the men who had nearly ended his own life barely minutes prior. He reached his bitter orgasm in moments. He abandoned her there sobbing. Although unhurt physically, she had been raped and humiliated. Jonas thrust the incident from his memory, especially as there was a great measure of guilt attached to it.

Several days later, his company were guests at Castle Rock, feasting with the famous leader of the Knights Templar, Sir Guy de Brussiers. An Arab Sheik appeared. After a brief conference with the Sheik, Sir Guy confronted Jonas. The Sheik accused Jonas of violating his young and previously virgin sister.

Jonas went pale, his guilt written plain across his youthfully innocent features. On the spot he had dropped to his knees and begged forgiveness. He tried to explain his vile actions by reasoning that he had been in the midst of battle and not entirely in charge of his wits. He claimed that he had not harmed the young woman and that she was an Arab anyway.

"Take him to the dungeon. We'll deal with him on the morrow!" Sir Guy shouted. In the booming timber of his voice, rage and disgust lashed down on the young Lithuanian's head like the snap of a whip.

And now Jonas waited. After a bitter night of anguish, he was prepared for whatever was to come. He feared the worse – that he might be executed. The Arab whose sister Jonas raped had been consumed by a fit of insane anger when he confronted Jonas. If it was up to that foreign heathen, there was no telling the torture Jonas would be subjected to, and death afterward almost a certainty.

Sir Guy de Brussiers was known for his wisdom and mercy, although he was also a strict Master. Jonas prayed it would be he who would decide his punishment and not the Muslim devil.

"Come with us, Jonas Dambrusk," a voice from out of the darkness snarled at him. The door to his cell swung open, and three Knights stormed in to seize him by the arms and haul him out to the corridor.

Jonas attempted to stand as erect as possible. He was determined to bear his punishment like a man and a Knight. Yet he could not prevent his limbs from trembling and dreaded his voice would betray him if he was required to speak.

Soon he was facing his accusers. Several Arabs stood among a gathering of Knights Templar with Sir Guy at their head. The Sheik Abdul, whose sister Jonas had violated, stood tall and implacable. His dark eyes scrutinized Jonas with utter loathing.

"You have raped an innocent woman, Sheik Abdul's beloved sister. A heinous crime without provocation. But you have admitted your guilt and are willing to accept your just punishment. Is this true?" Sir Guy asked this at once. His glare was as grim as the devil Sheik's.

Jonas' heart sank. If Sir Guy was not to champion him, he was lost. Jonas went to his knees and bowed his head, unable to face the contempt of the mighty Knight he so revered.

"Yes, sir. I am indeed guilty and remorseful. I accept whatever punishment you decide to inflict."

His voice was stronger than he anticipated. He came to the sudden realization that his terror was not quite as palpable as his contrition. He truly believed he had besmirched all Knights by his unchivalrous act. He deserved punishment.

"Strip him," Guy commanded sharply.

The two men holding Jonas pulled him to his feet and ripped his clothing from him. He did not struggle, but submitted in silence. The young Lithuanian was soon completely unclothed before the gathered audience of Christians and Arabs. His large, sturdy body quavered visibly with the humiliation of his nudity and his dread of what might follow.

Even in his wildest fantasies, he would not have guessed at the events that would transpire in the next few hours.

Sir Guy stepped forward to take Jonas' face in one of his large hands and gazed directly into his eyes.

"Jonas Dambrusk. This day you'll experience for yourself what your victim underwent at your hands. The abject degradation of that defenseless stranger will be yours to know, and taste, and suffer. You'll feel what it's like to be a woman

119

and defiled and used. Your humbling will be complete before
the men here at Castle Rock and at the feet of your victim's
brother. Your dignity will be stripped from you, beginning now
with your trembling nudity."

Jonas quailed at the Master Knight's withering gaze, his
own soft green orbs swimming with tears as he beheld Sir
Guy's disgust. Yet he offered neither plea nor quarrel, suffering
Sir Guy's regard with utter acquiescence and resignation.

Sir Guy seemed satisfied by the unequivocal display. He
released the youth's handsome face and turned to nod to two of
the waiting Knights. So swift was their response, Jonas hardly
had time to take a breath before he found himself again kneeling
on the floor. This time his face pressed to the cool tiles and his
buttocks were upraised in the air. Without question, he felt
completely humbled in that position. His naked buttocks were
up thrust for everyone to witness, his unprotected balls and cock
dangling between his legs, his face pressed to the floor by his
fellow Knights' merciless fists.

Further debasement followed. Warm water was dumped
over him without ceremony. Great buckets of it soaked him
from head to toe. Two men held out his arms while a third
rubbed his naked body with lathered soap. Another Knight
grasped his head and began to shave off his long raven locks
with a sharp knife. Jonas shivered uncontrollably, in a state of
shock, uncertain where that knife would be going, fearing for
his manhood, dreading that the worst might occur, and
castration would be part of this punishment.

The Knight shaving Sir Jonas performed expertly.
Within minutes the young man was completely bald. His pale
head gleamed in the morning light. Next his face was shaved
smooth, while being clasped tightly by other Knights. The sharp
knife traveled over Jonas' muscled back, stripping away any
suggestion of hair with the thick lather, even be it light down.
While Jonas submitted without a word, the knife found his
quaking ass cheeks, slicing across the hefty globes and
denuding the young man of any hair there as well. Jonas felt his

120

legs being kicked apart, and the unyielding knife descend into his widespread ass crack. That sharp blade worked around his anal hole, which he attempted to clamp shut in his terror and mortification.

When the barber Knight grasped Jonas' nut sack and worked the sharp knife across it, the Lithuanian was on the verge of a swoon. A wave of heat surged through his crotch and from there upwards through his gut and lungs and heart to his face and head. The sensation was undeniably sensual, but his head swam with horror at the image of that knife doing worse, unspeakably worse things to his vulnerable seed sack. The fact that he was being observed by all these Knights, and the Arabs, as he was indignantly shaved with his ass in the air magnified his confused dread.

Jonas managed to stay conscious, although blood radiated through his body in a rosy flush. Soon the bare skin of his head, back and buttocks gleamed lustrous and smooth. To the onlookers, his chagrin was readily apparent in the shivering luster of his pink-infused flesh. The sensuality of it was undeniable. More than one watcher's prick rose up rampant beneath a tunic or silken drawer.

After the poor miscreant's balls had been razored clean, they were thankfully released still intact. The knife-wielding Knight proceeded to shave Jonas' shaky legs, right to his feet. Jonas was twisted around and spread out on his back so that he peered up at the men gathered around him. Their avid interest at his abasement was clear, hanging over him like veritable devils in hell. Again he felt as if he would faint. The inexorable path of that knife shaved clean his hairy chest, his beefy arms and biceps, and then his smooth stomach. Lastly, the cruel knife reached his crotch and his flaccid manhood. Jonas stared down at the knife as it approached his cock and balls, his eyes wide with alarm, his limbs quaking. The knife was razor sharp and moving swiftly under the Knight's expert hands, but Jonas was all too aware that one slip might spell disaster for him.

His prick was grasped and held up as the hair around it was shorn away, its fat length throbbing slightly under the firm grip of the Knight who shaved him. Jonas once more experienced the sensual delight of his privates being touched, but fear and shame overwhelmed any other emotion.

In a short time the Knight's denuding was complete. More water was unceremoniously dumped over him. He was hauled to his feet and displayed for the gathering to ogle and heckle.

"Look at the dirty Lithuanian, shaved bare as a babe. What a delectably pretty ass he's got now," the Knight closest to him laughed in his face, the others joining him. Only Sir Guy and the Arab Sheik did not enter in the taunting, although neither stirred to discourage it.

Jonas presented a lush vision. A tall and muscular young man, he appeared more so now that his skin was divested of any hair. He glowed pink due to his shame, his limbs quivering with the intensity of his disgrace. His butt cheeks were pinkest of all. A flush centered on each smooth globe. Those mounds were most enticing to behold, as well as offering a tempting object for all those there to contemplate molesting.

His dangling dick and balls, hairless and defenseless as a child's presented an equally erotic vision for the watching men's perusal. Most of them were hard beneath their trousers, aroused to see the handsome young criminal exhibited so.

"Now you will become a woman for your ordeal. Gown him."

Sir Guy's simple command was immediately obeyed. A Knight produced a diaphanous Arab dress, dropping it over Jonas' head, drawing it down to cover his hairless form.

Jonas felt the smoothness of the gown as it covered his nakedness and the sensual touch of its silk over his freshly shaved skin. He was oddly stimulated by that sensation. His prick responded with the beginning of an erection. He was disgusted with himself and hung his head in further shame as all those around laughed uproariously.

Sir Guy's voice was stern, "Now, you'll experience your first taste of prick. Get on your knees like a whore."

Jonas obeyed, kneeling with his head bowed. The gown did nothing to support his balls and dick, and he felt them dangle between his legs as if he was still naked. But all his thoughts became focused on the figure of the Arab Sheik who strode forward and was now standing over him.

"Sheik Abdul will avenge his sister's violation with his male member in your gullet. Accept it like the slut you are," Sir Guy commanded.

Jonas' mouth was roughly pried open by the Arab's dark hands. As the Sheik parted his own gown, his thick brown prick was exposed and then shoved between Jonas' gaping lips. The Lithuanian feared he would gag, having never sucked a prick before, but the situation was so overwhelming he merely allowed his mouth to go slack and the brown flesh to slip inside undeterred. The taste of hot male shaft was not as unpleasant as he had expected. Its bittersweet aroma merely blended with the other sensations bombarding his consciousness. The fact that everyone was watching as an Arab's member was planted between his lips was worse than the act itself. His face was once again infused with rosy shame, yet he did not resist as the Sheik grinned down at him and began to work his hard manhood in and out.

"Yes! Suck that Arab spear, whore. Your mouth is a sweet cunt for him to use as he wishes," one of the Knights jeered as he held Jonas from behind. It was Sir Philippe de Chanson who clasped him. Jonas recognized the handsome auburn-haired Knight as they had chatted amiably only the day before. Now Philippe taunted him as he held Jonas' face for the Arab to fuck.

Jonas allowed the brown manhood to work inside his slack mouth, finding its hard girth strangely agreeable. He began to suck on it just as Philippe directed. Massaging inexpertly with his lips and cheeks, he slurped noisily. The vile, yet exciting taste of that hard Arab prick was enough to harden

Jay Starre

his own member. Shivers pulsed up his body. His prick rubbed against the silky material of the dress he wore, and as Philippe kicked his legs apart, he also felt its gossamer sheerness against his smooth freshly shaved ass cheeks.

He was shocked to realize he was truly beginning to feel as if he was a whore. His mouth was being fucked relentlessly with thick Arab cock sliding in and out. His shaved ass and legs were being rubbed sensually by the delicate material that covered him. He was further astounded when the Arab Sheik grunted deeply and abruptly spewed a load of jism deep into his throat. Jonas just managed to swallow without choking. The taste was again not unpleasant, a nutty flavor that he abstractly savored as the thick cream flooded his mouth and dribbled from his lips.

"Yes! That's right. Eat a man's cum, slut," Philippe whispered huskily in his ear, leaning close to watch as the Arab Sheik spurted, his body jerking with his orgasm. The Lithuanian's thick lips pouted around the brown prick as jism spilled out to drip onto the floor.

The Arab withdrew his still-hard prick, and Philippe at once inserted two big fingers. The Frenchman worked those digits inside Jonas' slack lips and played in the gooey cum still unswallowed.

The Sheik himself continued to grin evilly. Although having just cum he was not finished with the Lithuanian Knight. He turned and bent over. Shoving his ass in Jonas' face, he pulled down his silk pantaloons and exposed a brown, hairless bottom.

"Eat the man's ass whose sister you raped, you lowly whore," Philippe ordered while Sir Guy looked on approvingly. Philippe shoved Jonas' head forward, forcing his mouth between the Arab's warm ass cheeks. He pried open Jonas' lips and placed them directly at the entrance to the Sheik's tightly palpitating butt hole. The Burgundian Knight planted one hand atop Jonas' gleaming, shaved head and held him fast against the Arab's parted ass.

124

Jonas again felt heat flush his face and dizziness threaten to overwhelm him. The added warmth of the Arab's slick flesh as his cheeks were pressed against those brown mounds only intensified his breathlessness. He was forced to snatch great gulps of air, inhaling the Muslim's ass scent. He tasted the Sheik's hole as Sir Philippe's fingers pried his mouth open and pressed it against the intimate spot. Jonas was so mired in his own degradation, his compliance was unquestioned and immediate as he poked out his tongue and licked that asshole just as he was commanded. He plunged his tongue between the brown ass lips and slobbered and sucked with complete abandon. The lewd sounds of his ass-eating were loud in the room's bated silence.

The men surrounding him were incensed with lust as they witnessed the shaved Christian Knight snuffling in the Arab's Sheik's brown ass like a depraved sycophant. His feminine dress underlined his humiliation. As Sir Guy nodded in acquiescence, his Knights drew out their own raging fuck-tools to crowd around Jonas and masturbate over the scene of chastisement.

Philippe knew what was to come next, having discussed it all with Sir Guy beforehand. In fact many of the previous events were his own indecent suggestions! As he held Jonas' shaved head against the Arab's butt with one hand, he used his other to pull up the silken gown that covered the snuffling Knight. The woman's garb was tugged up over his lush bottom and past his waist, exposing the Lithuanian's naked legs and ass to the view of the crowded room. He nodded to another of the Knights, Sir Jan Hansen, who responded with swift enthusiasm. The copper-haired Dane knelt behind Jonas. He immediately dove between those exposed nether cheeks to begin licking and sucking ardently.

When the short Dane had grasped Jonas' buttocks and stuck his face between his spread cheeks, the young Lithuanian's body jerked with astonishment. His own face was driven deeper between the Arab Sheik's hot ass globes. Jonas

125

gasped for breath in shocked surprise as he felt a warm tongue playing along his virgin asshole. When a mouth began to suck directly on the tender anal lips, Jonas flushed with carnal pleasure and grunted like a pig at the trough around the ass he was eating himself.

Sir Philippe leaned over the poor Lithuanian, holding the dress at his waist and forcing his handsome face deep into the Sheik's parted butt furrow. Philippe grinned lasciviously at the sound of Jonas' labored pants. He whispered throatily in Jonas' ear. "Now you can feel your ass being eaten like the cunt it is, just like a whore feels. Spread your legs and open your pussy."

Jonas did as he was told. He spread his shaved thighs wider. The powerful muscles strained as he reared his ass up in order to accept with greater ease the attentions offered by the Danish Knight's enthusiastic tongue and lips. Jonas felt the slippery tongue enter his hole and part his virgin ass lips insistently. Again he nearly swooned with the overwhelming flush of heat that rushed from that sensitive spot directly up to his swimming head.

Jan grinned around the hole he tongue-fucked. His typically cheerful mood was hardly dampened by the seriousness of the situation. There was nothing he loved more than eating out asses. He reveled in the smooth feel of the freshly shaved ass he licked and the snug torridness of the virgin hole he tongued. He dug deeper with that probing tongue, tugging Jonas' muscular cheeks wide and exposing more of the hairless slot.

The Knights and Arabs encircling them had disrobed partially. Some were without their pantaloons while others were completely nude. All handled their rampant pricks as they observed the degradation of the Lithuanian rapist. The silken gown was bunched high above his waist. His lower back and wide butt cheeks, shaved of all vestige of manly hair, glistened with sweat as his ass was licked and sucked by the smaller, grinning Dane. His bald head was pressed deep between the

Sheik's plump brown nether buns. Jonas grunted and mewled in abject abasement over the Arab asshole he suckled, as if he was a hungry calf at the teat.

Jonas felt himself slipping into the role of victim, allowing his body to be violated and used, his ass and mouth the swirling vortices of his degradation. He realized abstractly that his prick was spear hard and his balls grossly swollen as they dangled beneath his widespread thighs. But his consciousness could barely venture beyond the twin whirlpools of lust, which were the orifices of his mouth and his anus.

He began to press back against the mouth that sucked out his virgin asshole. He began to mash his face deeper into the steaming ass in front of him. As he did, the men surrounding him continued to jeer. They called him cunt and pussy and other variously derogative epithets. The whirlpools of his asshole and mouth emanated searing heat. His shaved body writhing between the twin apertures became merely a conduit for that flooding desire.

The combination of the onlookers' derisive clamor, and the fruition of his own abject surrender, spawned a sublime rapture that his body utterly succumbed to.

All at once, he spurted cum in a rocketing spray over the tiled floor beneath him. He didn't even realize at first what was happening, his body was so infused with lust and humiliation. But as he ejaculated thick gobs and his prick began to spasm and his balls contract, he understood. He was indeed even further abased. His body lurched, alternately pressing back and jerking forward into the two bodies that held him. His asshole seemed to expand and open wider. The Dane's tongue slithered impossibly deep into his guts. Laughter assailed him as the men hemming him in witnessed his bucking orgasm.

"Look at the slut cum. He loves it! He was born to be a whore."

It was then Sir Guy interrupted. He stepped in to tap Jan on the shoulder and had him move away. Sir Guy was behind the crouching Jonas staring down at the twitching, hairless butt hole covered in saliva. He knelt to lightly run a large finger over the palpitating slot.

"You'll now experience the ravishment of the rape you committed. This time you'll be the prey, so know your own sin," Sir Guy admonished. That probing finger was harsh around the edges of Jonas' twitching hole.

Jonas was still in the throes of his orgasm, the most intense of his life. He continued to ejaculate the final gobs of cum onto the floor. His ivory-pale ass waved uncontrollably while he slobbered over the bent-over Sheik's brown butt hole. Jonas' tongue stabbed as far as he could force it, the ass juices of the Arab like honey to his fevered libido. He understood the stern mandate of Sir Guy with only a small part of his mind. He could not comprehend the full import without feeling faint once again. Not until he felt a mighty knob of flesh bumping up against his smooth ass cheeks did he allow himself to acknowledge his predicament.

Sir Guy had removed his own clothing and was in the full glory of his lordly nudity as he crouched behind the Lithuanian. His prick raged, his muscled chest heaved in anticipation of the violation of this virginal offender. He placed the crown of his member against that rosebud hole and began to press into its slippery confines. Sir Jan had succeeded in unfolding the sweet lips with his intensive tonguing and lubricated them as well. Yet the maw remained snug and hot as Guy shoved the fat knob between the slowly expanding nether lips.

Jonas' eyes snapped open and his mouth went wide as a shriek of pain and dread bubbled up and burst forth, only to be muffled by the Arab's ass that his face was mashed into by the pressure of Philippe's unrelenting grip. He felt as if he was being split asunder. He attempted to pull away, but Sir Guy held his hips with a vicelike clasp, and Philippe pinned Jonas' head and neck. The two men were both powerful, and Jonas was no match for them.

The young Knight's brief rebellion was enough to drive him to the verge of passing out again. But somehow he reached within and found the inner strength to abide his punishment. He inhaled deeply. Concentrating on tonguing the Sheik's quivering hole, he also willed his own expanding slot to part for the mammoth prick that probed it. His legs quaked frenziedly with the effort. Then, he was suddenly rewarded as Sir Guy's shaft popped within. The wide head disappeared between the fluttering lips.

The gathered Knights gawked with amazed wonder at the sight.

"Take that prick, you little cunt. Spread your hairless butt cheeks and get fucked up the ass!" Philippe was quick to chortle. The Frenchman gawked gleefully at the sight of Sir Guy's engorged shaft snaking deeper between Jonas's quivering ass globes.

Sir Guy groaned. His prick was enfolded painfully by the Lithuanians's narrow cleft. Yet, he gave no quarter to his victim, shoving harder, sinking the entire length into the hot butt maw. For his part, Jonas panted like a beast even as he slobbered over the Sheik's slippery bunghole.

He had capitulated to the agony in his asshole. He accepted the position of being fucked, of being violated and raped without a choice. His anus agreed with his heart. The hole eased open and surrendered to the brute dominion of the prick that was being stuffed between its tremulous lips.

Sir Guy sensed the abdication as Jonas's anal muscles slackened. He began to stroke in and out, slapping his hairy balls against the Lithuanian youth's smoothly shaved thighs. Jonas moaned louder and crowded back against the heated pole violating him. Miraculously, his hole gaped wide open. It became a slippery, sloppy sheath that massaged and welcomed Sir Guy's monster fuck sword.

"Fuck me! Make me a cunt! Fuck me like a slut," Jonas blubbered from between the Sheik's hot ass cheeks.

The gross words were audible to the crowd around him, and they jeered with heightened excitement. Their hands eagerly massaged their own pricks as they moved even closer, nearly touching the four men on the floor. Sir Guy's shaft plunged into the prostrate Knight, who sucked loudly on the Arab's ass while spreading his thighs wider to welcome further thrusts.

Jonas became nothing but a fuck hole. His ass burned with sensations he had never experienced. His degradation and transformation into a submissive slave was complete. He utterly surrendered to the men who raped him.

He sucked up the ass he tongued, reveling in the slippery heat, while his butt humped ardently back onto the prick that probed deep within him. He heard Sir Guy shout, followed by a blood-curdling ululation from the Arab Sheik. Guy ejaculated up his bruised butt hole while the Arab Sheik turned to spray a copious stream of cum across Jonas' lolling tongue and lips.

One after the other the rest of onlookers shot jism over Jonas' crouching body. Man spunk splashed his bare buttocks and soaked the sweaty gown that still covered his shoulders and upper back.

"Now, I must have retribution for my sister," Sheik Abdul shouted. He moved swiftly behind the exhausted and cum-soaked Lithuanian rapist. Jonas lay sprawled out in abject degradation, willing to accept whatever transpired. His resistance was totally shattered.

Yet he still feared. He realized the Arab had replaced Sir Guy behind him. The Sheik had taken hold of his hairless balls with one hand, yanking them back savagely. Through the corner of one eye, Jonas was aware the Sheik had a sword in his upraised hand and was preparing to strike. Jonas lay limp and without a shred of defiance, yet neither did he shrink away in fear or beg for mercy. He would accept the consequences of his action. He now comprehended what rape felt like and was utterly remorseful. He deserved whatever punishment was inflicted on him.

But the flash of the sword and imminent pain of castration was averted. Sir Guy's strong hand seized the Arab's sword.

"Hold. I will offer the perpetrator an alternative!"

Jonas couldn't believe his ears. He held his breath. He might be delivered from the Sheik's wrath after all.

"Sir Jonas Dambrusk of Lithuania. In recognition of your brave acceptance of your punishment, I would offer you a place in the Order of the Knights Templar. You will submit to our restrictions and commands, but will be spared castration and execution. Do you accept?"

Jonas was stunned. Through the delirious fog of his joy he managed to turn and grasp Sir Guy's powerful thighs with gratitude. Jonas gazed with adoring eyes up at the tall figure hovering above him.

"I promise to obey you with my life! I thank you from the bottom of my unworthy heart," Jonas promised fervently. His look of adoration was unambiguous.

Jonas' body was still half-naked. His ass was exposed where it continued to ooze cum from its recent violation. His entire body was covered with the sperm of other Knights Templar, while the Sheik's rank spunk drooled from his chin and lips.

"Then your punishment will be as follows," Sir Guy commanded. He regarded the young man offering himself so abjectly. "You'll remain shaved of hair for one year as a mark of your crime. You'll submit to the desires of your fellow Knights Templar as a common whore would, your ass and mouth ready recipients for one and all at any time of day or night. You'll perform your duties as a Knight as any of the others would, including fighting and working for our Order in the Holy Land. Is this acceptable?"

Jonas wept then. His answer was evident in the joyous sheen of those tears. Sir Guy then deigned to smile.

His companion, the Sheik Abdul, looked on with approval. He bowed to Guy's decision and the kneeling

Lithuanian's groveling promises. He smirked slightly. He had gotten what he came for and enjoyed every lusty minute of it. The young Christian Knight had been degraded and violated. He would suffer the loss of his dignity for a further year. This was much better than murdering the poor bastard Christian. All would be forgiven.

A round of cheering greeted Guy's proclamation. The thought of free access to the handsome Lithuanian's privates for the next year went over well with everyone. Naturally, Sir Guy understood all this. He was an astute Master.

Mercy was best after all, he chuckled to himself.

# Tale Eleven: The Harem Is Captured

*In which several of the Knights are victorious in battle, and during their plundering come upon a harem of young male playthings, and in their provoked state proceed to abuse them thoroughly.*

The Knights entered the chamber splattered in blood and gore, their swords and lances still dripping from the battle they had just won. The evil Sultan they vanquished had many chambers in his extensive pleasure palace, and they intended to search them all out for booty to bring back to Castle Rock.

Sir Jan Hansen was the first of that company to enter that particular apartment. He whooped with glee as he realized what they had stumbled on. In the far corner of the resplendently apportioned room, a group of men huddled, trembling with fear. Jan realized immediately that these were harem slaves. These were the Sultan's personal male playthings the Knights had heard lascivious whispers of.

The other Knights crowded around. The warriors eyed the cowering men with a great deal of curiosity. Also, with a great deal of battle-heightened lust. There were a half dozen of the slaves all in varying states of dress and undress. They clung together near a large bed, which was draped with silks and multi-colored woven cloths. One of the harem slaves separated himself from the clutches of his mates and stepped boldly forward.

He was a blond youth, his flowing pantaloons creating a bizarre counter to his distinctly European form. He was also very handsome in a lush, plump manner. His upper body was naked and apparently shaved of all body hair. His smooth flesh gleamed with a coat of exotic oil. The scent of delicate perfume wafted toward the Franks who gathered around to ogle the slave's half-naked body appreciatively.

"Fair Knights! We mean to offer you no resistance! We willingly surrender and throw ourselves at your mercy!"

The young man's speech was entirely in French. It seemed plain that he was a captured pilgrim who was now a slave. He bowed low and then prostrated himself at the feet of the Knights Templar gathered around.

Jan was unmoved by the eloquent gesture. The Dane snorted with laughter as he took one bloodied boot and nuzzled the lad's naked neck with it. Jan was hot, sweaty, bloody and bursting with intense sexual craving. He wanted nothing more than to show these perfumed slaves exactly what surrender to the Knights Templar would mean. He shouted out an order.

"Seize them! Since they offer themselves so freely, we'll make good use of them!"

Jan chortled, although it was not a cruel laugh. He was by nature a lighthearted man, but he fully intended to instruct these cowering lads in the art of submission.

The harem slaves grimaced in fear. Indeed, the sight they confronted would have frightened even the staunchest of men. The five Frankish Knights coming toward them were covered in gore. Those in their heavy armor appeared almost inhuman. All alike exhibited a gleam of lust in their eyes that was impossible for the frightened slaves to misconstrue.

The next few minutes were chaos. The harem slaves cowered in their corner as hot-blooded Knights descended on them. Their clothing was ripped from their bodies rudely. They were thrown on the bed, on the floor, or draped over knees. They were probed and spanked and jeered at. The Knights tore off their own clothing and armor in a mad frenzy. The killing they just partook in had incensed them. Now they were adamant about fucking.

Shrill screams and futile begging did nothing to halt the madness. In fact it only served to augment the Knights sexual frenzy.

Sir Xavier de Planta, a Spanish Knight from Navarre, was both disgusted and bewitched by the submissiveness of the harem slaves. He felt in his heart he could never be as they. He could never be a willing orifice for any male's hard flesh. He was the first to bend down and yank up the blond European, stripping off his pantaloons in one savage motion. He forced the youth over his knees and shoved his filthy hand between the slave's shaved and scented buttocks. Xavier grasped his quivering nut sack and squeezed.

The whimpering pleas of the plump young slave only goaded him into more savage treatment. He sought out and found the youth's soft anal orifice between the rounded butt cheeks. He inhaled his own sweat and the man's perfumed purity in one breath. Xavier gritted his teeth as he brutally violated the lad's warm, silken asshole with his blunt fingers. The blond slave's moans of mixed pain and pleasure were as music to his ears.

The other Knights were just as keen. The Spanish twins, Sir Alfonse and Sir Jaime pulled their own armor off with glee and attacked a groveling slave together.

The man's skin was midnight black and his nude body glowed obsidian in the light of day. He was shaved from head to toe, which made his enormous dick appear even larger. That dick was hard as steel once the slave understood the handsome twins meant to abuse him. His black eyes opened wide with tremulous anticipation as he was thrown on the floor, and the two nearly identical Knights each grasped an end of him to do with as they pleased.

A lengthy Spanish dick snaked between his bulbous lips. Another Spanish pole probed between his upraised thighs. The slave was amazed as his lips wrapped around a cock with a large silver ring embedded in the crown. How unusual! And between his thighs, the Spanish prick thrusting up his shaved quim was similarly adorned. Ringed cocks!

A grimy Spanish paw gripped his own black shaft fiercely. The slave, although impaled by twin pricks was still acutely conscious of that strong hand on his cock. The long elegant fingers were strangely soft and sensual. Those fingers slid up and down the slave's rampant black erection, eliciting gurgling moans and a bucking thrust upwards.

The two brothers leaned toward one another and kissed as they delved the black slave's opposite cavities. Of course, the slave's asshole was primed and oiled, as all the slaves' anuses were at the Sultan's whim. Alfonse's dick slid in and out of the palpitating asshole, the gold ring in the crown disappearing and reappearing. His balls slapped against the jet-black butt cheeks. Jaime's dick buried itself between the man's plump lips as the silver ring attached to the knob banged against the slave's teeth and tongue. This cock also produced slapping, lewd sounds as the two men avidly fucked the poor slave's moist and gaping orifices.

Sir Jan the Dane spotted his own prey. He caught the eye of a fair-skinned youth hiding behind the rest. He was voluptuously fat and entirely unclothed. The slave's rounded butt was lewdly displayed as he crouched down with his back to the others, quivering with fear. Sir Jan reached him in an instant. The Dane yanked him to his feet and leered. Jan's blood-spattered countenance was not overly reassuring to the blubbering young slave.

"Please don't hurt me! I'll do anything you want," the frightened lad begged.

Sir Jan continued grinning. He patted the youth genially but then proceeded to rip his own armor and clothing off in a frenzy as he trapped the young man in a corner.

"What are you going to do to me?"

The slave's lips quivered delightfully. Jan's blue eyes glittered. His shoulder-length copper locks were usually clean and shiny, but today they were tangled and sweaty. His naked chest heaved with his lust. His dick reared up slick and stiff. The combination of all this lent him an undeniably wanton appearance. He looked as if he was intent on fucking the cum right out of his terrified victim. But he had other nasty intentions on his mind.

Jan laughed as he reached out and shoved the boy to the floor. "Get on your hands and knees and spread wide your butt cheeks, like the plump puppy you are."

The lad quickly obeyed. Fear galvanized him, and he was on his knees with his ass in the air in no time at all.

Jan sighed with delight when he perused the superb butt displayed for his edification. Jan's favorite pastime was slurping asshole. While screams and shouts echoed in the room around him, he knelt down and buried his face between those perfumed butt cheeks.

The slave moaned as he pressed his face to the tiled floor. Expecting the plunging stab of a raging prick, he was delighted to feel instead smooth lips and slippery tongue. He thrust his nether cheeks well apart. He felt the silken tongue tickling at his anal door and shivered with delicious pleasure. His thighs split. His will dissolved.

"Please! Oh yes! Please! Lick my man-cunt! Tongue my man-pussy," the slave crooned in an accented French that hinted at a Germanic background.

Jan obliged the slave's plea, curious at the youth's choice of words. He reached between the creamy, parted thighs for a feel of the slave's dick and balls, and was amazed to realize the young man had no ball sack. He had been castrated! There was a long dangling dick there, but no seed sack beneath it. Only a small scar indicated there had once been a semen-filled pair of gonads there. No wonder the man derived such pleasure from his ass button! Perhaps it was the seat of all his pleasure now.

Jan was astounded but also galvanized by the strange disfigurement. He employed all his expertise on the palpitating cleft. His tongue delved deep. His fingers pulled the fluttering ass lips apart. He teased and tormented the writhing, kneeling slave. He was in heaven.

Meanwhile Sir Brian Howard of England had made another titillating discovery. This huge bear of a man was not as quick to action as his brethren. He stood back and observed the proceedings with a keen eye. There was no question of his own lustiness, but he was apt to think before he acted. And, the scene quickly unfolding was gratifying to behold.

His fellow Knights discarded their armor, weapons and clothing hastily. They attacked the slaves and unleashed their sexual ardor without a moment's hesitation. In contrast, the large slow-moving Englishman took his time. He shucked his own blood-drenched clothing, glad to be rid of the grimy filth, and stood legs akimbo. Large, hairy and naked he observed the bizarre orgy.

His keen eyes ferreted out the figure of one slave attempting to hide himself in a corner behind a curtain. Brian strode forward on beefy thighs and ripped aside the flimsy material. He was face to face with a quaking semi-naked young slave. Dusky and short with a lean, tight body, the Muslim youth hid in an alcove that also contained a strange contraption. The sight of this bizarre thing caused the huge Englishman's eyes to widen in astonishment.

"What is that behind you?" Sir Brian growled at the cowering slave.

"It's the Sultan's love saddle," the poor youth replied in accented French.

Sir Brian laughed out loud when he realized what the thing was. Perched on a solid stand of heavy polished wood, it was an elaborately carved saddle with stirrups of heavy leather. But on the seat, a huge, carved dildo was implanted into the leather.

"Let's put it to use," Sir Howard guffawed.

His own appetite had finally found its outlet. He craved to witness the quaking slave astride that dildo-saddle. Brian wanted nothing more than to watch the slave's butt cheeks part and lower down over that obscene, gleaming instrument.

Once his mind was made up, the bear of a Knight acted. He effortlessly lifted the struggling young Muslim and ripped off his silken pantaloons with one big paw. A gauzy, purple shirt floated around his shoulders and belly, but below that his body was now nude. The slave's prick and balls flopped free. His dusky butt cheeks jiggled as he writhed in Brian's fierce grip.

Sir Howard was still laughing as he lifted up the hapless young man and tossed him onto the grotesque saddle. Brian pulled each of the slave's shaved thighs apart to straddle the thing and then poised his parted ass cheeks directly over the stiff head of the immobile dildo.

"Please. You must oil the dildo! The Sultan always does," the slave screamed. His huge amber eyes were wide with fright.

Sir Howard saw no reason not to oblige the quivering slave. He reached out for the bottle of scented oil that stood on the delicate stand beside the saddle. Brian poured a liberal amount of the oil over that fake penis, which was twice the size of the poor slave's flopping dick. Sir Howard then took one hand and parted the slave's ass cheeks, pointing his quivering asshole right at the rounded knob of that freakish dildo. While still laughing, he began to lower the slave over it.

"Allah have mercy! Oh! It's so large! Oh! It's going inside me! Oh! Please! Oh!" The youth blubbered with histrionic wails.

Brian was no fool and saw through the wailed protests. He was certain the Sultan employed this love saddle often, and the young Muslim slave had more than once straddled it for this depraved Master. Brian actually enjoyed the caterwauling as he watched the youth's anal lips part and the monster dildo begin to enter him. Glistening oil trickled down the slave's smooth ass crack and over his dangling balls and finally onto the saddle itself. It was incredible. The image of that helpless slave being impaled on the rock-hard instrument was extremely arousing, as were his continuous cries for mercy.

As Brian guffawed above his prey, some of the other Knights took notice of the laughter and the loud begging. They gathered around with their own victims in tow. They also watched as the hapless harem slave was slowly impaled by the giant dildo.

As he groaned amidst copious and loud complaining, his pathetic butt hole expanded and accepted more and more of it. The head disappeared inside him. Then inch after inch of the gleaming shaft slid into him. Finally, after much dramatic screaming, he was seated on the saddle. Only the very bottom of the shaft was visible between his parted ass cheeks. The slave leaned forward and groaned like a gored beast as his body was entirely stuffed with the huge dildo.

Brian then commanded him to ride the obscene thing. The English Knight lustily slapped the slave's jiggling ass cheeks while shouting encouragement. The youth obeyed with labored, explosive grunts.

The gathered Knights cheered as they paid heed to the ludicrous ride. Eventually, the slave surrendered to the experience. His dick grew hard between his thighs and then abruptly shot. A load of heavy cream spurted all over the saddle.

"Well done," Brian chuckled.

Effortlessly lifting the young man off the saddle, he then tossed him aside as if he weighed less than nothing. Sir Brian was a giant of a man and strong as an ox. He turned to the onlookers and smirked. They understood immediately.

The Aragon brothers shoved their black victim forward. They had loosened up his rear orifice nicely and were eager to witness the inky flesh impaled by that well-oiled dildo. Brian laughed as he lifted the naked man up in the air and dropped him down over the saddle.

This slave also groaned with agony as his butt lips were pried apart and the giant dildo head crammed between them. He

140

was quicker to swallow the lengthy instrument. His black ass parted and his butt lips ate up the shaft as Brian lowered him over it. He rode the thing with grunting gusto. His swollen anal lips gaped wide and drooled oil as Brian slapped his butt harshly and shouted at him to fuck himself over the dildo.

One by one the other harem slaves were forced to take a turn on the saddle. Their anuses were stretched apart by eager fingers, dicks and tongues beforehand. Some of them even took to the saddle most eagerly.

Especially the young castrated male whom Jan had tongued. This youth seemed to have the most sensitive asshole. When he was dropped down over the dildo, he cried out not in agony but in rapture.

"Oh yes! Fill my poor cunt with hard dick! I love it! I need my hole stuffed! I'm just a slobbering hole for your pleasure," he shrieked obscenely.

When lifted over the grotesque instrument in Brian's huge arms, he had dropped down over it in one swift plunge. He swallowed the thing to the root. His chubby body rode up and down over the saddle with wild abandon. His dick never got hard. It was as if the entire center of his pleasure was in that palpitating, stuffed asshole getting reamed by the mammoth dildo. When he finally came, his dick was still limp. It spewed out a load of colorless juice anyway.

Sir Xavier of Aragon was appalled by this one scene in particular. He could not fathom what could transform a man into such a debased creature. He had been butt fucked by Sir Guy when initiated into the Knights Templar, yet that had been a holy experience. He had never since allowed anyone to repeat it. He had fucked plenty of willing male holes since then, but he had always been the one doing the fucking. Xavier had always felt a superiority over the man who took his stiff cock up the ass.

While he watched this last display and saw the utter abandon the slave demonstrated, the way his asshole seemed to gape open and suck in that stiff, inhuman dildo, and the look of

141

lust in his blue, half-shut eyes, Sir Xavier was almost sickened. He turned to the discarded harem slave closest to him and attacked him with a ferocity close to that he exhibited in battle. He threw the hapless youth to the floor. He rammed his dripping manhood to the root up the already abused asshole between the moaning slave's shivering butt cheeks.

Xavier fucked like a madman, one eye on the disgusting display in front of him. Little did the tall, dark-haired Knight realize what the future held for him. He never would have dreamed he would be forced to face this aspect of his personality at some time in the near future.

After the harem slaves had all ridden the saddle, their drooling dicks coated with slimy cum, their perfumed bodies now slick with sweat and oil, the Knights were still far from satisfied.

Brian glanced around and laid eyes on the naked and grinning Sir Jan the Dane. There was a look of evil amusement in his eyes before his big hands snaked forward and seized the laughing Knight. They were the best of friends, but Brian had become so inflamed with passion, he had only sex on his mind. And the more grotesque it was, the more satisfying.

While the lust-crazed Knights watched, Brian lifted his nude friend up and inflicted the same punishment on him as he had on the slaves. The dildo was liberally smeared with oil and ass juices from half a dozen others. It slithered around in Jan's ass crack sensually before finding the quivering asshole between. Jan still chortled like a madman himself as his English friend managed to stretch apart his ass lips and cram the dildo head between them.

Jan groaned and his eyes bugged out, but he accepted it. His muscular butt cheeks clenched, then relaxed as that greasy fake dick entered him. He grunted like a stuck pig as the shaft began to fill him.

The other Knights chanted and shouted out as they watched one of their number being so humiliated and violated. They were busy fucking, fingering and slapping the slaves in front of them as they watched. Alfonse draped a Templar tunic with its red cross over Jan so that only his muscular arms, bare legs and midriff showed. Every time he rose up and down over that obscene dildo, his naked buttocks clenched and his ass crack gaped open to accept the thing. The tunic was an indication that it was a Knight Templar being so rudely self-abused.

Jan only had one wish then, and Brian knew exactly what it was. He laughed aloud as he stepped up and perched on the saddle's sturdy stand in front of the moaning Dane. There was a wooden platform on either side of the saddle, perhaps for just this purpose. The Englishman spread wide his hairy ass. He reached back and clasped Jan's head in both big paws. Brian shoved Jan's face into his parted ass furrow. Jan's loud sigh of delight was clearly audible as his mouth gaped open, his tongue snaked out and he began to eat the hair-ringed asshole offered him. He was now in his own version of paradise.

The Aragon twins pulled their slave forward and placed him in front of Brian. They forced him to open his lush black lips wide and swallow down Brian's fat pole to the root. They took turns plowing his fertile black butt hole, first one would apply a deep stroke, pull out, and then the other would slide his be-ringed scimitar dick into the inky, gaping pit.

Xavier's own mental turmoil was dispelled by the overpowering combination of passion, sweat and exhilaration flooding his senses during the bizarre scene. He kept up the pace of his pounding fuck deep into the upturned butt beneath him, but reached forward to slide one of his hands down around the saddle's dildo. Xavier felt every bump and grind of Jan's hot hard butt as it fucked itself over the lewd instrument. His other hand moved in front of the Danish Knight and stroked Jan's equally hard dick. One hand in front, the other behind, and his own cock massaging a willing hole, Sir Xavier screwed himself into a frenzy of sexual pleasure.

When he eventually did cum, he was joined by the others in a mutual orgasm that defied belief.

They slept the night away in the captured palace, a pile of nude male bodies draped over one another. In the morning the harem slaves treated the conquering Knights to soothing baths, perfumed massages and other treats before they were carted away to Castle Rock as part of their booty.

One thing especially the Englishman Sir Brian Howard made certain to take with him to Castle Rock as his share of the spoils. That would be the bizarre love-saddle. He would ensconce it somewhere in the bowels of that huge stone edifice in the hopes of utilizing the grotesque thing some time in the future.

# Tale Twelve: Sir Guy Tastes Defeat

*In which an interloper, the Swede Sir Olaf Thorsen, makes a bid to wrest control of Castle Rock from Guy. In defeat, Guy tastes the mighty fist of the Swedish giant.*

Sir Guy de Brussiers perched on his wooden throne at the far end of his Council Chamber surveying the new arrivals who stood before him.

Guy grinned down at the tall Knight who was the newcomers' evident leader.

"And you've been ordered to remove me from my command, Sir Olaf?" he asked amiably.

"Yes, Sir Guy. By the Great Master himself. I'm to take over Castle Rock and assume control of the affairs of the Templar in this sector of the Holy Land." The man's deep voice boomed out over the assembled Knights.

There were smirks amidst the dismay of the congregated Knights. They all worshipped and obeyed their leader, Sir Guy, and were not pleased to have this interloper deliver such news. All congregated there knew Sir Guy and couldn't believe he would give in to such an order readily.

"But you have never been to the Holy Land before. You have no knowledge of the intricacies of this strange and exotic land's politics," Sir Guy replied smoothly, making no move to descend from his place on the throne. Or acknowledge Sir Olaf's superiority.

The men around muttered among themselves while they observed keenly the interaction between the two men. Sir Olaf strode forward without hesitation to place a sealed letter in Sir Guy's lap. He pointedly made no display of homage to the seated Knight.

The men's eyes locked before Sir Guy tore open the letter and read it silently.

Sir Olaf Thorsen stood implacably before the French Knight. He was a towering man well over six feet tall, which was at least a few inches taller than Sir Guy. The hair on the Swede's head was cropped short. The red bristles were just barely discernable. He boasted a clipped red beard as well, which suited his handsome but pale features. He had a bit of the aspect of a Viking to him – a trifle more refined and less brutish, though.

"I see. All is in order here. But again, I must say Sir Olaf, that you are ill prepared to command the Knights in our tricky business here in the Holy Land," Sir Guy stated mildly.

Sir Olaf's eyes clouded for a moment. He lifted his shoulders with haughty insolence. "I'm always prepared! And at any rate, you'll be my second in command and useful to me."

The crowded Knights gasped with shock, speculating on what their all-powerful leader would do now. His temper was slow to ignite, but he was not known to have patience with boorishness. They were surprised when Sir Guy did not answer at once.

The tension mounted while Sir Olaf's features gathered steam, and he seemed on the verge of an outburst. Sir Guy finally laughed and rose to clap the man on his shoulder in a friendly gesture.

"I tell you what, Sir Olaf. You'll have my obedience and cooperation if you'll agree to a contest between the two of us. Three trials, and the one who wins two of those will command the Knights Templar in the Holy Land."

The tall Swede was visibly taken aback by the challenge, yet his innate arrogance wouldn't allow him to refuse. He accepted with a smug grin, clearly certain of the outcome of any contest between the two of them.

On the instant, a table was brought in, and a chess game was set up. The two Knights hunkered over the board for an hour before Sir Guy soundly defeated the Swedish Knight amidst great cheering from the scores of observing men. Sir Olaf accepted the defeat with surprising grace and a confident smile. He seemed certain of the outcome of the next two trials.

Next the men moved outside to a walled-in courtyard where a verdant garden of lemon trees and lilacs lent a pleasant scent to the heat of the Palestine morning. Bright sunshine welcomed the Knights as they gathered around a central grassy area. Sir Olaf and Sir Guy stripped off their garments and were soon completely nude under the pristine blue skies.

They squared off then clasped each other's shoulders and gave out a great shout. Immediately, the two commenced to wrestle back and forth across the grass. The crowded Knights kept them from straying as they pushed and shoved in an attempt to throw one another to the ground.

Guy was a tall man himself with a thick chest, massive shoulders, and powerful legs, but Sir Olaf was half a head taller and a true giant of a man. His body was almost completely hairless in contrast to the light blond fur coating Sir Guy's muscular form. The sweat that trickled down the Swede's smooth chest and shoulders gleamed in the morning light.

Both men sported lengthy fat pricks that dangled and flopped as they strained to throw one another. But as Olaf began to press Guy to his knees, his cock began to rise and stab out like some kind of fierce weapon. It was fully erect when he finally vanquished the burly French Knight by throwing him to the grassy ground. Shouts mostly of dismay, but some of glee rang out in the morning air at the surprise outcome. Few hoped for Olaf's victory.

Sir Olaf's eyes gleamed in triumph when he helped the unfortunate Guy to his feet. His bare prick was engorged and throbbing with excitement as he made ready for the final test.

147

Jay Starre

Before Guy could recoup from his loss, the Swedish Knight seized him by the forearms and lifted him up to toss him violently on his stomach to the ground.

In a split second, Olaf leapt on the prostrate Guy. His stiff cock jabbed between the Knight's wide-spread ass cheeks and his heavy body pinned him unmoving on the grassy ground.

It was over before any of the Knights could truly comprehend the meaning of it. They had been so fascinated by the image of the Swede's lengthy, spear-stiff tool as it probed between their Master's potent ass mounds they hadn't thought beyond that lascivious moment. The lusty sight of Sir Guy buried under the massive Swede's nude form was too exciting to warrant any thoughts other than sexual ones.

While the Knights watched with mingled lust and growing consternation, the Swede shouted in triumph and pinned Sir Guy beneath him. His giant hairless body was too much even for the powerful French Knight to dislodge. Yet Guy continued squirming and wriggling mightily beneath the Swede in his effort to escape.

What transpired next brought a concerted gasp from the Knights surrounding the struggling pair. All Guy's wriggling had remarkably inflamed the Swedish Knight's lust beyond his control. Before their eyes, he kicked the squirming Guy's legs farther apart and began to hump up and down onto his bucking body.

A muffled cry could be heard emanating from Sir Guy's buried head. It was then obvious Olaf had penetrated Guy's defenses and was now driving his stiff shaft into their leader's unwilling asshole.

The gathered Knights were totally stunned by the display. Yet they had all heard Sir Guy's proclamation that the winner would be their Master. They could do nothing but watch the lewd display. They also knew Guy well and were absolutely certain he would not want them to interfere in any way. The Swede began to fuck Guy violently. The giant pounded his

148

prick deep between Guy's hairy butt cheeks, huffing and groaning with leering gratification.

Sir Guy himself continued struggling for a time. Eventually though, he began to lift his ass and meet the harsh thrusts of the Swede's inhumanly lengthy instrument. What was going through Guy's mind was impossible to guess. He was certainly aware his men watched his rape by the brutal Swede. It may have been unclear what Guy's thoughts were, but his body responded unequivocally. His beefy thighs splayed wide apart, and he appeared as if he accepted the Swede's prick willingly. Guy even took to moaning out loud with what clearly seemed to be undeniable pleasure.

There, under the branches of the lemon trees, in his own hard-won Castle, Guy was violated and humiliated by the newcomer for all to see.

But Olaf was not finished with his task of conquest. He withdrew his throbbing prick and rose up to poise over the vanquished Knight. He leered wickedly at the gathering.

"Bring me rope! Now," his booming voice commanded.

Instantly one of the Knights obeyed, and while Olaf hovered over the prostrate Guy, the remainder of the Knights waited breathlessly for the next course of events.

A long rope was placed in the titan Swede's hands. Expertly he bound Guy with the rope, placing him on his hands and knees with his arms tightly folded behind his back and his head pressed into the grass. The rope snaked around Guy's balls and prick so they jutted out and grew fat and thick with blood. Guy's legs and arms were so restrained that he was helpless.

"Now you will submit to your new Master," Olaf bragged, slapping Sir Guy's beefy ass cheeks with one of his huge pale palms.

Olaf called forward the shaved Knight Sir Jonas Dambrusk, who had been raped himself only a short time before as a punishment for his crimes. The Swede whispered into the Lithuanian's ear, then waited with his huge arms on his hips while Jonas scurried off to obey the new leader.

The Knights could do nothing but wait and watch. Dismayed, they were at the same time fascinated by the sight of their former Master, Sir Guy bound naked and humiliated before them. The smirking figure of the giant Swede was stationed over Guy possessively. Olaf's long legs, both muscular and hairless, were planted firmly on either side of Guy's nude body.

Olaf chided the kneeling Knight, as if his physical conquest was not enough in itself. "You are nothing now, French pig. I'll teach you to obey your new Master freely."

Stepping back, Olaf raised his foot. His huge toes pressed into Guy's butt crack to tickle his tightly bound ball sack. Olaf laughed brutally as he fondled Guy's butt with those massive toes.

Jonas returned with an obscene object in his hands. It was a huge dildo, veined and realistic with a monstrous knob of a head on it. It was one of Guy's special punishment dildos. Guy employed the giant tool only on rare occasions when some Knight deserved a painfully exquisite penalty. It glowed obscenely under the bright morning light in Jonas's hands. The shaved Knight had brought oil as well, and he worked a liberal amount over the fuck tool. Now it glistened and dripped with nasty readiness.

"You'll take this prick up your ass. You'll love it. You'll beg for more then you'll promise to be my agreeable fuck pig," Olaf said with a rude smirk. He then crouched behind Guy and placed the huge phallus against Guy's snug red ass aperture.

Guy had so far remained mute. His head bowed from the snug force of the ropes twisted around his forehead and neck, but his body was relaxed and powerful even in this position. There was much sympathy for him from those gathered around. Even in the extremity of the situation, his masculine beauty was absolutely undiminished. Yet all watching could not help but be enthralled by the picture of the huge dildo about to penetrate his bound rear end.

Olaf's forearms strained as he pushed against the resistance of Guy's asshole muscles. The fat head of the dildo spread the oiled hole impossibly wide. Olaf's face was a rictus of pleasure and profound satisfaction as he witnessed Guy's hole capitulate and the dildo's head finally glide within the French Knight's straining innards.

There was a concerted moan from the crowd as Guy accepted the dildo's head without flinching. His bound body moved not at all while the Swede pressed the flanged head of the fake phallus beyond Guy's quivering anal lips and began to pack him with the shaft.

"Take it, slave. You're nothing but a fuck receptacle for your new Master," Olaf shouted out. He punctuated the insult with a lusty slap across Guy's hefty butt.

Guy said nothing and reacted stonily. His ass swallowed the enormous dildo inch by immense inch. Olaf stood up and surveyed the bound Knight, half the monster dildo sticking out of his stretched anus obscenely, oil dripping down between his roped thighs. He grinned triumphantly and began to use his foot to press the dildo deeper into Guy's asshole.

Utter silence gripped the audience. The giant Swede's foot drove the dildo all the way up Guy's ass. And then amazingly, his brutal heel worked the base of it completely inside Guy's stretched hole to totally disappear.

Olaf laughed with cruel satisfaction. "That's it! Swallow that monster dildo like a good slave!" The men were amazed to see no sign of the huge fake cock, which was now completely embedded inside Guy's straining asshole.

"All right. That's enough. Time to expel it, dog-slave," Olaf commanded, his booming voice ringing out.

Again the men were amazed to see Guy's asshole expanding on command and the wide base of the dildo reappearing. The dildo slid out between Guy's big butt cheeks. The slippery shaft gleamed longer and longer until the flange of the head caught at his ass lips and was prevented from being expelled entirely.

"Go ahead, slave. Let's see the rest of it," Olaf shouted around a wicked smirk. He leaned down to smack Guy's heaving butt cheek at the same time.

Guy's body shuddered once and the head of the dildo popped out and dropped to the ground. Everyone stared at the quivering anal orifice as it slowly shrunk, yet remained obscenely distended and slick.

Olaf laughed with cruel pleasure. "Now you'll show your true mettle, slave. You'll accept whatever I deign to subject your poor ass to."

He knelt behind the bound Master of the Templar and placed his massive hand against the upended Knight's butt hole. Jonas moved forward without being asked and poured more of the scented oil over Guy's ass crack. The young acolyte was completely sympathetic to Guy's plight and hoped to alleviate the pain of whatever was to come.

Olaf still grinned like some depraved monster as his fingers began to work into Guy's stretched anal ring. But even the width of that enormous dildo did not compare with the girth of the hand Olaf began to press into Guy's fuck hole. Two, then three, then four fingers penetrated Guy's oiled rectum. The relentless fingers stretched open the butt maw while probing deep inside Guy's churning guts.

Guy had said nothing. His eyes were open and unreadable, but now as his hole was stretched to what must have been his limits he began to sweat and groan slightly. As Olaf pressed inward with his thumb to join his four fingers already rooting around inside Guy, the Frenchman expelled his breath, and a loud moan escaped his lips.

"That's right! Moan for us all to hear. You need a big fist up your greasy ass, slave pussy," Olaf shouted out with a sneer. He pushed all five fingers deeper, the wide part of his hand stretching open the straining sphincter. Guy's upraised and bound buttocks broke out in sweat and quivered with tension.

"Aggh! Oohhhh!" Guy finally shouted out. The pain on his face was plain to see. But then, unexpectedly, the big Knight smiled almost serenely, and with a bucking shove pushed his ass back against that huge fist. The violated hole abruptly sucked Olaf's hand completely inside to the wrist.

Olaf's eyes widened in awe. But even so, his passion was further inflamed at the feeling of his fist buried inside the warmth of Guy's guts. He groaned like a crazed beast as he began to fuck Guy with his fist. Olaf sank that big fist deeper, then cruelly withdrew to tease the anal ring with his wide palm.

"Yes, Master. Fist my willing hole. You're my Master now, and I'm your fuck hole," Guy shouted out.

Guy's mighty ass rose up and humped against the arm that fucked him. It was difficult to tell who was directing the scene as Guy's bound body wriggled and thrust against the fist impaling him. Even though he was tied and defenseless, it appeared as if Guy was the one who was fucking Olaf.

Guy's big solid bottom worked itself over the fist planted inside it. Olaf sat back and gave himself up to the bombarding of his hand by squishy asshole and the corresponding bombarding of his senses by the intense pleasure that invoked. His prick jutted straight up and continually leaked precum. Olaf's blue orbs fixed greedily on the sight of Guy's deliciously bound body humping itself obligingly over his clenched fist and halfway up his thrusting forearm.

The crowded Knights were beyond amazement. In shock, they watched as Olaf's prick abruptly discharged a load of cum straight in the air. As Guy writhed over his buried fist the gooey cream splattered upwards to smear Olaf's laboring chest. The Swede yanked his arm from Guy's butt hole and collapsed on top of him. He shot jism over Guy's roped back while muttering incoherently.

Some of the men could see their former master's face as he was buried under the cuming Swede. They were astounded at the satisfied smile on his lips as he also convulsed in the throes of an orgasm. Guy's pulsing prick splattered the ground and his own belly with gobs of spunk.

Both men remained on the ground writhing in their mutual orgasm for several minutes. The observing Knights waited in hushed silence. Their own pricks were rock hard under their pantaloons. Many stroked their engorged rods through the rough material and were on the verge of cuming themselves.

Olaf's powerful back and ass were spread over the sweating, bound Frenchman. The Swede's body quaked with the force of his orgasm. It was almost as if it was he who had just been fisted. And with his pale thighs spread and flopping as he squirted out the last of his seed, the Knights were treated to the sight of Olaf's twitching, bare asshole. It was as hairless as the rest of his fine body. Many there briefly fantasized diving between those pale butt cheeks and slobbering over that snug and defenseless aperture.

Finally, Olaf rose up and stood over the bound and cum-smeared former leader of the Knights Templar. He nodded to Jonas who at once began to untie Guy. In a few moments the French Knight was unbound and forced to kneel before the naked Swede. Guy was first made to kiss and lick Olaf's bare feet, then his calves, his thighs and finally his balls and cum-dripping prick.

But although Olaf grinned in triumph at each Knight gathered around, the kneeling Guy was also smiling, albeit secretly. His unbowed head did not go unnoticed among those watching. Many caught the glint of challenge still lurking in the Frenchman's eyes – especially so in the case of the Templar second in command, Philippe.

Throughout the entire ordeal Philippe had never for a moment believed Guy wasn't truly in charge of the situation, not this giant red-headed interloper. Philippe understood Guy's mind and heart more than any other.

Yet even he realized only time would tell who would become the ultimate Master. For now, it was Guy naked on his knees sucking Sir Olaf's lengthening prick. All the Knights gathered there were certain the day would prove more interesting yet.

# Tale Thirteen: The Knights Submit to Sir Olaf

*In which the Knights at Castle Rock are forced to submit to their new Master, the Swede Sir Olaf, and Guy is the butt of their abuse under the giant's commands.*

Sir Guy de Brussiers had been vanquished from his position of leadership by the newcomer. The giant Viking, Sir Olaf Thorsen, would henceforth become undisputed Master of the Order of the Knights Templar in the Holy Land at Castle Rock.

Olaf lounged in the throne that had a week earlier been occupied by the heroic Frenchman. Braziers and torches burned along the walls and next to the throne to light the Palestine night and lend warmth to the chill of the spring evening. Olaf presented a bizarre yet magnetic figure perched upon the elaborately carved wooden throne.

He was entirely naked.

Olaf's huge girth gleamed pale and hairless in the flickering glow cast by the nearby braziers. His close-cropped hair and beard glinted a devilish blood-red. His only adornments consisted of black leather bands. One surrounded each of his bulging biceps and thick wrists. One leather strap wrapped tightly around the base of his flagrantly erect prick. Another black strap encircled his seed sack. His balls were distended downward by that wide leather that had them bulging out in engorged ripeness between his monster thighs.

His eyes glinted icy blue. His teeth were a feral white within a savage grin. He glared down at his assembled Knights with implacable disdain. He intended to leave no room for doubt in any of their minds as to who would be their undisputed Master from that day forward.

Another figure knelt slightly below him on the steps leading to the dais the throne occupied.

Sir Guy crouched on all fours with his naked ass exposed and facing the assembled Knights he had governed until only a week earlier. Mimicking Sir Olaf, Guy also had been clad only in the simple black leather armbands over his biceps and around his wrists. His prick and balls were bound with leather exactly as his new Master's, their swollen mass dangling down between his wide-spread thighs.

One other piece of garb distinguished him from the Swede. Guy wore a thick leather slave collar around his bull neck. The collar was attached by a long chain to one of his new Master's ankles.

Olaf's abrupt shout boomed through the audience chamber, "Knights Templar! You're all to prove your obedience to me this evening!"

Thirty Knights convened in Castle Rock that evening. This was the number within a reasonable distance of Castle Rock and able to be called to this bizarre ceremony of submission. Most had witnessed the contest between the two Knights that had culminated in Guy's defeat. But a few had not. These amazed men jockeyed in the crowd for a glimpse of the man who could have vanquished their dynamic leader.

One of the number was called forward. It was the Lithuanian with the shaved head, Sir Jonas Dambrusk. As the lowliest of the low in the pecking order of the Knights Templar, Jonas was signaled out by the new leader to be the first to submit. Olaf also understood Jonas was the most easily tyrannized.

Olaf grinned when the comely young Knight approached and knelt in front of him. Jonas' shaved head glistened in the torchlight. Olaf leaned forward to speak quietly into the ear of the Knight. Jonas visibly flinched at his words before bowing his head in acquiescence.

Olaf offered the gathering his broad, sneering grin before shouting out over the hubbub of gawking Knights. "You're all to witness the submission of this Lithuanian Knight. All are to follow his example one after the other!"

The men's voices grew still as they stared ahead, wondering what sort of obeisance would be required of them. All could see the crouching, nude form of their erstwhile leader, the beefy Frenchman's upturned ass and winking asshole plainly visible with several torches and braziers surrounding him. Some sort of degradation of Sir Guy would undoubtedly be forthcoming!

Their eyes turned to the figure of the young Lithuanian as he began to disrobe with trembling hands. They had been ordered to follow Jonas' example, so watched his actions with more than mere curiosity. What would they be made to do? What awful degradation had this new Master conceived?

Jonas peeled off his tunic with the cross of the Templar emblazoned on the back, then discarded his other clothing, piece by piece. Every man present knew of Jonas' previous humiliation. He had been shaved head to toe, forced to wear women's garb, and submitted to rape as punishment for the rape he himself had committed. They also knew of his sentence, whereby he must remain shaved and a slave to all the Knights' whims for one full year.

The Franks were fascinated by his quaking body as he stripped before them. The hairlessness of his muscularity seemed more alluring because it was so all-encompassing. From his gleaming bald head to his flawless pale butt cheeks there was not a scrap of hair on his body. His strong thighs and bulging calves also were scraped clean of hair. He glowed pale and utterly naked in the flickering brazier light. Although he faced away from them, they all knew he owned no hair to hide his cock and balls either.

Jonas quaked visibly. That sight gave every Knight there an instant erection, even though most shared his trepidation. Again they had to wonder, what would the arrogant Olaf require of Jonas, and of them?

They were quickly to learn as Jonas moved forward and knelt at the Swede's feet. The grin on Olaf's refined features appeared demonic in the torch light. Jonas immediately bowed his bald head, opened his mouth wide, and swallowed whole the erect prick issuing obscenely from between Olaf's thighs.

The young Lithuanian could be heard slurping and gagging over the monster member. Olaf did not bother so much as to move a hand to compel him. Jonas was required to suck their new Master's sex stick with all the attention he could muster with no added encouragement from Olaf. The silence was total as the gathered Knights witnessed the young man lick and suck the immense prick, slobbering over it with his utmost concentration. Olaf continued to stare at the Knights with a wicked grin. His look clearly indicated that each and every one would be in that spot soon, down on their knees suckling at his horse prick with their own yawning mouths.

Jonas' naked thighs shook. His bent-over form was fetching as he knelt at the feet of the potent Swede. But it ended all too soon for some of them. A low word from Olaf and Jonas rose to his feet and stood back, half-facing the assembly. They saw the young man's prick for the first time, which was semi-stiff and twitching as it jutted out from his hairless crotch. He looked like a large child, naked as a newborn babe. His face was full of unease as he peered up at the enthroned Knight above him.

Olaf yanked on the chain that was attached to the collar around Guy's sturdy neck. The Frenchman had remained motionless throughout the activities thus far, his head pressed to the cold stone of the dais steps. But now he was forced forward, still on his hands and knees. Olaf pulled him irrevocably toward his spit-slick prick, which was boldly upright and primed for the next mouth to engulf it. That mouth was to belong to Guy.

Before the entire assembly, Olaf wrapped the silver chain around one of his large fists and hauled Guy's head into his lap.

While they all gawked in silence, Guy opened his mouth and swallowed Olaf's prick. And that was not all. Immediately, Olaf nodded and glared at Jonas with an evil smirk on his thin lips. Jonas' face was a mask of remorse, but he had been already instructed by the cruel new Master. The Lithuanian knelt on the steps below Guy and reached out with his trembling hands to spread the Frenchman's beefy ass cheeks. Jonas plunged his head forward and buried it in the naked, furry ass crack. He began to slurp loudly over Guy's asshole.

Olaf laughed loud and long. Finally he yanked on the silver chain to pull Guy's head off his big tool, then after laughing uproariously once more, shoved Guy's blond head back down into his lap. His long foot snaked out and kicked Jonas roughly. The Lithuanian was knocked backwards from the force of the kick.

"You know what to do, Lithuanian!" Olaf shouted.

Jonas was shaking uncontrollably, obviously reluctant to perform the next stage of this bizarre ritual. But he obeyed, having no choice in the matter. He stood behind Guy, two steps below him so that his own prick was even with the Knight's twitching butt hole. He began to force it between those snug anal lips.

There was a concerted gasp from the gathered men. They were witnessing the lowest of the low, the totally naked and hairless slave, Jonas the rapist, as he violated their previous Master's sacrosanct asshole. As the young man's hardening member began to stretch the opening and then popped inside, the men groaned, although each and every one hid a prick that was wooden beneath their trousers. Jonas continued to feed his prick into the French Knight's beautiful butt. Guy himself slobbered over Olaf's monster prick while he accepted the humiliation of his asshole being filled by the ignoble Knight's reluctant shaft.

Olaf laughed and laughed. He threw back his Viking head and thrust upwards to impale Guy with vicious stabs. Guy swallowed all that lengthy tool while his asshole accommodated the Lithuanian's rigid prick without complaint.

All this movement, and the awareness of the gathered Knights observing him, proved too much for the modest Lithuanian. His body rocked, his head went back, and it was plain he was being possessed by a forceful orgasm. Again a gasp flowed through the gathered men as they witnessed not only the rape of Guy, but also the flooding of his ass with the Lithuanian's man seed.

Jonas pulled out. Jism spilled onto the Frenchman's brawny butt cheeks before Jonas moved on shaky legs off to one side. He knelt with his head bowed and his eyes averted. He was mortified and heavy-hearted to have been forced to fuck his former Master. Guy had saved him from castration at the hands of the Arab Prince whose sister he had raped. Jonas worshipped the Knight.

Olaf plucked Guy's head off his lap and kicked him away. Guy crawled to the side and lowered his head again. No one was able to see the expression on his face, but everyone witnessed his silent acquiescence to his own humiliation.

Next to come forward was the Knight Sir Philippe de Chanson. This Burgundian was acknowledged second in command to Sir Guy. There were few so loyal to their vanquished leader. Philippe himself chose to be the one to lead the Knights. He would set an example for the others. The sight of Guy's large and delectable buttocks being licked and then fucked by the shaved acolyte was a lurid feast for the Burgundian's extremely avid libido. He had always desired access to his Master's private manhole and admitted to himself he would revel in the experience.

Not to say he did not love and respect Guy. That was why he elected to be first. He knew the proud Master well and was certain Guy would require Philippe to perform exactly as he intended.

Philippe stood before the assembly and stripped off his own garb even as the arrogant Olaf smirked down at him. Once naked, the lanky warrior smiled and bowed, almost as arrogantly as the seated Olaf. He shook out his auburn locks and strode forward, kneeling immediately to take Olaf's substantial prick between his full, sensual lips. Men muttered among themselves when they witnessed the second in command apparently betraying his former Master by submitting to the new Swedish Master.

More than a few guessed at what was in Philippe's mind. But whether they understood or not, everyone knew beyond any doubt that once Philippe performed this act of humility, they must all follow. There was no room for argument or rebellion.

Their eyes were glued to Philippe as his naked flanks shuddered in reaction to the taste of the giant's shaft. They were amazed as he sucked voraciously. Philippe's goateed face bobbed up and down quite zealously. Olaf's devilish grin was jubilant as he surveyed the silent gathering.

Olaf's massive hand plucked the sucking mouth from his turgid rod. He snapped a quiet order at the kneeling Knight. Philippe rose and stood aside. Once again Olaf yanked the crouching Guy's chain and drew him forward into his lap to suck up the prick that his second in command had just been licking so ardently.

Philippe moved behind Guy, as Olaf had quietly ordered, and knelt to lick at Guy's ample buttocks. The Burgundian took the time to grasp those wondrous cheeks in each hand and knead them lovingly as he slathered juicy kisses over the blond-furred globes. Guy's ass moved slightly, as if appreciating his friend's caresses. Philippe's tongue snaked out and dove between the delectable butt cheeks. He sought out the moist, recently fucked anus, still drooling cum from the young Lithuanian's ejaculation.

Philippe sucked up the warm ass juices, adding his own spittle as he plunged his tongue deep into Guy's hot crevice. He slobbered and moaned with unmistakable lust, and love, over the Knight's asshole. But shortly he was also booted away by Olaf's large bare foot.

Olaf shouted at Philippe. "Fuck him now! No mercy must be given the man. Understand?" His hand was on Guy's head, holding it over his prick while he lunged into Guy's mouth with savage jabs.

Philippe obeyed with athletic alacrity. He rose from the steps and crouched behind Guy. He drove forward with his long, slim prick. The throbbing flesh stabbed between Guy's spread butt cheeks and sank deep inside the steaming asshole, which was still delectably tight and hot. Philippe nearly shrieked as he began to fuck wildly.

The men were treated to the sight of the Burgundian's high tight butt as it clenched and fucked in an eager rhythm over the prostrate body of their former leader. Philippe raped his Master fervently, driving his prick deep and relentlessly into Guy's torrid guts.

Olaf continued to laugh aloud. His booming guffaws reverberated up into the high dark corners of the vaulted chamber. When Philippe eventually shuddered in ecstatic orgasm, Olaf again kicked him away from the Frenchman. Guy's tender and dripping asshole was revealed to the crowd.

Philippe staggered to the side and knelt in obeisance beside the already prostrate Jonas. Guy was pushed rudely away by Olaf with an offhand shove, which sent him sprawling beside Philippe. The Burgundian helped Guy back to his position on his hands and knees with his just-fucked ass spread out before the gathering. The men were aware of the two Knights exchanging glances, but could not see Guy's face or fathom what he might be feeling at that moment.

Guy's upturned ass once more caught their attention. Profuse streams of new jism ran down his butt crack and gathered on his swollen leather-bound balls. His prick and balls throbbed with purple tightness. The engorged member dangled with luscious fullness between his spread thighs.

Olaf shouted out for the next man to render homage. The crowd parted to allow Sir Gerhardt Slalciz to come forward. The gentle Swabian moved to the throne without any pretext of turmoil or fear. The dusky-skinned man with his short raven hair and innocent blue eyes was known among them to be the most religious of them all, bordering on the mystic. He displayed his inner harmony by the manner in which he bowed politely to the monster on the throne and disrobed without a word. He sank to his knees and took Olaf's swollen prick into his small mouth without any hesitation. While he sucked the Swede's hard flesh, the onlookers stared at Gerhardt's wide buttocks, hairless, amber-smooth, and firm as they were outstretched nude before them.

When he was forced to eat their Master's ass, he did it slowly and lovingly, tonguing the bruised hole tenderly. Guy actually spread his legs wider and accepted him freely even though his own mouth was again being brutally pounded by Olaf's up thrust rod. Gerhardt accepted the harsh kick from Olaf's bare foot without any display of anger and stood placidly to plant his hard prick at the entrance to Guy's pulsing butt hole. Gerhardt ran his hands adoringly over Guy's broad back as he penetrated the Knight's anal maw. Slowly and gently, he massaged Guy's innards with steady but considerate thrusts.

Guy could be seen to relax visibly and widen his legs to accept the slow ministrations of the mystic Knight. His beefy butt rose and fell with each leisurely but deep-felt penetration. The gathering held their breath at the display, but even Gerhardt eventually could no longer control his body's appetites. He threw his head back and uttered a prolonged , near-ecstatic sigh. His body convulsed as he spewed semen into Guy's abused butt hole.

He was kicked away by the laughing Sir Olaf and made to kneel beside the two other Knights who had already assailed Guy. The French Knight was again discarded disdainfully, although as he prostrated himself at Olaf's feet it was obvious that the Swede was extremely stimulated, his prick lurching and distended as if on the brink of ejaculation.

When they were treated to the sight of Guy's upended ass once more it was smeared with cum and ass juice. The mixture of several men's saliva and cum dribbled down his thighs and between his legs.

At once another Knight took his position and the whole ceremony was repeated. Knight after Knight suckled the big Swede's hard prick. Guy was forced to take it between his bruised lips time after time, while he spread his thighs to take up his ass one after the other every stiff manhood forced on him.

Sir Jan Hansen of Denmark had taken his turn after almost a score of others. His lighthearted nature refused to be cowed by the situation. Like Philippe, his confidence in Guy was undiminished. He chose to participate without remorse, leaving the niceties to be worked out later. He grinned when it was his turn to kneel behind the wide muscular buttocks of the famous Knights Templar leader. Staring up at Guy's ass crack, he was filled with lust at the sight of the man's swollen ass lips, smeared with other men's cum and oozing warm juices copiously.

At least twenty men's pricks had already seen action there, then deposited their sticky semen to lubricate the tender cleft. Jan loved to eat ass, more so than any other sexual practice. He dove into the greasy mess with genuine gusto. He beamed with delight as his tongue tasted the warmth of Guy's insides. He licked around the tender distended ass lips, tonguing up all the cum he chanced on. He clamped his mouth thirstily on that hole, stabbing inside with his lapping tongue to fuck Guy with noisy, slobbering relish. He was truly disappointed when Olaf's brutal foot forced him away. But he still tasted the wondrous juices of Guy's ass in his mouth and on his lips even as he pounded away at him with his thrusting prick.

Each of the Knights dealt with the abuse of their former Master in their own way. Without exception they respected Guy and either loved or worshipped him. He had been a considerate and brilliant leader. But also many there had tasted his displeasure and his punishment. Undeniably there was an undercurrent of savage enjoyment at the picture of the mighty Knight sucking Olaf's rampant, purple staff again and again, while his upturned ass was licked and then fucked by every single Knight.

Each and every one relished the feeling of his prick inside the sultry asshole they were forced to impale. And many enjoyed the taste of the arrogant Swede's giant meat as well. In fact several of them were so enthusiastic they were rewarded by Olaf's cum rocketing deep into their throats. Olaf never touched any of their heads, expecting them to suck him willingly and without coercion. And when Olaf first ejaculated – into the mouth of the bear-like Brian – the man swallowed the steaming semen without flinching. Brian did almost choke though as he attempted to accept the geyser of bubbling seed.

After that Olaf shot twice more, but never inside Guy's mouth, which was stuffed with that continually swollen prick more than any other's. The Swede shouted out when he orgasmed. He laughed uproariously but never slowed the pace. He urged man after man to render their new allegiance to him.

Guy himself had cum once. It was when Eric von Bartell had been snuffling at his ass and driving his tongue deep inside Guy's well-fucked and gaping void. The young blond had been punished himself by Guy previously. Eric experienced his first sex under the bondage and paddling of the Master's expert hand. When Guy convulsed in orgasm while Eric's tongue was deep inside his ass, the young Knight sprayed his own cum all over both their legs. The two men jerked and twitched all over the stairs while the others watched in fascination and Olaf shouted out for the "damn dogs to cum like the curs you are."

Eric was still able to plow a few strokes up Guy's convulsing ass with a prick that was semi-hard. He did not cum again, and Olaf booted him away in disgust and called forward the next man.

When the final man had done his duty and Guy sprawled on the stone steps near exhaustion, Olaf grinned evilly and surveyed the assembly. Guy's butt hole was red and gaping. It had become a sloppy hole that now appeared to welcome any invader that cared to subdue it. His head was buried in his arms at the Swede's feet and his own prick dripped from the last time he had cum at the hands of the final Knight to rape him.

Olaf yanked on Guy's chain, this time pulling him up to stand before him.

"All right then, Frenchman. The Knights have proved their homage to their new Master, now I order you to squat in my lap as the good slave you are. Show them all how you serve me!"

Olaf laughed brutally as he twisted Guy around and forced him to spread his thighs and sit down on Olaf's lap.

Before them all, Guy's spread ass sank down over the Swede's rampant prick. His asshole swallowed the monster flesh with ease. They watched as Guy rode their new Master's sex tool, rising up and dropping down, the Swede's cum-soaked prick appearing and disappearing like a monstrous, slithering snake.

Guy threw back his blond, sweaty head to moan loudly. His prick was swollen and purple, the constraining black prick-strap trapping blood in it and engorging it. But it was hard from carnal lust as well. The look of utter passion on the Frenchman's handsome face enthralled them all.

The Knights peered up from their kneeling positions. Everyone's own desire was quickly rekindled by the sight of the brawny Frenchman seated in the even larger Swede's lap, fucking himself senseless over his new Master's mighty phallus.

Both men roared with delight when they came simultaneously. Guy's jism shot out onto the stone steps in flying ropey gobs. Olaf closed his eyes in rapture for the first time. His roar was more of a loud moan as he enjoyed the final humiliation of the former Master at Castle Rock.

Olaf held the beefy Frenchman in that position while each of the Knights were forced to kiss his feet and lick Guy's thick but flopping prick before they again lined up to kneel before the two men.

Olaf stood, placing Guy beside him. The taller Swede put one hand behind Sir Guy and skewered him with three of his fingers, driving them deep inside the man's slimy, steaming ass and holding them there. He spoke to the crowd even as he fingered Guy's compliant butt hole.

Olaf bellowed at the crowd. "You will serve me, and serve Sir Guy as my second in command. There will be no debate, no denial. I am Master at Castle Rock in the Holy Land from now on!"

As one, the Knights bowed their heads and shouted out Olaf's name.

Yet when they raised their eyes many of them were unsurprised to see the slight grin on Guy's satiated, but placid features. Their former Master was not yet to be discounted.

# Tale Fourteen: Constantinople Lessons

*In which Sir Jonas Dambrusk relates in his own words a tale of a journey to Constantinople with Guy. On arrival, they are lured into the dungeon of the evil Lord Barabas Gerband.*

I am Sir Jonas Dambrusk of Lithuania. I joined the Order of the Knights Templar only four months ago. I was offered this membership in lieu of castration and imprisonment. I gladly accepted.

Sir Guy de Brussiers was the one who ordered my punishment, but he was also the one who delivered me. Due to him, I am shaved of all bodily hair, from my glossy bald scalp to the tops of my feet. Only my eyebrows remain. There is no hair between the slick cheeks of my muscular butt, and I feel the smooth flesh rub voluptuously when I walk or sit. I have come to enjoy this humiliation. When I am shaved by one of the Knights, all of whom crave turns at this pursuit, my dick remains stiff and dripping during the entire episode.

But now I will speak of the incredible journey I have just been fortunate enough to have returned from alive and thankfully in one piece. With my Master and mentor, Sir Guy de Brussiers, a dozen of us embarked on a journey to the fabled city of the East, Constantinople. We rode out of Castle Rock on a dawn morning while Sir Olaf, our new Master was trusted to hold the fortress against any infidel horde.

We rode north along the coast until we reached the citadel and city of Acre. Once there we set sail upon the aquamarine Mediterranean Sea. Our first landfall was the island of Cyprus followed next by the island of Rhodes. From there, we sailed until rounding the bulk of Asia Minor and made landfall on the shores of the Latin Kingdom of Constantinople. We found ourselves on the very doorstep of that fabled city.

When we finally rode through the bustling and exotic streets of the famous metropolis, I was transfixed by both the beauty and squalor that existed side by side. The Emperor's Palace and the splendid Hagia Sophia were heavenly in their magnificence, while everywhere were the marks of damage from Crusaders who had invaded and stolen artwork and architecture from the fallen city.

It had only been a few short years since the Venetians and Flemish Crusaders had sacked Constantinople. It was now ruled by Henry of Flanders as Emperor. The Latin Kingdom here was imposed upon a Greek and Byzantine populace, of which there were over a million. It was the largest and richest city in Europe.

Befitting our Master's station as Master of the Second Rank and due to the fame of the Knights Templar, we were admitted to accommodations in the Palace. Our lodgings were lavish and decadent. We lacked for nothing. Sir Guy as usual conducted his business with political expertise second to none, including to my belief, the upstart Sir Olaf Thorsen who now ruled as Master of at Castle Rock. Olaf had dispatched Guy on this mission due to this very political astuteness.

I will not regale you with the niceties of the political intrigues in the Court of Henry the Emperor. They are confusing and brutal. Suffice to say, we were required to tread carefully. It was during these tangled negotiations I found myself with Guy at my side in the bowels of the Palace. We were in the dungeons.

There were just the two of us. Sir Guy asked me to accompany him as a scribe – at least that is what we told the Vizier. We were escorted by the esteemed (and cruel) Lord Barabas Gerband. This man was the Emperor's right hand and was known to wield his power ruthlessly. He was tall and handsome, yet his hooked nose and beetling brows lent him the aspect of a predator. We were to learn shortly that his heart mirrored that brutal image.

It had been a glorious afternoon. The sky was full of pearl-grey clouds scudding across the horizon, sails floated in the harbor below the Palace, and the company of our fellow Knights was merry. Although my station was beneath all the other Knights, they treated me well.

Late that same afternoon, Sir Guy and I passed from this bright daylight and fair companionship into the very pit of hell. I do not exaggerate.

We followed the tall Vizier down stairs that wound deeper and deeper into the bowels of the dungeons. Torches lit our way while well-armed guards accompanied us. Soon we heard the sounds of men crying out. These pitiful souls wept or begged, or even emitted outright screams of agony. We were approaching the Pit.

I remained close beside my Master. The strong bulk of Sir Guy formed a protective calm around me when we came out into the hot and stinking chamber that sufficed as the Vizier's torture chamber. The sounds of men's torments wafted up to us, floating on a blast of heat from the dozens of wall torches and braziers. The stink of sweating flesh and body fluids invaded my nostrils like a foul miasma. The first images of naked and bound men evoked a flush of carnal fear in my loins.

The Vizier imperiously surveyed the Pit. "Here we find the men who deign to displease the Emperor. Or myself. And here they are educated to alter their misguided ways." Lord Barabas smirked as he reached out with one long arm and indicated the men inhabiting the room with a haughtily aimed index finger.

It was a truly cavernous chamber. Devices of punishment were spread throughout the room, and at least several score of men were scattered among them. A cacophony of screams, moans, weeping, and begging, mingled with crazed laughter and wicked commands. Amidst the agony of those castigated, the Vizier's men who inflicted these blandishments were obviously enjoying their handiwork.

The horror of the scene was only mitigated by the strong arm placed around my shoulder. Sir Guy had moved close, and I can attest his touch was more than welcome.

"Ah! I see you feel the need to protect your young protégé," the Vizier grinned as he witnessed Sir Guy's gesture. "Perhaps instead you may wish to test out our various instruments of correction on the young man?"

Lord Barabas stared directly into my eyes. His blue orbs commanded and chilled as they attempted to dominate me. I am a brave man, at least I think I am, and I was able to meet his gaze with head held high. It did help that Sir Guy tightened his grip on my shoulder.

"Well, well. At least let us look around then," Lord Barabas laughed.

Directly in front of us, two victims of Lord Barabas's correction hung upright in chains. Their bodies were spread-eagled, and both hands and feet were cuffed wide apart. They were completely nude. Their lean and attractive bodies were stretched taut so that every muscle gleamed in the wicked torchlight. As a bizarre touch, each of them had their heads encased in snug-fitting, black leather hoods. Only eye, ear, nose, and mouth openings lent them any aspect of individuality. My dick rose in freakish response, stiffening painfully under my woolen trousers.

The Vizier laughed. "As you can see, each of the men is very handsome. We don't bother bringing anyone here who isn't a wonderful specimen of manhood. It's so much more gratifying to degrade and humiliate the more superior examples of male animal. Don't you agree?"

"If punishment teaches, then it's of merit," Sir Guy replied enigmatically. Thankfully his arm never abandoned my shoulder.

The two men stared at us with beseeching eyes before they were accosted by two of the Vizier's henchmen. Burly, half-naked thugs, the two began to slap and punch the defenseless men, laughing when they cried out. While we watched, the two bound men were subjected to a pummeling by the brutes with their bare fists. They proceeded to pinch at the chained men's nipples and balls, and reach behind them to inflict some unseen punishment on their widespread ass cheeks and defenseless butt holes. Their hooded anonymity was grotesque, although it allowed me to picture anyone in their position. Either could have been one of my fellow Knights, or Sir Guy, or myself. Although I was appalled at the cruelty of the thugs and sympathized with their victims, there was no denying I was stimulated sexually. Every cry and whimper of the bound and hooded men both frightened and lured me.

The Vizier's laughter continued as he led us away to the next scene in the dungeon's evil din. We were confronted by another bound figure. A red-haired young German was lying back in a sling constructed of thick rope webbing. His arms were raised high and cuffed with leather. His legs were spread apart and similarly raised and cuffed. He was nude as it seemed everyone was in the vile chamber. He appeared to be in a state of extreme confusion or fear.

He muttered incoherently and moaned as his body writhed within his bonds. A flush of sweat dripped from his broad chest and around his semi-hard dick and dangling balls. His asshole was exposed and pulsing. It appeared as if he had been already penetrated. His ass lips drooled some kind of lubricant.

"He is awaiting castigation and has been fed stimulating herbs in order to cherish it the more so. And of course learn from it all, as you so graciously have reminded me, Sir Guy."

The Vizier smirked, laying a powerful clawed hand on Sir Guy's shoulder. Sir Guy only smiled in return, answering nothing.

We were moved onward, even as I stared back at the vision of the man in the sling, his head tossing, his asshole awaiting some manner of bizarre and harsh intrusion. I turned away and was confronted by another monstrous dungeon scene.

On a plank table lay a man turned on his side. He was naked and hooded. Only, his hood claimed neither eyeholes nor ear holes. He was confined to darkness and silence. All the better, I imagined, to experience his punishment. Three big men held him on the table. One was at his head, clasping his shoulders and hands firmly. Another was at his legs, grasping them in his beefy arms. The third was at his ass.

The man's ample and enticing butt cheeks were forced tightly together by the second man who pinned him. But between those big, smooth butt cheeks the man's quivering anus was being brutally violated. The third guard had his entire hand stuffed between those masculine cheeks, fist-fucking the hapless captive with rapid, intense thrusts. The victim squirmed as much as he could, obviously attempting to widen his legs so that he could accept the fist more easily, but the second man pinned his thighs together and laughed cruelly at his frantic struggles.

I could only imagine the captive's emotions as he accepted that huge fist up his butt, while that black hood effectively blinded him and made him deaf to any sounds. His only awareness of the world around him was that probing hand driving into his guts. The searing image of a greasy forearm protruding from the hooded captive's struggling ass was left behind as the Vizier gleefully moved us onwards.

"Here we have a particularly recalcitrant warrior. He has displeased us by taking another guard as his lover, and refused me when I offered him my own personal favors." The Vizier smiled almost sweetly, but his ice-cold eyes narrowed as he stared at the next victim we were to meet.

A man was spread-eagled on a plank table. Tall and lean with dusky Latin skin and honey-amber hair, he had an appealing, sweet complexion. He was entirely naked, but unhooded so that I could easily perceive the keen anxiety in his fearful expression. His dick and balls were tied together and pulled upwards by a silver chain from the ceiling. They were stretched uncomfortably taut, while his legs were stretched apart just as uncomfortably.

While we watched, the Vizier nodded to one of his men standing nearby. The bare-chested brute stood between the fearful soldier's parted legs and began to finger his exposed butt hole. Using ample grease from a bowl he proceeded to dig one finger after the other into the pulsing and expanding hole. The captive was shouting out, begging for mercy, promising to do whatever the Vizier wanted by the time his ass was being plied by three huge fingers and another was being added.

"Too late, my poor friend. You will taste the fist today, and who knows what tomorrow, and on and on until you are nothing but a quivering mass, whimpering at my feet!" Lord Barabas proclaimed.

He had moved to the man's head and was caressing his shuddering face with sinister, lingering strokes, grinning while the man's ass was violated. The burly guard added his thumb to four fingers and was pressing deeper. The poor victim, pleaded, writhing on the bench and self-inflicting more punishment upon his stretched balls and dick. Finally the entire fist drove into him, while he groaned and then passed out.

The Vizier only laughed, splashing cold water on the victim's face and then abandoning him to the fist in his ass while he could do nothing but whimper with pain and humiliation.

We passed several unusual contraptions that were designed to constrict and bind men, all of which were occupied by naked, robust sacrifices. Many appeared dazed, as if they too had been drugged, while others begged and pleaded for mercy, or lay still in resignation.

One particular individual stood out in my memory. He was light-skinned with piercing blue eyes and straw-colored hair. Obviously he hailed from some northern nation, like me. A large fellow, with bulging muscles, he was bound upright to a plank platform. Face against the wood, his broad back was stretched wide due to cuffed wrists fastened far apart against the platform. His legs were likewise stretched wide and ankles cuffed and fastened to the plank. His thighs were like tree trunks and covered with thick blond hair. His butt cheeks were also coated in the blond hair and just as massively muscular. The cheeks were parted, and a smallish, crinkled anus was visible. He stared backwards at us in trepidation, plainly in fear of what fate awaited his defenseless anal opening. His aquamarine eyes met mine briefly before we moved on. A shiver of empathy raced up my spine.

The next men we came on were four in number. They were on their hands and knees, totally nude and unbound. All appeared to be of similar nationality, blond and young. Greek, I guessed. These men were each being slowly and deeply fist-fucked by more of the Vizier's men. Their asses perched in the air, their heads pressed to the floor, and their legs stretched out as far as possible. Each of them accepted the punishment without attempting to escape.

Whether they, too, were drugged, or simply cowed into submission, I did not know. But each of them whimpered as their asses were filled with huge fists. Whether they were begging for mercy, or pleading for more, I honestly could not tell. The greasy hands of the cruel guards entered and exited the four holes rhythmically and without cessation, regardless of what the victims were uttering. I stared at one of the big fists and felt my own hole quiver between my shaved butt cheeks with sympathy, and I admit a touch of perverse desire as well.

Next, we came to the cruelest of the punishments. The screams of the victims warned us before we even approached them in their corner of the dank and fetid dungeon. Several bright torches surrounded them, and a large flaming brazier created a wave of heat that enveloped us when we approached.

"These are the worst of the worst. The mighty have fallen," Barabas grinned. "These are noblemen who have refused to adhere to the Emperor's commands on some level or another. They have plummeted from the height to the veritable bottom, and here they are!" He uttered a horrible laugh. His cruel eyes glittered in the light of the burning brazier.

A half dozen men were bound over rounded barrels, their arms and legs chained securely. That these naked men were proud nobles of the Eastern Roman Empire was hard to believe. Except, each was a fine specimen of masculinity. All were sinewy and muscular, and although several were obviously older men, they were still in fine shape. One was gray-haired, but his face was handsome, and his back and legs were substantial with muscle and vigorous. Another was so young he could not have been much older than I, at eighteen.

Regardless of age, each was being subjected to a similar correction. Several had already been freshly brutalized, their quivering butt cheeks seared and smoking from the cruel taste of burning iron. On each of those men's butt cheeks had been branded the words "fuck hole," obviously a message for any who would see those bare asses in the future.

At that point, another burning iron was being pulled from the brazier, and the youngest of the men was staring backwards in fear, his ass quaking, his mouth jabbering with incoherent pleas. I felt Sir Guy tense beside me and glance backwards, searching for something at the far entrance to the dungeon. He was disappointed and turned back to the scene with a resigned sigh.

I was both fascinated and appalled. The smooth and hairless butt cheeks of this victim reminded me of my own shaved ass. I could have been branded like this if Sir Guy was a cruel Master, which he was not. I could have been castrated, but he had prevented that. I wondered if these men would also be castrated. But for now, I was too caught up in the imminent branding to do other than gawk with wide, disbelieving eyes.

The hot iron was removed from the brazier and carried forward to hover over the poor youth's bare ass. It was wielded by an enormous unclad warrior, his own dick rampant and dripping, clearly aroused by his handiwork. The iron glowed red as it was lowered toward the unprotected ass. The instant it touched flesh, the lad shrieked, just as the sizzling sound and rank stench of searing skin reached us only a few feet away.

The brand was removed at once, its work done, the words imprinted forever on the hapless young man's butt. The naked warrior who had inflicted the punishment stood over the young man and with a final brute cruelty, crammed his dripping dick between those creamy ass cheeks and began to fuck him with swift, vicious strokes. It was over in seconds. The warrior jerked out his meat and came copiously over the fresh burn and the quivering ass cheeks.

I felt an iron grip on my arm. The Vizier yanked me away from Sir Guy. "I think we should let this delectable young Knight have a taste of the iron!"

I have to say I was not altogether surprised. The Vizier had eyed me keenly since we had arrived in Constantinople. I know he had asked Sir Guy about me and had been refused whatever his request had been. Now he apparently desired his own sweet vengeance. The man was drunk with his own power and would not suffer anyone to deny him.

Strangely, I was not afraid. But I was also not prepared to accept this disfigurement without a struggle. Three men grabbed me before I realized they were there, though. My clothes were stripped from me in a winking of an eye. I was naked and being forced over one of the empty barrels. My head turned to seek out Sir Guy's eye.

He was again looking over toward the dungeon entrance. This time his face broke into a bright beaming grin. Abruptly, he lunged forward and seized the tall Vizier. His dagger was out and pressed to the Lord's handsome throat.

"Come Knights!" Guy roared.

I was held over the barrel naked by the Vizier's cohorts, but by craning my head, I could see partially behind me. I witnessed the blessed sight of our compatriots, a dozen other Knights Templar. They flooded into the room with their swords raised and their bows trained on the guards and warriors that inhabited the dungeon.

"What is this?" the Vizier sputtered. He spoke haughtily but did not move. He was too fearful of Sir Guy's knife to attempt an escape.

"The tables are being turned, Lord Barabas. We're giving you a taste of your own vile medicine," Sir Guy said with a grin. Even as he spoke, the Vizier's men were being rounded up by my fellow Knights. I was released, and I hurried to Sir Guy's side still naked.

"What will the Emperor say, and how can you escape after this!" Lord Barabas shrieked with spittle flying. He was being divested of his garments by Brian and Heinz. Their rough treatment made clear their enjoyment of the experience.

"Your Master has offered us what we came here for. All our desires and treaties and monies. He would give us all this in exchange for one prodigious favor. We were to subdue you and rid him of your evil presence," Sir Guy explained with a broad grin.

His arm over my naked shoulder reassured me immeasurably. I had barely escaped the branding iron!

While the Vizier cursed us with profuse vitriol, he was thrown over the barrel I was to have covered. His high and haughty ass cheeks were spread, and his hands and ankles cuffed with iron chains. While we all observed, his own man was made to lay the burning iron on his upturned and fetchingly ample butt. The guard's dick was as stiff as when he had branded the other men. Lord Barabas' cursing changed to pleading just before the hot iron seared his skin, and then to shrieking as he experienced a taste of his own punishment.

Next, Sir Guy had him placed in one of the slings. The Vizier's legs and arms were chained high above his head. His tender butt hole was exposed. He cursed us again and threatened all kinds of recriminations.

Sir Guy did not gloat or laugh as it was not in his nature. But many of the other Knights did so. They taunted him

Jay Starre

wickedly and were joined in their jeers by some of the Vizier's own guards who had eagerly switched allegiance once it was offered.

While we left the Vizier to stew in his own rage and fear, we went to each of his bound victims and released them. I was given the honor of this duty as a reward for my bravery. I remained naked for this labor. My dick twitched stiff the entire time with the profound lust of reprieve. I unchained and unfettered man after man. They all fell to their knees before our Master, Sir Guy, and promised their undying gratitude.

For the final act, we gathered around the cursing and bound Lord Barabas. His naked body was pleasant to look at. He was no idle lounger and boasted a sinewy, long-limbed build. His handsome face was twisted up in a disfiguring rage, though. His fine, long legs were stretched wide and high above his head, while his equally long arms were attached beside them. He was completely helpless.

Men stood by with instruments for piercing. He was to have his nipples and his cock be-ringed after this. Meanwhile, we hovered around him while the grey-haired nobleman who had escaped branding straddled his parted thighs. While we looked on, the handsome Noble took a huge black dildo in both hands and began to press it against the Vizier's exposed butt hole.

I was still naked and standing beside Sir Guy. My erect dick swayed in the open air begging for attention. Sir Guy glanced at me and smiled. My reward was the touch of his calloused hands over my naked body. While I watched the huge dildo stretch and penetrate the defenseless asshole of the evil Vizier, I felt Sir Guy's kind hand probing my own hot hole. He jacked my dick slowly and sensually while he fingered my responsive anus. I squirmed under his ministrations before the entire gathering, my shaved body gleaming in the dungeon torchlight.

Meanwhile, the monster dildo's flared head had penetrated the Vizier's asshole. The silver-haired, muscular

182

nobleman shouted out with glee as he violated the cruel Lord's palpitating cleft. All those around shouted out with equal fervor, drowning out the vanquished Vizier's own screams of woe and humiliation.

As I felt the warmth of two of Sir Guy's thick fingers jabbing my own fuck hole, I spurted cum from the end of my throbbing dick. The ropey stream flew out and splattered the bare legs of the dildo-raped Constantinople Lord. Amazingly, the man's own dick ejaculated even as his mouth howled out his denial. He had cum while being fucked by a huge black dildo wielded by his formerly vanquished enemy.

We abandoned him there. The men who had been the victims now inflicted their own eager punishments on the Vizier and all his cohorts. Black hoods were placed over pleading warriors, while the asses of those same thugs were spread wide and violated with all manner of hands or instruments.

We rode out of Constantinople in the dark of night. The Emperor was rid of his distasteful henchmen, and free from blame as the real perpetrators disappeared in secret. Sir Guy had adroitly accomplished yet another mission.

And I had been blessed by his tender attentions, loving him all the more.

# Tale Fifteen: Initiation by Bonfire

*In which two young Russians who were rescued from the clutches of the Vizier Barabas in the dungeons of Constantinople are initiated by bonfire into the Knights Templar.*

I am Petr Stepov. My home was at one time far to the north in the Russian city of Moscow. I am now a Knight Templar, and my home is Castle Rock in the beautiful and arid Holy Land. I could have been a beaten and branded slave to the evil Lord Barabas Gerband in the dungeons of Constantinople, but Sir Guy de Brussiers and his men saved me. This is the story of the evening they initiated me into their Order.

We had fled Constantinople in the middle of the night. The Templar' mission of subduing Lord Barabas for the Emperor was complete. They had released me from the plank to which I had been cuffed, and I instantly begged to go with them wherever that was. When they agreed, I also asked that my younger brother be allowed to come as well. We were both grateful when the Knights hustled us off on horseback.

We rode our steeds hard across the hills and valleys of Asia Minor. The secrecy of the mission meant we should be far from the Empire's capital before any repercussions could descend on us. There were many weeks of this hard riding, broken by only short rests, before we reached a coastal valley in Lesser Armenia. We were just north of the Holy Land. It was here Sir Guy ordered us to rest and celebrate. It was here, he offered my brother and me membership in the Order of the Knights Templar.

A large bonfire was built up under the darkening sky. We camped on a sandy beach with the splashing waves of the ocean only a scant dozen yards away. The stars of the nearby Holy Land were bright across the sky. There was no moon and no human habitation within many miles. We were alone and would not be disturbed. Before the gathered Knights, Sir Guy made us his offer.

"Would you Petr Stepov and you Giorgi Stepov desire to join in our Order, follow the restrictions of our laws, and obey the commands of our leaders?"

He stood with legs apart. His heroic form was godlike in the bright reflection of the bonfire. His golden hair was free from his helm and flowed to his shoulders. His grey eyes, which were usually so kind, were now demanding and implacable. There was no mistaking the obligations and sacrifices required of us if we decided to accept this offer.

"Yes," I murmured, falling to my knees with my head bowed. My brother followed my example, as ever he had. The two of us were very alike, except that my hair was fair and his was black as a raven's feathers. He was not quite as tall and muscular as I, but very close in burly strength. Our faces were alike with wide cheekbones and small pug noses. Many had called us handsome. I imagined we were.

"And you will accept the ritual initiation willingly, and without complaint or resistance?" Sir Guy queried. His voice was steel in the quiet of the night. He had placed a hand on each of our bowed heads, and the incredible strength in those long fingers was indisputable.

As we murmured assent in unison, a shout went up among the gathered Knights, and a chant began. It was as if they all knew exactly what they were to do. I raised my eyes to the young Knight who was always at Sir Guy's side, the Lithuanian Jonas Dambrusk. He moved forward and lifted us up. He smiled reassuringly into our eyes before he began to remove our clothing. We stood passively as the Knight undressed each of us. The eerie chanting of the other men rose high into the night sky along with the shooting sparks of our bonfire.

Sir Guy stood before us and watched silently. His massive forearms folded across his wide chest. Jonas was swift, but courteous, and in moments, I was naked as the day I was born. I recalled with vivid nightmarish emotion the last time I had been thus – bound to a plank in the dungeon of Constantinople awaiting some punishment or mutilation, with my ass cheeks bare and undefended. I shuddered, although the night air was not cold. I turned my gaze to my brother, who was similarly becoming naked under the sure hands of the shaved Lithuanian. He stood proudly, even though I knew he was as fearful as I. Giorgi's pale flesh shone in the firelight, his hairless torso strong and clean, and at odds with the furry coat on his legs and buttocks. We both boasted hairy lower bodies, although mine was a golden, blond down whereas his was a silky, black fur.

We stood proud and naked, and a little fearful, for only a few moments before, a log was rolled forward, and now we were made to bend over it. Our naked asses faced the warmth of the bonfire's bright flames. I felt my legs pulled apart and held by the ankle. A Knight's powerful grip on each forced me to remain still. I was on my knees, as was my brother, with the soft sand beneath us. My upper body was pressed downward, and my arms were pulled behind my back.

I felt silken ropes, such as we employed for bridling the horses, being used to bind my arms tightly together. The soft ropes were pulled up and strung around my face, through my open mouth and back down to be reattached to my bound arms. My upper body was immobilized, and my mouth semi-gagged. It was almost as if I wore a bridle. I could scream or beg, but my words would be muffled and unintelligible. I could not close my mouth.

I was able to glance sideways and caught my young brother's eyes. They were wild with fear, but I was able to reassure him with the semblance of a nod. I was sure the ordeal would be difficult, but we would not be truly harmed. At least I hoped so.

It all had happened so swiftly, I had little time to assimilate all the body sensations of the experience. But then there was a pause, as we lay across the log and the chanting ceased for a moment. Someone reached between my spread legs and pulled down my cock and balls so they dangled between my thighs and were no doubt visible to the gathered men. Also, they were now vulnerable to whatever Sir Guy would order.

For several minutes, there was silence. Only the crackling of the fire and the steady rhythm of the ocean waves could be heard. It was then I found myself growing acutely aware of my position. My hands and arms could not move and my ankles were held tightly. My ass was wide open, and a trickle of sweat had run down the hairy crack, tickling it with maddening sensualness. When the moisture ran farther down and settled on my asshole, it twitched and pulsed of its own accord. I felt utterly vulnerable. Who knew what was about to be inflicted on my bare buttocks and unprotected anal cleft?

I jerked with surprise when the chanting commenced abruptly again. My head was pulled up slightly by the constricting ropes that were attached to my arms, and I could see that Sir Guy was now standing in front of my brother and me.

A wooden paddle was thrust in my face. Its flat blade caressed my cheeks, my nose and my gagged mouth. The wood was encased in black leather, with crisscrossed straps that wound down to the long handle. The smell of leather and an unmistakable stench of men's sweat and bodies penetrated my nostrils as the weapon was pressed against them. The thought of that leather having been recently used to slap against a man's heaving and sweating buttocks, and now being thrust in my face sent a flush of heat coursing through my naked body.

It was pulled away, and I watched as it was rubbed over my brother's face. The image of the black weapon stroking his roped mouth was profoundly arousing. I felt my cock stiffen for the first time. Its growing length throbbed against the hard log I was bent over.

Sir Guy stepped over our bound bodies and disappeared behind us. The chanting grew louder before I heard the first slap of leather on flesh and the muffled cries of my brother beside me. Sir Guy must have been striking Giorgi with the paddle. His bound body jerked, and his eyes went wide as he gazed over at me with an expression of pain and humiliation. I watched helplessly as the beating continued. Empathy for my brother mingled with the fearful anticipation of an identical pain being inflicted on me imminently.

A strange transformation occurred in my brother's demeanor. At first he jerked violently, as if attempting to escape the punishment. His eyes registered fear and pain and his mouth's mutterings were agonized. But then as the slow rhythmic beating continued, his face flushed with blood, his eyes closed, and his muffled cries ceased. His body rose from the log and crowded backwards just before each blow as if he was welcoming the slap of the leather paddle against his bare buttocks.

His experience only ended when mine commenced.

With a suddenness I was unprepared for, I felt the mighty thwack of leather against my defenseless buttocks. I jerked just as Giorgi had, and a stifled scream escaped my roped mouth. I, too, felt the impossibility of escape as strong hands held my ankles apart and the silken ropes bound my arms together behind my back. Other blows followed, and the chanting grew steadily louder in my ears. There was nothing but the pain and the chanting until with heated disbelief I realized I, too, was welcoming the blows.

Warmth suffused my body, emanating from my paddled pink buttocks. My ass was on fire! The leather paddle was a burning brand that stroked my soul. My thighs slackened, and I began to shove back just like Giorgi had. My asshole even opened. The slot pulsed and twitched as if it wanted the paddle to strike it, or enter it. I felt a rush of humiliation, realizing the other Knights were witnessing my capitulation and my lascivious enjoyment of the paddling.

I imagined the image of my red ass humping backwards and my twitching butt hole expanding and contracting. The sluttish orifice between my thighs begged to be violated, and all eyes could see this lewd truth.

The delicious paddling ceased as abruptly as it had begun. We were raised up to stand on trembling legs, then shoved back to back so that our burning asses were pressed together. The Knights' chanting was overwhelming. Now that we could see them, we realized they were naked and sporting huge erections.

My own cock was hard and drooling sex juice copiously. I breathed in harsh gasps. My recent beating still caused me to shake violently. Yet my brother's warm body and torridly heated ass against mine were reassuring and very sensual. His ass felt as hot against mine as the flames of the raging fire we stood before.

While we stood in that way, the naked and hairless Jonas approached us. Two strange contraptions were in his hands. I recognized them for tools of the depraved Lord Barabas of Constantinople. The Knights must have pilfered them when we fled!

One was employed on me at once. A long, thin metal cage, formed so that it could entrap a hard male shaft was slipped over mine and then attached at the base of my balls by a leather cock-ring. A leather harness wrapped around my upper thighs and waist to hold it firmly in place. It was constricting, as my cock is very large when erect, and it was even fuller with hot blood than normal. Although grotesque, it was definitely sensual and exciting. Yet, I would not be able to touch my cock or manipulate it as long as the instrument was in place. That thought had me longing to caress my cock and pull forth a hot steamy load of cum. But, alas, I could not.

A similar device was placed over my brother's staff, although with my back to him I could not witness the operation.

190

His burning ass cheeks clenched against mine, and that was message enough. Next Jonas came around to my chest. While my eyes widened with trepidation, he attached two evil-looking pincers to my erect nipples. At first the pain was agonizing, but in moments it transformed to the identical heat flushing my freshly-beaten ass cheeks.

Jonas disappeared to work on my brother; I imagined to similarly clamp his tender nipples. Then I felt Jonas unbinding the ropes around my arms, while next the silken length was removed from my mouth. I was turned around to face my brother. His soft blue eyes were a mirror image of my own as we gazed at one another.

The nipple clamps sent stabbing pains through my chest as I moved. As I was made to embrace Giorgi, the pain again raced through my body as our chests were crushed together. The same silken ropes were used to bind my arms around my brother's back, and his to mine in such a manner that we stood in a confining embrace. Our caged dicks mashed between our sweating bellies. The feel of the cold metal was peculiar against my skin. Our legs were kicked apart, although not roughly.

Now our asses were once more vulnerable, and I wondered if the paddling would recommence.

Instead, as the Knights chanted around us, Jonas was told to bring out another instrument no doubt liberated from the dungeons of Constantinople. This was indeed a bizarre tool. It was a double-headed dildo, gleaming jet black, with a thick leather guard at its middle. Attached to the guard were thin leather straps. Before I could wonder at its use, one end was forced into my open mouth, the other into my brother's. The straps were pulled behind each of our heads. As the straps were tightened, the cold wooden dildo was forced deeper into both our mouths. Our heads were forced closer until the dildo slid into our throats and our mouths came together as if in a deep kiss. The round leather guard prevented our lips from actually touching. We were effectively gagged, and our mouths stuffed with wooden cock. Fortunately, the dildo was short and thin enough to allow us to breath around it.

Then the paddling began again. This time each of the Knights took a turn, either by abusing my beefy butt or my brother's. We were bound together in a tight embrace, our mouths sucking on mutual dildo, and our caged cocks trapped between our heaving bellies. Our squirming bodies mutually stimulated our caged hard-ons, but we were unable to touch them or even massage them with the jerking movements of our hips. It was maddening.

The paddling had long ceased to be painful. It only grew miraculously more wonderful as my red-hot butt got even hotter. I found myself longing for something to slide between my widespread legs and penetrate my pulsing butt hole. I spread my legs farther apart and so did Giorgi. We practically gyrated with the wild thrusting of our hips as the paddle's blows landed on one pink ass and then the other. The Knights surrounding us in a seething, naked mass chanted so loud the sound was like thunder in our ears. More blows landed. The chant rose to a shrieking crescendo. Giorgio and I writhed together on fire from head to toe.

The paddling suddenly terminated and the chanting ceased for the second time.

Giorgi and I heaved and moaned around the dildo in our mouths. Our naked butts were blistered and inflamed. The silence lasted long enough for us to calm down slightly, before the chant began again. Only this time it was a deep and slow explosion of sound.

The Knights would shout once, then become eerily silent. Then they would shout again, and be silent. Their circle closed inexorably tighter around us with each explosion of sound until we were in the midst of fourteen sweating naked men. Their sweaty heat nearly smothered us. Their chant penetrated my ears as if it was the thrusting of a giant cock inside my brain.

I believe that was exactly the image they intended us to take in.

I felt a hand on my ass. Fingers caressed the burning flesh lightly. Those fingers moved between my ample butt cheeks and spread them apart. Other hands began to fondle my solidly muscular ass. They slid across the slick, sweaty skin and began to probe and pinch. The fingers between my ass cheeks teased my aching butt hole. They pulled apart the pulsing ass lips. They tantalized my sensitive opening but refused to enter. They pried apart the muscled ring and allowed cooling air to waft against the inner flesh. That sensation of being opened up and held that way was nearly as intensely stimulating, humiliating, and pleasurable as all that had gone before.

My hole yawned open and begged to be fed! And I was utterly certain everyone there knew it. My humiliation was total! Gazing into my brother's eyes, I realized exactly the same thing was happening to him!

I groaned around the dildo in my mouth and pressed my ass backwards, but the fingers would not oblige me. They merely played with the outer rim and grazed my sensitive flesh cruelly. My brother and I were crushed between naked hot men. Their hands roamed all over our bodies. I felt the thongs at the back of my head being undone, and then the dildo pulled from my mouth. When I gasped for breath, my lips lolling open, a thick warm tongue invaded my mouth and sucked with lustful abandon.

I recognized Sir Guy's handsome face. His soft grey eyes bored into mine.

The fingers teasing my ass entrance withdrew, and I felt the heat of a hard cock replace them. As Sir Guy's tongue stabbed into my mouth, I reared back against that cock head. My hole was finally going to be fed!

That cock centered on my pulsing anal maw while the hands on my ass pulled my hairy butt cheeks apart. My ass lips were spread and stretched while that fuck-pole filled my parting cleft. I moaned, Sir Guy's sucking mouth a cauldron of heat, my

193

asshole a burning opening entreating, begging, hungering to be violated.

I was rewarded! Hot cock began to penetrate my now slackened defenses. It slithered beyond the muscled ring. It was a searing poker that felt miraculous. My asshole simply melted apart and allowed the huge width of whoever's flesh that hard weapon belonged to inside me. The cock plunged into my warm guts. The fuck weapon stabbed deep, withdrew and then plunged deeper, and then even deeper. I was joyously thankful for every inch that possessed me.

Sir Guy released my mouth and then pressed my face into Giorgi's. I kissed my brother. His slobbering tongue penetrated my willing mouth even as the huge cock up my butt ploughed to new depths. I could feel Giorgi being pounded against me. He was taking cock up the ass, too.

I don't know how long it went on. My cock was hard throughout the ordeal. I could not console its maddening sensitivity with the cruel cock-cage guarding it. My aching prick dripped and drooled with fluid and so did my brother's. Our bellies were smeared with the juice that escaped the cages.

Our asses were reamed over and over by every man present. Hot cum was injected deep in our guts as each Knight attained orgasm before allowing the next access. The chanting voices and Latin prayers voiced by strong masculine men overwhelmed my senses. I felt as if I was floating. My brother's bound body pressed to mine was all that held me up.

Finally, we were untied, and allowed to lie face-down on a comfortable blanket in the sand. The roaring bonfire had quieted as had the men's lust. Yet they were not finished.

Our cock-cages had not been removed, and both Giorgi and I were still famished with carnal hunger. While the men chanted, we writhed on our bellies. Our slick and dripping assholes pointed upwards toward the starry sky. We tried to fuck the sand, but the cages would not allow sufficient sensation to reach our rampant cocks.

We were turned over on our backs and our legs raised. While one naked Knight fingered our butt holes, the cock-cages were blessedly removed.

Our hands were held by other Knights so that we could not touch our throbbing tools. But then the shaved Lithuanian was raised up in the arms of two burly Knights and lowered over my brother's fuck-pole. His slick asshole descended over Giorgi's erect shaft. The utter pleasure of it elicited a mighty shout from his lips. Jonas was moved up and down. His shaved body gleamed in the low firelight as my brother's cock appeared and disappeared. Shortly though, Giorgi shrieked out and shot his pent-up load deep inside the Knight's heated hole.

I was shaking all over when they lowered that pale ass over my pulsing cock. I screamed out in rapture when I felt the snug warmth of Jonas' aperture engulf it. After his time servicing the lusty needs of the Templar, he had become expert with his anal muscles. He massaged my cock with every up and down thrust of his muscular body. His hairless crotch and own fat drooling cock was almost in my face. I stared at that awesome sight as the jism built in my balls and rushed up to my cock head.

I spurted wildly inside the Knight. His talented butt hole clamped around my erupting cock and milked it dry.

Giorgi and I were made to sleep together naked. In each other's arms, we were wrapped in a woolen blanket beside the fire. In the morning the cock-cages were again placed over our stiff cocks. We were told to suck the raging boner of every Knight present.

Giorgi and I were then allowed to remove our cock-cages as symbolic entry to the Knights Templar. We lay across each other's firm bodies and sucked each other's throbbing pricks until we filled each other's mouths with warm jism.

Afterward, we rode proudly under the sun of the Holy Land on toward Sir Guy's Castle Rock. We were now Knights Templar.

Fate had truly blessed us when Sir Guy journeyed to Constantinople and rescued us.

# Tale Sixteen: Castle Rock Falls

*In which Sir Olaf surrenders Castle Rock to the depraved Sheik Tariz Abdulla and then suffers sexual humiliation in front of his own Knights at the Sheik's hands.*

Sir Olaf stood arrogantly inside the barred lower gates at the entrance to Castle Rock. Summer's blazing power gripped the Holy Land, and the heat outside was oppressive. Sir Olaf sweated. It was his first taste of that season, and he was very irritable. He snapped at his second-in-command in his booming voice.

"Philippe. Inform the barbarian Prince we'll acquiesce to his demands. It's my foremost duty to protect the Christian villagers. We have no choice but to surrender Castle Rock." His shocking words sent a chill through the crowd of Knights who stood beside him in the shade of the Castle Walls.

Philippe bowed his head without comment. The Burgundian Knight knew not to question this new Master. He only wished their fearless former leader, Sir Guy de Brussiers, was here. Guy would never have surrendered Castle Rock!

"Make certain our valuables are well-hidden. See that Mamluk escapes to warn Sir Guy and the other Knights who are on assignment. We can stall him for another hour," Olaf instructed.

The tall Swedish Knight was not entirely useless, Philippe thought. This was not the worst of all possibilities. At that moment, only eight Knights were in attendance at the Castle. The other sixty of the Order remained free. And Guy was still on an embassy to Constantinople and had not yet returned.

So it was that under the searing Palestine sun, eight brave Knights of the Templar walked out and yielded to the barbarian Muslim Prince, Sheik Tariz Abdulla.

The Sheik perched atop his ebony stallion. He towered over the Knights, even the giant red-headed Swede. He grinned triumphantly as the eight Franks were stripped naked before the very gates of their own Castle. They stood proudly but without opposition as their garments were ripped off among jeering insults.

Philippe peered up at the Muslim. He admired the Sheik's handsome chocolate-colored complexion and wide generous mouth. The infidel's flashing grin displayed fine white teeth, and his honey-colored eyes were full of humor. Greedy lust flamed in those amber orbs as well. The Burgundian Knight submitted to the stripping of his garb without protest as he observed the Arab. But, Prince Tariz only had eyes for the tall Master, Olaf. Philippe conjectured that the hungry look in the Arab's eyes boded no good for the Templar leader.

As the naked bodies of the Knights became exposed under the Palestine sun, their fit, muscular forms gleamed with masculine beauty, especially, the giant Swede, Olaf. His large body was pale and hairless. His bulky musculature rippled with a translucent sheen. His gigantic dick flopped between his huge thighs, and was for now quiescent and humble. But not so humble was his gaze, which locked with the Muslim Sheik's. Blue orbs clashed with amber.

The singsong voice of the Prince rang out over the gathering and was obeyed instantly.

"Put some oil on the pale barbarian, or he'll sunburn terribly. We wouldn't want to ruin his beautiful hide before we offer him on the auction block."

As the unclad Frankish Knights stood by helplessly, their leader was seized by several Arab lackeys. Others arrived momentarily with jars of oil. They slathered the glistening grease over Olaf's pale skin. Apparently, it was a sunburn preventative known to the local inhabitants.

The Arab men's hands slid provocatively over the Swede's muscled frame. Exploring, oiled palms and fingers slithered across his substantial pecs. They moved further down his chiseled torso, and then around his horse dick. His hairless balls were oiled with more attention than necessary, and sliding hands roamed even between the smooth globes of his powerful, jutting white buttocks with that close care.

The Arab Prince observed the spectacle with keen eyes and a feral grin. Olaf submitted without a sign of discomfort or dismay. His stoic attitude did much to bolster the courage of the other Knights. All had heard the Muslim announce they were going to the auction block, which naturally seemed to them a horrible fate. Whose slave would they become?

Their thoughts were further thrown in disarray when the Arabs went down the line of Knights and applied the natural sun screen to each of them. The bodies of the other naked Franks were in various degrees of tan, as they had been in the Holy Land for quite some time and had become accustomed to the sun. Many were tanned from head to toe, due to their habit of swimming naked in the nearby ocean. Others were much paler, especially the Knight Eric von Bartell. His blond good looks also bestowed on him an alabaster skin.

Regardless, their Arab captors applied the oil to each of them in turn. The men ran their lubricated hands roughly over the Knights' crotches and asses to prevent sunburn on those tender areas. More than one Knight felt his dick expand and lengthen under the hands of the grinning Arabs, notwithstanding the terrible predicament they found themselves in. Several of the laughing Arabs spent an exorbitant amount of time over the rather lushly muscular body of Sir Eric. They obviously enjoyed his fat dick but were especially keen for his luscious butt cheeks. They fondled and parted the mounds with leisurely, sensuous gropes.

After this, events proceeded rapidly. Metal collars snapped in place around the necks of the naked Knights, and a long chain was connected to the eight of them. They were prodded to march on foot while the Prince and his surrounding Arab army hemmed them in.

The blistering sun was alleviated by a cool breeze from the nearby sea as they marched northward. Even with the protective oils coating their nude bodies, most became sunburned under that baking sun by the time they reached their destination three hours later.

They marched directly into the grounds of the fortress of Prince Tariz. This fortress was a huge and foreboding pile of buildings surrounded by a high wall. It was set against a cliff and faced the Mediterranean Sea. Villagers gawked at their humiliating nudity and jeered at them as they were led through the Arab town at the foot of the fortress.

The Knights themselves strode erect and proud. They were yet unbowed by their captivity, although they suffered from sunburn and fatigue, and fear for their future. There was not a one that did not chafe at the surrender of Castle Rock. They keenly felt the dishonor of that capitulation. How it would disappoint Sir Guy when he returned from Constantinople to discover his Castle in the hands of the infidels!

When Sheik Tariz Abdulla had arrived at the gates of Castle Rock the previous evening with a large army, he had announced his intention of razing the countryside. He would burn the nearby Maronite Christian villages that usually sheltered under the protection of the Templar. With only eight Knights at the Castle, they had no way of preventing such an action. Although the Castle itself was impregnable, the villagers nearby would be at the mercy of the Sheik. Seeing no recourse, the Swedish Master of the Castle capitulated. Now the Knights found themselves naked, chained and exhausted in the fortress of that Muslim Lord.

The Prince wasted no time once they reached the safety of his citadel. The Knights were led into a large chamber which was thankfully cool with a splashing fountain in its center. They were allowed to kneel around the tiled pool and dunk their heads and upper bodies into the refreshing water. On their knees naked and defenseless, they were silent as they gazed at one another.

"Be firm men. We'll endure whatever rank humiliations these heathens choose to inflict on us," Olaf announced. His deep voice seemed no less strong than when he sat atop the Throne at Castle Rock.

The others took some heart in his encouraging speech. But their eyes were attracted by another sight which was both astonishing and arresting. Prince Tariz had entered the airy chamber.

Sheik Tariz strode triumphantly through the room. He grinned from ear to ear as he surveyed his captives. His cocky walk was startling, not because of the arrogance of it, but because he was entirely naked! He had shed his voluminous Arab robes during the interval when the Knights had knelt and refreshed themselves at the pool.

This was a thing unheard of. The Arabs rarely disrobed entirely, especially those of higher rank. And here was the Sheik strutting along without any apparent shame. In fact, his long brown member was fully erect and throbbing shamelessly.

The handsome Prince seated himself at a couch which was covered with large comfortable pillows in colorful Arab patterns. The imperious Sheik plopped down with his lean thighs spread and his hard dick jutting up from his hips in a rampant display. His eyes fixed on the kneeling form of the Swedish Master of the Knights Templar.

Philippe the Burgundian stared at the nude Arab with wide eyes. He was very handsome. His brown skin was creamy and smooth, and completely hairless as if he had it shaved. There was no sign of hair surrounding that jutting dick or the around the flopping balls beneath. The muscled thighs that lay on the couch were also hairless and smooth, as were his chest and arms. The dusky Prince sprawled back with a supercilious smirk on his face and snapped his fingers.

Three Arab attendants seized the leader of the Franks. One of them unlocked the fetters that connected him to the others and dragged him on his knees toward the Sheik.

"I will enjoy the services of you and your men tonight, for tomorrow you go on the auction block. If you value your men's lives, you'll perform obediently and to my satisfaction," the Prince demanded of Olaf.

Again he snapped his fingers, and the red-headed Swede was shoved down on his belly at the Arab's feet.

"Suck my mighty member, dog!" Tariz commanded.

Olaf showed no expression as he slowly crawled forward and raised his head to the Arab's lap. Philippe and the other men watched breathlessly as they witnessed their naked leader open his mouth and swallow the pulsing, coffee-colored flesh. They were so engrossed in the spectacle they were taken by surprise when they were roughly brought to their feet and dragged forward to stand in a circle around the pair. So close now they were unable to look away, the men gazed on their leader's humiliation with uneasy silence.

Olaf sprawled on hands and knees. His handsome Nordic face burrowed in the Prince's lap. His ass was bare and spread apart, while his balls and dick dangled down between his mountainous thighs. The naked Swede's body glistened from the oil that had been applied to it. The flesh had still become somewhat sunburned and glowed with a rosy-pink flush. His short red hair and beard contrasted sharply with this new rosy coloring of his skin. Somehow the sunburn lent him an aspect of eroticism, as though he was continually flushed from a state of sexual excitement.

The sounds of Olaf's mouth and tongue slobbering over the infidel Prince's lengthy prick added to the powerful carnality of the scene.

The Prince stared down at the Swede as he suckled his manhood. His eyes were full of desire, and his body arched up to lunge into the Knight's mouth. It was obvious how much he lusted for the giant Swede.

Philippe observed the Prince's body more closely now. The barbarian potentate although naked still displayed his Eastern penchant for luxury. Around his long, sleek black hair he wore a silk headband encrusted with glittering jewels. At his ears were several sets of long gold loops, and amazingly at his chest were another pair of gold loops which pierced each protruding brown nipple. Philippe's dick rose up and throbbed at the sight of those delectable, pierced nubs.

For Philippe, even more erotic was what appeared when Olaf allowed the head of the Prince's dick to slip from his lips now and then. The plump cock-head was pierced by another thick gold loop! Philippe had rarely seen such a thing. In fact, only twice before had he seen it. His fellow Knights, the Della twins, had been captured and pierced through their cocks by another Arab potentate.

The Prince moaned steadily as he pumped his dick into the Swede's obedient mouth, but then abruptly grasped the man's head and yanked it from his twitching member. It was apparent by the Arab's deep groans he was averting a precipitous ejaculation. Obviously, he desired more action before he unloaded his heathen sperm.

Again the Sheik snapped his fingers as he attempted to catch his breath. He and Olaf exchanged deep, challenging glances. Philippe read no sign of surrender or humiliation in the blank stare of the Templar Master, but the Prince merely laughed and nodded.

"Tie him and spread his legs. We'll see him groveling yet," the Prince ordered.

Six brawny half-naked Arabs grabbed the unlucky Knight and threw him to the floor onto his back. The intricately painted tiles of the floor were smooth and cool, but no doubt uncomfortable for the Swede. Olaf was forced to raise his hands and suffer leather cuffs placed around his wrists. Next, his pink legs were forced backwards toward his chest and attached to those cuffs at his wrists. Now his ass was raised and exposed to the crowded room. And to his own fellow Knights.

The Knights had only caught a brief glimpse of their Master's bare butt hole before. This had been when he toppled over Sir Guy during the culmination of their contest to command the Knights Templar. Now they were afforded a perfect view.

It was as rosy-pink as his sunburned skin. The hole palpitated nervously between his widespread, hairless crack. His buttocks were huge and firm, he was a giant of a man, but the rectal cleft was small in comparison. That hole also looked totally virginal and defenseless.

What diabolical, lewd plans did the Prince contemplate for the Swede and his small, unprotected anus? The Knights who surrounded them were confused and silent. Not a one of them had not felt their own dicks swell and rise at the sight of their leader in such a vulnerable and sexually exciting position. They all recalled his brutal humiliation of their beloved leader, Sir Guy. A part of their minds reveled in his degradation, and longed to witness a rape of that innocent and tempting butt hole.

Yet he was also a member of their order. Although arrogant and cold, he was undeniably brave. And he was as Christian as they were.

"Let me take Sir Olaf's place," a voice suddenly cried out in the expectant silence.

It was the courageous action of one of the lesser Knights. Sir Eric von Bartell had spoken those words. The plump and wealthy young Knight shamed the others by his selfless offer. They stirred and moved forward. It looked as though they would attempt a rescue of their leader, albeit they were fettered in strong chains and had thick collars around their necks.

But the Prince had anticipated such an event. The Knights each and every one found three Arab strongmen grasping them by the arms and neck. They were forced to their knees and held immobile while they endured the spectacle of their leader's degradation.

The Prince laughed fanatically. He was incensed not only by the erotic atmosphere, but also by the vision of the massive Olaf collared and cuffed at his feet. He again snapped his fingers and grinned as he stepped forward and knelt over Olaf's collared head. He took his long dick in hand and slowly fed it between the Swede's gasping lips. The Sheik's incredibly smooth, muscular brown thighs straddled Olaf's head. The image of the dusky Arab squatting over the red-headed and pink-fleshed naked Knight was highly erotic. But what occurred next was even more exciting, though depraved.

The blond Saxon Eric was dragged forward. An Arab propelled Eric's face between Olaf's spread butt cheeks. Arab fingers pried open his mouth and he was compelled to kiss Olaf's fluttering sphincter.

Eric's naked body was a delight in itself. He was a wealthy young aristocrat that Sir Guy had disciplined into an obedient member of their order. Still somewhat chubby from his former luxurious lifestyle, his enticing butt jiggled delightfully. His naked body shivered with humiliation and trepidation as he was forced to mouth his leader's snug anal opening. Eric was not fat, by any means. He was a stalwart young warrior, but his flesh was pleasingly plump over the solid musculature beneath. His pale skin had also sunburned, and his equally hairless skin matched their leader's as he sprawled between Olaf's shackled thighs.

He was soon slobbering eagerly over the butt hole. The musky taste was too wondrous for any pretense of dislike. The Prince guffawed with pleasure at the sight of the Saxon's blond head buried in Olaf's defenseless butt crack. He shoved his stiff dick deep down Olaf's throat and grunted nastily as he did.

The Knights watched helplessly as their Arab captors pinned them in place. Not one had a limp dick. Especially the auburn-haired Philippe. His eyes leapt eagerly from one exciting image to the next. The Prince's wet, dusky dick entering Olaf's full mouth, Eric's tongue licking up and down Olaf's spread butt crack, or Eric's own plump ass cheeks quivering fearfully.

This scene went on for some time, the participants and spectators equally engrossed in the steamy action. Eventually, the Prince snapped his fingers once more, and Eric was pulled away from the Swede's ass. The Knights' eyes took in the sensual sight of Olaf's spit-coated asshole. It was slightly swollen and fluttering open like a tiny mouth.

What happened next to that virginal anus shocked them all.

"Now we'll see how stoic our Swedish Knight remains," Tariz gloated.

The eyes of the Knights nearly popped from their heads when they saw what two of the Arabs held in their hands. The two naked warriors strode past the Knights and stood in front of the Prince and the prostrate Swede. Between them they cradled an enormous dildo. The thing gleamed jet black and evil. It was coated with glistening oil. The dildo was long and fat with a wide head. It was carved in the exact likeness of a veined and perfect, although inhumanly large, prick.

They placed the broad head at the entrance to Olaf's spit-slick asshole and waited. The Prince yanked his manhood from Olaf's mouth, but without a moment's hesitation scooted forward and sat down on the Knight's face. He sighed as his buttocks parted and smothered Olaf's nose and mouth. He relaxed over that impotent face and sighed again as his own hole buried Olaf's lips and mouth. He took his erect tool in his hand and began to rub it up and down. His honey-amber eyes glazed over with passion. The delicate gold ring embedded in the head of his glistening brown meat moved up and down with every stroke of the Prince's eager hand. He nodded to his two lackeys.

The naked Arabs knelt down behind Olaf. They began to shove the greased black dildo against the pink-flesh of Olaf's snug anal lips. It was an obscene image. Those tiny rosy-red ass lips stretched and gaped as the fake black prick began to part them. The oiled dildo entered the sanctity of Olaf's virgin butt hole.

A muffled groan could be heard as they witnessed Olaf's entire body stiffen with apparent agony. But there was no escape for the bound Swede from that invading dildo. The brawny brown arms that pressed it into his hole were steady and cruel. The fluttering lips parted, and the black head pressed deeper. Olaf's hips rose into the air, but there was nothing he could say with his mouth buried under coffee-brown ass. The Prince moaned at the lewd sight. He flailed his be-ringed dick faster as he eagerly watched Olaf's rape.

The long black invader steadily crawled up Olaf's tender butt hole. Inch after fat inch invaded him. His spread crack dripped oil from the well-lubed dildo, and his powerful ass shook violently under the relentless plundering. Soon the Arabs were plunging the grotesque thing in and out of that violated ass-pit with enthusiastic thrusts.

Philippe was incensed at the sight. A very large part of him reveled in the arrogant Swede's rape. Guy had suffered under Olaf's cruel humiliation, and Philippe worshipped the French Master. Philippe also delighted in and craved harsh and humiliating sexual scenes. Such a sight would probably have aroused any of the Templar. But when his eyes strayed to the Swede's prick, he was stunned to see it was growing larger and stiffer. As the black dildo was shoved deeper and deeper into his guts, his dick was actually swelling with passion. He was being sexually stimulated by his own humiliation and rape!

Philippe found himself floating into a state of passionate semi-consciousness. And the other Knights were just as delirious. Their exhaustion, sunburn, and confusion overcame them almost simultaneously. It was as if they were sharing identical thoughts – as if they were experiencing a common vision.

As the Arab Prince screamed out and ejaculated, a fountain of white sperm over the belly and legs of the bound

Olaf, so did the chained Franks. As one, they ejaculated from untouched pricks. Cum flew with gooey wings in every direction. Much of landed on the shackled Swede.

The monster black dildo was relentless. It plied Olaf's now gaping asshole without cessation as his body was splattered with warm cum. He must have felt that sticky fluid. His own tense body writhed with abrupt violence, his giant dick convulsed in wild spasms, and he suddenly creamed his own belly. Great gobs of milky cum oozed out of his fat dickhead. His palpitating asshole clamped around the invading dildo, which the Arabs rammed even deeper inside him.

What happened next was a blur to the exhausted Knights. They only realized they were eventually left alone, naked and fettered. Olaf was again chained among them. They had collapsed in a heap. Their nude, sunburned bodies piled together as if they sought comfort in each other's physical proximity. Even Olaf sprawled humbly amidst them. His head pillowed in Eric the Saxon's soft warm buttocks.

As dawn light filtered in upon the naked Knights, hefty Arab warriors arrived to seize them and march them off to the auction block. Below them, a multitude of jeering and screaming Muslims jostled for a closer look at the naked Franks. The locals were delighted to be treated to this highly unusual spectacle. The haughty Knights Templar in fetters, each and every one nude and up for sale, this was unheard of. Any one of them with sufficient monies was anxious to initiate the bidding.

Olaf Thorsen, Master of Castle Rock, stood upright and proud. It was as though he had not suffered the degradations of the previous evening. There was no hint in his haughty demeanor that he had swallowed down Prince Tariz' fat dick, or opened his mouth to the Sheik's brown ass crack, or that his own private butt slot had been brutally invaded by a monster black dildo. In front of his fellow Franks, his own dick had ejected an undeniable load of spunk while he was being fucked by a dildo in the hands of two naked Arabs. Yet, he appeared unbowed. His broad shoulders were thrown back, and his chains seemed almost inconsequential as they draped his nude but powerful form.

Philippe observed this apparent lack of emotion. He was amazed at it, but also rendered the man his grudging respect. He assumed that Olaf was too secure in his own self-image to allow the rape to damage his spirit.

Olaf's own thoughts were far different.

Although his cold blue eyes conveyed one message, his inner feelings were quite contradictory. He cursed himself for giving up Castle Rock to the Prince. He felt he had failed in his mission in the Holy Land. Guy was no doubt a better leader. As to the previous evening, the unusual sexual experience did not shake him too badly. His asshole ached with the memory of that massive dildo. But it was a strangely pleasurable ache. Recalling the feel of the smooth flesh of the Prince's buttocks against his face was arousing. Even the Sheik's asshole which he had secretly licked and sucked at with pleasure was a memory he treasured with private gratification. Sex had always been extremely exciting for him, although he had primarily enjoyed his conquest over others. Mastering staunch men like Guy was what he lived for.

Yet a part of him thrilled in his own degradation at the hands of the exotic Prince.

The other Knights were merely in shock. Fearful of the clamoring horde, they wondered where they would spend the remainder of their lives. Only Philippe was unafraid.

His serenity stemmed from his utter trust in Guy. As long as he was alive, he believed Guy would rescue him. Philippe was without question loyal to the heroic Knight and believed in the French Master's powers without reservation. He recalled his own initiation into the Order of the Templar, and the moment that Guy had ploughed Philippe's willing butt hole with his fat tool. Philippe had surrendered his soul to the French Knight. Guy returned that trust and loyalty with complete affection. Guy cared for Philippe deeply. Nay, he loved

Philippe. And Philippe loved Guy. The realization of that truth sent a thrill of hope through the heart of the naked, fettered Burgundian.

It was at that moment the Knights discerned a raucous hue and cry rippling through the hubbub of the auction. Their hearts soared with profound relief as they witnessed the crowd parting. Sir Guy had arrived with a score of their fellow Knights!

Guy flashed them a reassuring grin as he met with the Sheik at their feet. The Templar Master handed Tariz a bag of gold to purchase his men and that was that.

Several hours later, they rode from the Muslim fortress. They happily left behind the handsome but wicked Prince Tariz Abdulla. Olaf and Guy spoke together as they rode side by side. The giant sunburned Swede was acutely aware of his sore anus as he squirmed uncomfortably in the saddle.

"What would you have done when the Prince threatened to burn the villages? Would you have surrendered Castle Rock?" Olaf had to ask Guy. His deep voice was subtly altered. It was almost, but not quite, humble.

Guy let out a huge guffaw and reached over to clap the Knight on his sunburned shoulder. "My friend. The Prince was testing you! He had no intention of burning those villages. He has lived in peace with the Maronite Christians his entire life. He would never have harmed them. I would know that because of my experience here. It was merely something you could not know. Perhaps you need yet to learn something of this country." Guy winked at Olaf, but did not press the point.

"And what of Castle Rock? Must we attempt to retake it?"

"No, of course not. Mamluk reached me when I was a day's ride from the Castle on my return from Constantinople. We used the secret underground entrance to the Castle last night and were successful in evicting the Arab occupants. It was a wise move on your part to dispatch my loyal servant." Guy grinned as he willingly acknowledged Olaf's intelligent action.

Olaf said nothing for some time as they rode under the stars of the Palestine evening. Finally, he smiled and bowed toward Guy.

"I suppose we should share the leadership of the Knights Templar here in the Holy Land. What do you say?"

Guy grinned and nodded.

Philippe rode directly behind the conversing pair. He heard everything they said and could not help but smile. All Guy told Olaf concerning the Shiek, Philippe himself could have told him, too. Philippe, though, was not only intelligent, but crafty. He had allowed the Swede to make that blunder, and hoped for the best. His trust in Guy's timely rescue was great.

Also, Philippe was looking forward to getting the Swedish Knight alone. He had some hope that he had a more than even chance of teaching the egotistical Knight a few more lessons in humiliation. His dick stiffened. He was happy. They were on their way home.

# Tale Seventeen: The Tale of the Masks

*In which Sir Jonas Dambrusk of Lithuania and his companions are captured by the evil Lord Barabas and are tortured by masked men in the night.*

I again introduce myself as Sir Jonas Dambrusk of Lithuania, a member of the Order of the Knights Templar. My liege Lord is Sir Guy de Brussiers of Castle Rock in the Holy Land. He is a handsome and kind man, although he is also a firm master who brooks neither disobedience nor cowardly behavior. I believe I acted as bravely as possible in the situation I found myself in. Even though I have belonged to this Order less than one year, I have given my heart and soul over to it. And, to Sir Guy.

Three other Knights and I found ourselves on an errand some four hours north of Castle Rock. The day was fine. It was late autumn, and the sky was soft with recent rains but clear and pristine on that particular afternoon. We did not expect the approaching score of Franks on horseback to be a threat. Their dust rose behind them as they rode down into the quiet valley we were then passing through. The road was otherwise deserted with the nearest village nearly an hour's ride south.

Imagine my consternation when the riders were suddenly on us. They did seem a little odd as they came closer. The entire contingent wore neither iron nor bronze helmets. Instead, they were masked, with bizarre black hoods covering their faces and heads.

All were masked except for one, whom I recognized at once. I was stunned. It was the evil Lord Barabas Gerband! Tall in the saddle, he gazed at us from under those dark beetling brows and out of piercing blue orbs I recalled so vividly from the dungeons in Constantinople.

"Ride! Swiftly, before he sees you. Go to Sir Guy," I hissed to the young Knight at my side. We were still half-obscured by a lee of rock, and Sir Hillary Browning was slightly ahead of us. Perhaps he had not yet been seen by the advancing men.

Although I was only just nineteen and without any claim to authority among the Knights Templar, I was respected. This Knight was new to the Holy Land and naturally deferred to me in matters of importance. By the wild look in my eyes, he obviously understood my command must be urgent.

"Tell the Master we've come on Lord Barabas of Constantinople! Go!" I exclaimed as I slapped his horse. He was off in a gallop. Sir Hillary rode up through a twisted trail through the rocks over a ridge back toward Castle Rock. His horse disappeared only moments before the approaching riders surrounded us.

"Well! I surely recognize you!" The foul laugh boomed out over us.

We were entirely surrounded by over twenty men. I gave a secret hand signal to my companions. I cautioned them to wait no matter what happened. We would attempt to keep the enemy occupied until Sir Guy could come to the rescue. With the vile Vizier as their leader, I was absolutely certain these were wicked men, and Sir Guy would want them apprehended. Our own fate was not important. At least I told myself that.

We were swiftly disarmed and roped together as our horses were appropriated. Lord Barabas spoke to his minions in that cruel harsh rasp I recalled so vividly. Our captors dragged us through the remaining afternoon light to a clearing in the woods above the sea. It was off the road some distance, and the sinister-appearing men swiftly made camp and built up a large bonfire.

These were definitely bizarre men. They were Franks, at least most of them. Their clothing and their weaponry were similar to ours. What flesh of their bodies that we could see did appear to be fairer than the dusky skin of the Arabs of the Holy Land. But their faces were hidden. Each and every one wore the same mask.

This mask was really a black leather hood. It snugly encased their entire heads. It obscured all sign of their hair and most of their faces. Their eyes stared out from holes in the dark gleaming leather. Their nostrils appeared from similar holes, while their mouths and chins were left exposed. They seemed peculiarly alike in their anonymity, and they were absolutely obedient to their leader, the Lord Barabas.

He hovered over us like the predator he was. His smile was cruel. I wondered how he had escaped the dungeon in Constantinople. We abandoned him there screaming as those he had tortured were unleashed on him. What happened to allow him his freedom? And who were these minions so eager to obey his will?

"Sir Jonas is it?" He sneered as he towered over us. We had been forced to kneel in the dirt beside the rising bonfire.

I did not deign to reply and merely stared up at him with a blank expression on my face. I did not want to raise his ire, but I had no intention of pleasing him either. The truth is his every aspect from that sneer to his predatory stance sent a shiver of horror down my spine. His dungeon in Constantinople had been appalling, but it had also affected me in a deeply sexual and twisted manner.

I longed for Sir Guy's strong shoulder beside me as it had been on that occasion.

"Answer not. It hardly matters. We'll enjoy ourselves with you tonight," he said with a vile laugh. He gazed down at me with a hungry look that sickened me. Then his eyes narrowed with a gleam of additional cruelty. "One of you will

215

Jay Starre

suffer the worst fate imaginable for a man by dawn's breaking. It's only a simple matter for the three of you to decide who it shall be!"

He laughed again, and never before had laughter sounded so absolutely sinful.

I struggled to rise. Again I signed for my compatriots to follow my lead. Although my hands were bound, we had other body signals that we shared. My shrugs and the inflection of my head commanded the other Knights to remain quiet. Again, even though I was the youngest, they were all aware of my closeness to Sir Guy. They also understood I knew this evil man from Constantinople.

"I'll be the one," I heard my own voice speaking quietly. There was a slight tremor to it, which betrayed my deep-seated fear. I loathed this Vizier.

He laughed in my face. This boded no good. Then he gestured to a pair of his men. They leapt forward and grasped my companions.

"The brave Lithuanian! Well. You shall watch as we take one of your men and abuse him firstly. He will suffer the fate I planned for you and you must watch! By dawn, your own doom will match his. Every agony, every groan and cry, you will taste in the end as he will before you!"

Lord Barabas understood how to be cruel. It was the truest part of him.

I shuddered as he unerringly chose the weakest of us. He could sniff fear like an animal. His minions took hold of Sir Ivan Metrovosk, a blond Russian who had only arrived in the Holy Land a few brief weeks earlier. He cast a terrified look in my direction, but stiffened and retrieved his manhood, if for only a moment. My heart sank at what fate might await him, and myself afterward.

We were soon to find out. The fire had grown large and illuminated the small meadow brightly. I prayed for Sir Guy to come soon, although we were many hours ride from Castle

216

Rock. At least these idiots were building up a beacon to light his way.

The grotesquely masked men had been efficiently busy. A wooden frame had been hastily constructed beside the bonfire. The hapless Sir Ivan was dragged toward it. The contraption actually turned out to be a round barrel on the ground surrounded by a wooden framework.

While we were forced to stand and observe, the young Russian was stripped by the former Vizier's faceless minions. Lord Barabas stood by and looked on with a depraved, keen gaze.

Ivan was a fair young man. His flesh was pale and soft to look at, although he was athletic and muscular. There was a fine down of blond on his limbs, and a furry thatch of gold at the base of the long flaccid cock that flopped between his robust thighs. He trembled violently as he gawked at the strange contraption he was forced toward. He struggled at the last minute. Obviously, he was fearful of being helplessly bound, as it was certain to be his fate in moments.

And that was his fate. His youthful body was draped over the wooden barrel, his legs spread wide and attached to the wooden frame, and each ankle secured tightly with hemp rope. His arms were stretched forward and attached to the front of the framework. He was bent double, his naked buttocks spread apart and vulnerable. The corded muscles of his back stretched outward in helpless bondage.

The whipping began at a peremptory signal from the Vizier. One of the masked men, it was impossible to distinguish one from another, vigorously struck Ivan's back with a long lash.

Ivan did not scream. He was at least brave enough to endure the pain of the lash. And it was not as severe as it could have been. He was not even bleeding, although the pale flesh of his unblemished back became mottled and red with raised welts.

No snapping strikes found his beautiful buttocks. They quivered with every lash, but they were left pristine and unmolested. I knew this would not last. I recalled with horror all the various tortures and punishments I had witnessed in that dungeon in Constantinople. Lord Barabas had a fertile, if dark, imagination.

The whipping ceased. A deep quiet descended on the night. We could hear the quiet sobs of our companion. I knew it was not from the pain of his whipping that he wept. He feared what was to come.

Lord Barabas stepped in front of me. I was on my knees again along with my other two companions. He peered down at me with a look of total malevolence. I admitted to myself how much I feared him. But I don't believe I exhibited too much of this horror.

He grasped my face with one cruel hand and shouted at me. "You and your dung-smelling Master abandoned me to the mercy of my prisoners in Constantinople. And this is what they did to me!" He almost spit in my face in his fury.

Then he turned and bent over, ripping down his leather trousers and baring his ass. That naked butt was as hard as his heart. Each cheek was a mound of solid muscle that was barely hidden by a dark and silky fuzz. The naked mounds would have been perfect, except for one glaring disfigurement. Across the top of each cheek were emblazoned the words "fuck hole" in bold Latin. The scars were obviously inflicted by a heated iron. The seared flesh stood out red and angry on those otherwise unmarked posterior cheeks.

I was amazed to have his naked ass in my face, and secretly happy to once again see those vulgar words implanted on his flesh. I recalled his branding and punishment in the dungeons of Constantinople with pleasure. He had deserved it. He would never disrobe in someone's presence without them reading those words. The pain he suffered when the lewd words were seared into his sensitive flesh was a welcome memory as well.

I was swiftly brought back to harsh reality. Those ass cheeks were removed from my face. Lord Barabas stood up and without even looking at us, tore the remainder of his clothing off with violent passion. He was totally unclad, and his cock thrust up in a curving erection. It looked like a brutal saber. He was apparently filled with a cruel ardor. Perhaps this lust had been kindled by the memory of his own humiliation and pain when those words were burned into his upended bottom.

He sneered at Ivan, whose head hung down so that he was unable to see what was coming. Two of the masked men approached as if they already knew what would be expected of them. I suspected this scenario may have been acted out at other times. It was apparent by the twitching erection bobbing at the Vizier's thighs, he was anticipating it with great pleasure.

I shuddered, and my companions blanched white with horror as each of the two masked men raised a burning brand, red-hot from having been in the fire. Thankfully Ivan did not see the iron advancing. But we did.

"Ahhggg! Oh God have mercy on my soul," he shrieked.

Those irons had kissed his flesh. Swiftly but adequately. The pain must have been excruciating. Smoke and the stench of burned flesh rose to make us nearly gag. But the sight of those otherwise beautiful pale ass mounds now seared with the words "fuck hole" was undeniable erotic in some deep, perverted sense.

Ivan's body was stretched taut while all the muscles of his bound form clenched in spasms of agony. Fear of what other insults and pain were likely to occur sent shivers through his taut muscles. Totally nude, with his flesh now seared by those vulgar words, he still gleamed beautiful in the eerie light of that raging bonfire. Beads of sweat broke out all over his writhing body, from his pain, his fear, and the heat of that same bonfire. I myself sweltered in the heated atmosphere.

Ivan's writhing contortions abruptly ceased. He fainted. I heard the cruel Lord Barabas laughing loudly. "Put the salve on him. And wake him. We don't want him too occupied with his pain. More exciting tortures await him!"

I gritted my teeth and was only able to remain quiet by shear willpower alone. I longed to rise up and annihilate that filthy bastard. But I knew to wait. Wait for Sir Guy.

Men obeyed the naked Lord. True to his word, a soothing balm was rubbed over Ivan's bound body. It made his flesh gleam even more brightly in the firelight. Much like a basted pig for the roasting, I thought with a shudder.

The three of us were grabbed and rudely stripped of all our clothing. My two other companions were dragged forward and forced to their knees in the dirt behind Ivan. The Russian was rousing from his faint after cool water was poured over his lolling head.

As I watched, black hoods and masks were brought forward. First Sir Pierre de Lanset, an auburn-haired Burgundian, was held immobile. He struggled momentarily and cried out as a dark hood was pulled over his head and strapped around his neck. I could see it distinctly in the bright firelight and realized these were actually two-part masks. This leather hood fit snugly over the scalp, forehead, neck, and ears. But there were perforations around the ears, so one could hear. Then another black leather garment was placed across the upper face. With slits for the eyes and nose, it was pulled tightly back and tied behind the head.

Pierre's mouth and chin were still exposed. And the tightness of the fit forced his lips to stretch open like a gaping wound. It was strange, dehumanizing, and highly erotic. When he was completely masked, I could no longer recognize him. He became one of the others.

The same was done to our other fellow Knight, Sir Tonio de Slava of Tuscany. His beautiful black locks were quickly hidden by the hood. His full Etruscan lips were the only distinguishing feature left to him. Both men were on their knees while their naked bodies shivered under the dancing glow of the firelight. They knelt directly behind our bound companion and were forced to remain there to better witness his further tortures.

I was left without a hood, the only man to remain unmasked besides the tortured Ivan and Lord Barabas. He grinned at me. His handsome face was distorted by the hideous aspect of his soul, which shone out undisguised. Masked men dragged me closer and compelled me to stand directly behind my companions.

"Tie his balls and cock!" Barabas shrieked shrilly. Two men hastened to obey. His senses having returned, the greased and whipped young Russian heard the command. But there was nothing he could do other than submit. He did struggle briefly as one of the men reached between his spread thighs and grasped his dangling balls. The man also pulled down Ivan's flopping cock and stretched it out along the wood of the barrel Ivan was bent over. The man held Ivan's privates while the other began to wind a long thin leather strap round both cock and balls.

"Stretch them tight, especially those huge, delectable semen sacks!" Barabas cried. "By night's end, he may no longer have them!" He then laughed uproariously.

That was it then. He intended to castrate poor Ivan at dawn. And me afterward. Oh well, I had been threatened with just such a fate when I had raped an Arabian Princess. Sir Guy had staved off that punishment. Perhaps he would save me again, and poor Ivan. I prayed for the night to be long and the cursed dawn not to arrive too quickly.

Poor Ivan's balls were wrapped and separated expertly by the black leather strands. Each lay along the barrel surrounded by that leather, huge and swollen now. And the youth's cock had been encased in leather similarly, pulled downwards and lengthened so it appeared to be in a state of full erection. Those black-strapped genitals contrasted oddly against the paleness of Ivan's quivering butt cheeks. They almost looked as if they were not a part of him. And that was most likely Barabas' intention by the time the evil dawn arrived.

A grotesque chant began, not unlike the prayers we often intoned together during religious ceremonies. The deep

221

voices of the anonymous men chilled. Their actions were far worse.

First, they forced Pierre to crawl forward on his knees. They shoved his masked face against the barrel. His gaping mouth was pressed against the bound testicles and held there. One man bent down and whispered in his ear. The hooded Pierre began at once to lick and mouth those obscenely bound genitals. I do not know what was whispered to him, but it was enough for the Burgundian to take to his task with alacrity.

Another of the men began to rub a gloved hand over Ivan's quaking ass cheeks. Those beautiful mounds were slippery with the balm applied to his body, and the black leather of the man's gloves slithered over them effortlessly. That obscene, midnight-black hand slipped between the mounds and began to run up and down the parted crevice. Leather-encased fingers strummed the hairless butt hole that pulsed in a matching rhythm to the constant shudder of Ivan's ivory-pale butt cheeks. One of those gloved fingers pressed at the exposed anal cleft.

If Ivan made any sounds, they could not be heard above the chanting of the masked men. But his body spoke volumes. It writhed and convulsed as Pierre licked and sucked at his swollen balls, which must have been painfully sensitive. That big leather-encased finger dipped into his greased anus. It shoved all the way inside, which elicited a writhing struggle from Ivan, but to no avail. Another black finger slid in beside the first. The two fingers moved in and out. Grease oozed out of the violated rectal cleft, then was forced back in by the steady impalement of those black-gloved digits.

The man added another finger, slowly, deliberately and cruelly. When the fourth was pressed against that stretched hole, Ivan's voice was finally heard above the chanting.

He shrieked, "NO!"

His protest made no difference. The fourth went in beside the other three. That straining hole was forced wide open. It was filled with four huge black-gloved fingers. The masked man kept them planted firmly inside Ivan's butt as the Russian struggled and twisted his ass all over the barrel. Ivan's body strained against his bonds as his muscles clenched and spasmed. But then, he inevitably collapsed from all that fruitless effort.

I could see his quivering asshole abruptly surrender. The four fingers slid right to the knuckles. That violated hole was now a sloppy, welcoming pit. Ivan's assailant took immediate advantage of the Russian's capitulation. He added his thumb and worked it into the greased slot. Ivan's pale ass, rather than moving away, rose up and shoved back at the gloved fist. Amazingly, the young Knight swallowed that hand completely with his asshole.

I gasped, unable to believe what I was seeing. Ivan had found some strength within to not only bear what was being forced on him, but to go beyond. The black hand disappeared up that white chute. It was swallowed to the wrist. The anal lips pulsed with dripping grease all around the hairy wrist planted up it.

Then began the real violation of Ivan's poor asshole. That hand was removed, leaving a gaping and dripping anal cavity for all the company to witness. Ivan's body had collapsed over the barrel, his arms limp in their bonds. But he was not unconscious. He would feel the rest of his torture, and endure it.

First Tonio was compelled to bury his lush lips in that gaping maw. His masked face was pushed deep between Ivan's sweating buttocks. His mouth and nose were shoved into Ivan's yawning anal cleft. He was held there by the back of the neck until he nearly passed out. He was then commanded to stuff his own fist into that gooey hole. It did not readily go inside. Ivan's poor butt aperture had to be stretched out again, and he caterwauled loudly when his companion's fist finally sunk entirely out of sight.

Pierre was required to follow suit. Then others. One masked man, then another. It seemed to never end. But what could happen when the fisting did end was not something I wanted to contemplate.

Eventually, I was dragged forward. My hand was raised and two men held my arm while they shoved my fingers into that gaping mass of anal flesh. It was warm, and wet, and soft. I had no choice but to enter it, praying that Ivan would understand. We were buying time until Sir Guy would arrive. If only Ivan could survive. The pulsing flesh that enveloped my hand was incredibly wondrous. I would have relished it at some other time. Just as my entire fist was buried inside my friend's sloppy butt hole, two masked men grasped my head and began to slide a silken leather hood over it.

The feel of that leather over my bald scalp, which had been shaved as my punishment for almost a year now, was undeniably sensual and seductive. That the pulsing anal walls of the Russian I called a friend was massaging my hand at the same time was strangely erotic.

Then the mask came.

As it covered the upper part of my face, I also felt like an anonymous player in that horrid drama. My hand felt so good up that fleshy ass cavern, I began to massage back. I could feel Ivan's hole responding. I was making love to him with my fist. I think some part of his tortured mind realized it was someone speaking to him who cared. His asshole opened and closed over my hand. His body rose up and down as if fucking my fist willingly. The heat, the dark night and glowing bonfire, the fear, and the masks combined to convey us into another world altogether.

And there was Lord Barabas laughing steadily behind us.

Both my other fellow Knights were beside me on their knees. Their faces pressed up against Ivan's writhing butt, which they licked avidly. At that one moment I sensed Ivan knew it was his friends touching him, even though he could not see us.

But that did not last. Other masked assailants dragged us away. I suddenly realized there was another barrel set up, with a similar wooden frame around it. It was to be my turn!

I freely admit I felt fear. Still, I went to the barrel without struggle and draped my own naked body over it. When I was bound helpless and the whipping began, I smiled as my head was bent down and pain erupted over my back. I could hear Lord Barabas behind me laughing, but it was a hollow sound. I realized that nothing he did, for the rest of his life would be able to fill the void that was his soul. For me, I was fulfilled. I knew in my heart that Sir Guy would come. Even if it was too late for me and my companions, it would not be too late to punish this evil man and his crazed cohorts.

The burning brands did not come. Why, I do not know. Perhaps he was saving that for last. Just before he would remove my manhood from me. Anyway, he did tie my balls and dick with those leather straps, which felt incredible. My nut sack had never felt so full. And with my thighs spread apart, my asshole twitched in anticipation for what would come next. I did not bother to resist, and the feel of a tongue over my pulsing anal slot was a pleasure so intense, I was beyond pain or even orgasm.

My body surrendered to the bonds. I lay supine over the barrel in virtual comfort. My arms relaxed and stretched out in the frame in similar ease. The pain in my back from the whipping was mitigated by the soothing balm applied to it.

Even when the horrid countenance of Lord Barabas leaned close to my face and licked my cheek with a snaky, slobbering tongue, I did not quail. During the course of that vile night, he had somehow lost all power over me.

When his hand, and I knew it was his, began to violate my asshole, I did not resist. One finger after the other drove up my anal cleft. No mercy nor any thought of my pleasure could be read into those crudely probing leather-encased fingers. But it did not matter. Every thrust I answered. My asshole obeyed my will. It opened, and it opened further. He could not find my

225

limits. His entire hand slipped into me. He pounded me with his fist. He withdrew completely and punched back inside way up my guts. He screamed at me. He began to add another hand one finger at a time.

My asshole only opened wider. The amazing orifice accommodated his insinuating second hand with caressing ease. I laughed to myself. He could not beat me. The terrible chanting, the heat of the fire, Ivan's moans beside me, Barabas' awful shouting, my pain and my pleasure all melded into a floating dream of barbaric eroticism.

And then inexplicably, those violating fingers were abruptly removed. The incessant chanting around us was transformed to screams and cries of agony. What was going on?

I looked up from my euphoric fog. I realized it was growing light. It was near dawn. The clearing was filled with sword-wielding Knights.

Sir Guy had come.

I was released from my bonds. I found myself smiling groggily up at my Master's bearded face. His blond glory was such a welcome sight I fainted dead away.

When I came to, it was broad daylight. I looked up to see we were in that same clearing, but there were a score of Knights Templar roaming around the meadow now. I sat up. I bit my lip and winced at the pain in my back, buttocks, and anus. I noticed that at an edge of the clearing a number of men sat in a circle. They were bound together. There wore no masks, and of course I did not recognize any them. But I knew who they were.

"Come, my brave Jonas. How are you?" Sir Guy hovered over me with his beaming smile.

"I think I'll survive. How are Tonio and Pierre? And Ivan?" I asked fearfully. Had the Vizier carried out his evil plan for Ivan? Was he castrated or dead?

"He isn't much worse off than you. Except for his branding. But he has decided he likes it!" Sir Guy guffawed. He laid an affectionate hand on my shoulder. "You did well. We've apprehended a band of evil thugs this morning. And the worst of them shall rot in a dungeon for the remainder of his wicked life. I think you know who I mean."

I was led over to confront that heinous Lord. He was clothed now and huddled with the other captives. He looked up at me and glowered. He still appeared handsome and evil of course. But his hooded brows and cold blue eyes no longer held any menace for me. I had faced the worst and triumphed. I laughed in his face.

He spit at my feet. But it was an empty gesture.

I glanced at Sir Guy, whose own eyes were easy to read. I thought perhaps he contemplated offering his own disciplinary lessons to the recalcitrant Lord Barabas. Perhaps I would be allowed to participate. I recalled those firm ass cheeks with the words "fuck hole" branded brightly across their muscular surface.

How deep would the pulsing anal hole between those hard mounds be? Would the Vizier's ass take a fist, or two? Maybe we would find out. I laughed again.

227

# Tale Eighteen: The Prince Undergoes Initiation

*In which Prince Eros Ramozas arrives at Castle Rock and suffers an impromptu initiation at the hands of three Knights, Eric the Saxon, and the brothers Stepov, Petr and Giorgi.*

Prince Eros Ramozas trotted his horse toward the wide entrance to Castle Rock under the burning glare of a Palestinian summer sun. That heat and the intensity of the sunlight did not affect him. He was well accustomed to it. His home on the outskirts of the walled city of Palermo in sun baked Sicily was similarly sweltering and golden during the summer. He squinted up against the ramparts of the Castle and picked out a trio of men gazing down at him.

Knights, he guessed by their accoutrements. Two were blond. Their fair hair sparkled like golden helms. The third was dark-haired, but may as well have been fair his skin was so light in color. They looked to be Franks from the northern climes. He soon discovered they were.

From their high perch they scrutinized him with a measured intensity that was slightly disconcerting. He waved his arm and bowed from the back of his horse. He intended to commence his sojourn here in the fabled home of the Knights Templar under Sir Guy de Brussiers on a good footing. It never hurt to be courteous.

His horse was taken as he entered the courtyard. The Castle walls loomed high above him. It looked to be a substantial citadel, although somewhat foreboding and dark.

He heard a cry from the northern wall. "Welcome, sir!"

One of the trio who had been regarding him from there descended a set of steep stairs along the inner wall of the courtyard. That deep voice belonged to a handsome flaxen-haired young man who was adorned in the red-cross emblazoned tunic of the Knights Templar.

The two stood face to face in the shadowed courtyard.

Eric von Bartell surveyed the newcomer, whom he assumed to be the Prince from Sicily Sir Guy had cautioned him to expect. He was a comely young man. Tall, his back was straight and somewhat bold in his even gaze. His auburn hair was cropped exceedingly short about his skull. It was the style among many of the nobility in Sicily. That short dark-red hair, along with an amber complexion shaved smooth, and deep brown eyes created a fetching combination. There was a delicateness about him, though. No doubt this refinement came from his wealthy upbringing among the decadent nobility of southern Italy.

Eric sensed this at once, especially since he himself had grown up in a pampered environment, although it had been in the much cooler northern province of Saxony. Something inside the blond von Bartell responded to this gentle prince. Eric's dick leaped to attention beneath his leather trousers. He smiled brightly.

Prince Eros read that smile incorrectly. The boyish-looking young Knight before him, grinning jovially and taking his hand so kindly seemed to be the very image of trustworthy benevolence. He fell into the Knight's trap at once.

For his part, Eric von Bartell thought quickly. He turned his head upwards and gestured to the waiting Stepov brothers. They readily understood the secret sign and scurried away to make a chamber ready to "entertain" their new guest.

It was less than an hour later that the fair Eric and the dark Eros found their way to the chamber the Stepov brothers had prepared. The two men, of equally youthful age, had conversed convivially in Italian and German during that interlude. Both were exceedingly well educated. Eric even showed the Prince his spacious apartments, which were simple but comfortable. They had toured the Castle briefly, eaten a light afternoon dinner and then finally made their way to this private room hidden in one of the towers of the Castle.

Before arriving there, Eric had determined his assumptions about the Prince were close to the truth. The young nobleman was innocent, pampered, and utterly unprepared for the rough and ready life of the Holy Land, or for the coming evening.

Eric had been ordered to offer the guest Castle Rock's hospitality until the following week when Guy returned. He was also commanded to determine the mettle of the new supplicant to the Order of the Knights Templar. The exact manner of his determination had not been spelled out.

Eric had his own ideas.

He smirked behind the slim Prince's sturdy back as he ushered Eros into the specially prepared chamber.

"What is this room?" the amiable young Sicilian asked as he peered around at the strange cell.

The chamber was not large, but had an exceedingly high and vaulted ceiling. The only light entering the room fell down in shafts of gold from a series of slatted windows high up in the stone walls. It was deeply shadowed in the circular cell even though it was afternoon outside.

Dominating the center of the room was a slim pillar of marbled stone that reached straight up to that high ceiling. On it were attached iron manacles at various heights. A single table sat against the far wall, with instruments on it that were not entirely distinguishable in the dim light.

Eros was given no time to guess at the room's true use. Even as Eric slammed and barred the door behind them, the

Stepov brothers leapt out from behind that same door. They seized the Italian Prince and hauled him forward before he could even get out a decent yelp. Eric moved behind the hapless Sicilian while the two brawny Russians clutched either of his arms.

Although Eros was a swift and athletic young nobleman, it happened so quickly he had no opportunity to fend off his assailants.

As well, the young men knew what they were about, having plotted exactly their course of action. They yanked up each of Eros's lean arms and had them shackled by the wrists to the tall post in less than five seconds. That was enough.

There was now no escape for the prince.

"What is this? I demand an explanation, Sirs!" Eros shouted peremptorily. His deep brown eyes were wide with astonishment at the sudden turn of events.

The blond Saxon came around to face Eros. He smiled. The soft regard perplexed the captive Sicilian.

Eric already liked the amiable Eros. His smile was genuine. But, this was to be a Templar initiation. Eric could not allow his sympathy for the Prince to mitigate the severe nature of the induction.

"You've come a long way to join the Knights Templar. This is to be your initiation. My advice to you, as one who has undergone such an ordeal, is to brace yourself with courage. Any pain you may undergo will be balanced by a pleasure it is unlikely you have ever before experienced."

"But this is not what I expected!" Prince Eros blustered. His handsome face clouded with outrage.

Eric stared directly into that face. His body was only inches from the young prince. "Best not to have any expectations. The Knights Templar is an exemplary Order. Few are admitted. I have faith you are made of sufficient mettle. Now's your opportunity to prove it."

"But…" Eros began to protest again. At the same time his arms tensed as he tugged futilely on the shackles that restrained his hands above his head.

Even as he spoke, Petr Stepov reached around him and inserted a ball gag of silver and black leather into his gaping mouth. His outburst was muffled into an incoherent blubber. The black leather strap which held the gag was buckled on the back of Eros' head and over the brow and center of his scalp. His close-cropped hair made the contraption appear as if it was all of one piece with his skull. It looked like a reddish-dark helm gleaming in the dim light.

As he muffled Eros and leaned into the young Italian's taut body with his own, Petr experienced a rising erection beneath his woolen trousers. He had been excited beforehand when the three plotted this scene, but now that the prince was muffled and bound, Petr found himself aroused beyond any previous expectations.

It was then up to his brother, Giorgi, the dark-haired of the three to take the initiative. He grinned wickedly as he came forward to replace his older brother behind the shackled and gagged prince. He also leaned lewdly into the body of the man. His prick was also rigid as it pressed into Eros' firm buttocks. He wielded a razor-sharp knife that he began at once to implement with alacrity. With deft, swift strokes, he slit the prince's fine tunic from the back, and then followed by slicing the arms as easily. The expensive silk fell from the prince's body to flutter to the stone floor.

"You will first be made naked as the day you came into this world as a babe. Thus you will be prepared to be made anew as you join our Order," Eric intoned

His soft voice was steady as he stood close beside Eros and locked eyes with the muffled man. Eric was pleased with the fanciful word smithing. It sounded like something Sir Guy would say.

Giorgi stepped back for an instant while the men surveyed their handiwork. Eros' arms stretched above his head with the delicate wrists shackled by heavy leather and iron cuffs. His head was strapped with the bizarre ball-gag. His noble mouth stretched wide open around the gleaming silver ball that the leather contraption smothered his words with. He was naked from the waist up.

Eros was a lean young man, but broad of back with tightly packed muscles from shoulder down to a narrow waist. His skin was a satin-soft amber. His limbs were mostly hairless and without blemish. He was undeniably beautiful. His perfection, though, was more in the manner of an immature youth, without the world-hardened toughness of male adulthood and experience. He was an innocent!

All three men licked their lips and smirked as they contemplated their handsome captive and the events they had planned for the evening ahead.

Giorgi was the first to step forward, again wielding his sharp blade. With expert slices, the prince's light woolen trousers were shredded to pieces. Only a thick leather belt was left behind, with tattered strips of expensive cloth hanging from it. The man's finely tooled leather boots also remained, but otherwise he was now completely nude.

Light streamed down from the slatted windows above to illuminate their victim's manacled form. He seemed to glow in the dusty Palestine light, his amber flesh glimmering with that almost ethereal satiny smoothness. His lithe form had little body hair, except a thick black bush about the base of his dangling and substantial prick. The Sicilian's limbs were supple and muscular, yet there was softness there, and when the Knights' gaze fell to the pronounced swell of Eros' naked buttocks, there they saw ample, lush flesh that was tempting indeed.

Yet the beautiful youth, unblemished and not yet cowed, still seemed a prince. Even manacled, gagged and stripped naked as he was.

It was time to make him into nothing, and then remake him into a Knight of the Order Templar. The three gawking young men, the Baron's son Sir Eric, and the two Russian

234

brothers Giorgi and Petr were more than happy to commence the prince's initiation and introduce him into the exotic and erotic secrets of their Order.

"Begin with the banishing of his former attachments, through the coursing of the whip," Eric intoned.

He was in charge, as the senior member of the Order among the three. Of course he was making it all up as he went along. He had never done any such thing before. He only had the powerful memory of Sir Guy and the night they had spent, just the two of them, in that secret camp in the mountains. Eric employed that sweet recollection as his guide.

Giorgi moved speedily to the opposite end of the small cell. He fetched an instrument from the table ensconced there and brought it to his fair-haired older brother. Petr took the black leather handle in one big hand and stepped back to commence the whipping.

The crack of that whip as it sliced through the air and landed on the smooth back of the Prince resounded in the chamber and echoed toward to the vaulted ceiling. The gagged Prince's muffled cry was barely discernable. But the jerking of his body as the whip stung his back was apparent.

The Saxon locked eyes with Eros. While Petr stroked his quivering back with that evil whip, the victim and the master never looked away from each other. The Prince's eyes were full of appeal at first, then anger, then just simple pain. The whipping went on for some time. Petr was forced to remove his tunic and stand bare-chested, sweat streaming down his wide torso.

Then Eric glanced at Petr and gave him a soft nod. The whipping ended as abruptly as it had begun. Eros collapsed in his manacles, his head hanging down now that Eric no longer held his gaze. His back was trembling violently. Red stripes crisscrossed it. Sweat ran down in rivulets over the wicked stripes. The welts did not break the skin. Sir Guy would punish them severely if such a thing occurred. He might punish them anyway when he discovered their little escapade, but that was

235

something all three chose not to contemplate at the moment. Anyway, the trio had no intention of scarring such a beautiful young man. They only meant to have him feel the pain and the ignominy of the experience.

"We will now remove all vestiges of your masculinity from your flesh," Eric abruptly shouted in Eros' ear.

His voice snapped the young man's head up. Their faces were only inches away from one another. They could have kissed.

Eros had no idea of what Eric's shouted words meant. He was in agony from the whipping. He had never been punished in his life. This was a terrible humiliation for him. He was bound helpless and unable to speak out against the cruel behavior of his captors. It hurt his pride as well as his flesh. Now they were going to inflict some other bizarre action on him? What did they mean by removing his masculinity? God save him if they were intending to castrate him like some falsetto eunuch! Singing was not his forte!

When the proficient Giorgi again stood behind the Prince with his sharp knife, Eros shuddered and felt near to fainting from the fear he suffered. But then, he realized the Russian brothers were rubbing soapy water over his buttocks, between his legs, and even around to his crotch. They lathered up that area, along with eager explorations of his deep ass crevice, dangling ball sack and trembling, flaccid prick. This was not so bad, Eros thought. The slippery fingers actually titillated and almost excited him. But he was still too afraid to experience any real pleasure.

Giorgi began to scrape away what little hair he had in the crevice of his ass and between his thighs. Petr held the powerful butt cheeks apart to assist his brother. The knife slid sensually over the prince's sensitive ass flesh, right up into the crack and around his tightly clamped asshole. It was embarrassing to have all that attention on his spread ass and exposed hole, but Eros again found himself almost enjoying it. He had not expected to.

Eros shuddered though as that sharp instrument caressed his ball sack. Giorgi held each hefty nut in his palm as he stripped them of all hair. The knife scraped away at the base of Eros' limp prick and all around it. In no time at all, he was devoid of the only body hair he had, excepting the short reddish-black stubble on his head.

Petr and Giorgi washed away the soap and water. They slid their hands rudely into all the prince's private areas and enjoyed the satiny smoothness of that flesh now that it had been shaved clean. Their vulgar fondles finally stimulated even the fear-racked young Prince's libido. His formerly limp prick swelled and rose up to jut out from between his thighs. He was totally humiliated. But even so, his prick remained stiff and throbbing.

Eric was inflamed with lust when he witnessed the result of the Russian's handiwork. He had to feel that smooth flesh himself. He moved forward and slid his strong fingers along one protruding buttock. The skin was blood-warm, and clean and soft as a babe's bottom. He ran his fingers into the slick ass crack, up and down it, reveling in the silky warmth he also discovered there. Eros clenched his buttocks in an attempt to protect the quivering anal cavity buried deep in that crevice, but the Saxon sought it out and teased it with light strokes. Eric savored the way the small anal lips pouted and tensed under his manipulations.

Time for that area later, he smiled to himself. His ran his other hand down the quivering prince's supple abdomen and felt around the shaved base of that jutting prick. The flesh there, too, was smooth and devoid of any trace of hair. Giorgi had performed his labor exceedingly well.

Eric nodded to his companions who proceeded as planned. It was Giorgi this time who inflicted the demeaning punishment required on the new recruit. While the Saxon caressed the Italian Prince in front, Giorgi beat him from behind. The Russian employed another bizarre instrument from the table along the wall. It was a black leather paddle. With swift sure strokes, he belted each of their captive's freshly shaven butt cheeks.

Giorgi's muscled limbs at once began to break out into a sweat as he applied the paddle. He lay into the quivering Prince deliberately. Each timed blow was executed with all the power of his abundant strength. And each time the paddle struck, one of Eros's ample butt mounds quivered delightfully. The prince's buttocks grew steadily pinker with the flush of pain.

Meanwhile, Eric stroked the Prince's prick to a throbbing, twitching pole, while fondling his hairless balls and crotch. When that prick was ramrod stiff, Petr moved forward and handed their leader a long leather strap which Eric immediately began to wind and twist about the man's shorn ball sack.

Eros closed his eyes in a near faint as he experienced the twin sensations of the harsh paddling on his naked buttocks and the insistent stroking of the Saxon's hand on his aching prick. When Eric began to tie his sensitive nuts with that piece of leather, he bucked and moaned beneath the ball-gag muffling him.

Again, the trio stood back and surveyed their handiwork. They were in no rush. Giorgi had halted his paddling and Eros was left to catch his breath. The handsome Sicilian was bathed in sweat, his supple upper limbs trapped above him in the iron cuffs. His shaved ass was bright red from his beating. The hot cheeks trembled mightily in the painful aftermath. His prick was totally erect. The stiff meat strained against his flat, muscular belly. And below that rampant fuck stick, dangled his hairless balls. Wrapped in a long length of black string, they bulged swollen and undoubtedly ached painfully.

The scion of the Ramozas family was now ready for the next level of action. Before that, the three young captors themselves stripped. They had worked up a sweat in the warm chamber, and also worked up their libido. They were inflamed with lust. Enthusiastically, they divested themselves of what clothing they had remaining.

When all three stood facing their victim, they made a handsome trio. The muffled Prince Eros gazed at them with feverish eyes, impressed by their beauty, but also filled with fear of them, and fear of what devilish tricks they intended to inflict on him next.

The Russian brothers were almost identical, except for one being blond and one ebon-haired. As they stood side by side, their broad chests, only lightly hairy, glistened with beads of sweat. Their muscular forearms and biceps bulged. Their lower bodies were equally brawny, but covered with a fur of blond and black hair respectively. Between their thick thighs above dangling furry nut-sacks rose two massive and dripping fuck-sticks. Giorgi, the dark-haired brother, was slightly smaller in stature and build, but his wide face was similar in handsomeness to his brother's.

Beside them stood the sweetly-innocent appearing von Bartell Baron. He fairly beamed as he gazed at Eros. He relished this experience. Of course, he was recalling his own initiation at the hands of their leader, Sir Guy. This was his opportunity to apply those lessons to another. He felt certain Eros would in the end come to accept and even savor the initiation. At least he hoped so.

Eros gazed back at the Saxon. He was impressed by his beauty. Eric's body was strong, but also softly voluptuous with a layer of body fat from easy living, and an alluring light-golden tan from exposure to the desert sun. His thick mop of hair was as bright as spun gold. His boyish face was at odds with the situation. His forearms were heavy and muscular, and graced with a swirling down of thick blond fur, yet the rest of his body was practically naked of bodily hair, which added to his mien of boyishness.

Yet when his voice rang out in the cell and echoed to the ceiling, any trace of boyishness was dispelled.

"Prince Eros! You now have a choice. Do you allow us to continue, initiating you into the Order, or do you beg us to desist? That is your choice. Now is the only time I will offer this choice to you. In another minute, the choice will no longer be available."

Eros stared at the three naked men. Their protruding pricks aimed like weapons at him. His body was aflame with pain. But also he experienced some bizarre emotion new to him and as yet undefined. His balls ached, his prick ached, his ass screamed out with burning sensitivity. The three men were beautiful.

He wanted this to continue. Eros wanted more!

His eyes said it all. He could not speak, but he only had to shake his head and it would all end. The three men watching him waited expectantly. When Eros dropped his head and did nothing, they laughed in exultation, and went to work.

Eagerly they set about their business. They lit a myriad candles, setting the small cell aglow with glittering light. When this was done, they could see every bead of sweat on their victim's straining back. Eros observed everything with keen interest. Naturally he was fearful for what the men had planned next. The candles proved to be part of that.

With his soft, deceptive smile, von Bartell stood in front of Eros. The slim pillar was between them. He held one of the long burning tapers in his hand. Still smiling, he lifted up the candle and while Eros's eyes grew wide, he poised it above the prince's chest. One long drip of the burning wax landed on a small upright nipple.

Eros felt that searing pain as a jolt that coursed through his body. His muffled scream only excited the three assailants. When von Bartell repeated the maneuver on the other small nipple, they stared avidly as Eros' body writhed and bucked in apparent pain. Two or three more drips on the sensitive little nipples had each of them poking out in swollen agony.

That was just a tease for the poor prince. The men set to the real focus of their initiation. The dark-haired Giorgi was the one to present the instrument of that torture to Eros. With a bright smile, he raised up an object before the Prince's pain-wracked eyes.

Eros focused blurry, pain-wracked eyes on it. What was it? All at once he realized it was a fake penis carved of dark ebony. A bulbed head was followed by a long shaft and terminated in a rounded end. It was not as large as any of his captor's pricks. In fact it was rather slim and short. But it was menacing. There could be only one purpose for it, and one place it was intended to go.

Eros shuddered. His hefty, plump butt clenched unconsciously. His sphincter clamped down in dread.

"Yes! This dark dildo is intended for your anal cavity. We will insert it inside you, as a symbol of the breaking of your virginity, of the filling of your inner soul with the spear of our Order," Von Bartell intoned.

Eric was impressed with his own gibberish. It sounded perfect for the occasion. His stiff prick was what it was really all about, and from the looks of his fellow conspirators, they were thinking along similar lines. The Stepov brothers' erections bobbed and wove like eager snakes. The engorged rods drooled constantly.

The trio stood behind and to the side of the bound Sicilian. Each of the naked Stepov brothers clasped a butt cheek in their brawny hands and pulled it apart. They exposed the small, clenched anal cavity von Bartell had spoken of. It gleamed in the candlelight. Naked of hair, the anal lips throbbed with anxiety. Eric had the black dildo in his hand. He poured a liberal amount of glistening olive oil over the object. Now it gleamed in the light like a shining, dark spear, as he had indicated it was supposed to be in his fine speech.

With obvious relish, the Saxon planted the flared head of the thing directly against the Sicilian's quivering asshole.

Eros felt the firm wood against his clamping hole. He had seen it, and knew what was prodding at his sacrosanct sphincter. He trembled from head to toe. His prick, balls, and candle-waxed nipples all screamed with throbbing sensation, and now his tender butt hole was experiencing a warm, poking pressure. The ignominy of it all was almost too much. He let out a scream that was so profound, it could be heard even through the stifling ball-gag.

The Saxon was busy pressing the flared head of the dildo into that oiled opening. It was very snug. Eros' fear had the muscled anal rim clamped down like a vice. But Eric pressed ahead. He watched keenly as the inevitable occurred.

While the Stepov brothers also gazed intently at the exposed asshole, prying apart the large butt mounds as much as possible, that dildo began to stretch wide and then enter Eros' butt hole.

Eric persisted. He slowly inserted the dildo's head. The anal lips stretched apart as the flange at the widest part forced entry. The crown was inside, and the shaft began to follow.

Eros writhed in his cuffs. He squirmed and groaned as the invader implacably stretched him open. The pain was incredible, but his aching balls were somehow translating it into something entirely different. The thought of these handsome Knights, naked and with drooling, stiff pricks, manhandling his body like he was some tavern slut or worse, was so humiliating, the pain he was experiencing was only secondary. And the fact that his virgin anus was being crammed with a wooden dildo was equally mortifying.

Something in him unraveled. Some of his futile resistance dropped away. The dildo slid deeper. His asshole gaped open. He groaned and shoved back with his hips.

His torturers noticed this. The prince's legs came apart, and he dropped his hips down on the hand that held that dildo up between his parted thighs. The dildo slid deeper. Half of it was now inside the man's poor, distended hole.

Eric gently probed that slackening hole. In and out, he pressed deeper with every short thrust. The Sicilian felt that maddening teasing deep inside him. His quivering butt began to respond. He pressed back. Eric grinned and fed him more of the gleaming, oil-dripping dildo.

The Stepov brothers watched with rapt glee. Their own dripping pricks crowded into the Sicilian's warm outer thighs, while Eric forced the entire length of that dildo between the tight anal lips.

Suddenly it disappeared. The rounded lower end slipped inside and Eros' butt lips clamped over it. The Sicilian snorted and bucked when that had been accomplished. The sensation was so unexpected and incredible, his aching prick felt as if it might explode.

The Saxon rubbed his hands over the distended anal lips. He could feel the hard wood of the dildo just beyond being held inside by Eros' own snug anal muscles. Eric teased it, which drove Eros mad. Then Eric used his fingers to pry that tight ring apart, and the end of the dildo slipped back out into his hand. He pressed it back in, watching as it once more disappeared.

This bizarre humiliation was repeated over and over as Eric manipulated the dildo in and out of the Sicilian's straining anus. The Stepov brothers were incensed by the action. They humped their poor captive's sides with steady thrusts as they watched their leader play with his hapless hole.

Finally Eric stood back and laughed. The prince had somehow become captivated by that hard dildo squirming in his guts. Even without touching him, the Sicilian's palpitating butt hole would open up and the dildo head would be exposed. Poised on the edge of those tight anal lips, it was ready to shoot out, but remained held inside by the Prince's own greedy sphincter, and lusty hunger.

He was enjoying it!

And it was true. At some point the pain had disappeared. There was only profound, deep pleasure inside him. The hard thing planted up his butt teased his prostate and his tight anal lips. The pressure banged against his bound nuts and his aching, stiff prick. The heat of his whipped and paddled flesh only served to intensify his rapture.

Eric nodded to his companions. Giorgi was swift to respond. The men stepped away and abandoned Eros. Giorgi fetched a jar of unguent from the nearby table and brought it back.

All three naked Knights once more assaulted the shackled Prince. With gobs of the unique unguent in their palms they slathered the slick grease over Eros' entire body. Their lusty hands moved into every crevice and over every body part.

Eros howled beneath the ball-gag. Those hungry hands were full of a burning substance that inflamed his entire body, from neck to boot. The dildo still trapped in his clamping butt hole was only secondary to the heat pulsing in waves of agony over him. Abruptly, the men left him alone and stood back to observe.

Eric, Giorgi and Petr watched Eros writhe and struggle against the pillar. His body was bathed in sweat. The glow of the candles caught every droplet, while the grease they applied coagulated and emphasized the beading moisture. Eros had that bizarre contraption on his head, like a helmet, and the silver ball in his gaping mouth. He still wore the thick black belt around his waist, as well as his beautiful leather boots. Otherwise he was naked.

He twisted and moaned with his eyes half-closed in agony. His sturdy thighs were wide apart. His ass cheeks were parted. That black dildo embedded in his rectum barely glimmered as it hung suspended at the bulging anal lips.

He quivered and jerked, but then eventually a transformation began to occur.

The trio smiled as they watched. They understood what was happening to the prince. The unguent they had applied would at first sear his nerves with agonizing heat, then would cool and soothe him. His whipped back and paddled ass would no longer hurt. His body would become bathed in a cooling, relaxing balm. It was obvious this was occurring as his writhing slowed, his body slackened and eventually he slumped in his fetters.

Eric came around the Prince and stared directly into his eyes. Meanwhile, the Stepov brothers watched as his butt hole continued to open and shut over the captured dildo. It was fascinating.

244

Eric opened his mouth and covered Eros's with it. The silver ball was between their lips. Eric sucked at it, gazing deep into their prisoner's amber orbs. The bizarre kiss went on and on as Eros's battered consciousness became aware again of that dildo inside him. He was once more squirming and writhing around the invader. He somehow managed to fuck himself through his fevered gyrations.

He actually spread his thighs farther apart and humped up his large butt to better work his anal muscles around that wooden cock impaling him. The Stepov brothers had moved back in to clasp his butt cheeks, prying them apart. But they were no longer content to merely do that.

They began to run their hands up and down the slippery, shaved crack. They ran their fingers over the distended butt hole, feeling the dildo trapped inside, then poking at it as it appeared between the parting ass lips. Eros would almost expel the object, but could not quite open up his tight butt lips enough to do it. When he was on the verge of succeeding, either of the brothers would roughly shove the protruding end deep back inside his aching guts with a rude finger.

This crude stimulation was too much for the bound prince. With a violent convulsion, his prick erupted a stream of rocketing cum. He splattered his own hard belly and the more fleshy stomach of Saxon Knight in front of him.

At that moment, the dildo shot out of Eros' asshole, which suddenly gaped open at the ferocity of his orgasm. The slippery dark object was expelled in one swift eruption. The lewd instrument dropped to the floor at the Stepov brothers' feet. They had their hands down on Eros' plump butt. Spreading it wide, their eyes were glued to the sight of the young man's palpating bunghole as it drooled ass juices and oil. That hole gaped open due to the loss of the dildo that had been filling it for so long.

Eros convulsed with his orgasm, his lithe body wracked with trembling contortions. For the three torturers, this was the moment when their well-thought out plots deteriorated. The sight of the lean, but lush young prince in the throes of his orgasm, dangling from his shackles and gagged, with his tender asshole dripping and quivering, proved their downfall. No longer did they care one wit about the young man's initiation. They only wanted his beautiful body, to caress, and love, and fuck.

Petr was the first to react. With a whimpering moan, he crowded behind Eros and rammed his drooling member right up into the Sicilian's spread ass crack. The bulbous prick head pounded past Eros's gaping sphincter. That fat meat jabbed beyond and sank to the balls.

"I'm fucking him!" Petr shouted joyously. His blond head tossed backwards, his hips rammed forward, and his prick totally buried itself up the Sicilian's warm anus.

The others were as incensed. The dark-haired Giorgi's eyes went wide as he witnessed his brother's blond-furred buttocks pumping against their captive. The sight was so exciting he had to join in. Giorgi embraced the two of them from behind and ran hungry hands up and down their entwined forms. He thrust his own hard prick between his brother's heaving ass cheeks.

Eric and Eros were still kissing with the silver ball gag between them. Their eyes were locked. Soft blue on honey-amber. Eros was still shooting cum all over the Saxon's soft belly. It was at that moment the miracle occurred. Eric raised his hands and unshackled their victim, who with a moan, dropped to the floor on his knees.

Eros' face pressed into Eric's pale stomach. His cheeks rubbed against the smooth, warm flesh there. Eric's stiff prick slid over his mouth and nose. He wanted more than anything to lick it, to swallow it, to feel it in his gullet. Behind him a fat prick pounded his asshole, and two big Russians were running their hands all over him.

His balls were emptying. His seed was dripping onto the stone floor. He felt hands on his head. Suddenly the gag was released. He groaned. His mouth was wide open and empty. Then it was filled. A turgid, hot shaft slid inside.

Eric held the beautiful Sicilian's head as he fucked his mouth with his prick. Eros' hands came up and settled on Eric's butt cheeks. With greedy need they probed, pinched and finally searched out his asshole. The Sicilian was more than eager as he tongued Eric's prick. He sucked it deep into his mouth. He pulled Eric's lush hips forward while snuffling and moaning around the meat in his mouth. He was free of constraints, and free to do as he wished. This is what he wished! Cock in his mouth and up his ass!

This was the miracle. No longer was Eros the enslaved victim, but somehow he was the Master. The other three had become slaves to his beauty. They were unable to get enough of his body, his mouth, and his sweet, tender anus.

They had become a heaving mass of flesh. Their fevered hands explored, probed and even loved.

Eros nestled in the center of that vortex. He was enveloped in masculine heat. He had never felt so alive. The pain he had experienced previously was a dim memory. At that moment, he only wanted to be filled with prick forever. His guts ached with pleasure. Petr's large shaft massaged centers of sensation he hadn't known existed. He stared up at the beautiful Saxon who gazed down at him in return. There was lust there, but also more. Appreciation of mutual beauty.

The four men collapsed on the stone floor in a heap of writhing passion. The candles flickered about them. Bizarre shadows were cast on their contorting limbs. Mouths kissed, brother and brother, or Saxon and Russian, Sicilian and Russian. Pricks plied warm assholes, whose it did not matter any more. The oil flowed freely. They were slippery, tossing forms on their bellies and backs in the midst of unleashed desire.

This is how Guy found them.

Sir Guy had arrived in the night inexplicably, and unexpectedly. It was a habit of his that his Knights would have done well to pay heed to. Once he was in residence, Mamluk was obliged to inform his Master of the arrival of Sir Eros, and then lead him to the chamber where the initiation had gone awry.

The two stood in the doorway. The four men writhing on the floor were totally unaware of the onlookers. Guy watched for a few moments, then shook his head with a grin.

"Leave them for now," he whispered to Mamluk. "Time enough tomorrow to sort it out. Lock the door behind us."

Mamluk smiled as well as he left the room on the heels of the burly Sir Guy. He cast one last glance at the four sucking and fucking young Knights before bolting them inside.

They would no doubt find much to entertain themselves for the remainder of the evening. Sir Guy would discipline them at dawn.

Mamluk fervently hoped he would be present.

# Tale Nineteen: Sir Xavier Becomes a Slave

*In which Xavier de Planta of Navarre is captured by the Arabs and made into a slave, suffering the intimate and sexual whims of his new Masters.*

Sir Xavier de Planta was escorting a convoy of pilgrims toward Jerusalem on a blistering Palestine afternoon when he was captured. The Muslims appeared out of nowhere. The savage horde overwhelmed him before he could kill more than two of them. He lost consciousness as a blow struck his head.

He awoke to the sound of splashing water. The scent of incense was heavy in his nostrils adding to the ferocity of his headache. He did not open his eyes straightaway in an attempt to gather his thoughts before he moved too precipitously. His last conscious image was of the screaming Arab devils overwhelming him. He tested his body's capacities with slight movements of his hands and feet. His limbs were apparently stretched taut by something binding them, and he also realized he was standing upright, strangely enough. How could he have been unconscious and standing upright?

He opened his eyes just enough to peer about at his surroundings, but not enough to allow anyone who might be observing him to recognize that he was conscious. He found himself in a bright chamber facing a fountain at the far wall, which was the source of the splashing water. With eyes slitted half-shut he moved his head just enough to see he was bound hands and feet to some sort of framework. Sensations bombarded him as his consciousness became complete.

The beauty of the chamber around him was truly stunning. Gleaming tiles of intricate mosaic work covered both walls and floor. Several high windows bled Palestinian sunlight down on him. The fountain sparkled in that honey light. Pots of flowering trees, redolent with exotic aromas, were scattered about the walls. All this color and light assaulted his eyes like a fiery vision of some kind of gloriously adorned hell.

His body was unclad. He sensed that as much as he saw it. The hair on his limbs all at once stiffened in a bizarre charge of static electricity as a trembling shudder coursed through him. He felt pleasantly cool air caressing his nakedness. His balls dangled between his shuddering thighs, and he was keenly aware of their naked vulnerability. His quiescent dick jerked upright in sharp, unbidden lust.

Xavier was acutely aware of his thighs spread wide apart due to the manner in which his feet were clamped to the constricting frame. His buttocks were parted obscenely open. His deep ass crack experienced that same shudder, and a similar breath of cool air wafting over it. Even his small tight anus shuddered. The hole alternated between either clamping shut or gaping apart in quick, short convulsions. An unsettling sensation of expectation gripped his body, and his heart.

"Sir Knight. You're awake. And I see you're appreciating your circumstances. That is well. We are so looking forward to your future here as our biddable slave."

A quiet voice whispered those shocking words in his ear, which sent another shock wave coursing through his bound limbs. That voice was silken in tone, and uttered words in strangely accented French. The scent of the man who spoke to him invaded Xavier's nostrils. Exotic. Spices. Clean. And there was a certainty it was Arabic.

Xavier was unable to see the mysterious author of that voice. Xavier's head was held immobile in a kind of headgear that limited his movement. He wanted more than anything to turn and face his molester, but could not.

But then his thoughts were scattered, and focused at the same instant. Just as that voice lingered in his ear, Xavier sensed the barest touch of something against his asshole. He shuddered. Something was definitely touching him! That touch lightly teased the rim of his private hole. It stroked the small ringlets of dark hair that surrounded his sacrosanct anal entrance.

He shuddered again. It was a finger that had begun to caress his ass-button gently. Xavier was suddenly certain of that. And it must belong to the voice which had hissed in his ear. It was too much!

Xavier abruptly and briefly rebelled. He strained against his bindings. His hands and feet and his head all twisted and struggled with futile fury.

"No use in that. Submit, mighty Knight. We have much in store for you. Much for you to learn. Submit," that voice whispered again.

This time the finger at his asshole became suddenly wet and slippery with some slick substance.

Xavier went limp. His breath blew out in a loud gasp as the finger penetrated him. The unseen digit parted his convulsing anal lips. It dug into him. Deep. Deeper. The oiled finger probed into his insides, and into his very soul.

He bit back a scream. He had only been penetrated once in his life. It had occurred when Sir Guy and several other Knights had initiated him into the Order of the Knights Templar. He had submitted then, and never again. Now he found himself yielding to an ungodly Arab! It could not be! He would not suffer it!

He shook with rage and frustration. But also with an undeniable pleasure. The finger was slick and insistent. It did not hurt. It only teased and tickled and created a powerful heat inside him. The heat suffused through his guts down into his

251

dangling, vulnerable balls and then raced up into his stiff and jerking dick.

Through his denial, Xavier exploded in orgasm. Unwillingly, but with intense pleasure. Sperm rocketed out in front of him. He saw it clearly. Gobs of gooey cream gleamed in the bright light of the chamber. He heard laughter behind him. Cringing inwardly, he fainted.

This was the grotesque commencement of Sir Xavier de Planta's incarceration and training to become a slave to the Sheik Alballa Yusaref.

The frame in that gleaming chamber was to play a significant role in Xavier's debasement, and his ultimate exaltation as a slave to the Arabs he had always believed inferior.

Xavier awoke to his new life fettered hand and foot and collared with silver chains that were delicate and beautiful, but unbreakable. And he was naked. He would don no clothing for the next six months. Not once.

The palace he inhabited along with the Sheik and his minions was large and sprawling. Xavier was forced to labor throughout the royal buildings and their environs. He was set to backbreaking work in the fields. Or he carried and set heavy stones for walls and buildings.

The difficult toil made his already substantial muscles wax heavy and large with a masculine potency that enhanced his considerable comeliness. His body grew tanned and dark. His hair was cut short above his ears, but it became streaked with reddish glints from the innumerable hours of outside labor. His tall form became immensely appealing in its unclad, animal vigor.

But the beautifying of Sir Xavier's body was not left solely to nature's devices. The Sheik had plans for his new male toy. As the months went by, Xavier's masculine form was modified, time and time again.

The first time this occurred, Xavier had just finished a session at the Frame, as it was called by his torturers and masters. He was limp with exhaustion. His asshole twitched, his balls ached, his dick dripped, his mind was in turmoil, and his soul keened.

The Sheik, who was a short, dark, rotund individual, was the owner of that silken voice. It was the Sheik who penetrated Xavier's consciousness so deeply, as deeply as the fingers, tongues, and instruments that were daily penetrating Xavier's quivering and expanding anal entrance.

Naturally, the Sheik was in attendance as the first of the disfigurements (or enhancements, depending on one's perspective) was visited on the Spanish Knight's quaking body.

While Xavier was pinned and held by several large, half-naked Arabs, his tender nipples were pierced by a sharp, slender needle. Gleaming gold rings were then inserted. The searing pain transformed into throbbing pleasure due to the miraculous balm then applied to the swollen nibs. Xavier screamed anyway. He could not help himself. It was not the pain which elicited that anguished shriek; rather it was the debasement of his body into a pretty bauble for the Sheik's edification.

As he stared down at the golden rings in his nipples, he could only see himself as a golden toy. He had to rebel at the macabre image or lose his sanity.

It was only the first of his piercings. His ears were next. Delicate gold studs were inserted. Several graced each lobe, sparkling and contrasting with the darkness of his hair, yet catching the light along with the streaks of reddish auburn in his short but luxuriant locks.

His cruel owners pierced his navel and he howled his protest again. It was so utterly humiliating. When they pierced his dickhead, he fainted dead away. And each of these piercings was done after a session at the Frame.

The Frame: it was an exquisite torture, and at the core of all his subjugation as a slave to the Sheik Alballa Yusaref. Daily he was bound to it, hands and feet, and his head restrained by the leather contraption that forbade him to look behind and see who it was that would inflict that day's particular anal torture on him. It was always his tender butt hole that was the object of this experience.

Most of the time he knew it was the Sheik behind him.

"Open up your secret orifice for your master. Allow it to experience the pleasure you know it yearns for." That soft voice would insinuate in his ear and into his tortured psyche.

At first it was one finger. Then it was more than one. Sometimes as many as three, or two and a thumb, or the thumb alone would explore and tease his fearfully palpitating ass cleft.

Like small snakes they would slip inside him. They forced apart his tight anal lips, stretching them open, and digging beyond and into places he previously had no idea existed. He moaned, wept and sometimes begged for them to leave him alone, all to no avail. In every instance, his dick, like a traitorous criminal, rose up stiff and dripping. He always ejaculated volumes when they played with his hole. He loathed this result and felt it extremely demeaning.

Also, at first he had no control over that rear aperture the Sheik so loved to manipulate. It clamped tightly, or gaped open whether the Knight from Navarre wanted it to or no. The pain and pleasure he experienced from those intimate probes seemed not to have anything to do with his own will.

With time that began to alter, although it was a subtle change in the beginning. Xavier would be bound to the Frame. His muscular thighs quailed with fearful anticipation, and then those supple fingers would begin to caress him down there between his widespread butt cheeks. Somehow he began to realize he could open up his hole if he wanted to, or squeeze it tightly over those invading digits. If he wished, he could actually milk them with his anal muscles.

He was filled with a sickening humiliation when he realized he was doing just that. His shocked realization was followed by a whimpering moaning, then shouting, and finally by shooting out a tremendous load of jism all over the pristine, sun-drenched tiles.

The Sheik sometimes stood in front of him while another worked on his quivering slot. The man himself was really quite handsome. His swarthy features, though, were almost always screwed up in lust. His chocolate brown eyes under heavy brows were usually lidded half-shut while he gazed hungrily at his bound victim. His short body was admittedly fat, but when he sometimes disrobed to play with his thick member in front of Xavier, the Spaniard found that body to be curiously beautiful. There was muscle beneath the fat, and the rounded belly had a sensualness to it that mesmerized the naked Knight. The Sheik boasted grapefruit size balls which were shaved smooth beneath his fat dick. He would shoot his load on top of Xavier's on those tiles while laughing heartlessly.

It was during one of these occasions with the squat Sheik naked in front of him where Xavier experienced a tongue's caress on his tremulous butt hole for the first time. The tantalizing appendage slipped over his anal lips and sank into their depths with uncanny expertise. Xavier's hole opened to this foreign feeling as if it were a flower welcoming the spring sunshine. He even shoved his ass back to meet the slithering invader. His own moans were so loud, he startled himself. Xavier flushed with shame at his own actions, but his dick flushed with lust and shot a load even as that tongue fondled him mercilessly.

After one particular day toiling naked under the winter sunshine where he hauled stones with his delicate chains clinking at his every movement, he was brought into the chamber with the fountain and the Frame. Exhausted and with slack limbs, he allowed himself to be bound to that Frame.

The Sheik called two hulking Muslim warriors in. The two were naked savages with shaved pates gleaming with sweat, eyes alive with bizarre fervor, and wielded two sharp knives apiece. Xavier nearly fainted. What torture would they inflict on him now? Were they intending to mutilate him?

But no. They merely planned to divest him of his body's final covering. They were going to shave him. He had been naked for months, and now he was to be stripped naked of even his protective bodily hair.

The expertly wielded knives slid over his muscles. They scraped away all vestiges of his masculine fur. They cleaned his open armpits, his pectorals, down his belly, around the ring in his navel, and then with big Arab hands rudely holding each heavy nut in its sack, they even divested those of all their silken black hair.

A knife caressed each of his large butt cheeks. It slid over the firm mounds teasingly then slipped into the parted crack, which had Xavier quivering from head to toe. His asshole betrayed him as it palpitated rapidly like an eager dog wishing to be petted. There, too, his hair disappeared. When they completed their task, the Sheik surveyed the once proud Christian Knight with satisfaction. The gleaming rings at nipples, navel, and drooling dickhead were bright and shiny against his utterly smooth, tanned flesh. Only the lustrous red-black mane on his head remained. He whimpered and shook like a wild dog when the next grotesque procedure was inflicted on him.

From behind him, the same two naked Arabs shoved a strange type of bladder up between his shaved ass cheeks. They rammed a long stiff tube far up inside him. The bladder was squeezed, and its liquid contents gushed into Xavier's guts. He shook violently. The strange sensation was both erotically pleasant and horribly degrading. He felt his stomach distend with the liquid and his body tense around the invading juices.

He almost swooned. A delicious sensation began to emanate from his quivering asshole up through his guts and finally up to his head. He felt half-delirious. The bladder's spout was removed. A large Arab hand pressed against his distended, shaved belly and the liquid was unceremoniously expelled from his shuddering anus. He groaned. His thighs were splayed wide apart and his buttocks shaking as the liquid drained from his body. It was washed away with lemon-scented water.

One of the giant Arabs stood in front of him and began to massage his own massive prick. He coated it with glistening olive oil then rubbed it lasciviously until it grew to gigantic proportions. With a barbarous smirk, he moved behind the semi-delirious Xavier. While the Sheik laughed mirthlessly and played with his own hard dick, Xavier felt the huge Arab knob probe against his just-shaved asshole.

Oil eased the giant member's entrance, while Xavier's exhausted and drugged body was drained of opposition. He could only whimper incoherently as the Arab dick buried itself in his guts. He rocked back and forth in his bonds as that mammoth phallus fucked in and out, first stuffing his insides then leaving them empty, then filling them again. He could not rid himself of the huge, unholy prick. He spurted jism in a wild arc that landed on the Sheik's jiggling, naked belly.

That was his first prick fuck, but more was to follow, much more at the frightful Frame. But first he was tattooed. While immobilized in the Frame, his torturers decorated his body with vilely humiliating tattoos, while he could do nothing but writhe in pain and submit. They tattooed him a new collar to replace the silver one, so that afterward a permanent band snaked darkly around his thick neck. Other tattoos were inked around his bulging biceps, his wrists, and then one was made to writhe up from his left ankle to his left thigh. And finally as a sign of his slavery, his right buttock was tattooed with a tiny, but vibrant-red Muslim crescent moon.

How much time passed, Xavier was only able to fathom by first the waning of the autumn, and then the passing of the winter. When spring was near, he was still busy at his back-breaking labors outside the Palace. The first hints of that season were the sweet scents beginning to caress his nostrils and naked flesh. His responsive, well-trained body felt the power of that burgeoning season. New life was being infused in his hugely swollen muscles by the exacting labor he performed.

By this time he was being taken to the Frame as a daily ritual.

257

The Sheik and his minions utilized the strange bladder to clean his rear orifice, and would often add some bizarre drug to the contents of it. Some days he would feel drowsy and compliant, with his asshole opening up for fingers, tongue or dick after dick. Other days his anal lips would quiver with a wild burning and itching so that he craved something, anything, to fill the hole, stretch those twitching lips, stuff him deep and ease the throbbing itch. Of course that was exactly what would happen. The Sheik's men often fucked him with their vile pricks, but then they began to abuse him with all manner of instruments.

Dildos of every shape, color, and design were stuffed up his burning slot. The Arab savages would display the lewd monstrosity to him, glistening with perfumed or drugged oils, before they crammed it up his asshole,

In the Frame, Xavier was bound hand and foot. He was unable to move any of his limbs more than a few inches. And his head was immobilized by the leather strap encasing it so it too could move barely at all. The only parts of his body that were afforded some motion were his hips and buttocks. When spring arrived, and its seductive aromas and emotions overtook him, he found himself writhing in that Frame. His buttocks shoved back for more of whatever flesh or lewd instrument was fucking up between them. His dick thrust forward to rape the air. He would even roll his hips lasciviously to massage the dick or dildo that was at that moment violating his butt hole.

He had come very far from that first awakening when a single finger up his poor bunghole had felt like death itself. There seemed no turning back, now. When the Sheik himself was behind him, whispering grossly, fucking him with his fat dick, he would try not to listen. But those silken words would insinuate into his ears just as surely as the Sheik's engorged cock slithered into his asshole.

"Submit, mighty Knight. You are nothing now but a butt hole slave. You are a fucked and humiliated toy for my delectation. Your body is decorated, tattooed, be-ringed and shaved to make it ravishing. All solely for my pleasure. Surrender to it. Enjoy it. Make love to me with your hole. Make love to me with your soul," the awful words would chant in his ear.

He would resist. He would deafen his head and heart to those words, but his body responded otherwise. His traitorous body squirmed more and more willingly under the anal assaults. His buttocks parted with increasing obedience. His asshole quivered and spasmed and eventually gaped wide open for the numerous invasions it experienced.

The assault that sent him over the brink occurred some six months after he had been captured and enslaved.

The Sheik stripped naked in front of him. His rotund but exotically attractive body was oiled to a gleaming perfection. His fat cock was erect and throbbing between his dark thighs. He laughed as he stared into Xavier's soft blue eyes. He raised his right hand and while still laughing, he made a fist. He coated it liberally with the scented olive oil.

Xavier did not understand, or did not allow himself to understand the gesture.

He only understood when he felt the Sheik's fingers probing behind him. He understood when those fingers began insinuating themselves between his parted butt cheeks, spreading his quaking ass lips, and then digging deeper and deeper into his aching anus. With a groan of shocked understanding, he realized what the clenched fist had signified. He felt the increasing pressure of more and more of the Sheik's fingers, then finally the thumb added to press against his defenseless ass ring.

Xavier decided to save himself, to save his trembling asshole from pain, and to sacrifice his sanity at the same time. He let out one loud bestial shout, and then shoved back with his shaved, muscular buttocks. He took the fist in its entirety. He willed his spasming anal muscles to expand and to welcome inside the huge invader. His asshole swallowed the Sheik's fist.

Xavier gave up his asshole, and his soul.

He fucked himself on that monster fist. Once he had given in to the brutal invasion, the next step in his degradation was effortless. He writhed, bucked, and squirmed around that buried fist. All the while he listened to the Sheik's silken utterances, his minions' enthusiastic shouts of encouragement, and his own profane whimpers. The beautifully tiled, sunlit chamber reverberated with obscene song.

His orgasm was total. His entire body convulsed when his prick erupted. He was nothing more than a limp rag and a gaping, sloppy hole after that.

The Sheik was not satiated until he had teased and probed Xavier's stretched anus for another good hour.

The next time he was led to the Frame, he was totally subjugated. His dick grew stiff as soon as he entered the tiled chamber. When the bindings were complete, and he was spread-eagled and naked and immobilized, he sighed deeply and found himself writhing his bare ass backward into the empty air. His asshole gaped open. Expectant, willing, and even eager. He was now nothing more than an agreeable hole. He was a slave void that eagerly awaited his total debasement at the hands of his masters, the Arabs.

Xavier recalled with vivid detail the harem he and his fellow Knights had discovered months previously. He recalled the willing slaves who had not only allowed the Knights to fuck them, but had taken great pleasure in the debased violation. He had thought them disgusting. He had thought he could never be as they. Yet he had enjoyed using them. He had enjoyed making them grovel and worship his mightier self.

Now Xavier was the abject hole. Now Xavier writhed in the Frame, humping empty air, wanting his anal void filled with dick, tongue, fingers, dildos, fists, anything to make him whole. He wept as he realized who he had become, but he understood that did not want anything else. He was who he was now, a hungry, insatiable slot for the plugging.

At first, in his dazed stupor of lust and self-realization, he did not realize that the Sheik and the others had left the room. As he whimpered and writhed in his bindings his solid ass clenched and his hips slowly humped as if he was already being violated. All this was under a daze of expectation. What vulgar pleasure would his hole next receive?

No one was in the room. He was alone. Then he began to realize there was some kind of altercation going on outside the chamber. It went on for some time, and he remained alone, hanging vulnerably in the Frame.

When a strange man finally appeared in front of him, at first he did not recognize him.

Then, Xavier believed he must be dreaming, or in a delirium. Looming before him stood a powerfully huge Knight, with honey-blond hair and beard that was as beauteous as the morning sunlight. It was Sir Guy, the Master of Castle Rock.

His Master, Sir Xavier's Master. Or the Sir Xavier that had previously existed, but he had thought vanished.

The moaning Spanish Knight refused to believe that it really was Sir Guy. Instead he continued to groan and writhe within the Frame in a bizarre sexual stupor.

Guy gazed at his former friend. He was naked and bound up in a strange framework. But there was no denying Xavier was absolutely stunning in his bizarre beauty. Other Knights crowded around to stare in awe and disbelief at what Sir Xavier had become. They had just succeeded in capturing the Palace of Sheik Alballa Yusaref. Then they had discovered their friend and fellow Knight whom they had been searching for over the past several months.

They were astounded by the sight. Xavier had grown monstrous with muscle. His body was ebony-dark from the sun, head to toe, while the gleaming flesh had shaved of all bodily hair. The tanned, shaved flesh caused his spread-eagled muscles to appear larger than life. The bizarre tattoos around each massive muscle accentuated their brawny masculinity. The rings on his nipples made those protuberances seem highly sexual, and the one at his stiff, dripping dick was startling. All in all he presented an unbelievably shocking, and exotic sight.

Yet the most disturbing aspect of Xavier's appearance was the bestial moaning flowing from his slack mouth. He gazed at them as if they were strangers. And what he was uttering shocked them most of all.

"Fuck me. Fill my cavity with something, anything. Make me your hole, make me take your cock, your fingers, your fist up my slick manhole, please, please, please! I need something inside my poor slave butt ..." and on and on he begged with crazed eyes.

Sir Guy stepped forward. He stared into Xavier's eyes, recognized the madness there, and instinctively understood the cure. He smiled as he caressed the man's handsome face. Then he stepped behind Xavier, pulled down his own drawers and inserted his giant manhood inside the gaping anus Xavier presented so wantonly.

The other Knights also understood. To a man, they stripped and came forward. A dozen of them fondled, caressed and played with every part of Xavier's bound body. They made love to him, like he had never been made love to before. They milked several loads of cum from his stiff dick, which remained hard for the following hour.

Then they released him from the Frame and enveloped him in their brawny, familiar arms.

They had rescued Xavier, who eventually made a full recovery at Castle Rock. But at his request, Guy had another Frame installed in one of the myriad chambers in that huge Castle.

Every so often, when the craving would come on Xavier, he would have himself bound to it. One or many of the Templar would have their way with him. He would find himself suspended in the Frame with thighs widespread. His asshole would twitch wildly, as if it was calling for someone to tend to it.

And they would.

# Tale Twenty: Sir Guy's Triumph

*In which Guy is honored for his efforts in the Holy Land and celebrates with his men in an incredible orgy under the direction of Philippe.*

It has been three years since I became Master at Castle Rock here on the coast of Latin Palestine. For a time, I was dethroned by Olaf, but that proved temporary. On this third anniversary, I was fortunate enough to receive an honor that although it did not transcend my holy position as Master of the Order of the Knights Templar at Castle Rock, was still an incredible tribute.

I lounged contentedly in my bath on that morning. Scented steam from the hot water floated around my head as I looked out the open window and contemplated the nearby coast and cloud-filled skies. It would storm very soon. As I inhaled the redolent moisture, I recalled another morning three years previously when it had stormed violently while I lay in this same bath.

I grinned at that recollection. On that stormy afternoon, I had bent my loyal servant over in this very bath. I slid my heavy fist up his squirming buttocks while he moaned with pleasure and admitted to my dominance through his utter submission.

Now I awaited him so that he could assist me in my bath once more, as always. On this day, I was to be crowned Steward of the Middle Levantine Princedom. I was more than content to luxuriate in my hot tiled tub and contemplate the glorious career I had enjoyed in the Holy Land with the Knights Templar. It

had been exciting and exotic. It had also been exceedingly
fulfilling in a sexual sense. I had learned much about my own
inner desires, and as much about those of others.

As I pondered the gathering storm and basked naked in
the heated bath, I noted a disturbance behind me. I turned,
thinking it must be Mamluk.

"Are you here to assist your Master at last? You're not
usually so slow…" I began, but when I laid eyes on the two
men approaching, I was startled enough to halt in mid-speech.

Mamluk was there of course, but with him was my most
loyal of Knights, the Burgundian Sir Philippe de Chanson. The
two men were naked, or at least semi-naked. Mamluk preceded
the tall auburn-haired Knight. My slave's dusky flesh was
adorned only by a slim silver collar around his plump neck.
Attached was a lengthy silver chain Philippe held in one hand.

Philippe smirked. His sensual lips curved upwards in
that half-insolent smile he often sported as he spoke. "My Lord
and Master, I bring your servant, the Arab Mamluk. Chained, he
is a symbol of your glorious triumph over the infidel here at
Castle Rock!"

I rose from the bath, water dripping from my nude body.
My cock rose up at once as the sexual magnetism of the scene
engendered a surge of lust on the instant.

Philippe was attired in an elaborate harness of leather
and buckles that lewdly accentuated his muscular form. Thick
leather crisscrossed his chiseled chest while leaving his pecs
and nipples bare. More leather surrounded his lean waist and
jutting buttocks. The black leather wove under his cock and ball
sack with snug intimacy. His crotch and ass were exposed, as
were most of his fine long legs, except where heavy leather
boots encased these below the calves. He towered over the
shorter Arab. His well-formed hand firmly grasped the silver
chain that symbolized our power over the infidel here in the
Holy Land.

Of course, the canny Philippe had arranged this scene as
a commencement of the celebration of my ascendancy to the

264

throne of the new Stewardship. I had to ponder what other libidinous festivities he had in store for me.

I bowed my head to acknowledge the men's efforts. My grin matched Philippe's. The pair approached me at once, and Mamluk fell to his knees at my feet. His luscious lips opened, his sweet mouth reached forward, and he engulfed my stiffening cock to the root in one slippery gulp.

His eyes lifted toward mine. Those soft amber orbs overflowed with submissive love for me. I smiled down at him and caressed his dark curls. The ever present scent of lemon and Arabic spices wafted up from his nakedness to pleasingly invade my nostrils.

I looked up into the piercing green eyes of my fellow Knight. His gaze was not as submissive as the Arab's, but it was full of as much love. Philippe believed in me. He trusted me absolutely and saw in me the leader he would follow to his death. I returned that love in full measure.

I reached out to lay a trusting hand on his shoulder, even as I shuddered slightly from the effects of Mamluk's sweet lips bobbing over my member.

"Today is your day, Master," he said and nodded his head in obeisance. He looked up and smirked once more. He had definitely planned something! With his obscene imagination, it was sure to be wild and unpredictably bizarre.

In his free hand he held a strange contraption. Similar to the harness he wore, I knew it was handmade by our crafty Knights. After our journey to Constantinople and visit to the dungeon run by the evil Lord Barabas, we were stimulated to grow very inventive in our sexual experimentation. We created more and more unusual garb and instruments to further our gratification.

Philippe held a black leather belt, which he proceeded to fit onto my kneeling Arab slave. While Mamluk's satin lips massaged my hard shaft, Philippe pried apart his plump ass cheeks. He wound the studded belt around Mamluk's waist and snapped it in place. But there was more to the ingenious contraption. Another strap connected the front of the belt, which was pulled down between Mamluk's parted thighs and came up between those plump brown butt cheeks. As I gazed down at my exotically hairless Arab slave, I could see Philippe spread apart Mamluk's butt cheeks and expose the shaved anus. Philippe began to insert a thick, rounded plug that attached to the black leather belt that was being pulled up between Mamluk's parted cheeks.

Mamluk groaned around my cock in his mouth. He shoved his ass backwards and spread his thighs apart to accept the large implement forcing its way into his snapping anus. My cock went deeper into his throat as the black plug plunged between his ass lips.

The gross thing was large, and got larger before it tapered to a smaller base attached to the leather strap. Philippe panted as he shoved the plug deeper. Mamluk's greased anal entrance was shiny as it expanded to accept the increasing girth of that plug.

Finally, the plug popped entirely within, and Philippe pulled up the strap and connected it to the back of the belt around Mamluk's waist. The black thing had disappeared up Mamluk's hairless hole, and now hid behind the strap that snaked up along his crack and attached to the black belt surrounding his trembling waist. The plumpness of his buttocks was accentuated by the snug belt. The idea of that big plug jammed up his asshole was extremely arousing.

Philippe rose up and leaned forward to kiss me. His full lips covered mine and his tongue slithered inside. A deep soul kiss massaged my tongue and teeth. He pulled away and smiled into my eyes. His green orbs sparkled like a mountain lion's on the verge of pouncing.

"And now for the next event in our day's festivities," he announced gleefully.

"Ah. I'm certain you have an inspiring day planned!" I laughed outright with my cock jerking inside the warm confines of Mamluk's mouth.

My bobbing member was extricated from that mouth. Mamluk toweled me dry and combed my shoulder-length blond hair while the belted plug squirmed within his palpitating butt hole. Even though I laughed at the sexual implications, I caressed his head often and smiled into his submissive eyes. Although I loved Mamluk dearly, the thought of him attending me with that plug up his butt hole as a symbol of the Arabs whom I'd subjugated, was a pleasing experience.

I remained nude as Philippe led me on to the next event.

We ascended stairs to the Feast Hall, which was bright with morning light. The sun temporarily broke through the ominous clouds just as we arrived. This chamber was redolent with the scent of lemon and orange trees, which were planted in huge pots around the perimeter. The long wooden feast table was bare, except at one end, where a tall unclad man stood.

His wrists were bound in heavy iron shackles, and a thick chain dangled between them. His ankles were also bound by the shackles and a heavy iron bar prevented him from closing his widespread thighs, which were forced uncomfortably far apart. He faced away as we approached so that his alabaster-pale ass was exposed to our view. A dimpled and pink anus was just visible between the parted cheeks.

"Sir Olaf Thorsen at your disposal, Master Guy," Philippe announced with relish.

The gleam in my subordinate's eye made me chuckle with a similar emotion. Standing in front of me in chains was the man who had usurped my authority, albeit temporarily, when he arrived at Castle Rock with instructions to take over our faction of the Templar.

Philippe moved forward swiftly. The Burgundian yanked on the chain that held the tall Swede's wrists and unceremoniously drew him forward so that he sprawled out the length of the feast table. Olaf's long arms stretched out. Their heavy musculature gleamed pale against the dark wooden tabletop. His broad back stretch out as well, while he was bent over at the waist, so his rounded buttocks jutted out behind him.

He turned his head and glared back at me. Those sharp blue eyes were full of only partially cowed arrogance. He knew he had humiliated me at one time, but that I had proved to be the better man. There was respect there, and yet he was still not quite humble enough. As I gazed at his handsome face, the short red hair of his scalp and beard neat and perfect, I realized what I must do.

I glanced up to see Philippe grin and nod. He could very often discern my thoughts.

I stepped forward. My calloused hand slid down between those parted ass cheeks displayed so provocatively in front of me. The smooth flesh was practically hairless, particularly within the satin ass furrow. My fingers grazed the sphincter and Olaf's huge bent-over form quivered delightfully. A loud resigned sigh burbled out from his pursed lips. I think he surmised what I had in store for him.

Mamluk was there to assist as usual. The butt-plugged slave cradled a stone jar of white grease in his soft hands. He grinned as broadly as Philippe and I. We three shared the same thoughts.

I reached into the jar and scooped out a liberal handful of beef lard. I transferred the white grease to Olaf's quivering ass crack. The bar that connected his ankles prevented Olaf's hefty thighs from closing. Although he squirmed and attempted to bring his legs together as I poked at his defenseless hole, he was unable to forestall my onslaught. My fingers entered his rear sanctum. The squishy flesh parted, and as Olaf groaned and begged and called me his Master, I filled him with more and more fingers until I had all of them and my thumb pressing against his stretched rim. With steady pressure I forced my entire fist inside him.

As I stared down at my wrist protruding from Olaf's impossibly breached rectum, I laughed out loud. The dripping animal grease coating his quaking ass cheeks suited the situation perfectly. Olaf had fisted me in front of the entire assembly of Knights at one time, now the favor was returned.

"The Viking submits," Philippe chortled with satisfaction.

We both stared at the shaking Swede, whose brow was knitted in a mixture of both agony and rapture. Sweat poured off his body as he lay sprawled across the wooden table. A fist was crammed up his butt hole, his thighs were held apart by hard iron, and his mouth was open in a soundless moan of abdication.

I fisted him deeply. The torrid innards of his body were a pit of pleasure for my exploring fingers. But the most satisfying element of all proved to be Sir Olaf's loud grunts emitted after every deep gut-punch. He sounded like a mewling pig. His bulky body tensed, his big ass rose up, and he shoved back against my fist. Uttering another of those pig-grunts, he spewed a load of spunk all over the rough wooden table.

I did not achieve orgasm at that point, although I did savor a tingling sense of fulfillment at the undoing of the haughty Swede.

Philippe was already orchestrating the next event while this nasty one was winding down. The shuddering and just-fisted Swede was released. He was obliged to kneel down and fit my feet into a pair of heavy black leather boots. Those boots were to be my only attire. I was led by Philippe in his outlandish leather costume into another chamber previously prepared for our arrival. Following us were the butt-plugged Mamluk and chained Olaf.

I was confronted with another scene of sexual incredulity.

Suspended from the arched ceiling, two pairs of bound men dangled in midair. Each pair was wrapped in multi-colored silken ropes, which tightly bound their naked bodies together. Their thighs were upraised and wrapped around each other's backs leaving their asses exposed. They floated above us in the airy chamber.

This was one of the halls that led to the upper rooms. An arched high ceiling was dotted with windows that allowed the cloud-dappled light to play across the brightly painted stuccoed walls, and across the four trussed men.

I recognized them immediately. One pair consisted of the Della twins from Aragon. Their distinctively lean and dusky bodies were entangled and wrapped by the colorful silken ropes. The other pair was made up of the Stepov brothers from Russia. One was dark-haired and the other blond, but both were heavily muscled with bodies nearly identical. The sight of the two pairs of brothers in the forced embrace was definitely stirring.

Seated against the walls other men surrounded us. All had donned masks so I could not pick out their identity. Each played an instrument and exotic Arabic music beat through the chamber. The hanging brothers slowly revolved in their suspended state to the beat of that pulsing, erotic euphony.

Philippe stepped forward and gripped the end of a long chain that connected with a block and tackle in the ceiling. As I watched with curious interest, the bound Della twins were lowered slowly until they were at a height just above my waist and directly in front of me. Their plump brown buttocks were exposed, and their twin assholes twitched open between their elevated thighs.

Mamluk was close. This time the slave bore a brass vase that contained scented oil. He poured the oil over my bobbing prick, after which I stepped up beneath the suspended brothers. Philippe lowered them further until Jaime's sweet asshole just touched the flared head of my raging fuck tool. I moaned as he lowered the pair slowly. It was just enough so that Jaime's ass pit could encircle my oiled cock head. The warm orifice tantalized as it pulsed around the sensitive bulb. Philippe lowered them further and that throbbing hole swallowed the entire head of my cock and some of the engorged shaft.

Philippe deftly raised and lowered the pair of tightly bound Spaniards. Jaime whimpered as he was impaled on my stiff meat. Then, they were raised and their bodies slowly turned so that this time it was his brother Alphonse, who was lowered over my up thrust shank.

While I stared at the moaning brothers, they gazed into each other's eyes and then kissed. It was lewdly shocking to watch the brothers' tongues invading each others lush mouths. It was also feverishly thrilling to feel their quivering anuses rise up and down over my bone-hard cock.

Meanwhile, the giant Swede moved in beneath the suspended Russian brothers. He applied his revived fuck-meat to the same purpose. While the Arabic music beat and swirled around us, our two rods plowed the brothers' defenseless butt holes. Philippe was in charge as he raised and lowered the pairs in an obscene rhythm over our oiled shafts.

The red-headed Swede glistened with sweat as his alabaster body thrust to the beat of the music. Olaf shoved his monster pole between the Russian brothers' white ass cheeks, one after the other.

We traded places. I caressed the Stepov brothers broad Slavic faces as they also locked lips and tongued each other. My cock plied their well-oiled and dilated anal slots. They swirled around in front of me as they floated in mid-air. Their muscled bodies were wrapped tightly together, and they were unable to squirm or move away as they were fucked and fucked until their mashed bellies ran with mutual cum.

I was drilling the blond Petr's hefty white ass when I realized he and his brother were experiencing their orgasms. His asshole clamped over my slippery cock as his body tensed under an explosion of cum. The Russians were in the midst of a deep kiss with their mouths hungry over each other's lips. Their handsome faces dripped sweat. Their cocks were hidden between their tightly bound stomachs, but gooey man-cream dribbled from their sides to prove their orgasms.

Eventually the pairs of brothers were lowered to the floor and released. Nude and groveling on the floor before me, they licked my boots as their bare asses were fucked one more time for good measure by the eager Olaf. He was a giant rutting beast as he shoved his lengthy pole into each of their pliant ass clefts one after the other. Finally he shot a stringy load over Jaime Della's dusky back.

Philippe led us on after that stimulating interlude. This time an entourage of men followed. The naked Della and Stepov brothers were right behind Mamluk and Olaf, and the masked musicians, each of them naked, followed. I had recognized many of them, although their faces were hidden. I was familiar intimately with the bodies of my fellow Knights!

We arrived at the audience chamber. The lengthy pillared hallway had its huge doors at either end thrown open, so that we could take in the entire length of the room. In the center a high skylight bathed a circular area with illumination. Painted stone columns surrounded this circle and within that light-infused area another scene of bizarre bondage awaited us.

From a distance I could see a trio of slings suspended from the surrounding columns. Each was occupied by a naked man!

Their arms and legs were elevated and shackled wide apart. As we drew nearer, my stiff prick ached from anticipation. I had not cum and my churning balls were tested to their limits by the intensity of the sexual pleasure I had already experienced.

The Arabic music continued. That well-executed playing lulled us into a state of suspended tension. Heightening our experience, this music was both indolent, and inflaming.

Lit braziers lined the walls. Swirls of herbed smoke rose to curl and eddy in the slanted light above the naked and slinged Knights who awaited us in the distance.

I was tremulous with passion, and the music had increased to a feverish pitch by the time we reached the men.

I recognized them. A trio of blond Germans was surrounded by the floating mists of scented smoke. Their sweet young flesh was bathed in sweat. Their eyes were wild. They were obviously under the influence of the herbs. Their cocks pulsed where they lay on their trembling bellies. Each man's member was swollen with lust.

272

Two of the men were Saxons, von Bartlet and von Bartell. One was a young Baron, the other a son of a Baron, Siegfried and Eric. The third was Heinz Brauhauf of Bavaria. All three boasted a voluptuous muscularity. All three were fettered in their hanging slings.

My eyes zeroed in on their upended buttocks. Each ass was equally ample and enticing. Light blond fur covered Heinz's hefty bum, while the others were hairless and sleek. Heinz sported the biggest tool, which had swollen to nearly twice the size of the others. Each man's ass crack was spread wide open in the sling with his ankles elevated high above him. Each could only moan and gawk half-dazed at our approach.

This time there were many of us who caressed the fettered men. We walked around them in a slow circle. Their open asses were accessible to us all as we poked and prodded at the gaping holes between their spread butt cheeks. They jerked and groaned deliciously as fingers slid into palpitating anal cavities. Their cocks leapt up and leaked cum continuously. Their mouths opened in moaning pleas for us to use them, to touch them, and to fuck them.

We did.

Proceeding in a leisurely circle, my naked comrades and I teased the slippery, dilated slots one after the other. Each blond German reacted similarly to the fingers teasing his asshole. Their herb-induced state provoked them into focusing their physical sensations on those aching orifices.

I palpated the squishy interior of my secret favorite. I had taken Eric von Bartell to that secret pool in the mountains and taught him the meaning of submission more than two years earlier. I recalled how he became a willing vessel for my cock that night, and now I slid a pair of thick fingers deep into his pliant hole while he gazed up at me with profound passion.

We fingered the slick holes for some time. We employed three and four digits at once as the German Knights became more accustomed to the anal assaults. Finally, they seemed to reach a mutual crescendo of emotion. Their

273

combined moans grew into a thrilling song of lust. This sexual keening rose higher and higher with the chanting of the masked Knights and the irresistible beat of the erotic music.

Finally Heinz could not hold back. His huge cock reared straight up in the air, his hefty body writhed in his sling, while his steamy asshole was crammed with three of Petr Stepov's fingers. Heinz blew a load of spunk that splattered upwards onto his own sweating face. His tongue lolled out between his lips and licked at the juicy cream like a famished beast.

Eric followed. His cock erupted similarly while my fingers dug far up his squirming anal burrow. The blond-bearded Baron, Siegfried, was the final participant in the orgy of orgasm. His member jerked thrice dry before it also unloaded a gooey geyser of cream. His sloppy sphincter was being pried apart by three of Olaf's long fingers. The Swede laughed out loud at the pleasure of forcing the cum out of the herb-drugged Baron.

The three Germans were released. Their nude, sweat-dripping bodies were incorporated into the train of chanting men who followed us to the next destination.

Philippe led. The harnessed Burgundian strode ahead of us with his tight, high buttocks pumping up and down in front of me. Those perfect cheeks were surrounded by the leather harness that outlined each in black. My cock stood upright, drooling copiously, and hard as iron. I realized as I stared at Philippe's bizarrely accoutered body that I was also affected by the herbal smoke.

But I could not even think those thoughts clearly. The chanting of those following us combined with their drums, flutes, and stringed instruments into a wild cacophony of deranged music that only confused and intensified my cravings.

We descended to the bowels of Castle Rock. Our obvious destination was an apartment where I suspected what awaited us. When we entered the darkened room, braziers barely illuminated the rocky walls, and there he was.

He stood within the Frame that had held him for many months as a captive of Sheik Alballa Yusaref. In that Frame, he had learned ultimate submission. The man bound within that Frame was the comely, and somewhat alien, Sir Xavier de Planta of Navarre.

Flickering light played across his muscular body. He was spread-eagled in the wooden contraption brought here especially for his pleasure after I had rescued him.

Entirely naked, his heavily muscled limbs devoid of all bodily hair, the clump of lustrous auburn hair on his head a contrast to that total nakedness, he faced me now. His outstretched arms were tattooed with black bands that surrounded his massive biceps, his strong wrists, and his bull neck like a permanent collar. The bizarre tattoo that snaked up from his left ankle around his huge thigh and ended just below his dangling balls further accentuated his shorn beauty.

And then there were the piercings.

Each nipple held a thick gold ring which caused the nubs to stick out as if swollen with lust. Down in the midst of his flat, hairless belly another ring gleaming golden. Below that, on the head of his jutting, semi-stiff cock, another ring of gold glittered. His delicate ears were pierced by a dozen or more small gold studs. All that gold glinted luxuriously in the torchlight.

Our eyes met briefly. His were full of expectation and adoration. I had been his savior. Afterward, I allowed him at special times to continue with his own moments of profound pleasure in that Frame in our dungeon.

I smiled as I was led behind the Spanish Knight where I was treated to the sight of his spectacular backside. Sweat glistened over his muscular back. It ran down in rivulets to the furrow of his parted ass crack. His ankles were shackled far apart at either side of the Frame, which forced his buttocks to yawn open. That naked ass was truly glorious. A small crescent moon, a symbol of his subjugation by the Arabs, graced one butt cheek. But other than that, the ass globes were rounded, massively muscular, and as smooth as the finest silk.

While gazing at that perfect bottom, I first heard the voice of an angel.

At the sound I peered over Xavier's shoulder to notice a kneeling man remove his black leather mask. It was Gerhardt Slalciz, the Swabian Knight. His voice was the one that rose to echo magnificently up into the rafters.

Gerhardt was the mystical one among us. By natural intuition, he understood the mysteries of the Holy Land and interpreted their exotic significance to us often, as he did now through his song.

The naked Knight was beautiful in his rapture. His short raven hair and neat goatee accentuated the pallidness of his face. Wide innocent blue eyes lifted reverentially toward the ceiling and the heavens above. He uttered a softly ululating melody that both chilled my soul, and stabbed at my balls. My prick bobbed and leaked in a dance of mystery and lust in the wake of such a wondrous song.

Philippe and Mamluk stepped up beside me. One was on my right, the other on my left. Between them they held another bizarre contraption, which they immediately fitted to my waist. This was another sexual toy that our imaginative craftsmen at Castle Rock had created.

A heavy leather belt was strapped around my waist. Philippe then fitted a gargantuan fake cock over my own hard one. A wooden sheath surrounded my shank snugly. It was attached to the leather belt and secured by another strap that slipped between my thighs from in front and hooked onto the waist strap behind. It was all extremely tight, and constricted my cock, balls and ass almost painfully. Especially so now that my tool grew even larger and harder with the strange sheath encasing it.

At that point a monstrous wooden penis jutted out from my hips. It was thrice the size of any man's I had ever had the good fortune to look on.

The dizzying emotion coursing through me could not be gainsaid as I stared down at that heroic prick thrusting out at my waist. I felt a surging power that nearly overwhelmed me.

I wanted to stab forward with my new monstrous member and drive between Xavier's parted ass cheeks. I wanted to impale him to the hilt with the thing.

Before my unnatural ardor got the best of me, another Knight slid in between my prey and me. He was as naked as the singing Gerhardt, and he also removed his mask.

I recognized Jan the Dane. He knelt behind Xavier at once and reached out to grasp each of his silken butt globes. As I watched with lustful eyes, he buried his face between them. Even with the dazzling music surrounding us I could still hear Sir Jan's slobbering mouth and lips eating out Xavier's butt hole.

Xavier finally spoke. He began to beg as soon as he felt that expert mouth on his tender slit. "Oh! My hole! Yes! Lick out my swollen ass pit! Please! Stick your tongue up inside me!"

The nasty words vied with Gerhardt's mystical song and became lost in it. Xavier found a rhythm with that other voice and continued to chant his lewd pleas in a non-stop sing-song.

"Oh! Love my hole! Tongue my depths! Eat my soul! Please, oh please, oh please!"

I watched the busy mouth plying that reddened hole. Jan's big tongue slid up and over the anal lips, then dove between to rapidly stab at the inner flesh. My cock ached where it was trapped within the wooden dildo. My prick throbbed and drooled as it craved to find its way into that enticing Spanish asshole.

Jan's naked form shone with sweat as he worked over the asshole bound in the Frame and gyrating obscenely in front of him. The muscular mounds pressed back against Jan's face. The globes writhed with sexual abandon. The Dane's shoulder-length copper locks bobbed as he mouthed up and down the slippery crack and then zeroed in on that wet hole again and again.

I could not help myself and reached forward to force that handsome face deep into the Spaniard's crack. I held the Dane's mouth against that palpitating butt hole. In lieu of the Spaniard's sweet slot, I reached down with my other hand and fingered Jan's butt hole. The Dane's knees flailed wide as he welcomed my blunt digits into his own straining anus.

Eventually I could no longer control myself and thrust the kneeling Dane aside. Jan gasped out loud with drool and ass juices on his lips and cheeks. He fell to the floor beneath us on his back then reached up to grasp my potent, naked thighs.

Xavier's ass pit dripped with sweat and spit. Reddened, it was dilated and quivering. The sloppy lips clenched and parted with the Spaniard's depraved craving. His massive hamstrings bulged with muscularity below that high ass. The pillars of strength were in marked contrast to the quivering mass of flesh he had become. He whined with an eerie, keening whimper. He gyrated his shaved ass while he anticipated his own rape by the mammoth dildo I sported between my thighs.

Mamluk swiftly moved into the gap before I could accomplish that goal. He slid his nimble fingers into the Spaniard's ass crack and coated the flesh liberally with the same grease he had slathered on Olaf's alabaster ass.

I shoved him aside as hastily as I had the Dane and leaped forward. The jutting dildo was ahead of me. Its blunt though realistic head rammed into Xavier's pulsing pit. Amazingly, it sunk effortlessly into him and disappeared nearly halfway in only a scant moment.

"Oh-oh-oh-please ram it deep! Please Sir Guy. I am a hole for you, please..." Xavier screamed. His voice echoed up to float alongside Gerhardt's lilting song.

I fucked him.

With a staggering sense of mastery I rammed the big dildo in and out of the Knight's anal sanctum. Yet it was frustrating not to be able to feel his silky, palpitating flesh with my own cock, which was sheathed in the wooden dildo. This frustration only added to the ferocity of my attack. Poor Xavier's large butt heaved and jerked. That ass was slammed to the extents of his fetters as I plunged again and again into him.

The savage dildo fuck struck all the right chords in Xavier's depraved soul. His moans of orgasm, his body's convulsions, and his spurting cock all melded with the erotically mystic voice of the Swabian Knight. Gerhardt's face was plastered with Xavier's flying cum.

I withdrew the dildo and stepped back. I panted savagely myself. I was unable once more to achieve orgasm at that point. Philippe's strong arms supported me while I caught my breath, and then he turned and led me from the chamber. Our entourage followed with the beat of their drums steady and heavy as we moved on.

We ascended to a high tower. That jutting wood bobbed ever-erect and ever-potent between my thighs. My cock ached continually. The pleasure was profound, as if I was in a state of perpetual pre-orgasm.

We reached the East Tower. By this time it was late afternoon and the ominous cloud cover had thickened. The circular chamber was usually bright, but even with the windows thrown open, the heavy sky made the air dim and threatening. The sound of distant thunder warned us as we entered.

An edifying sight waited for us. One of the most evil of our enemies was there to greet us. The Lord of Constantinople, the cruel dungeon master, the Vizier Barabas was expecting us. Bound to a heavy wooden barrel in the middle of the room, he groveled at our feet.

Thunder boomed louder as I faced the evil man brought low. I could not help but smile at the sight of him. He was naked and bound to the barrel, his branded ass spread wide, and his long limbs extended and shackled tightly. The Vizier was utterly helpless.

My cock ached beneath the constricting wooden dildo. I recognized what I must do with it again. The Lord of

Constantinople, his beetling brows furrowed in fear and his teeth gritted in anger, glared backward at me. His piercing blue eyes were slitted in a fruitless attempt to appear defiant. But when he saw the monster cock jutting out from my hips, and my steely smile, he winced and his bound body shuddered all over

I stepped forward and returned his glare. He had been ingeniously bound. His ass was high and spread apart. The taut cheeks were graced with a silky black fuzz. The parted crack also boasted that light fuzz, which surrounded a small anal aperture. That slot clenched tightly in fear.

On one firm ass cheek the words "fuck hole" stood out in an angry red brand.

Beneath that delectable ass dangled his hefty ball sack. The sack was tightly wrapped in strands of black leather. Each nut was swollen and red. The agonizing pain of that constriction was apparent. Below that, his elongated cock was also wrapped in leather thongs. The stretched prick was pulled downwards snugly and strapped to the wooden barrel through rings of gold.

At the swollen tip, the gold ring that had been inserted into his cock head was stretched out and attached to the barrel by more leather straps.

His dick was hard as rock where it stretched down and was trapped by those bizarre bindings.

The only part of the Lord's body that could move was his head and neck, which he now craned around to watch my approach. His eyes dropped, then jerked wide as he took in the dimensions of the cock thrusting out at my waist.

I moved right in. Mamluk was quickly between us and this time coated the gross wooden dildo with a copious supply of grease. The rank smell of the beef lard perfectly suited my own frame of mind. My eyes narrowed as I recalled the punishment the evil Lord had inflicted on the Stepov brothers, and others. Among his victims was one of my favorite young Knights, Jonas Dambrusk.

I glared into those small, pig-like blue eyes as I planted the head of the dildo between Barabas' parted ass cheeks. The firm globes were bound and awaiting whatever I deemed their due. He was helpless.

I growled at him, "Suffer this instrument up your tight butt hole as a small measure of the punishment you deserve for all your evil deeds!"

The music beat savagely behind me, and I felt Philippe's hands on my bare ass as encouragement.

I held the Lord's gaze as I began to press into him with that monster dildo head. His asshole was tight. He resisted me with all his strength. Sweat beaded on his forehead, his teeth were clenched, his body taut as a strung instrument, but then the inexorable pressure proved too much.

I felt him give way.

His narrow cavity suddenly gaped open. His mouth also gaped open in a howl of rage. The greased dildo slid inside him. I looked down at the giant thing as it entered him. The small, hairy orifice was stretched impossibly wide and his sweat-soaked butt cheeks shuddered. But Lord Barabas was bound securely and unable to move so much as a muscle. He could only submit.

I fed him the giant cock inch by inch.

His howl was abruptly silenced by a Knight moving in front of him. It was Pierre de Lanset of Burgundy. His short auburn locks surrounded a wide handsome face that smirked with satisfaction and aroused lust. Naked like the other Knights, his tall and rope-lean form stepped in to straddle the Vizier's head. He grasped Barabas' hair, and with no preamble, shoved his long cock between the Lord's lips. Right to the root.

Barabas gagged, then slobbered and moaned as he was face-fucked. Pierre had been horribly abused by Barabas on the night of that evil bonfire before I rescued him. Now Pierre reaped his revenge. His golden eyes gleamed as he thrust his slim hips forward and fucked the Lord's slack mouth.

Meanwhile Philippe's firm hands were on my back and ass. He pushed my hips forward to drive the giant dildo up Barabas's tight hole. The anal furrow dripped grease. The stretched ass lips wrapped obscenely around the solid shaft that rammed in and out of it relentlessly. The bound buttocks could not move an inch. That greased ass was unable to do anything but passively accept its own violation.

Another Knight took Pierre's place after he had hastily unloaded his spunk all over the Lord's sweating face. This time it was Tonio de Slava of Tuscany who drove his fat cock between those gasping Constantinople lips. He also held Barabas's hair as he fed him cock. Tonio threw back his head, long black hair flying, and shouted out loud as he thrust his dick into that hot mouth. Tonio's ample butt cheeks clenched and thrust while his fat prick pounded into the unwilling face-hole.

He unloaded his male juice deep in Barabas' throat. To be honest, the Vizier's gagging moans were music to my ears.

Then it was Ivan Metrovosk who moved in to face-rape the Lord. His short, plump body was naked, pale and gleaming with sweat. His soft blue eyes were steel-cold as he fed his own cock to the moaning Lord. He had been fisted, whipped and branded by the evil Lord, and now he reveled in his vengeance.

When the blond Russian shot his cum all over the Lord, I had that giant cock buried deep in the Vizier's anus. Barabas's moans suddenly took on a distinctly altered tone.

I recognized words. Those words united, as surely and strangely as Xavier's had, with Gerhardt's mystical song behind me and the heavy beat of the Knights' drums all around us.

"Oh! Yes! Yes! Fuck me deep! Fuck my hole! Fuck my poor sluttish cavity! Yes! Make me into nothing but a hole! I'm your hole whore! I'm your hole toy," Barabas blubbered.

He was bound to the barrel helpless, his face coated with man-cream, his body bathed in his own sweat, his ass dripping grease, men chanting around him, and that monster dildo caressing his seared asshole. Now he was finally submitting. At last he was offering his obeisance.

"What did you say?" I shouted at him. I rammed that dildo deep into his gaping anal pit.

He screamed.

"OH! YES! FUCK MY HOLE!" Then he screamed again. "RAM MY HOLE! FILL MY HUNGRY HOLE!"

That was enough. Nearly exhausted, I pulled out

We left him there moaning. Grease ran down his hairy ass and thighs. His balls and dick were stretched out and also dripped grease. His own cum had shot out of the pierced head of his cock and splattered the barrel.

We moved on to the Throne Room. The wild entourage of chanting naked Knights strode behind me, while Philippe garbed in his leather harness was ahead.

I ascended my throne then turned and seated myself to gaze down at my fellow Knights. What a barbarous scene of depravity and male sexuality! All were naked, although many remained masked. Jutting cocks, flopping balls and tight asses packed the chamber.

It was time for homage. One by one the Knights approached to ascend the steps of the throne dais. Each took the fake cock in my lap between their lips and sucked it down as best they could while offering me their undying fealty.

There was Sir Daignold Assnault of Toulouse down on his knees. His delicate though masculine features gazed up at me. His small mouth engulfed the fake cock in my lap after promising his fealty. That enormous dick being suckled by the diminutive Captain's sweet mouth was an incredible sight.

Behind him stepped up the bear-like figure of the Englishman Brian Howard. He was massive in comparison to the French Knight on his knees before me. The dark-haired Englishman bent down and shoved his cock between the sucking Frenchman's parted thighs. Daignold's taut anus enveloped that big English dick and his pretty mouth opened wider as it swallowed more of the dildo encasing my own aching member.

And my dick was aching. Watching those delicate lips slobber and caress that fake dick had me yearning for the real thing. The chanting, the naked men, Sir Brian's big glistening cock riding far up Daignold's tight asshole, all combined to provoke me into a near madness.

Philippe read my mind. He moved in to take charge. Pulling Daignold's sweet lips off the fake cock, he reached down and unstrapped the thing from my waist. I groaned as I felt the constricting sheath being removed. My own stiff meat appeared. It was grossly swollen, reddened and smeared with all the drool I had oozed over the past hour.

Instantly the kneeling Toulouse Knight sucked it in with his wet mouth.

I moaned and sprawled back in the throne to relish the delicious sensation. But there was more. Two Knights stepped up to my side. Both were nude and unmasked. These men were extremely handsome in an almost ethereal manner. The first, Eros Ramozas of Sicily, was the most recent addition to our Order. The other, Hillary Browning, was a sandy-haired Englishman with a broad, cherubic face and compact pale body. Each of them bent down and immediately opened their mouths to suck in one of my nipples. A thrill of pleasure coursed through me.

I reached out with my hands to grope their meaty asses. One dusky and one pale, my fingers slid into their butt cracks and searched out their pulsating anuses. I dug into the hot pits. I moaned continually as a mouth sucked my hard cock and two tongues licked at my nipples.

Then Philippe bent down. Our eyes met briefly as he opened his own mouth and covered mine with it. His soft lips parted mine. His thick tongue entered to explore and caress my teeth and tongue and throat.

But there was yet more. Suddenly I felt my thighs being raised up, pulled back and each of them shoved over an arm of the throne I sat upon. My ass was now bared. I felt Daignold's body being moved aside, while his mouth still suckled on my stiff shank.

The most incredible sensation nearly overwhelmed me. A hot tongue probed at my parted ass crack and found my yawning asshole.

I had been violating asshole after asshole all day. Yet my own rear entrance had been twitching all the while in empathy. Now that it was spread apart, and an expert tongue tickled it, I realized that was exactly what I needed.

I had no trouble distinguishing whose tongue licked at my anal pit. The most accomplished bum-licker of our Order, Jan the Dane, had to have been the one down there so eagerly tasting my ass juices. He sucked outward at my yawning aperture, stabbed deep with his long tongue, and then withdrew and tickled maddeningly at my swollen anal lips. It was heaven.

I was being mouthed and sucked at all my orifices. I was by then a moaning mass of writhing flesh. It went on for some time. I don't know how long. The tongue up my asshole was a slippery snake, while the one on my cock was a twirling dancer.

I eventually felt that expert mouth move away from my quivering anus. Something large replaced it. It was very hard. I instinctively knew what it had to be.

That giant dildo.

I opened my eyes. Naturally it was the tall Swede Olaf who applied it to me. Our eyes met. Mine were delirious with passion, but were also fogged with a similar emotion. As I swam in the cold blue gaze of the red-headed giant, I felt that mighty phallus enter me. It stretched apart my adequately lubed ass lips and drove deeper and deeper into me. It filled the void of my guts with its brute power.

I was then utterly fucked. The thing was rammed to the hilt, my upraised and parted thighs wide open, with my slack orifice accommodating the violation joyfully.

That final explosive orgasm I had been awaiting for all day arrived as the giant dildo ploughed my fucked ass. Cum was sucked out of my cock.

Mouths were all over my body while hands groped and caressed me. My own hands were deeply buried in the two

285

Jay Starre

assholes I manipulated at my side. A rocketing eruption of sperm from deep in my balls coalesced in a fierce rapture so profound I swooned dead away.

The next thing I knew, I was being carried in a litter through hallways.

That male chanting and the beating of exotic drums surrounded me. The heavy boom of thunder could be heard over it all. The storm finally found us and engulfed Castle Rock with its rolling blast of natural energy.

We reached my bedchamber. I was aided to my feet and my boots slipped off. Now I was entirely naked. My spacious bed awaited me. The gauzy curtains obscured the soft bedding and the interior.

I moved them aside and was surprised to see a figure reclining there. A nude body peered up at me. I sighed with pleasure as I realized who it was.

Sir Jonas the Lithuanian sprawled on the covers, with arms upraised to greet me. I should have known. I had not seen him the entire day, this young man, my most loyal of servants other than Philippe and Mamluk.

His gentle eyes gazed up at me. His body was still entirely shaved, although his perfectly rounded scull was now graced by a cap of short black hair. He had been ordered shaved of all hair as a punishment for his rape of an Arab woman, but the year of his punishment had long passed. He still kept his body shaved, which I found very stimulating. He was young and his body was taut with muscle. Although Jonas was undeniably a large, tall man, his lack of bodily hair and pale flesh lent him an aspect of softness that appealed to me. Very much so.

I knew he loved me and he trusted me without reservation. I admitted then that I loved him, too. He had proved himself brave, as when he faced Lord Barabas and offered himself instead of other Knights for the depraved man's punishment. I stared down at him.

286

He lay with his muscular arms upraised to welcome me. His gentle eyes were full of love, his cock stiff, and his shaved balls were tight against his crotch. Jonas' hefty thighs were wide apart and lifted up. The rounded sensuality of his abundant buttocks were displayed voluptuously. Beneath those shaved balls I caught a glimpse of his puckered butt hole.

I fell into his arms. The warm flesh enveloped me tenderly. My fingers sought out and found his pliant anal slot. The heat I discovered there was welcoming. His vigorous body melted into my embrace. He smiled as he kissed my lips.

Above all the rest, including the absolute fealty of my Knights, all I had accomplished in the Holy Land for the Order of the Knights Templar, my loyal men and the numerous battles I had won; above all that, this was the very best.

It was this I truly treasured. The soft kiss of Jonas my loving Knight, and his arms around me, his plump buttocks, his willing butt hole and his stiff cock. His hot naked body.

I was content.

# About the Author

Jay Starre lives in Vancouver, British Columbia, where he burns up his keyboard writing hot gay erotica. His stories have been published in a number of gay men's magazines including *Torso*, *Mandate* and *Men*. He has contributed to over thirty gay erotica anthologies including *Kink*, *Lovers Who Stay with You*, *Wildest Ones*, and *Muscle Worshipers*.

g any underwear. "Excuse me," I said, having a hard time looking
d by that bulge in his crotch, "but don't I know you?" "Maybe," 
f to                                                    bout a m
Ray                                                    God, you
r?                                                     in?" he a
Lik                                                    s stronges
dy                                                     e on Gree
e l                                                    s I ever sa
o t                                                    any ideas'
ng                                                     ne same
ul                                                     ery long 
aci                                                    ne swell.
ith                                                    e in store
o c                                                    behind s
e u                                                    in public
he                                                     vent to th
y.                                                     grabbed
I                                                    
ci                                                    t, so firm
ha                                                   
m                                                     bing dick
;, I                                                  n cock, b
und or unzipping filled the small space. I don't know who's hand
before I knew it, I had his rod in my hand, and mine was in his. "
lo?" he asked, his tone challenging. I knew exactly, and sank to